PRAISE FOR ELLE KENNEDY

"Smart, sexy an  love with Tucker's strength and patie in the bedroom that made me swoon ai game!"
—#1 *New York* author Vi Keeland

"Tucker is mine, ladies. I called it. This series just keeps getting better."
—*USA Today* bestselling author Sarina Bowen

"Romance. The most adorable couple. The banter — omg the banter. The romance. The friends. The flirtation. The smiles it gave me."
—Mandi, *SmexyBooks*

"Absolute "new adult" angsty-romance reading PERFECTION!"
—*Maryse's Book Blog*

"This story is filled with witty banter, sexy tension and an overall warm feeling."
—*The Rock Stars of Romance*

"It had everything I crave in a romance; humor, depth, love and an over abundance of grand gestures. Highly recommend."
—*Book Binge*

"This story made me swoon, cry (and) I laughed, too. It's a story that gripped me from page one and kept me reading until the last line."
—*New Adult Addiction*

OTHER TITLES BY ELLE KENNEDY

Off-Campus Series:

The Deal

The Mistake

The Score

The Goal

Briar U Series:

The Chase

The Risk

Out of Uniform Series:

Hot & Bothered

Hot & Heavy

Feeling Hot

Getting Hotter

Hotter Than Ever

A Little Bit of Hot

As Hot As It Gets

A full list of Elle's contemporary and suspense print titles is available on her website: www.ellekennedy.com.

THE GOAL

AN OFF-CAMPUS NOVEL

ELLE KENNEDY

The Goal: An Off-Campus Novel

Copyright © 2016 by Elle Kennedy

Edited by Gwen Hayes

Proofed by Aquila Editing

Cover Art © Sarah Hansen, Okay Creations

1

SABRINA

"Crap. Crap. Crap. Craaaaap. Where are my keys?"

The clock in the narrow hallway tells me I have fifty-two minutes to make a sixty-eight-minute drive if I want to get to the party on time.

I check my purse again, but the keys aren't there. I run through the various locations. Dresser? No. Bathroom? Was just there. Kitchen? Maybe—

I'm about to pivot when I hear a jingle of metal behind me.

"You looking for these?"

Contempt lodges in my throat as I turn around and step into a living room so small that the five pieces of dated furniture—two tables, one loveseat, one sofa, and one chair—are squashed together like sardines in a can. The lump of flesh on the couch waves my keys in the air. At my sigh of irritation, he grins and shoves them under his sweatpants-covered ass.

"Come and get 'em."

I drag a frustrated hand down my flat-ironed hair before stalking over to my stepfather. "Give me my keys," I demand.

Ray leers in return. "Da-amn, you look hot tonight. You've turned into a real babe, Rina. You and me should get it on."

I ignore the meaty hand that's falling to his crotch. I've never known a man so desperate to touch his own junk. He makes Homer Simpson look like a gentleman.

"You and I don't exist to each other. So don't look at me, and *don't* call me Rina." Ray's the only person who ever calls me that, and I fucking hate it. "Now give me my keys."

"I told you—come and get 'em."

With gritted teeth, I shove my hand under his lard-ass and root around for my keys. Ray grunts and squirms like the disgusting piece of shit he is until my hand connects with metal.

I drag the keys free and spin back to the doorway.

"What's the big deal?" he mocks after me. "It's not like we're related, so there's no incest problem."

I stop and use thirty seconds of my precious time to stare at him in disbelief. "You're my stepfather. You married my mother. And—" I swallow a rush of bile, "—and you're sleeping with Nana now. So, no, it's not about whether you and I are related. It's because you're the grossest person on the planet and you belong in prison."

His hazel eyes darken. "Watch your mouth, missy, or one of these days you'll come home and the doors will be locked."

Whatever. "I pay for a third of the rent here," I remind him.

"Well, maybe you'll be in charge of more."

He turns back to the television, and I spend another valuable thirty seconds fantasizing about bashing his head in with my purse. Worth it.

In the kitchen, Nana is sitting at the table, smoking a cigarette and reading an issue of *People.* "Did you see this?" she exclaims. "Kim K is nude again."

"Goodie for her." I grab my jacket off the back of the chair and head for the kitchen door.

I've found that it's safer to leave the house through the back.

There are usually street punks congregating on the stoops of the narrow townhouses on our less than affluent street in this less than affluent part of Southie. Besides, our carport is behind the house.

"Heard Rachel Berkovich got knocked up," Nana remarks. "She should've aborted it, but I guess it's against their religion."

I clench my teeth again and turn to face my grandmother. As usual, she's wearing a ratty robe and fuzzy pink slippers, but her dyed blonde hair is teased to perfection and her face is fully made-up even though she rarely goes out.

"She's Jewish, Nana. I don't think it's against her religion, but even if it is, that's her choice."

"Probably wants those extra food stamps," Nana concludes, blowing a long stream of smoke in my direction. Shit. I hope I don't smell like an ashtray by the time I get to Hastings.

"I'm guessing that isn't the reason Rachel's keeping the baby." One hand on the door, I shift restlessly, waiting for an opening to tell Nana goodbye.

"Your momma thought about aborting you."

And there it is. "Okay, that's enough," I mutter. "I'm going to Hastings. I'll be back tonight."

Her head jerks up from the magazine and her eyes narrow as she takes in my black knit skirt, black short-sleeved sweater with a scoop neck, and three-inch heels. I can see the words forming in her mind before they even leave her mouth.

"You're looking uppity. Going off to that fancy college of yours? You got classes on Saturday night?"

"It's a cocktail party," I answer grudgingly.

"Oooh, cocktail, schocktail. Hope your lips don't get chapped kissing all the ass down there."

"Yeah, thanks, Nana." I wrench open the back door, forcing myself to add, "Love you."

"Love you too, baby girl."

She does love me, but sometimes that love is so tainted, I don't know if it's hurting me or helping me.

I don't make the drive to the small town of Hastings in fifty-two minutes *or* sixty-eight minutes. Instead, it takes me an entire hour and a half because the roads are so damn bad. Another five minutes pass before I can find a parking space, and by the time I reach Professor Gibson's house, I'm tenser than a piano wire—and feeling about as fragile.

"Hi, Mr. Gibson. I'm so sorry I'm late," I tell the bespectacled man at the door.

Professor Gibson's husband gives me a soft smile. "Don't worry about it, Sabrina. The weather is terrible. Let me take your coat." He holds out a hand and waits patiently while I struggle out of my wool jacket.

Professor Gibson arrives as her husband is hanging my cheap coat amongst all the expensive ones in the closet. It looks as out of place as I do. I shove aside the feelings of inadequacy and summon up a bright smile.

"Sabrina!" Professor Gibson calls out gaily. Her commanding presence jerks me to attention. "I'm so glad you arrived in one piece. Is it snowing yet?"

"No, just rain."

She grimaces and takes my arm. "Even worse. I hope you don't plan on driving back to the city tonight. The roads will be one sheet of ice."

Since I have to work in the morning, I'll be making that trek regardless of the road conditions, but I don't want Prof to worry, so I smile reassuringly. "I'll be fine. Is she still here?"

The professor squeezes my forearm. "She is, and she's dying to meet you."

Awesome. I take my first full breath since I got here and allow myself to be led across the room toward a short, gray-haired woman dressed in a boxy pastel suitcoat over a pair of black pants. The outfit is rather blah, but the diamonds sparkling in her ears are larger than my thumb. Also? She seems too genial for a professor of the law. I always envisioned them as dour, serious creatures. Like me.

"Amelia, let me introduce you to Sabrina James. She's the student I've been telling you about. At the top of her class, holds down two jobs, and managed a one seventy-seven on her LSATs." Professor Gibson turns to me. "Sabrina, Amelia Fromm, constitutional scholar extraordinaire."

"So nice to meet you," I say, holding out my hand and praying to God it feels dry and not damp. I practiced shaking my own hand for an hour leading up to this.

Amelia grips me lightly before stepping back. "Italian mother, Jewish grandfather, hence the odd combination of names. James is Scottish—is that where your family is from?" Her bright eyes sweep over me, and I resist the urge to fidget with my cheap Target clothing

"I couldn't say, ma'am." My family comes from the gutter. Scotland seems far too nice and regal to be our homeland.

She waves a hand. "It's not important. I dabble in genealogy on the side. So, you've applied to Harvard? That's what Kelly has told me."

Kelly? Do I know a Kelly?

"She means me, dear," Professor Gibson says with a gentle laugh.

I blush. "Yes, sorry. I think of you as Prof."

"So formal, Kelly!" Professor Fromm accuses. "Sabrina, where else have you applied?"

"Boston College, Suffolk, and Yale, but Harvard is my dream."

Amelia raises an eyebrow at my list of tier two and three Boston schools.

Professor Gibson jumps to my defense. "She wants to stay close to home. And obviously she belongs at someplace better than Yale."

The two professors share a contemptuous sniff. Prof was a Harvard grad, and apparently once a Harvard grad, always an anti-Yale person.

"From all that Kelly has shared, it sounds like Harvard would be honored to have you."

"It would be my honor to be a Harvard student, ma'am."

"Acceptance letters are being mailed out soon." Her eyes twinkle with mischief. "I'll be sure to put in a good word."

Amelia bestows another smile, and I nearly faint in happy relief. I wasn't just blowing smoke up her ass. Harvard really is my dream.

"Thank you," I manage to croak out.

Professor Gibson points me toward the food. "Why don't you get something to eat? Amelia, I want to talk to you about that position paper I heard was coming out of Brown. Did you have a chance to look at it?"

The two turn away, diving deep into a discussion about intersectionality of Black feminism and race theory, a topic that Professor Gibson is an expert in.

I wander over to the refreshment table, which is draped in white and loaded with cheese, crackers, and fruit. Two of my closest friends —Hope Matthews and Carin Thompson—are already standing there. One dark and one light, they're the two most beautiful, smartest angels in the world.

I rush over to them and nearly collapse in their arms.

"So? How'd it go?" Hope asks impatiently.

"Good, I think. She said that it sounded like Harvard would be honored to have me and that the first wave of acceptance letters is going out soon."

I grab a plate and start loading it up, wishing the pieces of cheese were bigger. I'm so hungry I could eat an entire block. All day I'd been sick with anticipation because of this meeting, and now that it's over, I want to fall face-first into the food table.

"Oh, you are so in," declares Carin.

The three of us are advisees of Professor Gibson, who's a big believer in helping young women along. There are other networking organizations on campus, but her influence is solely geared toward the advancement of women, and I couldn't be more grateful.

Tonight's cocktail party is designed for her students to meet with faculty members of the most competitive graduate programs in the nation. Hope is angling for a place at Harvard Med while Carin is headed for MIT.

Yep, it's a sea of estrogen inside Professor Gibson's house. Other than her husband, only a couple of other men are present. I'm really going to miss this place after I graduate. It's been a home away from home.

"Fingers crossed," I say in response to Carin. "If I don't get into Harvard, then it's BC or Suffolk." Which would be fine, but Harvard virtually guarantees me a shot at the job I want post-graduation—a position at one of the nation's top law firms, or what everyone calls BigLaw.

"You'll get in," Hope says confidently. "And hopefully once you get that acceptance letter, you'll stop killing yourself, because Lord, B, you look tense."

I roll my head around my neck stiffly. Yeah, I *am* tense. "I know. My schedule is brutal these days. I went to bed at two this morning because the girl who was supposed to close at Boots & Chutes bugged out and left me to close, and then I was up at four to sort mail. I got home around noon, crashed, and almost overslept."

"You're still working both jobs?" Carin flips her red hair out of her face. "You said you were going to quit the waitressing gig."

"I can't yet. Professor Gibson said that they don't want us working our first year of law school. The only way I can swing that is to have enough for food and rent saved up before September."

Carin makes a sympathetic noise. "I hear you. My parents are taking out a loan so big, I might be able to afford a small country with it."

"I wish you'd move in with us," Hope says plaintively.

"Really? I had no idea," I joke. "You've only said it twice a day since the semester started."

She wrinkles her cute nose at me. "You'd *love* this place my dad rented for us. It's got floor-to-ceiling windows and it's right on the subway line. Public transportation." She wiggles her eyebrows enticingly.

"It's too expensive, H."

"You know I'd cover the difference—or my parents would," she corrects herself. The girl's family has more money than an oil tycoon, but you'd never know it from talking to her. Hope's as down to earth as they come.

"I know," I say between gulping down bites of mini-sausages. "But I'd feel guilty and then guilt would turn into resentment and then we wouldn't be friends anymore and not being your friend would suck."

She shakes her head at me. "If, at some point, your stubborn pride allows you to ask for help, I'm here."

"*We're* here," Carin interjects.

"See?" I wave my fork between the two of them. "This is why I can't live with you guys. You mean too much to me. Besides, this is working for me. I've got nearly ten months to save up before classes start next fall. I've got this."

"At least come for a drink with us after this thing is over," Carin begs.

"I have to drive home." I make a face. "I'm scheduled to go in and sort packages tomorrow."

"On a Sunday?" Hope demands.

"Time and a half. I couldn't turn it down. Actually, I should probably take off soon." I lay my plate on the table and try to catch a glimpse of what's going on beyond the huge bay window. All I see is darkness and streaks of rain on the glass. "Sooner I'm on the road, the better."

"Not in this weather you're not." Professor Gibson appears at my elbow with a glass of wine. "The weather advisory is for sheets of glass—temperature's dropping and the rain is turning into ice."

One look at my advisor's face and I know I have to concede. So I do, but with great reluctance.

"All right," I say, "but I do this under protest. And you—" I tip my fork in Carin's direction, "you better have ice cream in the freezer in case I have to crash with you, otherwise I'm going to be really mad."

All three of them laugh. Professor Gibson wanders off, leaving us to network as best as three college seniors can. After an hour of mingling, Hope, Carin and I grab our coats.

"Where are we going?" I ask the girls.

"D'Andre is at Malone's and I said I'd meet him there," Hope tells me. "It's like a two-minute drive, so we should be fine."

"Really? Malone's? That's a hockey bar," I whine. "What's D'Andre doing there?"

"Drinking and waiting for me. Besides, you need to get laid and athletes are your favorite type."

Carin snorts. "Her only type."

"Hey, I have a very good reason for preferring athletes," I argue.

"I know. We've heard it." She rolls her eyes. "If you want a stats question answered, go to the math geeks. If you want a physical need met, go to an athlete. Bodies are the tools of an elite athlete. They take care of it, know how to push its limits, yada yada." Carin makes a yapping gesture with her left hand.

I flick up my middle finger.

"But sex with someone you like is so much better." This comes from Hope, who's been with D'Andre, her football player boyfriend, since freshman year.

"I like them," I protest. "...for the hour or so I use them."

We share a giggle over that, until Carin brings up a guy who brought down the average.

"Do you remember Ten-Second Greg, though?"

I shudder. "First, thank you very little for bringing that bad memory up, and second, I'm not saying there aren't duds. Just that the odds are better with an athlete."

"And the hockey players are duds?" Carin asks.

I shrug. "I wouldn't know. I didn't ax them from my list of potentials because of their performance in the sack, but because they're hyper-privileged jerks who get special favors from the profs."

"Sabrina, girl, you got to let that go," Hope urges.

"Nope. Hockey players don't make the cut."

"God, but look at what you're missing out on." Carin licks her lips with exaggerated lasciviousness. "That one guy on the team with the beard? I want to know what that feels like. Beards are on my bucket list."

"Go on then. My boycott against hockey players just means more for you."

"I'm on board with this, but..." She smirks. "Need I remind you that you hooked up with the manslut Di Laurentis?"

Ugh. That's a reminder I *never* need to hear.

"First, I was totally drunk," I grumble. "Second, that was sophomore year. And third, he's the reason I've sworn off hockey players."

Even though Briar University has a championship-winning football team, it's known as a hockey college. The guys who wear skates are treated like gods. Case in point—Dean Heyward-Di Laurentis. He's a poli sci major like me, so we've had several classes together, including Statistics in our sophomore year. That course was hard as fuck. Everyone struggled.

Everyone but Dean, who was screwing the TA.

And—shocker!—she gave him an A, which he absolutely did *not* deserve. I know this for a fact, because we were paired together for the final assignment, and I saw the garbage he turned in.

When I found out he aced it, I wanted to chop his dick off. It was so unfair. I worked my butt off in that course. Hell, I work my butt off for everything. My every accomplishment is stained with my blood, sweat and tears. Meanwhile, some asshole gets the world handed to him on a platter? Fuck. That.

"She's getting mad again," Hope stage-whispers to Carin.

"She's thinking about how Di Laurentis got an A in that one class," Carin shout-whispers back. "She really does need to get laid. How long has it been?"

I start to flip her off again when it occurs to me that I can't remember my last hookup.

"There was, um, Meyer? The lacrosse guy. That was in September. And after that was Beau..." I brighten up. "Ha! See? It's only been a little over a month. Hardly a national emergency."

"Girl, someone with your schedule isn't allowed to go a *month* without sex," Hope counters. "You're a walking ball of stress, which means you need a good dicking at least...daily," she decides.

"Every other day," Carin argues. "Give her lady garden some time to rest."

Hope nods. "Fine. But no rest for the pussy tonight—"

I snort in laughter.

"You hear that, B? You've been fed, you had an afternoon nap, and now you need some sexy times," Carin declares.

"But Malone's?" I repeat warily. "We just established that the place is crawling with hockey players."

"Not exclusively. I bet Beau is there. Want me to ask D'Andre?" Hope holds up her phone, but I shake my head.

"Beau's too much of a time commitment. Like he wanted to talk during sex. I want to do the deed and leave."

"Oooh, talking! Scary."

"Shut it."

"Make me." Hope tosses her head, her long braids smacking against my coat, and then exits Professor Gibson's house.

Carin shrugs and follows her, and after a second of hesitation, I do too. Our coats are drenched by the time we reach Hope's car, but we have our hoods on, so our hair survives the downpour.

I'm really not in the mood to chat up any guys tonight, but I can't deny that my friends are right. I've been plagued with tension for weeks, and these past few days I've definitely been feeling the...itch. The kind of itch that can only be scratched with a hard, ripped body and a hopefully above average-sized cock.

Except I'm extremely selective about who I hook up with, and just as I'd feared, Malone's is thick with hockey players when the girls and I stride inside five minutes later.

But hey, if that's the hand I've been dealt, then I guess there's no harm in playing it and seeing what happens.

Still, I have zero expectations as I follow my friends to the bar counter.

2

TUCKER

"Stay away from that one, kid. She's toxic."

Dean is dispensing his (usually misguided) wisdom to our freshman left wing, Hunter Davenport, as I walk into Malone's out of the pouring rain.

The roads are shit, and I don't particularly want to be here tonight, but Dean insisted that we needed to party. He'd been restlessly pacing our townhouse all day, grumpy as hell and obviously upset, but when I questioned him about it, he shrugged and said he was feeling antsy.

Which is bull. I might be considered quiet compared to my loud-mouthed teammates, but I ain't slow. And I sure as hell don't need to be a detective to put the clues together.

Allie Hayes, the best friend of our other roommate's girlfriend, crashed at our place last night.

Dean is a manwhore.

Chicks love Dean.

Allie is a chick.

Ergo, Dean slept with Allie.

Plus, there were all the clothes scattered around the living room because Dean is physically incapable of having sex in his bedroom.

He hasn't fessed up to it yet, but I'm sure he will eventually. I'm also sure that whatever went down between them last night, Allie's not looking for a repeat performance. Though why that should bother Dean, the one-night stand king, I've yet to figure out.

"She doesn't look toxic to me," Hunter drawls as I shake the water out of my hair.

"Hey Fido," Dean grumbles my way, "go dry off somewhere else."

I roll my eyes and follow Hunter's gaze, which is Krazy Glued to a slender brunette facing away from us at the long counter. I see a short skirt, killer legs, and thick dark hair streaming down her back. Not to mention the roundest, tightest, sexiest ass I've ever had the pleasure of admiring.

"Nice," I remark before grinning at Dean. "I take it you already called dibs?"

His face turns white with horror. "Not a chance. That's Sabrina, bro. She already busts my balls in class on a daily basis. I don't need her busting them outside of school."

"Wait, that's Sabrina?" I say slowly. *This* is the girl who Dean swears is his nemesis? "I've seen her around campus, but I didn't realize she's the one you're always bitching about."

"One and the same," he mutters.

"Damn shame. She sure is nice to look at." More than nice, actually. In the dictionary next to *fine* is a picture of Sabrina's ass. It might also be next to the words *gorgeous, goddamn,* and *smoke show.*

"What's the deal with you two?" Hunter pipes up. "She your ex?"

Dean recoils. "Fuck no."

The freshman purses his lips. "So I won't be breaking the bro code if I make a move?"

"You want to make a move? Go nuts. But I'm warning you, that bitch will eat you alive."

I avert my face to hide a grin. Sounds like someone may have turned Dean down. There's definitely some kind of history between them, but even after Hunter presses him about it, Dean doesn't give up any other intel. Across the room, Sabrina turns. She probably feels three sets of eyes on that ass—two of which are damn hungry.

Her gaze catches mine and holds it. There's challenge in her eyes and the competitor in me rises to meet it.

You enough for me? she appears to be asking.

You have no idea, darlin'.

A spark of heat lights her gaze—that is until it falls on Dean. Immediately, her lush lips thin and she jerks up her middle finger in our direction.

Hunter groans and mutters something about Dean ruining his chances. But Hunter's a baby and that girl has enough fire in her to ignite the world. I can't imagine her wanting to take an eighteen-year-old to bed, especially if he sees defeat in the first obstacle. Kid's gotta get stronger if he wants to play with the big boys.

I dig in my pocket for some cash. "I'm gonna grab a beer. You guys need a refill?"

They both shake their heads. Having discharged my friend duty, I make my way to the bar and Sabrina, arriving in time for the bartender to deliver her drink.

I lay down a twenty. "I've got that, and I'll take a Miller when you've got a minute."

The bartender grabs the bill and hustles off to the cash register before Sabrina can object. She gives me a contemplative look and then lifts the beer bottle to her lips.

"I'm not sleeping with you because you bought me a drink," she says over the rim.

"I hope not," I reply with a shrug. "I have higher standards than that."

I give her a polite nod and mosey back to the table where a few of my teammates are congregated. Behind me, I can feel her eyes boring into my back. Since she can't see me, I allow a smile of satisfaction to spread across my face. This is a girl who's used to being chased, which means I need to work a little surprise into my pursuit.

At the table, Hunter's eyeing another pack of girls, and Dean's head is buried in his phone, probably texting Allie. I wonder if the other guys know they did the dirty. Probably not. Garrett and Logan are in Boston with their girlfriends until tomorrow, so chances are they're still in the dark. But Garrett was adamant that Dean keep his hands off Allie this weekend. He didn't want any drama to interfere with his currently perfect life with Allie's best friend, Hannah.

Given that there haven't been any explosions or frantic phone calls, I'd bet that Dean and Allie are keeping last night's hookup on the DL.

Just as Hunter opens his mouth to deliver some bad line to one of the girls who's made her way over to the table, the lights flicker ominously.

Dean frowns. "Is it the Apocalypse out there or something?"

"It's coming down pretty hard," I tell him.

After that, Dean decides to take off. I stay put, despite the fact that I didn't even want to hit the bar tonight. I don't know why, but that brief exchange with Sabrina got me more than a little worked up.

It's not like there's a shortage of girls in my life. I might not brag about my conquests like Dean or Logan or my other teammates, but I get plenty of play. I even indulge in one-night stands if I'm feeling it.

And right now, I'm feeling it.

I want Sabrina under me. Over me. Anywhere she wants to put herself will do. And I want it so bad I have to rub my hand over my beard so I don't give in to the urge to slide it lower and rub something else.

I'm still not sure how I feel about the beard. I grew it around the time of the championship game this past spring, but it got mountain-man out of control on me, so I shaved it over the summer. Then it grew back because I'm lazy as hell, and trimming it close is a helluva lot easier than shaving it all off.

"Have a seat, man," Hunter encourages. His eyes actively telegraph that there are three of them and two of us, but these girls, as pretty as they are, don't interest me at all.

"All yours, kid."

I drain my bottle and return to the bar where Sabrina's still standing. A couple other predators have edged closer. I give them all a hard stare and slide into a newly vacated space beside her.

I lean an elbow behind me against the bar top, giving her the illusion of room. She reminds me a little of those untamed ponies, all wide eyes, long legs, and the unspoken promise of the best ride of your life. But you play your hand too soon and she's going to run off and there'll be no catching her.

"So you're a friend of Di Laurentis?"

The words are casually tossed out, but considering she and Dean don't like each other much, there's probably only one right way to respond and that's by denying everything.

Still, I won't do that to a friend, not even to get laid. And whatever issue Sabrina has with Dean doesn't influence me, just like Dean's opinion of Sabrina isn't going to shape what I'm looking for with her. Besides, I'm a big believer in the saying that you begin how you intend to go on.

"He's my roommate."

She makes no effort to hide her distaste and starts brushing me off. "Thanks for the drink, but I think I see my friends waving at me." She nods toward a group of girls.

I survey the crowd, none of whom are even looking in our direction, and turn back to her with a sad shake of my head. "You gotta do better than that. If you want me to go, tell me to go. You look like a girl who knows what she wants and isn't afraid to say it."

"Is that what Dean told you? I bet he called me a bitch, didn't he?"

This time I opt to keep my mouth shut. Instead, I take a drink.

"He's right," she continues. "I am and I'm not sorry for it."

Her chin juts out adorably. I'd pinch it, but I think I'd lose a few fingers and I'm going to need them later tonight. I have plans to have them all over her body.

She takes another sip of the beer I bought her, and I watch the delicate muscles in her throat work. Fuck, she's beautiful. Dean could've said that she sucks the life out of babies and I'd still be over here. She's got that kind of draw.

And it's not just me. Half the male population in the bar is throwing glares of envy in my direction. I cant my body slightly to hide her from view.

"Okay," I say lightly.

"Okay?" She gets the cutest look of confusion on her face.

"Yup. Is that supposed to scare me off?"

Her perfectly shaped eyebrows crash together. "I don't know what else he said, but I'm not easy. I'm not against a hookup, but I'm picky about who I let into my bed."

"He didn't say anything about that. Only that you liked to bust his balls. But we both know that Dean's ego can withstand a blow now and again. The question is whether you're hung up on him. Kind of seems like you are, because he's the only thing you can talk about." I shrug. "If that's the case, I'll skate right now."

While Dean said he didn't have feelings for Sabrina, I want to make sure there aren't any lingering emotions on her end. Her tone when she mentioned him was mad, though, not bitter, which I take as a good sign. Anger could stem from any number of things. Bitterness is usually hurt feelings.

When—not if—we get into bed together, it should be because she wants to be with me, not as a way to get back at Dean.

Her gaze flicks over my shoulder to where my teammate is still sitting, then back to me. She and I drink in silence for a bit. Her chocolate-brown eyes are tough to read, but I get the sense she's weighing my words carefully. It might be that she expects me to talk, fill the silence, but I'm waiting her out. Plus, it gives me time to inspect her close up. And from this distance, she's even more beautiful than I realized.

She doesn't just have a world-class ass and endless legs. Her rack is the kind that can turn a man religious. As in, *thank you, Jesus, for creating this glorious creature* and *please, Lord, make her not a lesbian.* Not blatantly staring at the pretty swells rising above her top is one of the harder things I've had to do.

Finally, she sets her bottle on the bar. "Just because you're pretty doesn't mean I'm interested."

I grin. "A guy's gotta start somewhere."

A reluctant smile tugs at the corners of her mouth. She wipes her hand against her skirt and sticks it out.

"I'm Sabrina James. I've heard all the jokes about being a witch, and no, I am not hung up on Dean Di Laurentis."

I take her hand in mine and use the contact to pull her an inch closer to me. It's baby steps with this one.

"John Tucker. Glad to hear it, but you should know that Dean is like a brother to me. We've had each other's backs on the ice for four years, lived together for three of them, and I plan to stand up at his wedding and hope he does the same at mine. That said, he's my friend, not my daddy."

"Wait, you're getting married?" she says in confusion.

It's kind of amusing that out of everything I said, that's the bit she's harping on. I smooth a hand down the outside of her arm and loosely circle her wrist with my fingers. "In the future, darlin'. In the future."

"Oh." She picks up her beer and then puts it down when she sees it's empty. "Wait. You *want* to get married?"

"Eventually." I chuckle at her astonishment. "Not today, but yeah, one day I want to be married and have a kid or three. You?"

The bartender comes by, and I nudge another twenty in his direction.

But Sabrina shakes her head. "I'm driving. One beer is my limit."

I order us waters instead, and he's back in a flash with two tall glasses.

The lights flicker again, sending a jolt of urgency to my gut. I'm going to have to close this deal soon or lose out entirely.

"Thanks," she says as she sips the water. "And, no. I don't see myself having kids or a husband in the near future. Besides, I thought you hockey players liked to play the field."

"At some point, even the great ones retire." I smirk over the top of my glass.

She laughs. "All right. I'll give you that. So what's your major, John?"

"Tucker. Everyone calls me Tucker or Tuck. And it's business admin."

"So you can manage all your hockey money?"

I still haven't let go of her wrist, and with each exchange, I'm eliminating all the distance between us.

"Nope." I nod toward my knee. "I'm too slow for the pros. I got banged up in high school. I'm good enough for a scholarship here, but I know my limits."

"Oh, I'm sorry." There's true regret in her voice.

Dean's a fool. This girl is as sweet as they come. I can't wait to get my mouth on her.

And my hands.

And my teeth.

And my hard-as-steel cock.

"Don't be. I'm not."

I slide my arm along the bar until Sabrina's essentially standing in the circle of my arms. Her feet are tucked between mine, and if I shift my hips slightly forward, I'll be able to make the contact my body is dying for. But if there's one thing I've learned in all the years I've played hockey, it's that patience is rewarded. You don't take an immediate shot when your stick gets the puck. You wait for the right opening.

"I never really wanted it," I add. "And I think it's one of those things you have to really want to pursue."

And then she gives it to me. The opening. "So what do you want these days?"

"You," I answer baldly.

Two things happen. The lights go out completely and she nearly drops her glass. The jukebox dies out and suddenly the bar seems way too quiet. Around us are a few shrieks of laughter, a few shouts of dismay.

"Keep your pants on, children," one of the bartenders yells. "We're going to see what's going on. Generator should kick in any second."

As if on cue, a humming noise fills the air and then a dim glow of light illuminates the crowded room.

"You still thirsty?" I ask, stroking the inside of her wrist with long, gentle strokes. Up toward the inner elbow and back down to the wrist. Repeat. Again and again and again.

Her gaze drops to our joined hands and widen as if she just now realizes we've been touching for the last ten minutes or so. I lean in close and brush my nose against the outer edge of her earlobe, filling my lungs with her spicy scent.

I could stand here all day. There's something great about drawing out the anticipation until it's nearly painful. It makes the release all the more explosive. I have a feeling that sex with Sabrina James will blow my mind.

I can't fucking wait.

After taking a deep breath, one that pushes her perfect tits into my chest, she eases back—not too far, but enough to create a sliver of distance.

"I'm not into relationships," she says bluntly. "If we do this—"

"Do what?" I can't help but tease.

"*This.* Don't play dumb, Tucker. You're better than that."

A laugh pops out. "Fair enough. All right..." I wave a hand. "Go on..."

"If we do this," she repeats, "it's sex only. No awkward morning after. No phone numbers."

I give her one last caress before releasing her, letting her read into my silence what she needs to. I highly doubt that one time is going to be enough for either of us, but if that's what she needs to believe tonight, I'm okay with that.

"Let's go then."

Her lips curve. "Now?"

"Now." I moisten my bottom lip with my tongue. "Unless you want to sit here a while longer and keep dancing around the fact that we want to rip each other's clothes off."

She lets out a throaty laugh that goes straight to my balls. "Very good point, Tucker."

Lord. I love the way my name rolls off those full, pouty lips. Maybe I'll ask her to say it when I'm making her come.

The need surging through me is so strong I have to squeeze my ass cheeks together and breathe through my nose to try to curb it. I take Sabrina's elbow and muscle my way to the door. A few people call out my name or pat me on the back to tell me good game. I ignore them all.

Outside, it's still pouring. I pull Sabrina close and raise my black-and-silver hockey jacket over her head. Fortunately, my truck is nearby. "Over here."

"Nice parking spot," she comments.

"Can't complain." It's a perk of being a starter on a championship-winning college hockey team.

I help her into the truck, then slide into the driver's seat and start the engine. "Where to?"

She shivers a little, though I'm not sure if it's from the cold or for another reason. "I live in Boston."

"My place then." Because there's no fucking way I can wait the hour it'll take to drive to the city. My dick will explode.

She puts her hand on my wrist before I can shift into reverse. "You live with Dean. That's not going to be uncomfortable for you?"

"No, why would it?"

"I don't know." Her index finger slides forward to rub my knuckles.

I grit my teeth as my erection nearly breaks through the zipper. The only reason I didn't kiss her the second we were outside the bar is because if I'd started, I probably would've taken her against the side of the building. But now she's touching me, and my self-control is more elusive than a puff of steam.

"Let's do it here," she says decisively.

I frown. "In the truck?"

"Why not? Do you need candles and rose petals? It's just sex," she insists.

"Darlin', you keep saying that and I'm going to start wondering if it's really me you want to convince." My breath catches when her thumb strokes a tiny circle in the center of my palm. Fuck it. I need her too bad. "But fine. You want to do me in this truck, then the truck it is."

Without another word, I reach beneath me and push the seat back as far as it can go. Then I shrug out of my jacket and toss it into the backseat.

"You got any guidelines for your just-sex hookups?" I drawl. "Like no kissing on the lips?"

"Hell, no. Do I look like Julia Roberts?"

I scrunch up my eyebrows.

"*Pretty Woman?*" she prompts. "Hooker with the heart of gold? No kissing the johns?"

I grin. "So what you're saying is that you'll kiss *this* John?" I tap my chest so she knows I'm referring to my name and not implying that she's a hooker.

She snickers. "If you don't kiss me, I'll be pissed. I need kissing. Otherwise I'd just stay at home with my vibe."

A smile creeps across my face. With my back against the window and my boot up on the console, I create a cradle for her hot body and beckon her toward me. "Then come and get what you need."

3

SABRINA

Tucker sits there with a slight smile on his face and a huge erection in his pants. My tongue sneaks out to wet my lips as excitement buzzes through my veins. God, that monster is going to feel so good inside me.

My gaze falls to his neatly trimmed beard, and I wonder, briefly, whether I should've given Carin a shot at him. After all, beards were on her bucket list. But now *I'm* wondering what that scruff would feel like between my legs. Soft? Scratchy? I squeeze my thighs together in anticipation.

Hope and Carin were so right. I do need to get laid, and hockey player or not, I believe Tucker is the guy for the job. He has confidence without the ego, which is the biggest turn-on ever. When he'd said "you" in response to my question about what he wanted, I nearly came in my panties.

And he seems steady, as if an earthquake wouldn't shake him. I even admired the way he stuck up for Dean, even though I know the loyalty is misplaced. Tucker had to have known that if he'd lied about his friendship with Dean, he could've stood a better chance with me, but he chose honesty, which I value most out of everything.

"Need some direction?" His voice is low and gravelly, drawing out those syllables. *Die rehhhc shun.*

Sweet Jesus, that accent.

"Just considering my options." I love that he's just sitting there, instructing me to take what I need. As if his big cock exists just for me.

I can't wait, but I can't decide what I want to do first, either. My mouth waters at the thought of his shaft dragging against my tongue, but my core aches at the anticipation of him stretching me, filling me all the way up.

"Why don't we start with the kissing you're so fond of?" he suggests.

I meet his hot gaze. "Where?" I ask coyly, which is weird, because I'm never coy. But there's something about the surety in him that draws out the woman in me, and I find I don't mind it at all.

He taps one big finger against his lower lip. "Right here."

As seductively as possible, I crawl over the console and onto his lap, allowing my heels to drop onto the floor of the truck. His mouth parts in invitation, but I don't immediately press my lips to his.

Instead, I run my fingertips across his beard, from one side of his jaw to the other. "Soft," I murmur.

His eyes darken and grow so full of lust that it's hard to breathe. And then he grabs me, tired of waiting and tired of talking.

Our mouths slam together. He tangles a hand in my hair and I'm not sure if it's to get a better angle or provide more leverage for the force of his invasion. Either way, his tongue is making me feel magical things downstairs. I'm forgetting why I almost turned him down.

I mean, tall, hot, dark auburn hair, scruffy beard? Why did I even hesitate? Oh, that's right. Because he's a hockey player.

Tearing my mouth away, I pant, "Just for the record, I hate hockey players. This is a one-time-only deal."

He sweeps my hair to the side to expose my throat. "Noted. I won't even remind you of this when you're begging me for a second round."

Laughing, I grab his head and hold it against me as he tongues his way down my throat to the tops of my breasts. "Never happening."

"Don't tie yourself to absolutes. It makes it easier to back away. More graceful."

His words are somewhat muffled as he buries his face in my cleavage. A callused hand pulls at my shirt, and then I hear a frustrated growl when the neckline doesn't lower enough to give him access to what he wants.

Good thing our needs are aligned. I reach between us and yank my sweater off, and his mouth latches on to my nipple before I can get my bra undone. When I reach around to undo the clasp, his hands bat mine away.

My laugh at his eagerness dies in my throat as his palm closes around one bare breast. I arch into his rough caress. Oh gosh, it's been way, *way* too long. As Tucker's mouth gets busy sucking on one puckered nipple, his fingers pinch and tease the other one.

He's good at this. He knows how deep to suck, how hard to bite, how tender to kiss, and despite the rod in his pants, he acts like he could do this nipple-sucking deed all night long.

I rock my lower body over his erection, fumbling to push my skirt out of the way so I can really feel him. I want it off, damn it. I want his naked body rubbing against mine. I want him inside me.

I want it all.

I fish for the bottom of his T-shirt. He offers me zero assistance, because he's too intent on my breasts right now. I find the hem and pull it hard. Only then does he separate from me, and the cool air in the truck causes my nipples to tighten even more.

"I don't need more foreplay," I tell him as I drag his shirt up over his head.

Oh God, muscle alert. Lots and lots of tight, smooth, rippled muscles glide beneath my palms. Gotta love athletes.

His hands tunnel under my skirt. "Is that right?"

There's nothing graceful about the way his fingers shove aside my thong, and there's no warning when he thrusts two of them inside of me. It's dirty and so hot. Air whistles between my teeth as I inhale sharply.

"Like that, do you?" he murmurs.

"It's okay," I lie, and am immediately punished when he withdraws. "Fine. It feels good."

He withdraws again and uses his now wet fingers to lightly circle my clit. My entire body strains and clenches and screams for more.

"Just good, huh?" he taunts.

I give in. "Great. It's great."

"I know." He looks smug. "I hate to tell you this, Sabrina. But you've made a big mistake."

"What? Why?"

His fingers draw my thong tight, the fabric cutting into my swollen lips. "Because I'm going to ruin you for all future guys. I apologize in advance."

Then he jerks the fabric aside and slams three fingers in. The graphic rawness of it comes as a giant shock. I can feel it—him—everywhere. Even down to my toes. A wave of excitement crashes over me. Holy shit, he's making me come. Is that even possible?

I stare at him open-mouthed, and he grins back, white teeth against his tanned skin and his beard, fully aware he's blowing my mind. His fingers move again, two of them rubbing against that spot that hardly anyone ever finds but me.

And he keeps rubbing it as he jacks his fingers inside me. And I keep coming. I let my head fall back and my eyelids fall closed and I give myself over to the pleasure that spirals up and through my body until I'm one shuddering mass of sensation.

When I drop back to Earth, I find myself lying against his chest, gasping for air. I've never come this hard in my life, and the guy hasn't even been inside me yet. My heart is pounding insanely fast, and my sluggish mind is having a hard time keeping up.

He's just a guy. A normal guy, I remind myself. One dick and two balls. This is nothing special.

"I haven't had sex in a while," I mumble as my breathing starts to normalize. "I've been super stressed. My body really needed a release."

Three long fingers flex inside me. "Whatever you need to tell yourself, darlin'."

There's smug amusement in his voice, but the guy just fingered me to orgasm (which *never* happens to me), so I guess I can't blame him. He drags the pads of his fingers along my sensitive nerve endings as he withdraws, pulling another involuntary shudder out of me.

Between us, his hand rises and the wetness shines on his fingers even in the dark cab of his truck. I'm not prepared for the shock of arousal that hits me when he sucks them clean.

I gulp.

One swift jerk of a lever and his seat falls completely flat. Tucker lies down and beckons for me again. "C'mere and fuck my face. I need more of that."

Oh. My. God. Who *is* this guy?

Maybe I shouldn't hike my skirt up around my waist and crawl forward, but I do. It's like he's cast a spell on me and I'm helpless to disobey him.

"You're gonna want to brace yourself," he rasps, "because I'm going to make you come again."

"You're so fucking cocky."

"No. I'm sure. And so are you. Now gimme that sweet pussy and ride my tongue."

Oh, sweet baby Jesus. Sex with Tucker is dirtier and hotter than I thought it would be. He doesn't look like he'd be this way, but isn't it always the quiet ones?

I like it, almost too much.

His hot breath warms my skin as I lower myself over his face.

"Fuck yeah," is the last thing he says before his mouth latches on to me.

He doesn't just use his tongue. He uses his lips, his teeth to scrape across my hypersensitive clit. One hand is clamped around my hip while he uses the other to finger me. And his tongue? He licks me in long, sweeping strokes until I'm muffling sobs against my wrist. Then he parts me with two fingers and holds me open while his tongue stabs hard inside me.

He's right—I do need to brace myself. I grip the sides of the seat and then I'm gone. He brings me right to the edge of the cliff and throws me over.

While I'm still shuddering from my second orgasm of the night, Tucker lifts me off his face and down to his lap where somehow his dick is free of his jeans. I reach between us and grab him.

"Wait," he barks, but it's too late.

I suck in my lower lip as the broad head slowly penetrates me. Greedily, I push down, wanting to fill myself up. His hands find my hips, and I breathe out a sigh of anticipatory satisfaction only to yelp with dismay when he pushes me off.

"Condom," he says grimly.

I glance down between us in surprise. I never make that mistake. Never. My hand flies to my mouth. "I'm sorry. I wasn't thinking..."

He fumbles in his jeans, finds his wallet and tosses it to me. "No big deal. It was just the tip."

A sly wink draws a startled laugh out of me. I bite open the foil and then position the rubber over the head of his shaft.

"I'm clean," I feel compelled to tell him. "I get tested after..." I trail off, feeling like talking about past hookups is bad form when I'm naked and about to impale myself on someone else's dick. "Well, after. And I'm on the pill."

"It's all good on my end," he says. His eyelids flutter shut for a beat as I roll the condom down the thick, hot column of flesh. A low moan escapes his mouth, and then he brushes my hand aside to take hold of himself.

"Ready?" he asks, positioning the head at my entrance.

I don't know if I nod or whimper or beg, but whatever sound comes out of my mouth must sound like assent, because he shoves upward with one swift motion until he's seated to the hilt.

"Fuck, you're so tight," he hisses through gritted teeth.

"And you're damn big," I croak, wriggling around on top of him.

He grabs my hips to hold me still and shallowly pumps into me. "Don't move."

"Can't stop." The friction feels so good. If I thought his fingers and tongue were magic, his dick is supernatural. I can feel him *everywhere*.

I dig my knees into the leather seat and rest my hands on his chest. The muscles flex beneath my palms, and I rake my gaze over his ridged abdomen, the light hair on his chest, and the thin line that leads directly down to heaven.

He's as delicious to look at as he feels. I wonder how he tastes, but that will have to come later. Right now, I need him to fuck me until my anxiety about Harvard, money, and my home life is driven out completely. I want to be wrecked and he's the perfect man for the job.

I slam down on him. A feral look crosses his face and then a large palm clamps against my ass. He powers upward, finding the leverage from somewhere, and even though I'm on top, he's clearly in control, which is exactly what I want.

His teeth are clenched and I feel the bite of his fingers on my ass, pushing me downward with each thrust forward. I squeeze my thighs tight around him and give myself over to his care, allowing him to power me into oblivion.

"Come for me," he mumbles. "Take what you need."

Inside of me, his cock pulses, and then his fingers find my clit, stroking and teasing it until I go off like a rocket, shaking so hard I can barely stay on top of him.

Tucker rises part way to clasp me to his chest, pounding into me so hard that I have to raise trembling hands to the truck's roof to prevent my head from slamming through it.

He drives into me, over and over, until suddenly he's the shaky, mindless mess who has a hard time maintaining any control. He collapses back against the seat, taking me with him.

I allow myself a few selfish moments to catch my breath, luxuriating against the big chest beneath me. Tremors give way to contentment. A part of me wants to stretch this moment out endlessly, curled up in this guy's lap while his hand runs soothingly up and down my spine.

"You sure you don't want to crash at my place?" he asks.

For a second, I nearly say yes. Yes, to going back to his place. Yes, to another round of sex. Yes, to breakfast in the morning, skipping work, and spending the entire day in bed with him. The need surprises and scares me.

I take a deep breath and gather up the pieces of my composure that he fucked into tiny bits. "No. I need to get home."

Just sex.

Right. It's just sex. John Tucker is good in bed. So good that he should be getting a trophy. But it's not better than I've had before. It only feels that way because of the stress I'm under. Or even if it was the best I've had, that doesn't mean anything other than he's one more data point in the *athletes make good lovers* theory. Stamina. World-class fingers and tongue. A dick that could serve as the model for the large versions at a sex shop.

I root around for my shirt and jacket. I throw them on, not even caring that they're likely on backwards. I need to get out of this truck and into my car.

"I'm ready," I announce. "My car is only a couple blocks from here."

His handsome features soften. "You look a little shocky."

I twist in agitation, but his expression shows nothing but concern. "I'm good," I assure him.

Tucker sits up and removes the condom, tying it off and then dumping it into a nest of napkins. He fingers his keys for a moment and then starts the truck. "Where to?"

I let out a breath of relief. "Over on Forest. Big Victorian."

"Got it."

We drive the short distance in silence. At the first glimpse of my car, the urge to flee is hard to resist. I have the door open before he comes to a complete stop.

"See you around," I say lightly.

"I'm walking you to your car."

He lifts his hips to pull his jeans up, alerting me to the fact that he's still half-naked. I try not to stare as he tucks his semi-hard dick away. He could go another round, easy.

My body pleads for more contact, which I ignore by climbing out of the truck. When Tucker joins me, his T-shirt is back on and his jeans are riding on his trim hips, the zipper undone. He still has his boots on.

A gurgle of hysteria shoots into my throat. He fucked me that good and he didn't even take his boots off?

"I'll follow you home," he says.

"I told you, I live in Boston."

He shrugs. "So? Roads are shit and I want to make sure you get home okay."

"I'll be fine. I've made this run dozens of times before."

"Then text me when you get home."

"No phone numbers," I remind him, feeling weirdly panicked.

"It's either the text or I follow you." Finality rings in his voice.

Figures I'd have a one-night stand with the last remaining gentleman on this planet.

"Fine." I fish my phone out of my coat pocket. "But you're killing off all the good feelings."

His light brown eyes twinkle. "Shouldn't matter, right, because this isn't going to be repeated?"

He has a fucking answer for everything. "You should be pre-law," I mutter. "Give me your number."

I tap it in as he reels it off, then unlock my car and practically hurl myself into the driver's seat. Thankfully, the engine of my some-times-unreliable Honda starts immediately.

I crack my window down an inch and murmur a hasty, "Night, Tucker," and he responds with a quick nod.

I watch him in the rearview mirror for nearly a block, a lone figure against the moonlit backdrop, before forcing my gaze forward. That's where my focus has to be.

The drive home passes by in a blur, though, as my mind replays the hot sex scene on repeat. Stupid mind.

But...the sex was *so* good. Would it really hurt to see him again?

I park on the cracked asphalt of the carport behind my house and just sit there for a moment. Then I rake a hand through my tousled sex-hair and reach for my phone.

Me: *I'm here.*

The response is immediate.

Him: *Good. Glad to hear it. Feel free to use this number again.*

Do I want to use it—him—again? It's so tempting. John Tucker was hot as hell, fucked like a god, and was so laidback nothing seemed to faze him. He didn't ask me any difficult questions and didn't seem interested in wanting more than I could offer. How often does a guy like that come along?

Me: *I'll keep that in mind.*

Him: *U do that, darlin'.*

I run a thumb over my lip, remembering how good it felt when he kissed me. Argh. Maybe I *will* use that number again.

Exhaustion hits me the moment I step out of the car. I need some sleep, STAT. Tomorrow's going to be as long and tiring as today was, and I can't say I'm looking forward to it.

When I stumble through the door, Nana is sitting in the same spot I left her. I suspect the only time she moved in the four or so hours I've been gone was to pee out the empty two-liter Coke bottle on the kitchen table. The bottle was full before I left. There's a different magazine in front of her, though. I think it's the *Enquirer*.

She takes in my disheveled appearance. "Thought you had a cocktail party." A smirk forms. "Looks like you were on the menu."

Heat floods my face. Yup. Nothing like a word from Nana to set the world back in order.

I ignore the jab and head for the doorway. "'Night," I mumble.

"Goodnight," she replies, her chuckles following me into the bedroom.

After I've closed and locked the door, I pull out my phone and bring up Tucker's name. For one long moment, I stare at it. I'm tempted to text him something. Anything.

Instead, I go to the info screen and press "BLOCK."

Because no matter how sexy he is or how many orgasms he can wring out of me, there's no place in my life for a second round with him.

4

TUCKER

The sound of a car engine revving jerks me awake. It's still dark out, but I can make out the tiniest sliver of light on the horizon, a grayish stripe in a black background. I flip the lever of my seat and allow the mechanism to push me upright, just in time to see a small Honda Civic pulling out of Sabrina James's drive.

Blearily, I check the time on the dash. Four a.m. As her car drives past, I catch a glimpse of dark hair, and before I know it, I've pulled out in traffic behind her.

I followed her to Boston last night because the roads were still icy and I was worried about her. And I wasn't convinced she was going to text me. After she'd come that last time, she'd totally shut down. It was obvious that being intimate isn't something she feels comfortable with. I got the sense I could say about any filthy thing I wanted to her and she'd be completely fine, but a tender, caring word and she'd jackrabbit out of there.

Hell, she almost jumped out of my truck in her haste to get away. I didn't take it personally, though.

I stretch my back as best as I can. I haven't slept in my truck for a long time, and my body's reminding me the exact reason why. But it was either catch a few zzzs or take a chance driving back on the slick roads. I chose to sleep in my cab.

Sabrina's car zips through a yellow light and then takes a sharp left. By the time I catch up, she's pulling into the employee parking lot of a south Boston post office. A second later, she stumbles out of the driver's seat wearing a work uniform, her long hair tied back in a ponytail.

A smile curves across my face. Smoking hot, bright as the sun, and a hard worker? Damn. My mom would love this girl.

I DRIVE BACK to Hastings with a silly-ass grin on my face and throw myself on my bed to sleep for three measly hours. Then I hop right back in the truck and drive to campus to meet up with my study group, because we've got a big marketing test tomorrow. Though I'm not sure this nine a.m. cram session is going to help me much in my groggy state. Two cups of coffee succeed in waking me up a bit, and I feel much more alert when the session breaks up around eleven.

Rather than head home right away, I grab a third coffee and pull out my phone. It's time to do a little digging, and I'd rather do it at the coffeehouse than at home where my nosy roommates might ask questions.

I know Sabrina has classes with Dean, but Dean's not exactly reliable when it comes to her, so I hit up the only other poli sci major I know—Sheena Drake. She's an ex but still a good friend of mine. Actually, I can't think of a single ex I'm not friends with.

Me: *What do u know about Sabrina James?*

Sheena answers right away, which tells me she either didn't party too hard last night, or she partied so hard she never went to bed.

Her: *Ugh. Hate her.*

I frown at the screen.

Me: *Why?*

Her: *b/c she's hotter than me. Bitch.*

My loud snort draws the attention of the trio of students at the neighboring table. Another text from Sheena pops up.

Her: *But she's hotter than EVERYONE. So I guess I can't b mad? Why r u asking about her?*

Me: *Ran into her last night. She seemed cool.*

Her: *I wouldn't know. Got 2 classes w/ her but she's not too chatty. Super smart, tho. Rumor is she only hooks up w/ jocks.*

I sip my coffee as I ponder that. Guess it makes sense, seeing as she hooked up with me last night. My phone buzzes with another message from Sheena.

U crushing on her?

Considering I had my tongue, mouth, fingers and dick all over her last night, I think I might be past crushing. But I just type, *Maybe.*

Her: *U so are!!! Tell me everything!!!*

Me: *Nothing 2 tell. CU in Econ tmrw?*

Her: *Yup.*

Me: *K. Thx, babe.*

Her: *<3*

I scroll through my contact list in search of anyone else who might know Sabrina, but only one name pops out at me. Hell, it's probably the person I should've spoken to first.

I gulp down the rest of my coffee, then head for the door. I shoot off a quick text, but there's no insta-response, so instead of waiting I send another message, this time to Ollie Jankowitz, the roommate of the guy I'm trying to track down.

Me: *U with Beau?*

Him: *Negative.*

Me: *Know where he's at?*

Him: *Gym.*

Well, that was easy.

I leave my truck in the student lot and decide to make the trek on foot, since the football stadium is only a short walk from the coffeehouse. My Briar hockey ID doesn't give me access to the training facility, but luckily I reach the door at the same time as a sophomore lineman, who lets me in.

I find Beau Maxwell in the weight room, working on his chest and arms. Beau is Briar's beloved quarterback, and, as far as I know, the last guy who'd held Sabrina's interest for any significant period of time.

He's a friend of mine, closer to Dean than any of us, but we're still buddies and I'd rather he hear that I'm chasing after Sabrina from me than the gossip mill. Athletes spend as much time as anyone talking about hookups, girlfriends, and future lays.

"Maxwell," I call as I cross the room, which smells like sweat and industrial cleaning supplies. "Got a minute?"

Beau doesn't look away from the mirror. "Sure. I'm gonna do bench presses in a sec. You can spot me."

"Sounds like a plan." I take a seat on the bench next to him and mentally count his reps as he does them. At ten, he drops the fifty-pound kettle bell and turns to me.

"I'm doing light weights, double reps," he explains, feeling the need to justify the two-fifty weight on the barbell.

"Should you even be lifting anything at all?" I don't know much about the quarterback position, but it seems to me that any extra muscle could affect his throwing arm.

"Light weights only," he reiterates.

As he lies back and reaches above him, I move to the head of the bench. With these weights, I doubt he could hurt himself, so the spotter position is sort of unnecessary. But it gives me something to do while we talk.

"Heard you hooked up with Sabrina James this fall," I start awkwardly. "You still holding a torch for her?"

Beau tilts his head backward so he can stare at me. He's got vivid blue eyes that I'm pretty sure half the chicks at Briar have gotten lost in. Or have dreamed about getting lost in.

"Naah, no torch here," he finally answers. "Why? You aiming to tap that?"

Already have, dude. But I repeat what I told Sheena. "Maybe."

"Gotcha. Well, if you're looking for more than a hookup, she's not your girl."

"Yeah?"

"Oh yeah. Seriously, Tuck, she's closed tighter than a clam. She doesn't have time." Beau wrinkles his forehead. "She's got like four or five jobs and you have to fit in on her schedule. Like a doctor on call."

"That's good to know."

He finishes out his reps in silence. When he's done, he pushes upright, and I toss him a bottle of water I find next to the bench.

"Need any more help?" I ask.

"Naah, I got it."

"See you around then." I take a step, then glance over at him again. "Do me a favor and keep this convo between us?"

He nods. "Gotcha."

I'm at the exit door when Beau calls out to me.

"Hey, what if I said I was still interested?"

I turn around to meet his eyes. "That'd be too bad."

Beau chuckles. "I thought so. Well, more power to you, dude, but I'm warning you—there are easier women than Sabrina."

"Why would I want someone easy?" I flash him a grin. "That doesn't sound like any fun."

5

SABRINA

I'm having one of those days. The kind of day where I'm living in a cartoon and I'm the Road Runner, speeding from one place to another without a single opportunity to sit down or breathe.

Well, technically I do a lot of sitting in my morning classes, but it's not relaxing at all, because we're gearing up for our con law papers which make up the entirety of my grade, and I stupidly chose one of the hardest topics—the differing legal standards applied to examine the constitutionality of laws.

Breakfast consists of a cheese croissant that I scarf down on the way from Advanced Political Theory to Media and Government. And I don't even get to finish it, because in my haste I trip on the cobblestone path that winds through campus and end up dropping the croissant in a puddle of slush.

My stomach growls angrily during the Media lecture, then gets louder and angrier when I meet with my advisor to talk finances. I didn't find any acceptance letters in my mailbox this morning, but I have to believe that I at least got into *one* of the programs I applied to.

And even the second tier schools will cost a pretty penny, which means I need a scholarship. If I don't get into a top law school, there'll be no BigLaw job offer with its BigLaw paycheck, and that means crushing, demoralizing, endless debt.

After the meeting, I have a one-hour tutorial for my Game Theory class. It's run by the TA, a skinny guy with Albert Einstein hair and the annoying, pretentious habit of incorporating REALLY BIG WORDS in every sentence he utters.

I'm an intelligent person, but every time I'm around this guy, I'm secretly looking up words on my phone's dictionary app under the table. There's really no reason for a person to use the word *parsimonious* when they can just say *frugal*—unless they're a total douche, of course. But Steve thinks of himself as a big shot. Though rumor has it, he's still a TA because he's failed—twice—to defend his dissertation and can't get an associate professorship anywhere.

Once the meeting wraps up, I shove my laptop and notebook in my messenger bag and make a beeline for the door.

I'm so hungry that I'm feeling light-headed. Fortunately, there's a sandwich place in the lobby of the building. I fly out the door, only to skid to a stop when a familiar face greets me.

My heart somersaults so hard it's embarrassing. I've spent the last day and a half forcing myself not to think about this guy, and now he's standing here, in the flesh.

My gaze eats him up eagerly. He's wearing his hockey jacket again. His auburn hair is windblown, cheeks ruddy as if he'd just come in from the cold. Faded blue jeans encase his impossibly long legs, and he's got his hands hooked lightly in the tops of his pockets.

"Tucker," I squeak.

His lips quirk up. "Sabrina."

"W-what are you doing here?" Oh my God. I'm stuttering. What's wrong with me?

Someone jostles me from behind. I hastily step away from the doorway to let the other students out. I'm not sure what to say, but I know what I want to *do*. I want to throw myself at this guy, wrap my arms around his neck, my legs around his waist, and maul him with my mouth.

But I don't.

"You're ignoring my texts," he says frankly.

Guilt tickles my throat. I'm not ignoring his texts—I haven't gotten them. Because I blocked his number.

Still, my heart does another silly flip at the knowledge that he's been texting. I suddenly wish I knew what he'd said, but I'm not going to ask him. That's just looking for trouble.

For some stupid reason, though, I find myself confessing, "I blocked you."

Rather than look offended, he chuckles. "Yeah. I figured you might've. That's why I tracked you down."

I narrow my eyes. "And how did you do that, exactly? How'd you know I'd be here?"

"I asked my advisor for your schedule."

My jaw falls open. "And she gave it to you?"

"He, actually. And yep, he was happy to do it."

Disbelief and indignation mingle in my blood. What the hell? The faculty can't just hand out students' schedules to anyone who asks for them, right? That's a violation of privacy. I grit my teeth and decide that the moment I pass the bar, my first order of legal business will be suing this stupid college.

"Did he give you my transcript too?" I mutter.

"No. And don't worry, I'm sure your schedule isn't being passed around in flier-form around campus. He only gave it to me because I play hockey."

"That's supposed to make me feel better? The reminder that you're a privileged jackass who gets special treatment because you skate around on the ice and win trophies?"

I take off walking, my pace brisk, but he's big enough that his strides eat up the ground and he's beside me in a heartbeat.

"I'm sorry." He sounds genuinely regretful. "If it helps, I don't normally play the athlete card to get favors. Hell, I could've asked Dean for your schedule, but I figured you'd like that even less."

He's right about that. The thought of Tucker talking to Dean Di Laurentis about me makes my skin crawl.

"Fine. Well, you tracked me down. What do you want, Tucker?" I walk faster.

"What's the hurry, darlin'?"

"My life," I mumble.

"What?"

"I'm always in a hurry," I clarify. "I've got twenty minutes to get some food in me before my next class."

We reach the lobby, where I instantly get in line at the sandwich stand, scanning the menu on the wall. The student in front of us leaves the counter before Tucker can speak. I hurriedly step forward to place my order. When I reach into my bag for my wallet, Tucker's hand drops over mine.

"I've got this," he says, already drawing a twenty-dollar bill from his brown leather wallet.

I don't know why, but that annoys me even more. "First drinks at Malone's, and now lunch? What, you're trying to show off? Making sure I know you've got cash to spare?"

Hurt flickers in his deep brown eyes.

Fuck. I don't know why I'm antagonizing him. It's just...him showing up here, admitting he pulled favors to find me, paying for my lunch...

It was supposed to be a one-time thing, and now he's in my face and I don't like it.

No, that's not true. I *love* having his face near mine. He's so sexy, and he smells so good, like sandalwood and citrus. I want to bury my nose in the strong column of his neck and inhale him until I get a contact high.

But there's no time for that. Time is a concept that doesn't exist in my life, and John Tucker is too big a distraction.

"I'm paying for your lunch because that's the way my mama

raised me," he says quietly. "Call me old-fashioned if you want, but that's how I roll."

I gulp down another rush of guilt. "I'm sorry." My voice shakes slightly. "Thank you for lunch. I appreciate it."

We edge to the other end of the counter, waiting in silence as a curly-haired girl prepares my ham and Swiss sandwich. She wraps it up for me, and I tuck it under my arm while uncapping the Diet Coke I'd ordered. Then we're on the move again. Tucker follows me out the door, watching in amusement as I try to juggle my drink and messenger bag and unwrap my sandwich at the same time.

"Let me hold this for you." He takes the bottle from my hand. There's a gentleness on his face as he watches me sink my teeth into the lightly toasted rye bread.

I barely chew before I'm taking a second bite, which makes him laugh. "Hungry?" he teases.

"Famished," I admit, and I don't even care that I'm being rude by talking with my mouth full.

I quickly descend the wide steps. Again, he keeps up with me.

"You shouldn't eat while you walk," he advises.

"No time. My next class is all the way across campus, so—hey!" I exclaim when he takes my arm and drags me away from the path. "What are you doing?"

Ignoring my protests, he leads me to one of the wrought-iron benches on the lawn. It hasn't snowed yet this winter, but the grass is covered with a silver layer of frost. Tucker forces me to sit, then drops down beside me and plants one hand on my knee, as if he's afraid I might bolt. Which I was totally considering doing before that big hand made contact. The heat of it sears through my tights and warms my core.

"Eat," he says gently. "You're allowed to give yourself two minutes to recharge, darlin'."

I find myself obeying, same way I obeyed the other night when he told me to ride his face, when he ordered me to come. A shiver shimmies up my spine. God, why can't I get this guy out of my head?

"What did you text me?" I blurt out.

He gives a mysterious smile. "Guess you'll never know."

Despite myself, I smile back. "It was something sexy, wasn't it?"

He whistles innocently.

"It was!" I accuse, and then experience a jolt of self-directed recrimination, because, damn it, I bet it was filthy and delicious and wonderful.

"Listen, I'm not going to take up much of your time," he says. "I know you're busy. I know you commute from Boston. I know you have a few jobs—"

"Two," I correct. My head tips in challenge. "And how would you know that?"

He shrugs. "I've been asking around."

He has? Crap. As flattering as that is, I'm kind of scared to know who he's been asking and what they've been telling him. Aside from Hope and Carin, I don't spend much time with my peers. I know I come off as aloof at times—

Fine, bitchy. Aloof is just a nice word for *bitchy*. And while I'm not thrilled that my classmates think I'm a bitch, there's not much I can do about that. I don't have the time or energy to make small talk, or to grab coffee after class, or to pretend that I have anything in common with the wealthy, elitist kids that comprise most of this college.

"The point," he finishes, "is that I get it, okay? You're swamped, and I'm not asking you to wear my varsity jacket and my class ring and be my steady girl."

I have to laugh at the *Pleasantville* picture he's painted. "Then what *are* you asking me?"

"For a date," he says simply. "One date. Maybe it'll end with us fucking again—"

My body sings in delight.

"—or maybe it won't. Either way, I wanna see you again."

I watch as he rakes a hand through his reddish hair. Damn, who would've thought that gingers could be so hot?

"I don't care when. You want to grab a bite late at night, fine. Early in the morning, cool, as long as I don't have practice. I'm willing to play by your rules, adapt to your schedule."

Pleasure and suspicion war inside me, but the latter wins out. "Why? I mean, I know we rocked each other's worlds, but why are you so hard up on seeing me again?"

I gulp when he fixes me with a steady, intense gaze. Then he freaks me out even more by asking, "Do you believe in love at first sight?"

Oh my fucking God.

I start to shoot to my feet.

He tugs me back onto the bench with a deep chuckle. "Chill, Sabrina. I'm not saying I'm in love with you."

He'd better not be! Taking a calming breath, I set my half-eaten sandwich on my lap and try to muster up a tone that doesn't convey the scared-shitless feeling racing through me. "Then what are you saying?"

"I'd seen you around campus before the night at Malone's," he admits. "And yeah, I thought you were hot, but it's not like I was desperate to find out who you were."

"Gee, thanks."

"Make up your mind, darlin'. Do you want me to be infatuated with you, or do you want me to not give a shit?"

Both! I want both, and that's the problem, damn it.

"Anyway, I'd seen you before. But the night at the bar, when we made eye contact from across the room? Something magical happened," he says bluntly. "I know you felt it too."

I pick up my sandwich and take a small bite, chewing extra slow in order to delay having to respond. He's freaking me out again, with his confident gaze and his matter-of-fact tone. I've never met a guy who can throw out phrases like "love at first sight" and "something magical happened" without at least having the decency to blush or look mortified.

Finally, I force myself to answer him. "The only magical thing that happened was that we liked what we saw. Pheromones, Tucker. Nothing more."

"That was part of it," he agrees. "But there was more to it than that, and you know it. There was a connection the moment we looked at each other."

I raise my Diet Coke to my lips and chug nearly half of it.

"I want to explore it. I think we'd be stupid not to."

"And I think..." I struggle for words. "I think..."

I think you're the most fascinating guy I've ever met.

I think you're amazing in bed and I want to fuck you again.

I think if I was capable of having my heart broken, you'd have the power to break it.

"I think I made myself clear that night," I finish. "I'm not in the market for a relationship, or even a fuck buddy. I wanted sex. You gave it to me. That's all it was."

I don't miss the disappointment that floods his eyes. It brings a pang of regret and makes my stomach twist painfully, but I've already set this course and now I need to see it through. I'm very good at staying the course.

"I know you athletes are stubborn as hell and that you don't give up when you want something, but..." I take a breath. "I'm asking you to give up."

His jaw tightens. "Sabrina—"

"Please." I cringe at the desperate note in my voice. "Just give up, all right? I don't want to start anything up. I don't want to go on a date. I want..." I rise on wobbly legs. "I want to get to class, that's all."

After an interminably long silence, he gets up too. "Sure, darlin'. If that's what you want."

It's not a taunt, nor does it contain even a hint of promise, as in *sure, darlin', I'll give up—for now. But expect me to keep chasing you until I wear you down.*

No, there's a finality to his words that makes me sad. John Tucker is clearly a man of his word, and while I ought to admire that, I've suddenly become a hypocrite, because now *I'm* the one feeling disappointed.

"I'll see you around," he says gruffly.

And then he strides off without another word, leaving me to stare after him in dismay.

I did the right thing. I *know* I did. Even if I had oodles of free time to pursue something with him, there's no room in my life for someone like Tucker. He's sweet and earnest and clearly has money, whereas I'm bitchy and stressed and live in the gutter. He can talk all he wants about connections at first sight, but that doesn't change the reality of this.

I'm not the girl for John Tucker, and I never will be.

6

TUCKER

Practice is shit. The team's just not clicking this season, and Coach Jensen is riding us mercilessly now that we've got a few losses tarnishing our record. Yesterday's loss bummed us out pretty hard—we were up against a Division II team who should *not* have wiped our asses all over the ice like that.

The new defensive coach, Frank O'Shea, is only making things worse. I've been thanking my lucky stars that I'm not a defenseman. O'Shea seems to have a vendetta against Dean, constantly calling him out and harping on his mistakes.

Dean's cheeks go redder than apples every time O'Shea opens his mouth. According to Logan, the man used to be the head coach at Dean's prep school. They obviously have a past, but whatever it is, Dean's not sharing. But he's not happy, either. Not only are the d-men constantly ordered to stay late, but apparently Dean got forced into coaching the kiddie team at the elementary school in town.

I skate to the bench after my shift and heave myself over the wall, then squirt some water in my mouth and watch Garrett's line fly across the blue line. Today's scrimmage is non-scoring so far. Seriously, that's how bad we suck. We can't even score on each other during practice, and it's not because our goalies are in top form—none of the forwards can get their shit together, myself included.

A whistle blows. Coach starts screaming at one of our junior d-men for icing the puck.

"What the hell was that, Kelvin! You had four passing opportunities and you decide to ice the fucking thing!" Coach looks ready to pull his hair out.

I don't blame him.

"I could've made that pass if I was out there," Dean grumbles beside me.

I glance over in sympathy. One of O'Shea's first orders of business had been to rearrange the lines. He'd paired Dean up with Brodowski, and Logan with Kelvin, when we all know that Logan and Dean are unstoppable together.

"I'm sure O'Shea will realize his mistake soon."

"Yeah right. This is punishment. The motherfucker hates me."

My curiosity is once again piqued. "Why's that again?"

Dean's expression goes cloudier. "Don't worry about it."

"Not sure if you know this," I say pleasantly, "but secrets kill friendships."

That makes him snicker. "You really want to talk to me about secrets? Where the fuck were you all weekend?"

I instantly shutter my expression. I'm cool confiding in my friends about my love life, but I don't want to discuss Sabrina with Dean, especially when I know his opinion of her. Besides, what the fuck is there to talk about, anyway? She shot me down. I asked her out and she flat-out told me no, it was never gonna happen.

If I thought there was even the slightest chance that she wanted me to chase after her, maybe I wouldn't have taken no for an answer. Maybe I would've shown up after her classes a few more times, bought her a couple more sandwiches, wooed her with my charm and worked the southern accent whenever I felt her drawing away.

But I saw the look in her eyes. She meant what she said—she doesn't want to see me again. And although I have no problem being the pursuer, I'm not going to chase after someone who's not interested.

Still, it fucking sucks balls. When we were sitting on that bench the other day, I wanted nothing more than to pull her onto my lap and fuck her right there, and to hell with anyone walking by. The Dean himself could've been standing there tapping his watch and I still wouldn't have stopped. It had taken all my willpower to suppress the primal urges, but man, something about that girl...

It's not just her beauty, though that doesn't hurt at all. It's...it's... damn, I can't even put it into words. She's got this hard exterior, but inside she's as soft as butter. I see flashes of vulnerability in her bottomless dark eyes and I just want to...take care of her.

The guys would laugh if they knew what I was thinking right now. Or hell, maybe they wouldn't. They already rag me daily at home about my "nurturing" side. I'm our resident cook, do most of the cleaning, make sure shit around the house is in working order.

That's how my mom raised me, though. I didn't have a dad. He died when I was three and I barely remember him. But Mom more than made up for him not being there, and the father figure I was lacking came in the form of my hockey coaches.

Texas is a football state. I probably would've gone that route if it weren't for a vacation we took to Wisconsin when I was five. Once a year, Mom and I would visit my dad's sister in Green Bay. Or at least we tried to. Sometimes money wouldn't allow it, but we did our best.

During that visit, Aunt Nancy bundled me up and took me skating. It's goddamn cold in Green Bay—I imagine that's most people's worst nightmare, but I loved the chill on my cheeks, the frigid air hissing past my ears as I skated on that outdoor pond. A few older kids had a game of hockey going, and I got a thrill watching them whiz across the pond. It looked like so much fun. When Mom and I got back to Texas the following week, I announced that I wanted to play hockey. She'd laughed indulgently, but humored me, finding a year-round rink an hour from home.

I think she thought I would grow out of it. Instead, I grew to love it even more.

Now I'm here, at an East Coast Ivy League college, playing hockey for a team that's won three national championships—consecutively. But I have a feeling there won't be a fourth, not the way we're playing lately.

"What, you've forgotten how to talk?"

I look over and find Dean watching me with a wary expression. What? Oh, right, he wants to know what I was up to this weekend.

"Just hanging with some friends," I say vaguely.

"What friends? All your friends are here—" He waves a hand around the rink. "And I know for a fact you weren't with any of them."

I shrug. "You don't know these friends." Then I shift my gaze back to the ice as Dean grumbles beside me.

"Jesus fuck, you're worse than Antoine and Marie-Thérèse."

My head swings back. "Excuse me?"

"Forget it," he mutters.

Who the fuck are Antoine and Marie-Thérèse? Just like Dean knows all my friends, I know all of his, and I'm pretty sure we don't know anyone with those names. But whatever. I don't want him pushing me for answers, so I'm not about to push him.

"Fuck yeah!" a voice yells from the other end of the bench.

I refocus on the ice in time to see Garrett slap a bullet past Patrick, our senior goalie. It's the first and only goal of the scrimmage, and all the guys on the bench thump their gloves against the wall in celebration.

Coach blows his whistle and dismisses us, so we end the practice on a good note. Sort of. The d-men are asked to stay behind as usual, and I don't miss the frustration in Dean's and Logan's eyes. O'Shea's gonna need to lighten up if he wants to win the respect of this team.

In the locker room, I strip out of my sweaty jersey and pads and drop my hockey pants on the gleaming floor. We've got a state-of-the-art facility here. The room is huge, the lockers are padded leather, and the ventilation system is top-notch. It only *slightly* smells like old socks in here.

Garrett comes up beside me and whips off his helmet. His dark hair is damp with sweat and sticking to his forehead. As he reaches up to smooth his hair away, I glance at the badass flames tattooed on his biceps. It always makes me think I want to get inked myself, but then I remember the travesty on Hollis' leg that he got after our first Frozen Four win. Three years later, and he still wears long socks to cover it up most of the time.

"Think we'll ever remember how to play hockey again?" he says wryly.

I snort. "Season's just started. We'll be fine."

He doesn't seem convinced. Neither does Hunter Davenport, who lumbers over with a sour look.

"We keep getting worse," the freshman growls, and then, in eighteen-year-old fashion, hurls one glove against the wall.

I quickly glance around and sigh in relief when I don't spot Coach. The man would shit a brick if he saw one of us throwing a temper tantrum in the locker room.

"Chillax, kid," Mike Hollis, a junior, tells Hunter. He's bare-chested and in the process of undoing his pants. "Who cares if we lose a scrimmage in practice?"

"It's not about the scrimmage," Hunter snaps. "It's that we *suck*."

Hollis tips his head. "You got laid last night, didn't ya?"

The dark-haired freshman furrows his brow. "What does that have to do with anything?"

"Everything. We embarrassed ourselves in that game, got our asses kicked, and you still had chicks lining up to suck on your knob. Doesn't matter if we win or lose—we're still hockey players. We rule this school, dude."

"Spoken like a man without ambition," Garrett says, his lips twitching.

Hollis shrugs. "Hey, not all of us have a hard-on for the pros like you do. Some of us are happy doing this for the pussy."

A heavy sigh sounds from the end of the long bench spanning our lockers. Colin "Fitzy" Fitzgerald, an enormous junior with scruffy hair and more tats than a biker, saunters over and smacks Hollis on the ass.

"Do you ever *not* talk about pussy?" Fitzy asks.

"Why would I talk about anything else? Pussy's great."

He's right about that. Unfortunately, I won't get to experience any great pussy for at least...oh, a month? Two? I'm not sure how long it'll take my cock to forget about Sabrina James. If I hooked up with anyone else right now, I'd only be comparing her to Sabrina, and that's not fair to anyone involved.

"Oh hey," Hollis says suddenly. "Speaking of pussy..."

Garrett rolls his eyes. Hard.

"I'm hitting up Boston this weekend," Hollis continues. "Crashing at my brother's place. You guys want to come with? Barhopping, a few clubs, hot girls. It'll be a good time."

Our team captain frowns. "We've got a game on Saturday."

Hollis waves a hand. "We'll be back in time."

"You'd better be." Garrett shrugs. "But I can't go anyway. Got plans with my girl this weekend." His face takes on a faraway expression, a mixture of wonder and pure bliss, before he saunters off toward the shower area.

I tamp down the envy that rises in my throat. Garrett's been with Hannah for a year now, and it doesn't seem like that new love glow is ever going to wear off. He's so in love with his girlfriend that it's almost disgusting. Ditto for Logan, who recently got back together with his girlfriend Grace and professed his love for her on the radio.

It feels a bit...wrong, I guess, that the two biggest players I know have settled down. Out of all of us, I'm the guy who's into all that commitment stuff. When I first came to Briar, I figured I'd meet the woman of my dreams—*the one*—during freshman orientation, date her for the next four years, and propose after graduation. But it didn't turn out that way at all. I've dated lots of girls, slept with a lot of them too, but none of them were *the one*.

Meanwhile, Garrett and Logan found their ones when they weren't even looking for them, those lucky bastards.

"Tuck?" Hollis encourages. "Boston? Dude weekend? You in?"

My first inclination is to say no, but my mind trips over the word *Boston*. I know Sabrina said she didn't want to see me again, but... would she really tell me to get lost if we happened to run into each other in the city? I mean, she lives there, and I happen to know her address, so...who knows, right? Maybe a stellar Yelp review will take the guys and me to some amazing bar in her neighborhood. Maybe we'll bump into each other. Maybe—

Maybe you're turning into a stalker?

I stifle a sigh. Fine, my mind's definitely treading into Stranger Danger! territory. But even knowing that, I can't stop myself from saying, "Sure, I'm in. Wouldn't mind catching a Bruins game at a sports bar or something."

"Me too," Fitzy decides. "I want to pop into this gaming store downtown. They've got a role-playing game there that I can't find anywhere online. I'll have to suck it up and spend some actual money."

Hollis' horrified gaze travels from me to Fitz. "A Bruins game? A gaming store? How am I friends with you two?"

I arch a brow. "You'd rather we bail?"

"No." He heaves a sigh. "But at least *try* to pretend you're in it for the pussy."

I snicker and pat him on the shoulder. "If that makes you feel better, then sure. Fitzy and I are—"

I look at Fitz, prompting him with my hand.

"—in it for the pussy," we finish in unison.

7

SABRINA

I'm dragging by the time I arrive home from Briar.

I can't decide what I hate more—the weekends, when I'm at the club until two or three in the morning and then have to sort mail and packages from four until eleven. Or the weekdays, when I either have classes in the morning and the post office afterward, or an ungodly early post office shift followed by classes. Today was the latter, so I'm dead-ass tired as I drop my backpack on the hall floor.

Even if I wanted to be with Tucker again (and most of my body parts are in favor of a reunion) I'm too exhausted to do anything but lie on my back.

Although...that wouldn't be half bad, either. He could rub me down, fuck me slow, and I could just lie back and enjoy it.

I give myself a mental head slap. Tucker and his big wang is the last thing that should be on my mind.

In the kitchen, Nana is stirring a pot at the stove, dressed in tight jeans, a lycra top that's losing its elasticity, and her ever-present fluffy pink slippers.

"That smells great," I tell her.

The simmering red sauce is filling the kitchen with the most heavenly scent. My stomach gurgles and reminds me I haven't had anything to eat since the bagel I grabbed for breakfast before work.

"Girl, you look like you're about to fall over. Go and sit down. Dinner will be ready in a sec."

I don't need to be told twice, but when I see the empty table, I make a detour to grab plates and silverware. Through the doorway, I spot the top of Ray's head as he stares at the television. He's probably fondling himself. I shudder as I pull the plates out of the cabinet.

"You want milk or water?" I ask as I begin to set the table.

"Water, babe. I'm feeling bloated. Did you know that Anne Hathaway is lactose intolerant? She doesn't eat any dairy. Maybe you should think about cutting dairy out of your diet."

"Nana, that means no cheese or ice cream. Unless a doctor tells me that dairy is going to kill me, I'm all in on the cow."

"All I'm saying is, dairy could be why you're tired all the time." She shakes her spoon at me.

"No, I'm pretty sure it's because I'm working two jobs and taking a full course load," I answer dryly.

"If she stops eating dairy, will she be less of a baby bitch?" Ray asks as he strolls into the kitchen. He's wearing the same sweatpants that he always does. The fabric is so worn around his crotch, I swear I can see a faint hint of pink skin.

I nearly gag, turning away before he ruins my appetite.

"Ray, don't you start," Nana complains. "Babe, will you get the strainer for me?"

My stepfather nudges me as I walk by. "She's talking to you."

"No shit. Because she knows talking to you is like talking to her couch. She gets the same results."

I set the glass of water next to Nana's plate and then hurry over to the sink to get the strainer out. Nana dumps the sauce into a bowl while I take care of the noodles.

Ray, meanwhile, leans against the refrigerator like a lazy toad, watching us bustle around the kitchen.

I hate this man with all my heart. From the first moment my mom brought him home to meet me when I was eight, I knew he was trouble. I told Mom as much, but listening to her daughter was never something she was very good at. Neither is sticking around, apparently. Mom ran off with some other slimebag when I was sixteen, and we haven't seen her since. She calls a few times a year to "check in," but as far as I can tell, she has no plans to ever come back to Boston.

I don't even know where she's living these days. What I do know is that there's no reason for Ray to be living *here*. He's not my father—that title is reserved for the piece of shit who abandoned Mom after knocking her up—and he's definitely not part of the family. I think the only reason Nana keeps him around is because his work comp checks pay a third of our rent. I assume she fucks him for about the same reason. Because he's convenient.

But, God, he's so worthless I think even worms would turn up their noses at him. If worms had noses, that is.

Only when the table is completely set and the steaming pasta is ready for serving does Ray take a seat.

"Where's the bread?" he demands.

Nana flies up from her chair. "Oh damn. It's in the oven."

"I've got it," I tell her. "You sit still." As much as Nana's offhand comments might hurt, the woman still raised me, clothed me, and fed me while Ray sat on his fat ass, smoked weed and masturbated to sporting events.

I cast a glare at his back and notice, for the first time, a white envelope stuck down his pants. It's probably a bill. The last time he hid a bill from us (because he'd watched a dozen pay-per-view pornos) we had a three-month late fee to pay. Our budget works only if we don't have unexpected surprises like that.

I grab the rolls from the oven, dump them into a basket and carry it over the table. As I bend over, I pluck the envelope out from the back of Ray's sweatpants. "What's this?" I demand, waving it in the air. "Some bill?"

"It's not those dirty shows again, is it, Ray?" The sides of Nana's thin lips pull down.

He flushes. "Course not. Told you I don't watch that shit anymore." He shifts in his chair to give me a smarmy smile. "It's for you." He snatches the envelope out of my grip and drags it under his nose. "Smells like uptight bitch to me."

A flash of crimson at the edge makes my heart beat faster. I lunge toward the envelope, but Ray holds his arm out high and away from me, making me press against him. God, I *hate* him.

"Give her the letter," Nana chastises. "The food is getting cold."

"I was just funnin'," he says, dropping the envelope by my plate.

My eyes lock on the crimson shield in the upper left corner.

"Open it," Nana urges.

There's a hint of eagerness in her tone. She may taunt me about my worthless education and ridiculous dreams, but I think that deep down she's damn excited. At least she'll have this to lord over the other ladies at the hair salon whose granddaughters are having babies instead of getting into Harvard.

Except...the envelope is wafer thin. All of my college acceptance letters were in giant envelopes stuffed full of pretty brochures and catalogs.

"She's scared. She probably didn't get in." Ray's words are both lined with disdain and ringing with glee.

I snatch the letter and rip it open with Ray's knife. A single piece of paper falls out. It's got several paragraphs, none of which I fully read as I scan for the important words.

Congratulations on your admission to Harvard Law School! I hope you will join us in Cambridge as part of the class of—

"Well?" Nana prompts.

The biggest smile known to mankind spreads across my face. My hunger, my exhaustion, my irritation with Ray, is all wiped away.

"I...got in." The words come out on a squeak of breath. I repeat myself, and this time I'm screaming. "I got in! Oh my God! I got in!"

I wave the letter in the air as I dance wildly around the kitchen. I don't usually allow myself to drop my guard in front of Ray, but the bastard doesn't even exist to me right now. Excitement pulses in my blood, along with a sense of relief so weighty that I can't stay upright for much longer. I fall on Nana's shoulders and give her a huge hug.

"I suppose you're going to be extra uppity now," she gripes, and I don't even care.

"Naah, this doesn't make her special or anything," Ray drawls. "She's got two holes like any other bitch. Three if you count her mouth."

I wait for Nana to defend me, but apparently jealousy is winning out over pride right now. She laughs at his disgusting comment, and just like that, I'm done celebrating with these people. I cannot *wait* to get out of this house.

Still, I refuse to let anything affect my happiness right now. I spin on my heel and waltz down the hallway to call my girls.

"What about dinner?" Nana yells after me.

I ignore her and keep walking. In my bedroom, I throw myself on the bed and text my friends.

I got in.

Hope beats Carin by a millisecond.

OMG! Congrats!!!!!!!!

Carin replies, *PIC! PIC! PIC!*

I snap a picture of the acceptance letter and send it off. While I'm waiting for their responses, I run down the hall, fill my plate with pasta, stuff a roll in my mouth, and run back to my bedroom. Nana and Ray say something, but none of it processes. Only sheer joy fills my ears.

There are a dozen responses when I get back.

Hope: <3

Carin: *LOVE! LOVE! LOVE! UR so awesome!*

Hope: *I'm so proud of u. UR going to make the best lawyer EVER. Please say you'll represent me if I get sued for malpractice.*

Carin: *THIS IS THE MOST BEAUTIFUL THING!*

Hope: *When do we get to take u out? And no, never, not happening R unacceptable responses.*

I chew on my roll as I text them back.

Me: *A) U both get free legal services 4 life.*

B) Let's celebrate tomorrow. I promise to order enough to make your credit card weep.

Hope: *Not possible! I'm making reservations for Santino's.*

Carin: *That place needs reservations?!*

Hope: *I dunno! Figure of speech. But we could go to Malone's again if u want celebratory sex.*

Me: *I still have the number from the guy from last Saturday. What about u? Your lady garden get a private tour last night?*

The two of them had gone out without me to a party at Beau Maxwell's house. I wonder if Tucker was there. And if so, I wonder who he took to his truck this time. The thought of him running his big, callused hands over some other girl's breasts makes me grit my teeth in envy, but I don't have the right to be jealous. I blocked his number, after all. I told him in no uncertain terms that I wasn't interested in going out with him.

So why did you unblock him, hmmm?

The taunting voice in my head has me biting my lip. Fine, so I unblocked his number. But that wasn't because I want to go out with him or anything. I just figured it might be handy to have in case of... an emergency.

God, I'm so pathetic.

My phone dings, pulling me out of my thoughts.

Carin: *No. I was an angel.*

Hope: *Liar! OMG, what a liar. She came downstairs with sex hair bigger than Cher. Text her a picture of ur chest. Right now or I'll do it.*

Carin: *Fine. I hate u.*

Sometimes I do wish I lived with them. I gobble up more pasta as

I wait for the picture from Carin. When the image comes through, I nearly choke on a noodle.

Me: *Did u make out with teen wolf last night?*

Carin: *No. Brad Allen.*

I search my memory banks and come up with a six-foot, four-inch guy with a round, sweet face.

Me: *Defensive lineman? He looks like a cherub!*

Carin: *Yup. Turns out he has a sucking fetish. Good thing it's cold out because tank tops would be out of the question.*

Me: *Other than him trying to actually suck the blood through ur chesticles, did u enjoy him?*

Carin: *It wasn't bad. He knew how to use his equipment.*

Me: *Ha! My athlete theory is holding strong!*

Hope: *Between Tucker and Brad Allen, it appears B's hypothesis is accurate.*

Carin: *U both know that's not how the scientific method works, right?*

Me: *Yup, but we don't care.*

Hope: *Does that mean Tucker is getting a repeat?*

Me: *Doubtful. He's good, but when do I have the time?*

We text for a few more minutes, but my spike of adrenaline is wearing off. I set my partially finished plate on my nightstand and hug the Harvard letter to my chest. It's all happening. All the good things I've worked so hard for are coming to fruition. Nothing can stop me now.

I fall asleep with a big, happy smile on my face.

———

RAINCHECK, chickadees, I text my girls the following day, after Hope messages to ask if I want to have lunch with them.

Hope: *Aw, why??*

Me: *Professor Fromm invited me for a campus visit. I'm back in Boston, skipping out on my last class. FYI, I'm officially 2 good for u.*

Hope: *Kisses! Text back on how it goes. Can't wait until next year and we're all in Boston as grad students!!!*

Carin's in class, but I know I'll get a text from her as soon as she's out.

I take the Red Line to Harvard Square. I swear the subway station even smells good here, unlike any other stop on the line, which reeks of garbage, stale urine, and bad BO. And the campus is gorgeous. I want to swing my arms out wide and spin in a ridiculously happy circle.

According to my map, the eighteen or so buildings that make up the law school are on the other side of campus. There's no hurry, though, so I take the time to walk through slowly, admiring all the massive brick buildings, the dozens and dozens of trees that are still holding on to the very last of their leaves, and the acres of grass—some of which is still green in places. It's Briar on steroids. Even the students look smarter, richer, more important.

Most of them are wearing what I like to call the rich girl uniform: Sperry topsiders, Rag & Bone jeans, and a Joie sweatshirt—the kind that looks like it came from the bottom of a trash can but actually costs a couple hundred bucks. I know this only because of Hope's closet.

But just because my black skirt and white top came from a discount store doesn't mean I don't belong. I might not have as much money as anyone here, but I'd stack my brain up against any of these students.

I pull open the doors to Everett, the building where Professor Fromm's office is. At the receptionist's desk, I introduce myself. She has me write my name in an entry book and then gestures for me to take a seat.

I'm not there for more than a minute when a young man wearing a blue-and-white checked shirt and a dark blue tie strolls out from a side hall that I didn't notice when I first arrived.

"Hello. I'm Kale Delacroix." He offers his hand.

I shake it automatically, unsure of why he's here while at the same time wondering why anyone would ever name their kid *Kale*. "I'm Sabrina James."

"Great. Welcome to Harvard Legal Aid. Here's our intake form. If you need any help, give me a holler."

He shoves a clipboard toward me. I scan the document, not quite understanding why I need to fill out a form to see Professor Fromm. I tug the pen out from under the clip and start to print my name. Then I stop. While I'm not a fan of looking stupid, I figure it's better to ask what the hell is going on. "Is this Legal Aid? Because I'm not—"

He cuts me off. "Don't worry about it. That's what legal aid is for. For the indigent." The last word drips with condescension.

My neck hairs bristle. "I know what—"

"Do you not read English? *Hablo español?*" He jerks the clipboard out of my hands, flips the paper over, and then shoves it back toward me. The form is now in Spanish.

"I speak English," I growl between clenched teeth.

"Oh, okay. I can fill out your form if you can't read or write. There are many people with your kind of problem here. Is it a domestic issue? Landlord/tenant? We don't handle torts here." Again, he gives me a patronizing smile.

"I'm a student," I tell him. "I mean, I will be a student."

We stare at each other for a moment as I wait for my words to register. I see the moment that they do, because the pale white guy grows even whiter. "You are? Christ, I thought..."

I know what he thought. He took one look at my frayed coat and pegged me as a poor person in need of free legal services. And the most humiliating part of this is that he isn't wrong. If I needed a lawyer, I wouldn't be able to pay for one.

"Is there a problem here?" a new voice interrupts. A giraffe of a woman appears behind Kale, her hands clasped behind her back.

"No, there's no problem, Professor Stein." Kale gives me a tight smile, but his eyes flash a warning, as if to say to not fuck this up for him.

The smile I give him in return is full of teeth. "Dale here thought I was a client, but I'm actually here to see Professor Fromm."

The professor studies me, quickly assessing the situation. As she relieves me of the clipboard, she tilts her head toward the stairs. "Second floor, first door on the left." She hands the clipboard back to the Kale.

"It's *Kale*," he hisses as he stiffly marches away.

The professor shakes her head. "New students," she says in a flimsy apology before walking off in the opposite direction.

As Kale disappears down the hall, I hear a high-pitched voice greet him. "Oh my God, that was too funny. Did you actually mistake that girl for a Spanish-speaking immigrant?"

I should move on, but my feet are rooted to the spot. The receptionist gives me a pained look.

"Did you see what she was wearing?" Kale protests from the corridor. "Looked like a reject from the domestic violence clothing drive we have each year."

A new voice chimes in. "What are you guys laughing about?"

"Kale mistook a student visiting Prof Fromm for a homeless person."

With burning cheeks, I meet the eyes of the receptionist. "You gotta do something about those acoustics."

She shrugs. "If you think that's the worst thing I hear every day, you're in for a sore surprise."

What a cheerful thought. The idea of lingering here isn't so appealing anymore, so I take the steps two at a time. Professor Fromm's door is at the top of the stairs. She's talking on the phone but notices me right away.

"Sabrina, come in." Placing a hand over the receiver, she gestures for me to enter. "I'll just be a minute." To the person on the phone she says, "I have to go. A student walked in. Don't forget to pick up the dry cleaning."

The office is lined with books, most of them legal publications marked by the olive hardcovers with the North Eastern Reporter words in gold lettering on the spine.

I take a seat in the black leather chair in front of the desk and wonder what it'd be like to sit on the other side. It would mean I'd arrived, and no one would mistake me for a legal aid recipient ever again.

"So... Congratulations!" She beams at me. "I wanted to tell you the other night, but I didn't want to ruin the surprise."

"Thank you. I can't tell you how thrilled I am."

"Your credentials are impeccable, but..." She pauses and my heart starts beating wildly.

She can't take away my acceptance, can she? Once it's mine, it can't be revoked, right?

"Kelly mentioned that you work two jobs?" she finishes.

"Yes, I wait tables and sort mail." Professor Gibson knows exactly where I wait tables, but she told me it wasn't necessary for Harvard to know, so I keep that under wraps. "But I plan to quit both jobs before classes start this fall."

This makes Fromm happy. "Good. I was hoping you'd say that. While the old *Paper Chase* saying that if you look to your left and right and one of you won't be here next year is no longer the case, we do have a few students that drop out after the first year. I don't want you to be one of them. Your focus this coming fall needs to be on your studies. You'll be expected to absorb more information in one night than most undergrads do in a semester."

She plucks two books off a stack on the floor and pushes them across the desk. According to the titles, one is on administrative law and the other is on the art of writing.

"When you have time, and I suggest you make it, practice your writing. The pen is your strongest weapon here. If you can write well, you'll go places. The other is on ad law. A lot of people get stumped on regulatory practice versus corporate and tort law. It's good to be a step ahead." She gives the books another nudge toward me.

"Thank you," I say gratefully, gathering the books and placing them in my lap.

"You're welcome. Tell Kelly I said hello when you get back to Briar."

Okay then. I'm clearly dismissed.

"Thank you," I repeat awkwardly, and then I take the books and rise to my feet.

I skipped class, rode the subway, and endured a humiliating encounter with a jerk named Kale, and for what? A five-minute conversation and two book recommendations?

When I reach the door, Professor Fromm calls my name again. "And Sabrina, allow me to give you a tip. Spend a little of your loan money on a new wardrobe. It will help you feel at home here, and the playing field won't seem so uneven. You dress for the job you want, not the one you have."

I nod, hoping that my cheeks aren't completely red. And here I thought the *Humiliate Sabrina* hour was over.

On the walk across the campus, everything looks a little duller. This time I notice that the large patches of lawn are really mostly brown and that the trees are naked without the leaves. The students have an unrelentingly sameness to them—rich and privileged.

When I get home, I toss the books on my dresser and lie down on the bed. There's a corner near my window where the plaster is cracked and yellowing. Water has been seeping in for as long as I can remember, but after bringing it up to Nana once and getting a blank stare in return, I haven't mentioned it again.

I roll onto my back and stare up at the ceiling. There are cracks in the plaster up there too, along with brownish stains that I've always wondered about. Maybe there's a leak in the roof?

A rush of shame washes over me, but I'm not sure what I'm feeling ashamed about. My ugly, rundown home? My cheap clothes? Myself in general?

Pity yourself later. It's time to pay the bills.

God. The last thing I want to do right now is leave one place of shame and go to another one, but I don't have much of a choice. My shift at Boots & Chutes starts in an hour.

I force myself to my feet and grab the booty shorts and bra that serve as my uniform. I'm only going to have to do this for ten more months, I remind myself as I shimmy into my outfit and then apply my makeup. I slip on my six-inch platform stripper shoes, throw on my tattered wool coat and head for the strip club. Which, sadly, is the one place where I really do fit in.

I'm trashy. I live with trashy people. I belong in a trashy place.

The question is, will I ever be able to rub off the stench of my past to belong at Harvard? I thought I could.

But tonight, I honestly don't know.

8

TUCKER

"We suck," Hollis gripes.

"We're not great," I acknowledge.

Today's practice was another disaster, which doesn't bode well for tomorrow's game against Yale. I was hoping the road trip to Boston would distract us from how badly we're playing, but we've been sitting in this bar for almost an hour, and so far all we've talked about is hockey. The Bruins game flashing on multiple screens all around us isn't helping matters—watching a good team play good hockey is just the icing on the shit cake.

I peer at my empty beer bottle and then wave it in the air to signal the waitress. I'm going to need about five more of these if I want to snap out of this sour mood.

Hollis is still grumbling beside me. "If we don't start playing some defense, we can kiss our chances at another Frozen Four goodbye."

"It's a long season. Let's not throw in the towel yet," Fitzy says from across the booth. He's sipping on a Coke because he's our DD tonight.

"Are you guys going to talk hockey all night?" Hollis' brother, Brody, complains. He's twenty-five, but looks way younger with his clean-shaven face and backwards Red Sox cap.

"What else are we gonna talk about? This place is a sausage fest." Hollis tosses a napkin at his brother.

He's not wrong. There are only two women in this bar. They're around our age, hot as fuck, and they also happen to be making out with each other in a corner booth. Ninety-five percent of the men here—myself included—have already snuck glances at the lip-locked chicks. The other five percent are busy lip-locking each other.

"Fine, you losers." Brody heaves out an exaggerated sigh. "You don't like this place? Let's go."

"Where?" his little brother asks.

"Where there's girls."

"Done and done."

Three minutes later, we're climbing into Fitzy's car and following Brody's Audi across town.

"Nice wheels," I remark, gesturing to the shiny silver car ahead of us.

"He leases it," Hollis informs me. "He likes to act like a big shot, but he's really not."

"Gee," Fitzy drawls from the driver's seat. "Sound like anyone you know?"

That gets him a middle finger from our teammate. "Dude. I'm more of a big shot than *your* pansy ass. You didn't even get laid on your birthday this week."

"I wasn't looking to get laid. Trust me, if I was, you wouldn't have seen me at all that night."

"We barely saw you, anyway! You went home early to play video games!"

"To demo the game I designed," the other guy corrects. "I don't see *you* doing anything productive with your time."

"Actually using my dick is *very* productive, thank you very much."

I hide a grin. It always boggles my mind how these two could be such close friends. Hollis is a loud-mouthed bro with only one thing on the brain—chicks—while Fitzy is serious and intense with only one thing on *his* brain—gaming. Or maybe two things, seeing as the guy loves getting tattooed. Somehow they make the friendship work, though it seems like it's mostly through bickering and flipping each other off.

We pull into a gravel driveway and park in the spot next to Brody's. His Audi doesn't look out of place with the rest of the cars, but it doesn't fit the bar, either. A neon sign over the nondescript building blazes with the words "Boots & Chutes," which are positioned underneath a half-naked girl riding a bull.

Hollis gapes at the sign. "Seriously? A western-theme titty bar in *Boston*? This is gonna suck." He looks like he wants to punch his brother.

"Aren't you Miss Mary Sunshine." Brody throws an arm around Hollis and waves for us to come forward. "You babies wanted pussy—well, here you are."

"Is this what happens after you get out of college? You have to pay for pussy?" Hollis hangs his head. "I'm never leaving Briar, bro. Ever."

I chuckle. "Hey, think of all the leftover hockey groupies you'll have access to when Garrett or Logan start playing for the pros."

That immediately perks him up. "Good point. And look—" He points to the sign "—now you don't have to leave Boston either. Who needs to move back to Texas when you've got cowgirls right here for you?"

"Tempting," I say dryly, "but I think I'm sticking to my original plan."

Unless my mom suddenly acquires a taste for the East Coast, I'm moving back to Patterson after I graduate. I'm not sure our small town is a good place to start a business, but I could always try to open something up in Dallas and come home on the weekends. Mom sacrificed a shitload to get me to where I'm at now, and I'm not leaving her alone.

The strip club reeks of sweat, smoke, and desperation. At the front of our group, Hollis' brother slaps something into the hands of the bouncer, and they have a short conversation.

"No touching. Private dances start at five bills." He waves a waitress over. "Front row, stage right," he tells her.

Everyone starts moving.

Everyone but me.

"Got a problem?"

The bouncer's sharp voice gets me moving. "Nope," I say easily.

But I kinda do. I have a big problem, in fact. A fucking huge problem.

Because under the heavy eyeliner and the big hair, I recognize the waitress. Hell, I've had my hands and mouth all over that exposed skin.

Sabrina's startled gaze locks with mine. I see all the color drain from her face, which is saying a lot because she didn't go easy on the blush when she applied her makeup.

"Right this way," she mumbles. She spins around with a swish of dark hair, but not before I see the flash of warning in her eyes.

Got it. She doesn't want me telling the guys that we know each other. I don't blame her. This is probably awkward as fuck for her.

"What kinds of chicks work this joint?" Hollis says as he leers at Sabrina's incredible backside, which is barely covered by the tiny shorts she's wearing.

"Hot ones," Fitzy replies dryly.

That's an understatement. The girls here are more than hot. They're goddamn spectacular. Source: my eyeballs.

Tall ones, short ones, curvy ones. Light, dark, and everything in between. But my gaze keeps snapping back to Sabrina, as if it's attached to an invisible string that's controlled by her perfect ass.

"I take back every rude thing I said about cowgirls in the parking lot. Any of these girls can ride me."

Heat curdles in my gut. I don't like the idea of Hollis—or any of the dudes in this place—getting ridden by Sabrina. She's mine.

"You okay?" Fitzy asks. "You look pissed."

I take a breath. "Yeah, sorry. I was thinking about the team."

He buys that. "That's enough to make anyone mad. Come on. Let's get a drink and forget about hockey."

I nod absently, too mesmerized by the center of Sabrina's back. It's completely bare except for one measly string that looks like it would unravel if I blew against the bow. My gaze drops lower, taking in the elegant indentation of her spine, all the way down to the top of her black satin booty shorts.

By the time we arrive at the stage, I'm sporting a semi, which is fucking embarrassing. Getting a hard-on at the mere sight of a girl's ass isn't something that's happened to me since high school.

I force my eyes upward in time to avoid a table full of frat boys. One of them reaches out to slap Sabrina's ass as she sways by him.

A jolt of rage shoots up my spine. I shove forward, but a bouncer sitting at the base of the stage reaches the punk before I do.

"No touching, asshole." He hauls the polo-shirted kid to his feet. "Let's go."

"Hey, I'm sorry," the asswipe protests. "It was reflex."

But the bouncer doesn't listen and the guy is dragged out anyway. His friends just watch him go.

Hollis grins. "Strict fuckers here."

"We need that guy on our team," Fitzy observes.

"No lie."

Sabrina holds out her hand. "Anything I can get for you boys?" Her voice is barely audible over the loud dance beat blaring through the club.

"Whatever you have on draft." I keep my eyes fixed above her chin, which is a fucking miracle.

I don't miss the unhappiness washing over her face. It doesn't take a rocket scientist to guess she's embarrassed, and I don't know how to tell her that where she works doesn't make a shit's worth of difference to me.

Brody flops down in the chair next to mine. He rests his forearms on the tabletop and leans forward to watch the half-naked woman dancing five feet away from us. The tall redhead is in the process of wiggling out of her G-string, leaving her in nothing but a leather holster around her waist and two fake guns.

"And for you?"

Hollis' brother tears his gaze off the naked cowgirl and glances at Sabrina. "Whiskey, neat."

"Coming right up."

"Thanks, baby."

With a strained smile, Sabrina disappears, and somehow I manage not to lunge across the table at Brody. Sabrina's not his baby. If he calls her that one more time, I'm not sure I'll be able to restrain myself from beating the living crap out of him.

"She looks familiar," Hollis yells in my ear. "The waitress. Doesn't she?"

I shrug. "Don't know."

Fitzy turns to study her as she leans forward to take orders at a nearby table. "I guess she looks a little like Olivia Munn?"

"No way. She's a million times hotter than her," Hollis declares. Then he shrugs. "Whatever, maybe I don't know her."

His brother grins. "I'll ask her later why she looks familiar. You know, when she's on her knees in front of me."

I clench my fists against my thighs. I have to, or I'm going to pound Hollis' brother into mincemeat and then Hollis will be pissed off. I like Hollis.

Luckily, Brody decides to stop being a creep, as if on some subconscious level he figured out how close I was to straight-up murdering him. He turns to me and says, "Mikey mentioned you're going to start your own business?"

I nod. "That's the plan."

"Got something in mind?"

"I'm kicking around a few ideas, but I haven't settled on anything yet. I've been focused on hockey."

"Yeah, I hear ya."

"But once I'm done with school, I'll evaluate my options."

"If you need help, let me know. I've got a couple ins with some new opportunities. Really ground-floor stuff. I'm not sure how much cash you've got, but these investment opportunities aren't open to the public. One day you're in for a couple hundred Gs, and three years later you're a billionaire when Facebook buys you out." He snaps his fingers as if it's just *that* easy.

"Sounds interesting. Maybe I'll give you a call when I'm ready to make some decisions." I'm nodding again, but really, I have no plans on calling Brody Hollis for investment advice. I'd rather not get suckered into some pyramid scheme, thank you very much.

Sabrina returns with a tray in her hand, and all my attention instantly belongs to her. She sets down our drinks, standing right at my shoulder. I figure it's because I'm the least likely to play grab-ass with her and not because she wants to rub her tits across my cheek.

"I'll be back in a bit to check on you," she murmurs before darting off.

Jesus. I stare at her in admiration, wishing I could run after her and give her a hug. Serving a bunch of Briar guys—not to mention one she's slept with—can't be comfortable for her. She could've asked her boss to be switched to another section, but she didn't. She's continuing to do her job as if our presence doesn't affect her at all.

For the next half hour, the guys and I watch the strippers do their thing. Well, the guys watch. Me, I'm wholly focused on Sabrina. I sneak glances at her every other second, barely paying attention to what's going on around me. I vaguely register laughter and catcalls and snippets of conversation, but my entire world has been reduced to Sabrina James. The sensual sway of her hips as she walks. The high heels that make her long legs look impossibly longer. Every time she walks past our table, I fight the urge to pull her into my lap and kiss her senseless.

"How much does a girl like you cost?" a loud voice slurs from behind me.

"I'm not a dancer."

My shoulders stiffen when I recognize Sabrina's voice. The woman on stage has just finished up, and the music volume has dropped a few notches while the next girl gets ready to go on. When I twist around in my chair, I find that the obnoxious frat boys are at it again.

"But you would be if the price was right," one of the douchecanoes drawls.

"No. I just serve drinks." From where I sit, I can see the tension in her slender shoulders.

"What if I want more than a drink?" Douchecanoe taunts.

"Trust me, you don't want to waste your money on me. I'm a terrible dancer." Her tone is light on the surface, but steely beneath it. "You need anything else?"

"Sweetheart, I'm not asking for a Broadway show. I just want you to shake your tits and ass in my face. Maybe rub up on me a bit—"

That's it. I've had enough.

I don't miss Fitzy's look of confusion as I push out of my chair and march over to the Douche Table.

"She said no," I growl.

The main douche smirks at me. "She's a fucking stripper, dude."

I fold my arms across my chest. "She said no," I repeat.

From the corner of my eye I see Sabrina edge backward.

"Where do you get off?" Douchecanoe demands. "Mind your own business or I'll—"

The chair legs behind me scrape against the floor, and Douchecanoe shrinks in his seat as over six hundred pounds of angry hockey players stare down at him. Fitzy is particularly menacing with his two full-sleeve tattoos and the cut over his eyebrow that he got during our last game.

"You'll what?" I ask, lifting a brow.

"Nothing," the frat boy says sullenly.

"That's what I thought." I bare my teeth at the assholes before the boys and I settle back in our chairs.

It takes me a second to realize that Sabrina is halfway across the room. She turns, briefly, to glance at our table. When our gazes meet, there's unmistakable sorrow in hers.

Before I can stop myself, I pull out my phone and send her a quick text. I don't know if she still has me blocked, but it can't hurt to try.

I'm sorry about that.

I don't expect a reply, so when my phone buzzes three minutes later, I'm genuinely surprised. But then I'm pissed, because she texted back:

Did u follow me here?

It takes me a minute to regroup. I sip my beer, take a breath, and then answer her with, *Meet me at the restrooms?*

This time she responds right away.

5 min.

For the next four minutes, I have to force myself not to stare at my phone. Or set a timer. Impatience bubbles in my gut, intensifying with each passing second. By the time I rise to my feet, I'm tense as fuck.

"Hitting the head," I mutter, but the guys pay me no attention. Hollis and Brody are too busy shoving dollar bills in a stripper's G-string, while Fitzy watches them with a bored expression.

I thread my way through the crowd of mostly men toward the doorway on the other side of the dark room. Boots & Chutes has gone overboard with the western theme—saloon-style doors separate the bathrooms from the main room, and the wooden signs on the restrooms read *Gunslingers* and *Fillies*. From behind the Fillies door, I hear the muffled sounds of female moans intermingled with male grunts. Classy.

"So, did you?"

I whirl around at Sabrina's voice. She stalks up to me, her arms crossed tightly over her chest in a way that causes her cleavage to spill over her bra.

"Follow you here, you mean?" I flatten my lips. "No, darlin', I did not."

She studies me for several seconds before nodding. "Okay. I believe you." Then she turns to walk away.

Oh hell no.

"Sabrina," I say in a low voice.

She stops. "W-what?"

Something inside of me melts when I hear the crack in her voice. She keeps her back to me, her spine like a metal rod. By the time I reach her, any indignation I felt over her unfair assumption has faded away. I gently touch her arm to shift her around so we're facing each other.

"Sabrina?" I keep my voice soft, safe.

She visibly swallows. "This is where I work."

I give a slow nod. "This is where you work."

"That's it? You've got nothing else to say about that?"

I stroke her bare shoulder with the pad of my thumb, gratified to feel her shiver. "This is your place of employment. You get paid to work here. You use those paychecks to pay your bills, I'm assuming. What else do you want me to say?"

But I know what she expected from me. Judgment. Contempt. Maybe a lewd comment or two.

I'm not that man, though.

She keeps watching me, until finally a small smile plays on her gorgeous lips. "I'm waiting for the part where you tell me you *never* come to these places, your friends just dragged you here against your will, yada yada."

"I'd be lying if I said I've never been to a strip club. But I kind of did get dragged here tonight—I voted for the sports bar. And the only reason I even came to Boston was because..." I trail off, because the last thing I want to do is scare her off again.

"Because what?"

Fuck it. I shrug and say, "I was hoping maybe I'd run into you."

Sabrina laughs. "Boston's a big place—you really expected to randomly run into me?"

"Expected, no. Hoped? Abso-fucking-lutely."

That gets me another laugh.

We stare at each other for a beat. My voice comes out gravelly as I murmur, "You unblocked my number."

"I unblocked your number," she agrees.

Then she moistens her bottom lip with the tip of her tongue, and I swallow a groan. Fuck, I want to kiss her.

"I should...get back to work."

There's only the tiniest sliver of reluctance in her words, but a sliver is all I need. "When do you get off?"

"Two."

"Do you want to hang out when you're done?"

She doesn't answer right away. I stand there, holding my breath, hoping that the raw, overpowering lust I feel for her doesn't show on my face, praying that she'll say—

"Yes."

9

TUCKER

I wait for Sabrina in the parking lot. Almost all the cars are gone, except for a half dozen that probably belong to the employees. The guys went back to Brody's apartment a couple hours ago, where they'll probably stay up all night drinking. I told them I was meeting a girl for a late bite, which got me a high-five from Hollis even as he griped about what a shitty person I was for not making sure she had a friend.

After they dropped me off at an all-night diner a few blocks from the club, the site of my supposed date, I killed an hour by grabbing a burger and chugging some coffee so that I wouldn't fall asleep within five minutes of seeing Sabrina. Then I walked back to Boots & Chutes, and now I'm leaning against the driver's side of Sabrina's Honda, monitoring the front entrance in anticipation.

When she appears, my excitement kicks up a notch. She's wearing a wool coat that goes down to her knees. Below that, her legs are bare.

My dick twitches as I wonder if she's still wearing those booty shorts. Then I chastise myself, because I could tell how embarrassed she was earlier by the skimpy outfit.

"Hey," she says as she reaches me.

"Hey."

I want to kiss her, but she's not sending any *c'mere, big boy* signals. I need to touch her, though, so I step closer and tuck a strand of hair behind her ear.

Hesitating, she bites her lip. "Where are we going?"

"Where do you want to go?" I'm leaving the decision entirely up to her.

"Are you hungry?"

"Nope. Just ate. You?"

"I had an energy bar during my last break."

I wink at her. "You thought you'd need energy, huh? Why's that?"

Her cheeks take on the cutest shade of pink. I see her fighting a smile, and when it breaks free, I do an internal fist pump. She's so gorgeous when she smiles. I really wish she'd do it more often.

She glances around. "Your truck's not here."

"Yeah, it's back in Hastings. We drove up in Fitzy's car."

She nods and nibbles on her lip again. "I...well...what should we do, then?"

"No pressure." I move even closer, loosely resting one hand on her hip while the other traces the line of her jaw. My pulse speeds up when she doesn't shy away from my touch. "We can walk around. Just chill in the car and talk. Whatever you want."

Sabrina lets out a sigh that leaves a white puff in the cold night air. "I don't feel like walking. It's cold out and my feet hurt from being on them all night. And my car is way too small for you. You'd be uncomfortable in five seconds."

"Do you want to go back to your place?"

She tenses up. "Not really." Another breath slides out. "I don't want you to..."

"To what?"

"I don't want you to see where I live." She sounds defensive. "It's shitty, okay?"

My heart squeezes a little. I don't respond, because I'm not sure what to say.

"Well, not my bedroom," she relents. "That's not shitty."

Sabrina goes silent, as if she's fighting some internal battle.

"I meant what I said before," I tell her in a soft voice. "No pressure. But if you're worried that I'm going to judge where you live, stop right now. I don't care if you live in a mansion or a shack. I just want to spend time with you, wherever and whenever."

When I rub her lips with my thumb, the tension seeps out of her shoulders. "Okay," she finally whispers. "Let's go to my house."

I search her face. "Are you sure?"

"Yeah, it's fine. I'd rather be somewhere warm and cozy right now. Not that my house is warm and cozy, but it's definitely warmer in there than it is out here."

Having made her decision, she unlocks the driver's door and slides behind the wheel. I get into the passenger side. And she's not wrong—my legs are not digging this vehicle. Even when I push the chair back as far as it can go, there's still no room to stretch out.

She starts the car and pulls out of the lot. "I don't live too far from here."

After that, she doesn't say much for the rest of the drive. I don't know if she's nervous or if she regrets agreeing to hang with me, but I hope to hell it's not the latter.

I don't push her to talk, because I know how skittish she can be. Patience is the name of the game here, and patience with Sabrina James comes with a reward. She's got so much passion that it's simply a matter of helping her reach a level of comfort that allows her to let go.

When we turn onto her street, I pretend it's the first time that I've ever been here. That I don't recognize the narrow, ramshackle row houses. That I hadn't slept in my car right over by that uneven curb the night I followed her home to make sure she got there safe.

Sabrina turns into a driveway at the side of the house, steering toward the small carport in the rear. She kills the engine and exits the car in silence.

"This way," she murmurs when I round the vehicle.

She doesn't take my hand, but she does check to make sure I'm following as she climbs the three low steps of the back stoop. Her keys jingle softly in the quiet night as she unlocks the door.

A moment later, we step into a tiny kitchen. It has ugly yellow-and-pink-patterned wallpaper, and in the center sits a square wood table surrounded by four chairs. The appliances look old, but they're clearly in working order because dirty pots and pans are strewn atop the stove burners.

Sabrina blanches at the mess. "My grandmother always forgets to clean up after herself," she says without meeting my gaze.

I glance around the cramped space. "It's just the two of you here?"

"No. My stepfather lives here too." She doesn't elaborate, and I don't ask for details. "Don't worry, though. Friday is poker night—he usually stays out and then stumbles home sometime around noon the next day. And Nana takes an Ambien every night before bed. She sleeps like the dead."

I wasn't worried, but I get the feeling she's not trying to reassure me, but herself.

"My room's this way." She ducks into the corridor before I can say a word.

I trail after her, noting how narrow the hall is, how dirty the carpet is, how there aren't any family photos hanging on the walls. My heart starts to ache, because the droop of Sabrina's shoulders tells me that she's ashamed of this place.

Fuck. I hate seeing her look so defeated. I want to tell her about the peeling paint in our place down in Texas, about how for the entirety of high school I slept in the tiniest room in the house so Mom could use the larger bedroom for her in-home hair salon that supplements the income from her hairdresser job in town.

I keep quiet, though. I'm following her lead here.

Her room is small, tidy, and clearly her source of refuge. The double bed is perfectly made with a pale blue comforter. Her desk is immaculate, overloaded with neatly stacked textbooks. It smells clean and fresh in here, like pine, lemon and something addictively feminine.

Sabrina unbuttons her coat, shrugs it off, and drapes it over the desk chair.

My mouth waters. She'd thrown a T-shirt over the skimpy bra that constitutes a work "uniform," but she's still in those little shorts. And the heels. Jesus fuck, those heels.

"So," she starts.

I unzip my jacket. "So," I echo.

Her dark eyes track the movement of my hands as I toss the jacket aside. Then she shakes her head abruptly, as if trying to snap herself out of...checking me out, I guess? I hide a grin.

"I meant it when I said I didn't want to get involved," she says.

"I know you did. That's why I haven't called." I wander over to the desk, scanning the titles of her textbooks, all gazillion of them.

There's a small cork bulletin board on the wall, with pictures tacked on it. I smile at a shot of Sabrina sandwiched between two other girls. The one on the left has bright red hair and she's sticking out her tongue while squeezing Sabrina's butt in an exaggerated fashion. The one on the right has long, thin braids, and she's smacking a kiss on Sabrina's cheek. They obviously adore her, and I feel a spark of approval knowing there are at least two people out there who have her back.

"My girls," Sabrina explains, coming up beside me. She points to the right. "That's Hope—" She points to the left. "And Carin. They're my angels sent from heaven. Seriously."

"They seem cool." My gaze travels over the other pictures before landing on a white piece of paper with the Harvard emblem in the corner. "Holy shit," I breathe. "Is that what I think it is?"

Her entire face lights up. "Yup. I got into Harvard Law."

"Fuck yeah!" I swing around and yank her toward me for a hug. "Congrats, darlin'. I'm proud of you."

"I'm proud of me too." Her voice is muffled against the side of my neck.

Oh boy. This hug was a bad idea. Now all I can concentrate on is the way her round, full tits are pressed up against my chest. I swear her nipples are hard too.

Sabrina's breath hitches the moment she feels the change in my body.

"Sorry," I say ruefully, easing my hips back. "My dick got confused."

A laugh pops out of her mouth. She tilts her head to look up at me with humor. And heat. I'm definitely seeing a spark of heat there.

"Poor guy," she murmurs. "Do I need to explain to him the difference between a hug and a fuck?"

Je-sus. This girl is not allowed to say the word *fuck*. It sounds too much like a promise when it's leaving those pouty lips.

"I think that's wise," I answer solemnly. "Though he's not the smartest fella—you might need to give him a hands-on tutorial."

She lifts an eyebrow. "What happened to no pressure?"

"Ah, I'm just playing. No pressure at all, babe." Except for the pressure behind my zipper, that is.

She goes quiet for a moment. We're no longer hugging, but still standing only a few inches apart.

"Honestly?" she says. "I tend to function better under pressure. Sometimes I need...a little push."

I hear the unspoken question, but although my cock gets harder, I force myself to show restraint. "I won't push you. Not unless I'm a hundred percent sure it's something you want." I study her expression. "Is it what you want?"

She moistens her lips. "It...is."

"Not good enough. Tell me exactly what you want."

"You. I want you."

"Be more specific." Fuck, I'm a masochist, apparently. But this girl has turned me down twice since we slept together. I need to make sure we're on the same page.

"I want you. I want *this*." Her palm covers my package, and my erection nearly hammers its way out of my pants.

"Where do you want it?" My voice is pure gravel.

"In my mouth."

Goodbye, restraint. Sabrina James literally took a wrecking ball to it with those three lust-drenched words.

I'm kissing her before either of us can blink. And it's the kind of kiss that goes from zero to sixty in a hot second. My tongue slides through her parted lips in a greedy stroke. She gasps with delight and kisses me back, her tongue tangling with mine for a few mind-melting seconds before she kisses her way toward my neck. Her breasts rise as she inhales deeply, and the soft moan she gives zips right to my balls.

"You smell so good," she whispers, and then her lips are all over me. Traveling along the tendons of my neck, rubbing over my collar-bone, tickling my chin. Pretty much driving me crazy.

She slides one hand between us and rubs me over my pants. She doesn't unzip them. Doesn't reach inside. I don't know if it's because she's teasing or waiting for the push she supposedly needs. Since I don't have patience for the former, I seize onto the latter.

"Take my dick out," I say roughly.

Her lips curve teasingly. "Why would I do that?"

"You said you wanted me in your mouth." I clench my fists to my sides. "So put me in your mouth."

She makes a sweet little sound, a cross between a whimper and a moan and a sigh. I feel her fingers trembling as she pops open the button of my jeans, but I know it's not nerves because her expression is smoky with excitement.

"I wanted to do this that night in your truck," she confesses. "But I was too impatient to feel you inside me."

She delicately draws my stiff shaft out of my boxers and curls her fingers around it. I kick off my boots, then yank my jeans and under-wear down. Kick those away too.

"Shirt," she orders, sounding amused. "I want to see your chest."

This girl is gonna kill me. I peel off my shirt and then I'm standing there naked in front of her. She remains fully clothed, if you could call booty shorts and a whisper-thin T-shirt *clothes*.

As her heated gaze eats me up, I send a quick thank-you to the hockey gods for inventing such a grueling sport. Hockey's a tough, dangerous game that requires hours of training. It's given me muscles in places I didn't even know had muscles. And now, all that hard work is paying me back twofold by putting this hungry look on Sabrina's face.

"Your body's insane," she informs me.

I chuckle. "Pot, kettle," I reply before cupping her tits over her top.

She swats my hands away. "Don't distract me! I have a job to do."

I flash her a look of challenge. "I figured you'd be good at multitasking. Considering you're always so busy."

"Oh, I can multi-task like a pro. I just don't want to right now. I want to savor this." She voices the seductive promise while slowly sinking to her knees.

Her hair falls over one shoulder as she peers up at me. Christ, I've never seen a hotter sight. I reach down and rub her mouth with my thumb. I want to see those lips wrapped around me. I want to see her throat working to take me in.

"Suck me," I rumble when she continues to kneel there without touching me.

She hears the tortured note in my voice and takes pity on me, leaning forward to kiss the tip of my cock. She offers the tiniest flick of tongue, but that alone is enough to send an electric current up my spine. Oh man, I'm not gonna last long at all.

I cup the back of her head and urge her closer. On command, she opens her mouth and half my length slides in. Wet heat surrounds me, making me groan. It's fucking amazing, and that's *before* she starts working me with her tongue.

"Ah, fuck," I choke out when she licks the sensitive underside.

Sabrina laughs, and the sound ripples through my shaft and pulses in my balls. She torments me with slow, lazy pumps of her hand. Deep, wet pulls of her mouth. Sweet, gentle licks of her tongue. And the entire time, she's making the hottest noises I've ever heard. Tiny whimpers of arousal and breathy moans that confirm she's as close to losing it as I am.

I stroke her hair. It's so damn soft, silky as it moves between my fingers. I rock my hips, slowly, because I want to make this last. But when her mouth suddenly slides forward until her lips are wrapped tightly around my base, there's no stopping the orgasm.

Buried in her throat, I go off like a firecracker. It happens so fast I don't even have time to warn her.

"Sabrina," I croak, trying to pull out.

She just moans and tightens the suction, taking everything I have to give.

The pleasure is so intense it almost fells me. My knees knock together. My brain stopped producing coherent thoughts right around the time she put her mouth on me.

Eventually I register the soft caress of her hand over my thighs, the tickle of her fingers along my shaft as she gives one final stroke before rising to her feet.

"That was fun," she tells me.

I sputter with laughter. Fun? Talk about an understatement.

"It was fucking incredible," I correct, yanking her toward me.

I kiss her until she's breathless. My legs are still shaking but my hands are rock steady as I methodically pull off her T-shirt and then tug on the string that's keeping her bikini-style bra in place. Our mouths still locked, I nudge her toward the bed, advancing on her until she has no choice but to fall onto her elbows and stretch out on her back.

I pop her heels off, one by one, taking the time to kiss each of her shapely ankles. Then I get rid of her booty shorts, whip them across the room, and reach for the heels again.

Sabrina raises a brow. "You're putting them back on me?"

"Hell yeah I am. You have no idea how hot you look in these heels."

I ease one small foot back into a stiletto, then the other. When I'm done, I stare at her for a long, long moment and wonder how I ever got this lucky. She's all long limbs and sweet curves and smooth olive-toned skin. Her dark hair is fanned out behind her head, her red lips are glossy and parted. And those fuck-me heels... Christ. She's the ultimate wet dream.

I rise on my knees and shuffle closer. My dick is waking up again, but I ignore him. He can take five while I play a little.

"I can't get over how beautiful you are," I rasp, bringing my hand between her legs.

When I rub the pad of my thumb over her clit, her hips jerk off the bed in response.

I smile. One barely there touch and she's already hot for me. Or maybe she got hot when she was giving me a blowjob that belongs in the history books.

I trail my finger down her slit toward her opening, groaning when I discover that she's soaking wet. "Did I do this?" I mutter.

Mischief dances in her eyes. "Sorry, but no. I was pretending you were Tom Hardy the whole time I was blowing you."

"Bull. Shit." I push one finger inside her and she squeaks loudly. "You knew exactly whose dick was in your mouth."

Sabrina squirms against my probing finger. I add another one, curl them both, and stroke her inner channel while my thumb teasingly circles her clit.

"Fine, I knew," she gasps out. "Who needs to picture a movie star when you're already a fantasy come to life?"

Damned if my ego doesn't like hearing that. And my cock definitely likes the way her pussy is clenching around my fingers. I remember how tight she was the last time, how good it felt, and once again I forget that I'm trying to be patient.

Groaning, I spread her thighs with my free hand and lean down to bury my face where my dick wants to be. When my tongue touches her, she moans loud enough to wake the dead. Hopefully that sleeping pill her grandmother took is doing its job, otherwise we're in for a mighty awkward interruption.

I kiss and lick and suck and play until my body can't take it anymore. Until my mind shuts down again, empty save for one thought: *need to be inside her.*

Wrenching my mouth away results in Sabrina's grumble of disappointment. My beard has left pink splotches all over her thighs, but she doesn't seem to care. She's squirming and scissoring her legs, a sexed-up look on her face.

"Tucker," she begs.

"Hold on, darlin'." I lean over the edge of the bed to grab my pants, then whip out the condom in my wallet.

She watches me suit up. Her gaze is no longer cloudy with frustration. It's on fire, blazing with anticipation.

"Get inside me," she orders.

"Yes, ma'am."

With a grin, I crawl back to her, one fist grasping my dick to guide it inside her. We both groan when I drive in deep. But apparently it's not deep enough. Her legs, long and silky and incredible, instantly wrap around my waist. She digs her heels into my ass and lifts her hips to deepen the contact, and it's the best fucking feeling in the world.

I drop down until my elbows are resting on either side of her head. "Beautiful," I mumble, staring down at her flushed face. I dip my head and kiss her again, while my cock pulses in the tight heat of her body.

I try to keep it slow. I try my fucking hardest. But Sabrina has other ideas.

She shoves her hand in my hair and pulls until our mouths break apart. "I need more." She sounds as desperate as I feel.

"Tell me what you need."

"This." She grabs my hand and pushes it to where we're joined.

Her fingers cover my knuckles as she urges me to stroke her clit. "And this." She bucks upward and starts fucking herself on me.

And that's the game, ladies and gentleman.

My slow, measured pace explodes to dust. In its place, pure animal fucking. I drill into her with everything I've got. The heel of my hand stays glued to her swollen clit, rubbing in time to each frantic thrust. Within seconds we're both sweaty, breathless messes. The mattress springs creak from the force of our fucking. The head-board slams against the wall in a rhythmic *thump-thump-thump* that matches the wild pounding of my heart.

She comes before I do, clutching my shoulders as she shudders beneath me. The blowjob had taken the edge off, so I last longer. Hell, longer than I want to, because I'm dying to come. Every muscle in my body is coiled tight, screaming for release that's still out of reach.

"Let go," Sabrina murmurs.

And then her fingers dig into my ass cheeks, one drifts along the crease, and—

That's the game.

I shoot with a hoarse cry. I forget my name. I probably black out for a minute. I feel loopy and wonderful and my balls are still tingling, but I think I might be crushing her, so I force my weak body off hers and collapse onto my back.

"Holy fuck," I mumble, staring up at the ceiling. "That was—"

A knock on the door cuts me off.

"Having fun in there?" a slurred male voice drawls. "Because it sure sounds like it."

Sabrina freezes like a deer in the middle of a country road. The sex glow she'd been sporting fades instantly. Her face turns ashen, her fingers curling into the bedspread.

"Go away," she snaps at the door.

"What? You're not gonna introduce me to your friend? Don't be so rude, Rina."

"Go away, Ray."

But the son of a bitch isn't going anywhere. He starts rapping on the door again, drunken laughter echoing in the hall. "Lemme meet your friend! C'mon, I'll be nice."

Sabrina jumps off the bed and starts snatching up pieces of clothing. I quickly do the same, because it's obvious that lying around naked isn't in the cards.

She throws on a tank top and a pair of cotton shorts, then stalks to the door and flings it open. "Get the fuck away from my door, Ray. I mean it."

The man in the doorway pushes past her, craning his neck to get a good look at me. When our gazes lock, he laughs again.

"Aw, you've got yourself a little jock buddy! Check out the muscles on this one!" His greasy hair flops onto his forehead as he swings his head toward Sabrina. "You like the muscles, huh? Yeah, you definitely like 'em. Heard you squealing like a bitch in heat all the way from the living room."

"*Get out*," Sabrina growls.

"You sound hot when you come—"

Fuck *this*. Anger boils in my gut as I charge forward. I don't give a shit that this man is Sabrina's stepfather. The sick fuck is not allowed to speak to her like that.

"That's enough," I say in a low voice. "She asked you to leave."

His eyebrows shoot up. "Who the fuck are you to give me orders? This is *my* house, boy."

"And this is her room," I retort.

"Tucker," she starts, but Ray interrupts her.

"Rina, tell your jock to shut his trap. Otherwise I'll shut it for him."

Yeah right. I could knock this fucker out with one punch. He's so drunk he's swaying on his feet.

"Ray." Sabrina's voice is deceptively quiet. "I'd like you to leave, please."

Silence hangs between the three of us. Finally, Ray rolls his eyes in a dramatic fashion and edges back to the door. "Jeez, you really are a stuck-up bitch, aren't ya? I was just playing around."

"Play somewhere else," I say coldly.

"Shut up, jock boy." But he doesn't stick around.

We hear his unsteady footsteps in the hallway. A moment later, a door shuts.

Slowly, I turn back to Sabrina. My stomach twists with concern. And there's a pang of fear too, because I hate the idea that the asshole sleeps only two doors down from her.

Before I can speak, she tucks her hair behind both ears and says, "I'm really tired. You should probably go now."

My gaze darts to the hallway.

"He won't bother me," she whispers, as if reading my mind. "I lock my door at night."

I'm not sure a locked door will keep that fuckhead out. Ray isn't as tall or bulky as I am, but he's not puny, either. Doughy, yes, but not puny...

"I'll be fine," she insists, and the look on her face tells me she's as eager for me to go as I am to stay.

"Are you sure you'll be all right?" I finally ask.

She nods.

"Okay. I...guess I'll go then." I slide my phone out of my pocket and pull up my Uber app. Then I take a needlessly long time with it, hoping that she'll change her mind.

She doesn't. She waits silently while I track down a car, then walks me to the kitchen, holds the door open for me, and murmurs a soft, "Good night."

She doesn't kiss me goodbye.

10

SABRINA

I'm not sure if u've blocked me again. On the off chance u haven't, ur fucking spectacular in bed. Ur hot body almost eclipses that sexy brain of urs. Almost. I want to see u again. In bed, out of it. Whatever.

I like to pretend that I'm impervious to ordinary things like feelings. That my focus is so precise and laser-like, nothing can push me off the path I set for myself back in sixth grade. But as I stare across the quad at some girl rubbing up against Tucker, thoughts of Harvard and perfect grades and sticking it to all the haters are pushed aside by a rush of green jealousy.

I want to march over there, whip out my phone, and shove a screenshot of his sext in front of her face. *See, he's mine,* I'd snarl and then I'd drag him away. Or maybe I'd throw him down and ride him in front of the entire Briar campus.

"B, you're looking like you don't know if you want to kill Amber Pivalis or fuck Tucker. Either one is illegal on school grounds." Hope laughs in my ear.

Amber? Her name is going in my burn book.

"I don't have time for this," I mutter, shifting my books higher in my arms. I'm not sure if I'm talking to myself or Hope at this point. Both of us, maybe.

"How are we defining 'this'? Your sudden obsession with Tucker or your maddening refusal to actually allow yourself to enjoy life?"

"If your eyebrow goes up any higher on your forehead, it will officially be part of your hairline," is my non-answer.

"Being around you causes these weird tics." Hope waggles both eyebrows.

"Do you make these faces in bed with D'Andre? Is it some strange fetish of his?"

"You know what D'Andre's fetish is and it's not my eyebrows."

"Oh God. Right. I'm sorry I brought it up." D'Andre's ass preference has not gone unnoticed by any of Hope's friends, but it's not something I like to dwell on, not even as a distraction from Amber.

Miss Thang is currently walking her fingers up Tucker's arm while he listens intently to every stupid thing that comes out of her stupid mouth. I mean, she could be telling him about Nietzsche's theories of nihilism, but it'd still be stupid because Tucker's enraptured.

"Are we going to stand here all day and watch the Amber/Tucker show, or are we going to eat?"

Their names don't even sound right together. Their celebrity nickname would be Tamber or Aucker, and both options are dumb.

Mine and Tucker's celebrity name would be *Sucker*, which could either refer to sex or to the way I feel right now—like a sucker. Because why the hell is he flirting with some other chick after sending me that sext?

"Eat," I grumble, but my legs are propelling me west, which is not the direction of the dining hall.

"You know Carver's to our left, right?" Hope sounds like she's trying not to bust a gut.

I barrel to a halt, but it's too late. Tucker's head lifts and he spots me. I can feel the warmth of his smile from here.

Oh shit, this was a mistake. Three nights ago was a mistake. A week ago was a mistake. Stomping across the quad like a jealous girlfriend is definitely a mistake.

I grab Hope's arm and walk very quickly in the opposite direction. "I'm starved. Let's go eat."

"You realize that running is something I only do on the treadmill while wearing my sneaks and running gear, correct?" She trots next to me, trying to keep up on feet that are clad in expensive suede boots with a heel as tall as my hand.

I walk even faster. "Can't hear you. Embarrassment is short-circuiting my nervous system."

"If embarrassment is causing your malfunction now, I'd love to know what it was that caused you to run across the quad."

As if she doesn't know. Before I can respond, though, Tucker shows up on my right.

"Where's the fire?" he drawls.

Hope grinds to a halt. "Thank God you caught up with us." She runs a hand across her forehead in an exaggerated motion. "I'm not cut out for outdoor exertions."

"Stow it, Hopeless," I hiss out of the side of my mouth.

She grins unrepentantly. "I'm going inside to save us a seat. When you're done, come find me." She reaches past me to give Tucker's biceps a squeeze. "You're welcome to join us, handsome."

Someone growls. I hope everyone thinks it's my stomach, but by Hope's broad grin and Tucker's smirk, I know I'm busted. At least Tucker has the decency to wait until Hope's out of earshot before he opens his mouth.

"Ignoring my texts again?"

"It was one text, and it's only been three days." I stare stubbornly ahead and not into his gorgeous face or his deep brown eyes.

"But who's counting, right?"

I don't even need to look at him to know he's smiling. It's in his every word.

We stand there for a moment, neither of us speaking. I suppose he's looking at me while I'm looking at everything but him. Finally, I find my ovaries and turn to face him.

The smile has worn off. Now he sports a slightly quizzical frown, as if he's decided I'm a puzzle that he's trying to solve. A dozen questions whirl around in my head, and I take a moment to sort through them until I arrive at the one that bothers me the most—the horrible scene with Ray before Tucker left my house on Friday night.

"I went to Harvard the other day," I begin awkwardly. "I sat in the lobby and some student mistook me for a poor person in need of legal aid."

"Shit."

I wave off the sympathy. "After I told him I was actually going to be attending Harvard with him next fall, I went to see the professor who's good friends with my advisor and she told me to buy new clothes. Up until this weekend, that was probably one of the more humiliating events in my life. Well, if you don't count the day in middle school when I unexpectedly got my period during gym class. While climbing a rope."

He chuckles. "Ouch."

"But...you hearing all that shit that my stepdad said?" I pause to shudder. "That's a scene I'd like to erase."

"Sabrina—"

I cut him off. "My life is like one horrible episode after another of the *Real Housewives of South Boston: Slum Edition*. And if I don't keep getting perfect grades, if I can't compete—" My voice cracks slightly and I have to stop.

Tucker doesn't say anything. He's watching me with an indecipherable expression.

I clear my throat. "If I can't compete, then I can't get out of there, which, frankly, is unacceptable to me. So while sex with you is so goddamn amazing, it's distracting. You're distracting," I confess.

He lets out a slow, steady breath. "Baby. You think you're the only one with an embarrassing family member? My Uncle Jim is literally one of those creepy guys that give the uncle stereotype life. He's always touching his family members in weird ways. None of my female cousins want to be around him. If I brought you to a family reunion, he'd be making some gross statement and trying to grab your ass. I don't think you'd hold that against me, would you?"

"No, but..." I start to say that it's not the same, but we both know that's not true. It is the same. Ray isn't my dad. He's some douchebag my mom married and left behind like an unwanted piece of luggage. Like me.

"And despite what you think, I don't have money. I'm here on a full-ride hockey scholarship. If Briar hadn't offered that, I would be at a state school in Texas." He shrugs. "I have some savings and I plan to use that to jumpstart my post-college life, but I'm not the asshole you think I am."

"I don't think you're an asshole," I mumble, but I don't deny that I'm leery of guys with money.

He studies me for a moment. "Let me ask you this. Dean's trust fund earns more in interest in one quarter than what my entire inheritance is worth. Did his dick feel different when you were with him?"

I cringe for a moment, because my drunken hookup with Dean Di Laurentis isn't something I like to dwell on. At the same time, the thought of Dean's money making his dick feel different is so silly, I can't stop a snort from coming out. "I don't remember. I was wasted and so was he."

"Did you feel like a million bucks the next day?"

"God, no."

"So money doesn't matter once you get down to it. It doesn't matter how thin or thick anyone's wallet is. We all hurt. We all love. We're the same. And your past, who you live with, where you came from, it doesn't have to matter. You're creating your own future, and I want to see where the road forward takes you." Tucker slides a finger under the strap of my messenger bag. "We should get some food in you. How about I carry this while I walk you to the dining hall?"

Apparently philosophy class is over, which I'm happy about because I'm not prepared to respond to anything he just said.

Instead, I let him take the bag. We walk in silence for a few steps before I'm compelled to ask, "Does nothing shake you?"

He nods solemnly as he hitches the bag higher onto his shoulder. Anyone else would look slightly ridiculous with a backpack strapped to his back and a messenger bag hanging off his shoulder, but somehow, probably because of his massive chest and height, he pulls it off.

"Yeah, all kinds of things, but I try not to let them get me down. It's a waste of energy."

"Just name one," I beg. "One embarrassing thing. One flaw. One thing that bothers you."

"You not calling me back bothers me."

"That's self-effacing, not embarrassing."

"You've turned me down. Twice," he reminds me. "How is admitting that it bothers me self-effacing?"

"Because we had good sex, so you know I'd sleep with you again under different circumstances," I argue.

Somewhere in the back of my mind, I acknowledge that this conversation is reaching ludicrous levels. I'm arguing with a guy I slept with about how I can't sleep with him again because he's too good in bed. My life is officially a farce.

"What's a normal circumstance for you?" he asks curiously, matching his long stride with my shorter one.

"I don't know. I can't see that far ahead."

He pulls to a stop right before the entrance of Carver Hall. "Bullshit."

"What?"

"Bullshit. You know exactly where you want to be in probably fifty years, not just the next five."

My cheeks heat up, because he's right.

"Listen. Here's how it is." Tucker reaches out and grabs a stray lock of my hair, rubbing it between his fingers before tucking it behind my ear. "I enjoyed sleeping with you. I enjoyed hearing those sexy little moans you made when I sucked on your clit, and I enjoyed feeling you shake like a leaf when you came apart underneath me." His dirty words are in stark contrast to his matter-of-fact tone and the steady way he stares into my eyes. "But I didn't like the way your dad—"

"Stepdad," I correct.

"—Stepdad treated you. I hated it, actually. I hate that you live with that and I'm glad you're making your way out of it, because that's what you're doing, right? You're killing yourself to get perfect grades, top scores, admission to the best schools, all so you can escape."

His thumb drags along the apple of my cheek. "I don't want to be a distraction, but I do want you. I think there's something here, but I'm a patient guy and I'll take what you have right now. I'm not here to add pressure on you or make things harder. I want to ease your load."

My heart thumps loudly in the space between us, the space that he closes with one step.

"My dad died when I was three," he says gruffly. "It was a car accident. I have almost no memory of him. I do remember waking up hearing my mom cry at night, though. I remember seeing her face when she couldn't get me a new pair of skates or a new video game. I remember how she got angry with me when I was roughhousing in the living room once and I put a lamp through the television. She reamed me out good for that." His expression is rueful rather than angry. "She worked two jobs to make sure I could play hockey, and when I graduate this spring I'm going to take her away from all that hard work. But I also know I want someone to share my life with. My mom's lonely. I don't want that for me. And I don't want that for you either."

When he kisses me, it's not anything like our previous encounters. Those were rough, hot, and sexually charged. This kiss is petal-soft and sweet as the syrup he ladles onto his words. It feels like he's pouring tenderness over my head by the gallon. With each press of his lips against mine, he's repeating his promise to give me nothing more than what I ask for.

And it's this kiss. This sweet, tender, thoughtful kiss that scares me more than anything I've ever felt.

11

TUCKER

A couple days after my talk with Sabrina in the quad, I heave myself off Fitzy's couch and get ready for a brutally early morning practice. I didn't plan on crashing at his place last night, but our video game session lasted until two a.m. and there was no point in driving home when we had to wake up at five-thirty for a six o'clock practice.

Fitzy lives alone in a shoebox-sized apartment in Hastings. His "bedroom" is separated from the living room by a curtain he hung from the ceiling. Getting to the tiny bathroom pretty much requires me to climb over his bed.

The big tattooed hockey player is sprawled on his stomach, sleeping like the dead, so I not so nicely smack his ass as I head for the bathroom.

"Wake up, dude. Practice," I grunt.

He mumbles something unintelligible and rolls over.

I find a spare toothbrush in a drawer next to the sink and tear it open. As I brush my teeth, I scroll through my phone to see if Sabrina texted when my phone was on silent last night.

She didn't. Damn. I was hoping my speech—and that amazing fucking kiss—might've changed her mind about going out with me, but I guess it didn't.

I do, however, find the most mind-boggling conversation in the group chat I have with my roommates. All the messages are from last night, and they're bizarre as fuck.

Garrett: *The hells, D?!*

Dean: *It's not what you think!!*

Logan: *It's hard to mistake ur romantic bath with that giant pink thing! In ur ass!*

Dean: *It wasn't in my ass!*

Garrett: *I'm not even going to ask where it was*

Dean: *I had a girl over!*

Garrett: *Suuuuuuuuuure*

Logan: *Suuuuuuuuuure*

Dean: *I hate you guys*

Garrett: *<3*

Logan: *<3*

I rinse my mouth out, spit, and drop the toothbrush into the little cup on the sink. Then I quickly type out a text.

Me: *Wait... what did I miss?*

Since we have practice in twenty minutes, the guys are already awake and clearly on their phones. Two photos pop up simultaneously. Garrett and Logan have both sent me pics of pink dildos. I'm even more confused now.

Dean messages immediately with, *Why do you guys have dildo pics handy?*

Logan: *ALINIMB*

Dean: *??*

Me: *??*

Garrett: *At Least It's Not In My Butt.*

I snort to myself, because I'm starting to piece it together.

Logan: *Nice, G! U got that on the first try!*

Garrett: *We spend too much time 2gether.*

Me: *PLEASE tell me u caught D playing w/ dildos.*

Logan: *Sure did.*

Dean is quick to object again.

I HAD A GIRL OVER!

The guys and I rag on him for a couple more minutes, but I have to stop when Fitzy stumbles into the bathroom and shoves me aside. He's got crazy bedhead and he's buck-naked.

"Gotta piss," he mumbles.

"Mornin', sunshine," I say cheerfully. "Want me to make you some coffee?"

"God. Yes. Please."

Chuckling, I duck out of the bathroom and walk the four or so steps into his kitchenette. When he finally emerges, I shove a cup of coffee in his hand, sip my own, and say, "Dean shoved a dildo up his ass last night."

Fitzy nods. "Makes sense."

I snicker mid-sip. Coffee spills over the rim of my cup. "It really does, huh?"

He gives another nod and chugs the rest of his coffee. I'm already dressed and ready to go, so I leisurely finish my drink while Fitzy dashes around the apartment in search of some clothes.

Five minutes later, we step outside into the early morning chill and head off to our respective cars. Luckily I've got my gear in the back, so I don't have to stop at the house first. And although it's stupid as fuck, Fitz and I race to campus like a bunch of speed demons. He wins, because my truck is old and slower than molasses.

We make it to the arena with ten minutes to spare, which is good because my phone chooses that moment to ring. My pulse quickens at the thought that it might be Sabrina.

It's not. I'm slightly disappointed when I see Mom's number and then feel bad about it because I love my mom.

"I'll see you in there," I call out to Fitzy, who's hopping out of his car. He nods and ambles off, while I answer the call. "Hey, Mom. Practice is about to start, so I don't have a lotta time."

"Aw, I won't keep you then. I was just calling to check in and say hi."

Her familiar voice causes something inside of me to soften. I swear, Mom always has that effect on me. I could be tense as shit, and one word from her loosens all my muscles. I guess I'm a mama's boy, but it's not like I could be anything else, seeing as how I don't have a dad.

"You're up early," I remark. It's only five o'clock in Texas, which is early even for her.

"Couldn't sleep," she admits. "I'm styling an entire bridal party this morning. I'm nervous."

"Ah, there's nothing to be nervous about. You're the hair whisperer, remember?"

Mom laughs. "That I am. But makeup, not so much. Those courses I took last summer helped, but jeez, kiddo, I'm freaking out here! How could I ever live with myself if I was the woman who ruined a bride's big day by painting her face like a clown!"

"You'll do fine," I assure her. "I guarantee it."

"Oooh, a guarantee? Not even a simple ol' promise? You've got a lot of confidence in your mama, John."

"Of course I do. Because my mama's a rock star."

"I really raised a charmer, huh?"

"Yup." I grin as I balance the phone on my shoulder and slide out of the pickup.

"Okay, give me a quick rundown of what you've been up to," she orders.

I make my way to the massive front steps of Briar's hockey facility. "Not much," I confess. "Hockey, school, friends—the usual."

"Still no girlfriend?" There's a teasing note in her voice.

"Nope." I hesitate. "I did meet someone, though."

"Oooh! Tell me everything!"

Laughing, I reach into my pocket for my student ID to unlock the front doors. Security is tight here. "Nothing to tell yet. But when I've got more details, you'll be the first to know. Anyway, I gotta go. Walking into the rink."

"All right, call me when you've got more time to chat. Love you, baby."

"Love you too."

I hang up and swipe my ID in the keypad, then barrel into the sleek, air-conditioned lobby where framed jerseys hang on the walls and colorful championship pennants stream down from the ceiling.

I wish I'd had more time to talk to Mom, but when it comes to Briar hockey, there's no such thing as slacking. Coach Jensen runs a top-notch program that prides itself on excellence and hard work. Just because we're sucking balls these days doesn't mean those fundamentals have been lost.

In a brisk stride, I head for the locker rooms. I still have my phone in hand, and after a moment of hesitation, I give in to the urge to text Sabrina.

Me: *Mornin, darlin. Give any thought to what we talked about? I've got a first date offer here with ur name written all over it...*

Then I put my phone away and go to practice.

SABRINA

I'M ALREADY LATE to meet the girls, but when I fly outside after my evening tutorial, I know instantly that I'm about to be even later.

Beau Maxwell and a few of his buddies are congregating at the bottom of the steps, surrounded by half a dozen football groupies. From where I'm standing, it's obvious that the boys are enjoying the attention. Although Briar is primarily a hockey college, the football players get plenty of limelight around here too.

"S!"

Beau breaks away from the group when he spots me on the steps.

His blue eyes light up, which brings ugly scowls to the faces of the girls around him. They clearly don't appreciate my poaching their quarterback slash potential hookup for the night, but I don't particularly care. I haven't spoken to Beau in weeks, and I can't deny that I'm happy to see him.

I descend the stairs while he ascends them and we meet halfway for a hug. Strong, muscular arms wrap around me and swing me right off my feet. I laugh, ignoring the groupies who are murdering me with their eyes.

"Hey," I say when he sets me back on my feet. "How've you been?"

"Not great, actually. Not great at all. My bed is cold and lonely without you in it."

I can tell he's joking because his pout is exaggerated. And even that silly expression doesn't make him any less handsome. With his dark hair and chiseled features, Beau's sexy as hell. We met at a party last spring where, within seconds, he sucked me in with his dimpled grin and easy-going charm. I think we fell into bed with each other about ten minutes after that, and he's one of the rare guys I allowed myself to see more than once.

Except now we're standing face to face, and he's doing nothing for me. No tingles. No heat. No *I want to hit that again*. As gorgeous as Beau is, he's not the one I want to be naked with these days.

That honor falls to John Tucker. AKA the sweetest, hottest, most patient guy on the planet. AKA the guy who asked me out via text this morning and who I still haven't texted back.

"Seriously, baby, what did I do to deserve such punishment?" He clutches his heart with mock pain, and the scowly, fumy groupies get scowlier and fumier.

"Uh-huh. I'm sure your bed's been miserably empty since I left it. I bet you're living the sad, lonely life of a monk."

"Not quite." He winks. "But you could at least *try* to act like you miss boning down with all this—" He sweeps a hand in front of him from head to toe.

And yeah, "all this" is mighty appealing. I'm talking big chest, sculpted arms, long legs, and muscles to spare.

But Tucker has all those things too.

"I see your ego is still as massive as ever," I say cheerfully.

Beau nods fervently. "It is. Not as big as my dick, of course—"

"Of course."

"But I'm not complaining."

"Other than your big dick and ego, how's life? How's Joanna?" I'd met Beau's older sister Joanna at one of his parties, and watching the two of them bicker had been highly entertaining.

"She's great. Still doing that show on Broadway and killing it." He sighs. "She asks about you all the time."

"She does?"

"Oh yeah. She thinks I'm an idiot for not making you my girlfriend."

"Making me?" I echo dryly.

"I tried to tell her that I'm too much man for you, but Jo insists that you're too much woman for *me*. She's wrong, obviously."

My lips twitch in humor. "Obviously. What else? How's the season going?"

His laidback expression falters slightly. "Team's lost two games already this season."

Sympathy tugs at my chest. I know how important football is to him. "I'm sure you can still turn things around," I assure him, though I have no idea if that's even true.

Apparently it's not. "Naah, we're fucked," he says glumly. "Two losses pretty much guarantees we won't make the playoffs."

Ah, crap. And it's his last year at Briar too. "Hey, but at least you led the team to *one* championship during your time here," I remind him. "That counts for something, right?"

"Sure." But he doesn't sound convinced of that. He clears his throat and offers a smile that lacks the luster from before. "Anyway, I'm glad I ran into you. I promised not to say anything about this, but I figured it's cool to bring it up to you since you're the other party."

I wrinkle my forehead. "The other party of what?"

He grins broadly, and this time it *does* reach his eyes. "Tuck's epic pursuit of you."

Oh God.

"What are you talking about?" I squeak.

"Ha. Don't play dumb, baby. It's been like a week since he tracked me down at the gym, and I know the guy—no way did he go a week without tracking *you* down."

Anxiety pricks my belly. Beau and I might have ended things on fantastic terms, but that doesn't mean I feel comfortable discussing other guys with him.

As if he senses that, he softens his tone. "It's all good, S. You don't have to give me deets if you don't want to." He shrugs. "I just wanted to make sure you knew he was a decent guy."

Wait, what?

"Wait, what?" I say aloud.

Beau laughs. "Tucker," he clarifies, as if I don't know who we're talking about. "I know you have this vendetta against hockey players—"

"I do not!" I protest.

"You totally fucking do!" He's laughing harder now. "Do you want me to list all times I had to sit there and listen to you trash Di Laurentis? Actually, I wouldn't even be able to list them. That's how often you did it."

"There may have been a couple of occasions," I concede with a grumble.

"A couple, a hundred, same diff, right? But yeah, I'm not even gonna try to defend Dean—who's fucking awesome, by the way. I know you won't change your mind about him. But Tucker is legit cool. He's one of the nicest dudes I've ever met."

Same, I think wryly. Out loud I ask, "Why are you telling me this?"

"Because I know you." He reaches out and tweaks a strand of my hair. Behind us, an outraged gasp sounds from the groupies. "You've probably already thought of a million reasons not to give Tuck a shot. And if one of those reasons is that you're really not into him, then great, don't go out with him then. But if you *are* into him, don't let this big brain of yours—" He gently taps my head "—talk you out of it, 'kay?"

"You should probably stop touching me. Your fans are getting upset."

He snorts. "You really think me touching you is gonna stop one or two or all of them from sucking my dick tonight?"

I blanch. "Gross, Beau."

"Truth, Sabrina." He waggles his eyebrows. "I'm a god around here. I can do no wrong."

Huh. Must be nice to live in a world where everything gets handed to you on a silver platter, where your mistakes mean nothing.

I keep my cynical thoughts to myself. "So what exactly did Tucker say to you?"

"That he's into you." Beau gives another shrug. "He wanted to know if our history was gonna pose a problem for him. I told him no."

My jaw falls open. "So he pretty much asked you for permission to date me?"

"Permission?" Beau snorts loud enough to cause all his buddies to glance over at us. "Yeah, right. More like he announced that he wanted you, and that if I had a problem with it, too bad so sad."

I fight the grin that's trying to surface. For all his sweet words and *aw shucks* smiles, Tucker really is an alpha fucker. I don't know why that thrills me so much, but it does.

"Anyway, don't be stupid about this," Beau says sternly. "Someone like Tuck might be good for you. He can keep you from studying yourself to death."

"Oh!" I exclaim. "Before I forget—I got into Harvard!"

"For real?" His face breaks out in the biggest, broadest smile. "Congratu-fucking-lations!"

And then he hauls me into his arms again for a bear hug, while his gorgeous groupies glare bloody murder at me.

12

SABRINA

Hope's Beemer is waiting for me in the parking lot. When I climb into the backseat, I find Hope and Carin singing along to some awful pop song, and I don't feel guilty anymore for making them wait. Clearly they've been having a great time.

"So what's this new place we're going to?" I ask once the song ends.

"You'll see," Hope chirps from the driver's seat.

My friends exchange amused glances, which immediately raises my suspicions.

"If it's the weird hippie bar you took me to in Boston that served wheatgrass shots, I'm jumping out right now. Not even kidding."

"You'll like this place," she assures me. "It has all your favorites."

I don't need to see their faces to know they're both smirking at me. "I'm trusting you," I warn. "Don't break the friend code."

Carin turns around. "Forget the friend code. What were you and Beau talking about?"

Leaning forward, I fill them in on the conversation I just had with Briar's star quarterback.

"Shit, this boy is serious," Hope exclaims.

"Beau or Tucker?"

"Tucker. Duh. He spoke to one of your exes and declared his intentions? Girl, this man is all in."

"That's weird, right? I mean, he's actively pursuing me. It's *weird*." I direct this mostly toward Carin. Hope's a romantic. She believes that everyone on *The Bachelor* is actually there to find love when the rest of the viewing public knows it's all about nobodies seeking fame.

But Carin disappoints me. "It's not weird—it's awesome. I mean, I've had hookups. Met a guy's eyes across the room or struck up a conversation, but I've never had someone pursue me."

"Same," Hope says, flicking a glance toward me in the rearview mirror. "D'Andre asked me out while I was walking on the treadmill. He said he'd never seen a girl look prettier sweaty than me." She sighs dreamily. "I said yes immediately. If there was any chase at all, it lasted all of five minutes. I put out on the second date, remember?"

"How does it feel?" Carin stares at me as if I'm some fascinating new discovery she just smeared on a microscope slide.

"When Hope puts out? Well, she's a good kisser, but the rest of her technique needs work." The joke is lame, but I'm not ready to acknowledge that I feel like a giddy kid by Tucker's steady, determined pursuit.

Hope holds up her middle finger. "I'm an awesome lay. My technique is perfect. If I were any better, D'Andre wouldn't be able to get out of bed. As it is, I have to kick him out."

"It's true," Carin confirms. "D'Andre always begs like a sad child when he has to leave in the morning."

"Is that how it is with Tucker?" Hope teases.

"You really want to know how I feel about it?" I exhale a long, heavy breath, deciding to be honest with my friends—and with myself. "I feel silly and weak and I don't like it. I should be immune to this. I mean, he's just a guy. I've slept with lots of guys before and I'm sure there'll be many in the future. So why am I all weak-kneed and fluttery around this one?"

"Why is feeling something for someone a weakness?" Hope chastises. "I know you don't think *I'm* weak."

"God no. But you're..."

You're rich and gorgeous and smart, and I have to work my ass off for everything.

Frustrated, I dig the knuckle of my thumb into my temple. "You're more together than I am. I always feel like I'm one day away from disaster. The other night I had a dream that Professor Fromm walked into Boots & Chutes while I was on stage wearing nothing but glitter and a G-string. I woke up in a panic because I was fucking convinced there'd be an email on my computer informing me that my admission to Harvard was being rescinded."

In front of me, Hope shakes her braids. "Honey, you said it yourself. Your schedule is terrible. The reason you're so stressed out is because you only give yourself an hour or two a week to just relax."

"She's right," Carin says. "And look, I think it's awesome that you meet up with us once a week, but at this rate, you're going to flame out before you even get to Harvard. *That's* what your dream is telling you."

"Briar's full of super students. Law school isn't going to be more competitive than what you've already faced." Hope fixes me with a stern look in the mirror. "Slow down, B. Or at least slow down while you still can."

"You don't have to marry the guy," Carin chimes in. "Going on a date or having great sex isn't a commitment. He's a student too, which means he has to study. He plays hockey, which means he's got practices and games. If you were going to date anyone, it should be someone who's got his own busy life, right?"

Hope raises one eyebrow. "He's got a game tonight..."

I gape at her. "Are you stalking him? How do you know he has a game?"

"I looked up the team's schedule on the Briar site."

Carin nods enthusiastically.

"Who are you guys and where are my friends?" I demand. "You don't even *like* hockey."

"I like it," Carin protests. "My dad throws a Stanley Cup party every year!"

I turn to Hope, who shrugs. "I neither like nor dislike it. And I have nothing against going to a game if it means watching my bestie finally have some fun."

"Come on," Carin urges. "We don't have to stay for the whole thing. We'll watch a bit of the game, and maybe afterward you can go up to Tucker and tell him how awesome he played and how sexy he looks in his uniform. In fact..." She waves a hand out the window. "Here we are."

"This is where we're eating dinner?" I stare at Briar's multi-million-dollar hockey facility and all of the students streaming inside.

Carin grins. "Yup. Love a good hot dog, don't you?"

"D'Andre's meeting us inside," Hope adds.

I sigh. "So he was in on this diabolical plan of yours too?"

"Of course. He's my partner in crime." Hope kills the engine, and she and Carin unbuckle their seatbelts. "All right, let's do this shit. Time's a-wasting, B."

I peer at the arena again, feeling oddly nervous. "I don't know about this."

"Aw come on," Carin coaxes. "This place is full of your favorite things—athletes."

I stick my tongue out at her, but she merely laughs.

"Hey, if you don't want Tuck, then I'll see if I can check *beard* off my bucket list." She blinks innocently. "I mean, if you're really not into this hot, built guy who gave you the best sex of your life, then you should totally be on board with me and Tuck hooking it up."

The image of Carin's petite body underneath Tucker's big frame roils my stomach. "It's Tucker. Not Tuck." I flush when I hear the stiffness in my own voice.

Hope dissolves into a fit of giggles.

"God, if you could see the angry look on your face right now..." Carin giggles. "Honey, you've got it bad."

Hope produces a flask from her purse. "If the game is terrible, we'll just get super drunk while we watch a bunch of white boys skate around with knives on their feet."

Her description of what she thinks hockey is makes me and Carin burst out in laughter. And as my friends hop out of the car, I find myself getting out and following them to the entrance of the arena.

They're right about a lot of things. I do need a break, and maybe, just maybe, I need Tucker.

I DON'T WATCH a lot of sports. Not because I don't like them, but because I've never had time to get into one. I know a little bit about football because of Beau. And some baseball because that's all Ray watches in the spring.

Hockey, not so much.

But I have to admit, watching Briar's team play is more exciting than I thought it would be.

I'm squished between Hope and Carin, with D'Andre sitting on Hope's other side. I don't know if we have good seats or not. Carin says yes, but I would've preferred to be sitting right behind the home bench so I could stare at Tucker all night. Instead, I have to satisfy myself by watching him on the ice.

Hope told me that his jersey number is 46. I guess she found that out on the school website too. So I glue my eyes to the black-and-silver jersey that reads #46, marveling at the way he confidently wields his stick. I don't think I could ever hold on to a hockey stick while I was wearing those bulky boxing gloves.

When I mention this to my friends, D'Andre laughs his ass off. "Those are hockey gloves, baby girl. Not boxing gloves."

"Oh." I feel stupid now.

In my defense, I've never been to a hockey game before, so why should I be expected to know what the equipment is called? I know there are sticks and pucks and nets. I know some players are forwards, because that's what Tucker told me he was. And I know other players are defensemen, because that's what Beau told me Dean was.

Other than that, I'm completely ignorant about this game. There was no reason to ever study up on it, since hockey players have been on my *hell no* list.

So have boyfriends, for that matter.

Argh. I can't believe I let my friends talk me into this. I don't have time for a boyfriend. And even if I did, Tucker isn't the guy. He's too nice. And sweet. And amazing.

That trickle of shame I felt when Ray interrupted us having sex still flutters through me every time I think about it. It was so humiliating. And even though Tucker assured me that it didn't make him think any less of me, a part of *me* thinks less of me.

I hate where I come from. I hate Ray. Sometimes I even hate my own mother. I know I'm supposed to love her because she gave birth to me, but the woman abandoned me. She just *left*.

"You got this, boys!" an enthusiastic fan shouts, jerking me out of my bleak thoughts.

I glance at the ice to see Tucker skating again. The night we met, he'd admitted that he was slow because of an old knee injury, but holy hell, he doesn't *look* slow. He's a blur of motion, getting from one end of the ice to the other before I can even blink.

His teammates are equally fast, and I can barely keep up with the puck. I thought Tucker had it, but then the crowd roars with disappointment and I swivel my head to see the black disk bounce off one of the net posts. I guess someone else had it, but Tucker scoops up the rebound. He passes to one of his teammates. When the guy slaps it right back to Tuck, I find myself bolting to my feet so I can get a better view of him taking a shot.

He misses. I groan in frustration. Carin laughs as I flop back down in my seat, but she doesn't make fun of me for my sudden burst of fangirldom.

The game remains scoreless all the way into the third period. I can't believe we've already watched thirty minutes of hockey and no one has scored yet. You'd think I'd find it boring, but I'm on the edge of my seat, wondering which team will draw first blood.

It's Briar.

As the lamp over the net lights up, a rock anthem blasts over the PA system and the home crowd screams in celebration. The announcer calls the goal for someone named Mike Hollis and the assist for...John Tucker.

I jump to my feet again, cheering loudly. This time, my friends do say something.

"She's got it bad," D'Andre remarks.

"Told you so," Hope says to her boyfriend.

"What?" I mutter defensively. "That was a very nice scoring maneuver."

Carin doubles over. "Scoring maneuver?" she echoes between giggles. "Jeez, B, get with the program. It's called a *goal*."

"You're called a goal," I retort childishly.

D'Andre snickers. "Good one."

I sit down and watch the fast-paced game with bated breath. To my relief, Briar holds the other team off, and we win 1-0 when the final buzzer goes off. Everyone is in good spirits as they shuffle out of the arena, myself included.

I'm happy I came tonight. And as unsure as I am about whether to get involved with Tucker, I can't deny I'm excited to see him and give him a hug and tell him what a great game he played. He'll hug me back. Thank me. Maybe he'll suggest we get in that truck of his for some celebratory sexytimes...

If he does that, I honestly don't think I would say no this time.

"Apparently all the bunnies hang out outside the locker rooms," Carin whispers to me as we file into the main lobby. "So let's wait for him outside. It'll be less crowded."

"The bunnies?"

"Puck bunnies. Hockey groupies. Whatever you want to call them." She shrugs. "You know, the chicks looking to get nasty with a hockey player."

"Ah. Gotcha." I shrug back, because I have nothing against girls who want that. After all, my own requirement for hookups is *athletes only*.

But when the athlete I'm waiting for finally emerges from the building, he's not alone.

My spine stiffens as I watch Tucker pause on the steps with his arm slung around a short blonde. He's in his hockey jacket and she's bundled up in a bright red parka, but the way my stomach twists up with jealousy, you'd think they were buck-naked and brazenly fucking on the stairs.

"Let's go," I hiss to my friends.

A firm hand circles my wrist. "They're just talking," Hope says quietly.

My cheeks hollow as I grind my teeth. "He has his arm around her."

I am *not* about to make a fool of myself over some hockey player, especially one who says how much he wants to go out with me and then comes out for a postgame celebration with his arm around some other girl.

I sneak another peek. Yep. Arm's still around her. And he's laughing at whatever Blondie's saying.

My molars are being crushed to dust, but I can't seem to look away. Blondie wraps both arms around Tucker's waist and gives him a tight hug. She tips her head up at him. He smiles down at her.

And then my heart is shredded to pieces, because Tucker's head is dipping toward hers. His mouth drops lower and lower and lower, until finally he kisses her...

13

SABRINA

On the forehead.

Tucker kisses Blondie on the forehead.

And then ruffles her hair as if she's a toddler.

"Damn. She got the forehead kiss?" D'Andre murmurs. "That's rough."

Whatever. It was still a kiss! And I don't even want to know who this chick is anymore. I feel stupid for coming tonight.

Tucker is Mr. Popular, with his swarm of admirers and impeccable manners and that reddish hair that makes him look like he belongs in some old-timey family sitcom where life is perfect, perfect, perfect.

I'm the overachiever, the bitch who studies her ass off and works every second of every day to try to climb out of the gutter she was born in so she can stand next to all these Briar kids without feeling inferior.

"Let's go," I repeat.

My friends must realize how serious I am, because they all take a step forward. We're about two feet from the base of the steps when I hear my name.

"Sabrina!"

Crap. I've been spotted.

"Wait up." His voice sounds closer now.

I turn to Carin in a silent plea for help, but she simply grins. When I turn to Hope and D'Andre, they're pretending to be studying her phone. Traitors.

Sighing, I swing around and meet Tucker halfway.

He's visibly thrilled to see me, his eyes bright and his sexy mouth curved in a smile. "What are you doing here?"

I say the first lame thing that comes to mind. "I was in the neighborhood."

"You were, were you?" His smile widens. "And did you happen to catch any of the game while you were in the neighborhood?"

"All of it, actually. That was a nice assist."

"I thought you didn't know anything about hockey."

"I don't. I'm just repeating what the announcer said on the PA."

"Tuck!" someone from the group of players calls. "You coming?"

He twists around to shout back, "I'll meet you there!" Then he's smiling at me again. "Want to come back to my place to celebrate the win with us?"

I shake my head. "I have to get home. I work tomorrow. Besides —" *Don't say it...* "I don't particularly feel like—" *Don't fucking say it, Sabrina!* "—being a third wheel," I finish, and want to punch myself for it.

His dark auburn eyebrows shoot up. "What are you talking about?"

I clench my teeth.

"Darlin'," he prompts.

"Little Red Riding Hood over there," I mumble, jerking my head toward Blondie, who's now chatting with one of Tucker's friends. "You two looked like you were on a date."

"A date? Um, no." He starts to laugh. "That's Sheena, a friend of mine." He pauses. "Well, an ex."

I pounce on that. "See!"

"See what? She's an ex, but she's also a friend. I'm friends with lots of my exes."

Of course he is. No girl on this damn planet would ever Carrie Underwood this guy and key his truck or bash it in with a baseball bat. He's too fucking nice. It's impossible to hate him.

"You're jealous," he teases.

"No," I lie.

"You totally are." Delight dances across his face. "You like me."

"No," I lie again. "I told you—I was in the neighborhood. I figured I'd say hello."

"You're better than this, baby. Why don't you put us out of our misery and say yes already?"

"Yes to what?"

"A date. Just say yes."

My mouth opens to form words. Or rather, one word. *Yes.* I want to say it, I really, really do, but I hate being put on the spot. I can feel my friends' amused gazes on us, and now some of his friends are glancing over too. And Tucker is too good and sweet, and I'm trashy and aloof, and my stepfather is a total creep, and it's all too fucking overwhelming right now.

So when I finally answer, it's not with the word he wants to hear. "Your friends are waiting for you," I mutter, and then I hurry back to my crew before he can object.

Carin takes one look at my face and steers me toward the parking lot where D'Andre parked his car.

"Ugh!" I groan when we're out of Tucker's sight. "I'm so freaking stupid!"

"You're not stupid," Hope objects.

"If anything, you're too smart," Carin says. "Your brain is your biggest enemy."

"What's that supposed to mean?"

"It means you think too much. We all saw your face just now—you like this guy. You really like him."

"He scares me," I blurt out.

Three sets of eyes blink in surprise.

"He's too perfect, you guys." I groan again. "And I'm a total mess most of the time. I'm scared that if he gets to know me better, he'll see that."

"So what if he does?" Hope counters.

My teeth dig into my bottom lip.

Carin touches my arm. "You need to go out with him. Seriously, Sabrina, you'll regret it if you don't. And the one thing I know you hate is regrets."

She's right. I always kick myself after I let an opportunity pass me by.

"Tell you what," she says when I hesitate for too long. "Let's make it a double date."

"A double date?" I echo weakly.

"Oooh, threesome." Hope waggles her brows. "Kinky."

"Calm your tits, Hopeless," Carin orders. "I'm talking normal, wholesome double date."

I think it over. It *does* take a lot of the pressure off. "Okay... I can do that."

Carin beams. "Good. Now text him before you change your mind. Oh, and whoever you pair me up with better be hot. And make sure he knows how to use his tongue."

"I'm standing right here, you know." D'Andre waves one meaty hand in the air. "How 'bout you pervs quit objectifying my man clan?"

Hope giggles.

"Who's objectifying?" Carin replies. "I'm just saying I want a guy who's good with his tongue. That should be the prerequisite for every member of your 'man clan,' D. Like in middle school, they should teach reading, writing, and really good tongue movement."

"Girl, I think you can get locked up for those thoughts," he warns.

Hope continues to giggle uncontrollably for another minute before gaining enough composure to reach over and squeeze my arm. "This'll be good for you."

"If it crashes and burns, do I get to say I told you so?"

"I'll write it across my forehead in black magic marker for you," she vows.

As my friends head for Hope's car, I gather all the courage I can find and text Tucker before I talk myself out of it.

If I say yes, it doesn't mean anything.

His answer is immediate.

Him: *It means yes.*

Me: *But I'm not committing to anything beyond this one date.*

Him: *Kinda presumptuous, no? I only asked for one date.*

I stare at my phone. Had I read this whole thing incorrectly? The guy talked about love at first sight, wanting to be married and have kids, and he only wants to see me one more time and fuck me?

Him: *Kidding, darlin. I'm holding back the marriage proposal until the 3rd date. When?*

Me: *I'm bringing my friend Carin and u need to bring the hottest guy u know.*

Him: *I'm the hottest guy I know. Will look for 2nd hottest guy on campus. She have any preferences?*

Me: *Someone who knows how to use his tongue.*

Him: *Again, that'd be me. Not sure how I'll find out how good the other guys are w/ their equipment. Not a topic that comes up a lot.*

Me: *That's the price of my time.*

Him: *On it.*

There's a short delay, and then another message pops up.

Him: *You won't regret this.*

I HAVE the perfect date idea, Carin texts an hour later. It's eleven and I'm getting ready for bed because I have to be up at four to sort mail. The text is followed up with a slightly blurry pic. I pinch and zoom until I manage to make out a few words.

Me: *Paint night out? I have no artistic skills. Even my stick figures look terrible. U know this. U mocked my hangman once.*

Her: *That was NOT a hangman. That was...I mean, the arms shld come out from the side of the body, not the neck. Anyway this is EZ. It's like a paint by numbers thing. We drink/paint/enjoy ourselves. If the date is crappy then u and I can drink ourselves into oblivion.*

Me: *Fine. When is it? I'm only available Sun, M, W, Thur.*

Her: *I know. It's why I picked this, dummy. It's every other Sunday, as in tomorrow night.*

How would I know? The picture she sent is small and blurry and could say it's a church group meeting on Saturday morning.

Me: *I'll see if T is available.*

Her: *Bet u he is.*

I'm not taking that bet. Instead, I text Tucker.

Me: *You in 4 some paint by numbers?*

My phone dings the message alert just as I'm pulling on my sleep shirt and boxers.

Him: *Is that like naked Twister?*

Me: *I have no clue.*

I send him the picture. Maybe he can make some sense out of it, because I sure can't.

Him: *Was this taken with an actual camera or drawn by tiny leprechauns?*

Me: *Carin's a scientist, not an artist. Btw did u find someone?*

Him: *Yes. My buddy Fitz is coming and b4 u ask, I have no idea re: his oral skills. But he's hella smart, has a mean slapshot, and I've never heard any complaints.*

I take a screenshot of that text and send it to Carin.

Me: *Is this OK?*

Her: *Can I have a pic?*

I text Tuck, *Can she have a pic?*

Him: *Of what?*

Dear God. This is a ridiculous game of actual telephone.

Me: *Tucker says: of what?*

Her: *Face, abs, ass. No dick*

I take yet another screenshot and shoot that off to Tucker. While he considers the request, I wash my face and brush my teeth. By the time I climb into bed, there's a message waiting for me. A picture of a gorgeous dark-haired guy flipping Tucker off fills my screen.

Wow. It's incredible how hot these Briar hockey players are. Is that a requirement of making the team? Be able to slap the puck a hundred miles an hour and also star in the calendar?

I forward the picture to Carin, who sends me a thumbs-up emoji in return. Then I text Tucker again.

Me: *We're good to go.*

Him: *Time/place? Srsly can't read this thing.*

Me: *Tomorrow. 8 p.m. Carin says there's booze.*

Him: *K*

I'm about to put my phone away when three dots appear. And then disappear. And then re-appear again. Finally, the message comes through.

Him: *Dick pics that bad?*

I smother a giggle. That's his question?

Me: *Why? RU going to send me one?*

Him: *Feel like that may be a trick question. Do u want one?*

Me: *Depends on context. Random dick pics = no. Otherwise? I dunno. I haven't gotten one that I've really liked. U've sent one? Or several?*

Him: *My thumbs are tired. Hold on.*

The phone vibrates in my hand a second later.

"Hello," I answer.

"Hey." He pauses. "So what made you change your mind about the date?"

"My friends said it would be good for me," I admit.

"Your friends are right." I can hear the smile in his voice. "Anyway, I feel like this is a conversation we should have in person so I can see your face. Eggplant emojis don't have enough nuance."

This makes me laugh. "True."

"But you're in Boston and I'm in Hastings, so we're going with the phone call. I may have sent a pic once, but it was solicited. She sent me one first."

"Really? I'm not a fan of that. Too many revenge pics online." Besides, I never really hung around a guy long enough to want to send him a picture, but I don't share that with Tucker. "So there are pics of Tucker's mighty wang on the internet?"

"I haven't been tagged on Instagram yet, so I'm hopeful they aren't out there. But thanks for calling my dick mighty. We appreciate that." Amusement colors his words.

"We? As in you and your penis?"

"Yup," he says cheerfully.

I snuggle deeper under the covers. "You have a name for your penis?"

"Doesn't everyone? Guys put a name on everything that's important to them—cars, dicks. One of my teammates in junior hockey named his stick, which was dumb because sticks break all the time. He'd gone through twelve of them by the end of the season."

"What were the names?"

"That's the thing. He just kept adding a number to the end, like iPhone 6, iPhone 7, except in his case it was Henrietta 1, Henrietta 2, et cetera."

I snicker. "He should've used the hurricane naming convention."

"Darlin', he wasn't smart enough to come up with two names, let alone twelve."

Darlin'. My heart trips at the endearment. When he used it before, it seemed like a throwaway. But now? After he just said guys name things that are important to them?

I quell my fantastical interpretations before they lead me to a dangerous end. *We're flirting. Keep the tone light.* "What's your dick's name?"

"Uh-uh," he scolds. "That's wife knowledge. I can't tell you until the honeymoon."

I wait for the inevitable sense of discomfort to start tickling my neck, but it doesn't come. Apparently the offhand jokes about marriage no longer bother me.

"So what makes a good dick pic?" he asks. "Not that I'm sending you one."

"Is that also wife knowledge?" I tease.

"I'd consider it engagement stuff."

I put that thought aside and consider his question. "Completely graphic doesn't do it for me. I need context, like I said before. Your fist around it would be hot. You have good hands."

There's a rustling sound, footsteps, and then a door latch clicking shut. He's gone somewhere private, and that knowledge makes certain parts of my body pulse excitedly.

"I had to leave the living room. We've got people over, and you thinking about my dick is hot as fuck. I'm too hard to be in public."

My breasts feel so heavy that I'm finding it hard to breathe. As I shift underneath the blankets, I hear his breath catch.

"What are you thinking about?" he murmurs.

I drag in some air to fill my suddenly depleted lungs. I know where this is going. If I stay on the phone, we're going to end up turning each other on to the point that I'm going to have to masturbate once I'm done. Tucker remains silent, leaving the decision up to me. I dip my hand between my legs as if the pressure could make the ache go away, but the contact only intensifies my desire.

My voice is hoarse when I start speaking. "I'm fixated on you holding your dick. Only now you're moving your hand, stroking yourself."

When there's no immediate response, I blush, thinking I've gone too far for him. But his next words tell me he's right with me.

"You're killing me."

I bite my lip and rub harder. "I'm getting worked up too."

"That doesn't help, because now I'm picturing you all flushed and needy. You wet, Sabrina?"

My fingers slip across my pussy. "Very."

"Fuck. What would I be doing if I was there?"

"Licking me," I say instantly. He has a great tongue.

On his end, there's more rustling and then a husky, "You need a toy?"

"Yeah, give me a sec." I fumble in my desk drawer and find the box of tampons where I hide stuff from Ray—some cash rolled up in an empty tampon cartridge and my vibe. I fish the latter out and flick it on.

"Ready," I tell him as I place the quivering toy against my clit. My hips arch up and a small cry escapes me.

"Goddamn," he groans. "Slide it inside, slow and steady. It's my hand on that vibrator and my tongue is on your clit."

As he issues his commands and paints an erotic picture, I work the toy in and out. It's such a relief not to have to think, to give myself completely over to him. I don't say anything more. I can't, really. I'm too focused on listening, letting his southern drawl pour over me like warm syrup, listening to the hoarse, dirty instructions telling me to pump the vibe harder, imagine him licking my pussy, telling me how gorgeous and sexy I am, and how he's never been harder in his life.

I come as the sounds of him working his own flesh mix with my gasps of pleasure. His voice fills my world.

"Night, darlin'," he says when my breathing slows.

"Night," I manage. And then I fall asleep, deep and long and utterly satisfied.

14

SABRINA

"Naked painting?" Suspicion floats through me as I pull open the door to Wine and Brush. The sign cheekily displays a pair of art dolls arranged in a sordid embrace. Fitting for a college town wine bar, I guess. "You took that blurry picture on purpose," I accuse my friend.

"Of course I did," Carin says smugly. "I didn't want you to have an excuse to say no." She strolls in and then stops about two steps from the threshold, her gaze glued to the bar across the room. "Nice." She whistles under her breath. "You did good, B."

I grin. "I'll happily take credit were none is due."

We each snag a wine glass from a tray by the table before moving forward. Our dates are leaning against the bar talking to each other. Even slouching, they're about a head taller than almost any other person in the room. I notice other girls eyeing their dates and then casting covetous glances toward Tucker and Fitzy.

It's those glances that propel me across the room and onto my tiptoes to give Tucker a kiss on the lips.

The corners of his sexy mouth curve up as if he knows exactly what I'm doing. "Good to see you, darlin'. Sleep well last night?"

"I did. You?"

"Like a baby."

Carin doesn't miss a thing. "Did you sleep in Boston last night?" she teases.

He shakes his head. "Just heard a good story."

I use the wine glass to smother a smile while Tucker introduces our friends. "Carin, this is Colin, but everyone calls him Fitzy."

"I like that better," she announces. "Carin and Colin sounds too cutesy together."

The six-foot-plus guy smiles shyly and takes Carin's hand in his, carefully shaking it as if he's afraid he's going to hurt her. He doesn't have to worry, though. She's small, but tough.

"Are you roommates?" Carin asks, and she's not at all covert as she admires him from head to toe.

I can't deny that I'm kinda doing the same thing. Fitzy is incredibly appealing. He's got messy dark hair that you just want to run your fingers through. And those tats...yum. He's wearing a T-shirt that reveals two full sleeves of intricate designs and a lot of fantasy-type imagery—I make out several dragons and at least one sword. And there's ink peeking out of the collar of his shirt too. Carin's not usually into tattooed guys, but her eyes are glued to this one.

"Nope. I live alone," Fitzy tells her. "Tuck lives with the glory boys."

"The glory boys?" I echo, but I suspect I know the answer.

Tucker's expression grows amused. "Garrett and Logan are the stars. Both guys are going pro. And you know Dean."

I wrinkle my nose at the mention of his name.

"Don't get her started," Carin warns.

Fitzy gives a lopsided grin. "A girl who doesn't love Dean? I didn't know they existed."

"He got an A because he was sleeping with the TA!" I grouse.

Carin places her hand over my mouth. "I warned you. Come on, Fitzy." She drops her hand and crooks her finger toward the big hockey player. "Let's find a place to sit. I've heard this story before and it's not a good one." She hums a few bars from *Frozen* as she leads him away.

I make a frustrated sound in the back of my throat, but since half my audience is gone, I turn to the only person who's left. "Are you going to tell me to let it go too?"

"Naah, you hold on to that as long as you want. It's not my place to dictate what you get mad about." He cups the back of my neck with one large palm and leans down to whisper in my ear. "But I'll be happy to tell you what to do later on tonight."

My body tightens immediately. Sex with Tucker is about the least stressful, most enjoyable thing in my life, and as I lean into his solid grip, I realize I'm no longer interested in fighting the attraction between us. My friends are right—I *do* need this. Not only the sex, but the company. Hanging out with a smart, cute guy who wants nothing more than to be with me, any way he can.

I think I'm just going to roll with this and see what happens.

"It's a deal."

He winks. "I've got ideas now."

"As if you didn't have them before," I scoff.

"I've got more ideas. You're very inspirational."

His hot gaze has me stepping forward and lifting my hand to his chest—his very ripped, very lickable, very gorgeous chest. Under my palm, his muscles flex and his heart beats quickly. I rise up on my tiptoes to—

A loud cough behind us has me dropping down.

"Yeah?" Tucker says to Fitzy without taking his eyes off mine.

"You might want to grab a seat. Everyone's waiting on you."

I shift around to see that most of the room is turned in their chairs, either waiting for us to sit down or hoping we start mauling each other in front of them. The long tables are set up in a C-shape, and there's a small riser in the center where I assume the model will stand. We each get our own easel, canvas, and an array of brushes and acrylic paints. It's pretty cool.

"Unless you're stripping and going to serve as our models, come and sit," Carin orders.

Tucker's hand drifts downward, managing to raise a thousand goose bumps on the way to my hand. I clasp it and lead him to the chairs next to Carin.

"You're supposed to wait until after the date to jump his bones," she whispers as I sit down.

I set the wine glass aside and pick up a paintbrush. "Rules are for suckers and boring people, Careful."

She runs a brush over my nose in mock disgust, but then the instructor starts speaking and we shut up out of habit.

"Hey everyone! I'm Aria and I'll be your instructor for the night! I'm so pumped by the turn-out!"

Oh boy. Our teacher is one big ball of energy, bouncing on her feet as she addresses the room. On her head is a crazy swirl of Medusa-like dreadlocks that swing around like snakes as she bounce-talks.

"First thing I'm going to do is introduce our model! This is Spector—"

Spector?

Tucker sways in his chair, and I turn to find him fighting waves of laughter. I plant a hand on his knee to still him.

"Be nice," I hiss.

"Trying to." He chuckles while muttering "Spector" to himself.

A tall guy in a white bathrobe steps forward and waves at the group. His black hair is longer than mine, and he has those squinty James Franco eyes that make him look perpetually stoned.

"Hi," is all he says.

Then he takes off the robe.

I choke on a gasp, because oh my God, his penis is *right there.* And it's impressive.

Beside me, Carin is also quick to examine the goods. "Now *that's* what I'm talking about! Well, hello there, Manaconda!" she calls to the model before sweeping her gaze over the other females in attendance. "Ladies, I think Spector deserves a slow clap right now, no?"

Now I'm the one fighting laughter, because damned if the ladies don't all break out in a slow, slow clap that leads to a burst of applause followed by whistles and catcalls. The shade of poor Spector's face is so red it belongs on the palette in front of me.

Tucker snorts loudly in the chair next to mine, while Fitzy leans around Carin's and asks me, "Is she always like this?"

"Usually she's worse," I say cheerfully.

He doesn't seem put off by that. Our instructor, meanwhile, is starting to get annoyed.

"Guys!" She claps her hands together. "Focus! There's beautiful art to be made!" Her stern expression cracks, replaced with a grin. "Which, of course, will absolutely include Spector's equipment."

This is the weirdest fucking date I've ever been on.

Aria gives us a rundown of how it all works. It's not very complicated. We drink wine and paint Spector's penis. Surprisingly, Tuck, Fitz and the other men in the room are instantly on board. Paint tubes are opened, brushes are raised, and then we're making beautiful art.

Sort of.

I awkwardly drag my brush over the canvas. I tried to mix yellow, white and brown to create a peachy skin tone for my canvas Spector, but it looks like he has an awful spray tan.

Tucker runs one of his dry brushes across a knuckle that's sporting a bruise. "I can think of a dozen good uses for one of these. Might take it home."

I roll my eyes. "Paintbrushes aren't sex toys."

"Says who?"

We work steadily for the next hour. Carin is awesome at this. So is Fitzy, who, according to Tuck, designs his own video games. Tucker is surprisingly decent, though he seems to be avoiding the dick region on his canvas.

"You're gonna have to paint his junk eventually," I taunt.

He winks. "I'm saving the best for last."

From the other section of the tables, a guy with floppy blond hair and a Red Sox T-shirt raises his hand. "Teach, I can't do the pubes! They look like little ants!"

A burst of laughter roars through the room. I think Red Sox is on a double date too, because he and his date are sitting next to another couple, who are in hysterics.

"Seriously, Spec," Red Sox's friend calls out. "You couldn't have done a little manscaping before you came here tonight?"

"Can't," Spector replies from his perch, sounding bored. "My contract doesn't allow it."

He has a *contract*? To pose naked at a college bar paint night?

"The pubic hair adds texture to the painting," Aria explains to the group. "But art is about interpretation, remember? Paint what you see in here—" She taps a hand over her heart, "not what you see here —" She points to her eyes.

"What the hell does that even mean?" I whisper to Tucker, whose entire face is flushed from laughing so hard.

"Like *this*!" Aria declares suddenly. "*This* is interpretation!"

I glance over to find her swiping Fitzy's canvas off his easel. The big guy rumbles in protest, but she ignores him and holds up the painting with a grand flourish.

My jaw drops when I see what Tucker's friend has painted. It's Spector, but a badass version of him in a helmet and wielding a shield. Instead of the much talked about penis, Fitzy painted an elaborate-looking sword jutting from the guy's crotch. Like, a sword worthy of *Game of Thrones*.

"*Dude*," Tucker exclaims, suitably impressed.

"That's amazing!" a wide-eyed Carin gushes to her date.

He shrugs. "It's all right."

His modesty makes me smile. I only grin harder when Aria gives him back the canvas and then begs him to leave it with her instead of taking it home with him.

We resume our painting, cracking jokes and sipping our wine. Every so often, Tucker leans toward the elderly gentleman beside him and helps the poor guy out.

"Naw, man, you want to shade under *here*," he advises. "Imagine that the light is hitting his arm from up there. So the shadow would be down here."

The old man harrumphs loudly. "This whole thing is a waste of time."

"Hiram!" his wife scolds.

"What? It's true," he says in a crabby voice, then gives Tucker and me a surly look. "This was *her* idea."

"Because I thought you would enjoy it," the gray-haired woman protests. "You've always told me how much you envy my artistic skills."

The couple appears to be in their late sixties. Or hell, maybe their late seventies. I've never been a good judge of age. Besides, seniors look so young these days. Nana could pass for my older sister.

"Gee, I'm sorry, Doris, but I never learned how to draw naked folks when I was getting shot at in 'Nam!"

Doris slams her brush on the table. "We talked about this! Dr. Phillips said you weren't allowed to discuss Vietnam anymore. It's destructive to our relationship."

"It was the most taxing time of my life," he says stubbornly.

"And you think it was easy for me?" she challenges. "Being at home and raising two children in diapers while you were off hunting Charlie?"

He squawks in outrage. "You were wiping bottoms! I was killing human beings!"

I bite my lip to stop from laughing, even though this isn't a particularly funny conversation. Maybe the wine has gone to my head.

"Now, now," Tucker drawls. "Hiram, my man, your wife is gorgeous and obviously devoted to you. And Doris, Hiram here fought for his country to keep you and your children safe—think of how much he must love you for him to have done that. So let's not fight, huh? Why don't we just focus on painting this nice fellow over there and doing justice to his equipment?"

Fitzy snorts from the other side of Carin.

So does Hiram, whose voice becomes gruff as he addresses his wife. "I'm sorry, Dorrie. You're right—this was a lovely idea."

"And you were very brave in the war," she says magnanimously.

Hiram leans over and pats Tucker on the shoulder. "All right. Show me that shadow trick."

My heart melts as I watch Tucker help the older man. Doris, meanwhile, is blushing prettily, probably thinking about how he called her gorgeous before.

"I like you, kid," Hiram tells my date.

Yeah. I like him too.

TUCKER

WE'RE all feeling stupid and giddy when we troop out of the bar with our wrapped-up canvases tucked under our arms. Well, except for Fitzy—our instructor made him leave his masterpiece behind so she could show it to future classes.

Outside, the air is frigid, but that doesn't stop Hiram from saying, "I saw an ice cream parlor down the road. Let's check if it's still open."

And yup, our double date has turned into a triple date and suddenly we're going out for ice cream with an old war vet and his sweet-as-molasses wife.

I hold Sabrina's hand as we amble down the sidewalk. I honestly didn't expect to have this much fun tonight. I mean, a painting class? There are a million—dirtier—things I would've rather done, but this wasn't bad at all. Even Fitzy has laughed more times tonight than I've ever heard in the past.

The ice cream place is just closing when we arrive, but the kid who's about to lock the door takes pity on us and opens the cash register. Thanking him profusely, we order waffle cones and then head back to the bar parking lot.

Now that they're no longer bickering, Hiram and Doris regale us with stories about their forty-six years together. They've lived through some pretty harrowing times, but I'm more interested in the happy memories they describe.

Forty-six years. It's fucking surreal to think of being with someone for that long. Am I totally nuts for wanting that?

Sabrina seems equally mesmerized by their tales, and when the elderly couple climbs into their little car and drives off, she seems genuinely disappointed to see them go.

"We're going to finish our ice cream in my car," Carin announces, and there's nothing stealthy about the way she says it. With a mischievous smile, she tugs on Fitzy's hand and drags him toward the blue hatchback parked across the lot.

He glances over his shoulder and grins at me.

"They're totally going to hook up," Sabrina says.

"Yup."

I drag her toward my own vehicle. Once we're settled in the front seat, I flick the ignition and blast the heat. Ice cream was probably a bad idea—Sabrina is visibly shivering as we wait for the truck to warm up.

"So," I say.

"So."

"That was entertaining."

"Which part? When the Red Sox guy painted ants for pubes? Or when Hiram and Doris described what it was like to live through the boob job craze in the eighties?"

"Holy fuck. When she said she'd considered getting her 'bosom done'?"

"Oh my God. I *died!*" Sabrina is in stitches beside me, the sound of her high-pitched giggles bringing a rush of warmth to my chest.

Damn. I really like this girl. She's...incredible. She's not the ice queen Dean insists that she is, not in the slightest. She's smart and funny and caring and—

And I might be falling for her.

My laughter dies off.

"What's wrong?" Sabrina asks immediately.

"Nothing," I lie. It's either that or tell her what I'm thinking about, and I'm pretty sure she doesn't want to hear it.

I don't even want to imagine what her response would be if I admitted that I'm falling for her. We've fucked twice and gone on *one* date. It's way too early to bring the L-word into the conversation.

"You sure?" She sounds concerned. "You got a really deep crease right...here." She smooths two fingers over my forehead.

"Naah, I'm good." I shift in my seat and ease closer to her. "I'm having a great time."

"Me too." Her bottom lip pokes out a bit. "I wish..."

"You wish what?"

She sighs. "I wish we could go back to my place, but I've got to be up at four in the morning. This isn't a good night for me to be up late."

"Same. I've got practice at seven."

"So no sex," she says glumly.

"Not unless you want to get it on in the truck again."

Interest flickers in her dark eyes before fading to resignation. "Tempting, but I'd feel weird having sex when Carin is like ten feet away."

"I'm pretty sure Carin isn't paying any attention to us right now."

Sabrina shakes her head. "Trust me, they won't be in there for long. She has a strict no-sex-on-the-first-date rule. Fitzy's only going to get a make-out session." She snickers. "And probably blue balls."

"What about me? Are my balls gonna hate me when I get home?"

"I don't know. You tell me." Then she slides over the console and kisses me.

When her tongue swirls seductively over mine, it sends a bolt of lust to my balls. I groan against her soft lips. "Yeah," I croak. "I'll defi-nitely be icing the boys tonight."

"Aw. You poor baby," she whispers, then proceeds to torture me with hungry kisses and the lazy glide of her palm over my crotch.

We make out for a while, neither of us anxious to take it further. But it's still hot as hell. The windows of my truck fog up, and I'm hard as a goal post by the time we break apart.

"I should get home," she says regretfully.

I nod, offering a wry smile. "Rock, Paper, Scissors to decide who knocks on their window?"

It turns out to be unnecessary, because suddenly there's a knock on *my* window. I roll it down to find Carin's flushed face peering down at me. Her lips are swollen, her hair a tangle of red curls.

"Sorry," she says with a sheepish shrug. "But B said she needed to leave by ten-thirty. It's past that already."

Very, very reluctantly, I slide out of the pickup and then hurry around to Sabrina's door to open it for her. Her expression is as reluc-tant as mine.

A tousled-haired Fitzy is leaning against the side of my truck, and Carin smacks his ass as she makes her way back to her car.

"We'll do this again?" I murmur to Sabrina.

"Naked paint night? I don't know. Once might be enough."

"Another date," I correct. "You'll call me when you have some free time?"

I half expect an argument, but she simply lifts up on her tiptoes, kisses me on the lips, and pulls back to say, "Absolutely."

15

TUCKER

December

Me: *I miss u*

Her: *I miss u 2*

Me: *Any chance we can change that by meeting up? I'll bring my dick...*

Her: *LMAO isn't that sort of a given? U 2 are a package deal*

Me: *Package is the right word. A really big package ;)*

Okay, so I'm laying it on pretty thick, but damn, I miss this girl. I haven't seen her in a week, which is about, oh, seven days too long. Since our double date last month, we've tried to see each other at least two or three times a week. With our hectic schedules, it's a miracle we've managed to find the time, so it was bound to happen that our schedules would catch up to us.

These past two weeks, we've both been busy with school. I've had some brutal practices and games, and then Thanksgiving rolled around and I'd already committed to spending the holiday with

Hollis and his family. I was tempted to bail and see Sabrina instead, but she was working and admitted she'd rather I didn't hang around at the strip club while she waited tables. Apparently Boots & Chutes is Bummer Central during holidays.

I'm dying to see her, so when I read her next message, I do a mental fist pump.

Her: *If u don't mind the drive, come to Boston 2nite? Working on my Con Law paper, but I can take a bunch of breaks if u wanna keep me company.*

I don't even hesitate.

Me: *On my way.*

I already showered and changed in anticipation of possibly seeing her tonight. I hurry downstairs, hoping to slip out of the house unnoticed.

"Tuck, get in here! We need a grown-up's opinion."

Damn. So close.

I follow Garrett's voice to the living room, where I find him and Hannah on the armchair. She's in his lap, he's got his arms around her, and they look so happy and at ease that I feel a pang of envy. They're not alone, though. Logan, Fitzy and Logan's friend Morris are on the couch, video game controllers in their hands. The first-person shooting game they're playing is paused on the flat screen.

"What's up?" I try to hide my impatience. "I'm on my way out."

From the couch, Logan arches a brow. "You've been on your way out a lot lately."

I shrug. "Places to go, people to see."

"Are you ever going to tell us her name?" Hannah asks in a cheerful voice.

"I have no idea what you're talking about," I reply innocently.

Garrett waves a hand. "I don't care about Tuck's mystery girl right now. I need someone to back me up—pronto."

I grin. "Back you up on what?"

"Dean and Allie."

Ah. I was wondering when we'd be having this powwow. We all

came back from our various Thanksgiving trips to discover that Dean and Allie are officially a couple.

I wasn't surprised to hear it, because I already suspected they'd hooked up, but I am a bit stunned that they're actually going out. Dean hasn't had a girlfriend since I've known him.

"Apparently I'm the only one who thinks this is the worst fucking idea since horses," Garrett says irritably.

"Horses?" Logan and Fitzy echo in unison.

"Like, horses in general?" Morris asks in confusion.

"As in, domesticating them," he grumbles. "They belong in the wild. End of story."

"Babe," Hannah hedges in, "are you just saying that because you're scared of horses?"

His jaw drops. "I'm not scared of horses."

She ignores the denial. "Oh my God, it's all coming together. That's why you wouldn't go to the Thanksgiving fair in Philly." She glances at the rest of us. "My aunt and uncle wanted to take us to this festival thing with all these cool booths and a petting zoo...and horseback riding. He said his *stomach hurt.*"

Garrett visibly clenches his teeth. "My stomach *did* hurt. I ate too much fucking turkey, Wellsy. Anyway, I don't like this. I'm going to be so screwed when they break up."

"They might not break up," she points out.

I furrow my brow. "And how would that even affect you?"

Since I'm not seeing his logic, he slowly spells it out for me. "Sides, dude. People break up, their friends take sides. Dean's my buddy, so obviously the bro code says I have to side with him. But this one—" He jerks a thumb at Hannah, "is my girlfriend. Girlfriend trumps buddy. Wellsy'll take Allie's side, and I'll have to take Wellsy's side, vis-à-vis, I'm taking Allie's side."

"I don't think you're using vis-à-vis right," Morris pipes up.

"Yeah, I believe the word you're looking for is *therefore.*" Logan's lips are twitching wildly.

"I wouldn't expect you to take Allie's side on my behalf," Hannah protests. "And you're being such a jackass about this. We're adults. If they break up, we'll all still be able to co-exist peacefully."

"Ross and Rachel co-existed," Logan agrees.

Fitzy snorts.

Garrett is too busy glaring at Hannah. "I can't believe you're cool with this. She's your best friend. He's going to blow this—you *know* that."

His girlfriend shrugs. "All I know is that Allie is happy. And if Allie's happy, I'm happy."

"Tuck?" Garrett prompts.

I hesitate. On one hand, Dean seems genuinely into Allie, at least from the limited interactions between them that I've witnessed. On the other hand, the guy doesn't have a serious bone in his body. Allie's a nice girl. I don't want to see her get hurt.

Either way, it's none of my business.

"Wellsy's right. They're adults. If they want to be together, then who cares?"

He glowers at me. "Traitor."

"Dude, the girl TKO'd him yesterday," Logan says with a grin. "You know how big his ego is—if it could take that kind of hit and he still wants to be with her, then it's the real deal."

Despite myself, I start to laugh. Fuck. I wish the other guys were here last night for all the chaos. After the team's road game to Scranton, Dean and I came home to a dark house where Allie and Dean's sister were watching a horror movie. The girls freaked, Allie accidentally knocked Dean out with a paperweight, and now I'm equipped with enough ammo to torture him for the rest of his life.

"Oh hey, speaking of last night," Hannah says. "Did Dean's sister get back to Brown okay? I wish I got to meet her."

"Trust me," Fitzy mutters from the couch. "You're lucky you didn't."

Logan snickers. "You poor thing—a hot blonde was throwing herself at you. How dare she!"

The other guy flushes. "She asked to see my dick!"

"And that's a problem because...?"

As Morris and Garrett start laughing their asses off, Fitzy just shrugs. "Aggressive chicks aren't my thing. I like going at my own speed, all right?"

I'm tempted to call bullshit, because he sure didn't seem to mind when Sabrina's friend Carin dragged him to her car for a hookup. But Fitz and I haven't really spoken about that night, so I stay quiet. Besides, if I mention the double date, everyone will demand to know who *I* was with.

The last time we saw each other, Sabrina teased me that I'm not telling people about us because I'm ashamed of her. Which is so not the case. My friends have a bad habit of sticking their noses into each other's love lives—case in point, Garrett's obsession with Dean and Allie. So yeah, I'd rather not have my relationship with Sabrina dissected by everyone, not when it's still so new.

And anyway, I know she's secretly relieved that we're on the DL. The one time I used the word *relationship* to describe us, she got all weird and fidgety on me.

"Okay, I gotta bounce," I tell the room. "Any other grown-up issues we need to discuss, or can I go?"

"Go," Garrett grumbles, making a shooing motion with his hand. "You were no help anyway."

SABRINA

TUCKER'S TONGUE is in my mouth before I can even close the front door. Despite the ripples of heat that assault my body, I force myself to wrench away from the kiss. Nana's in the kitchen, and I don't need her walking out and witnessing this.

"My grandmother's home," I murmur.

I expect disappointment, but he simply nods. "Cool. Want to introduce me?"

The one thing I've learned from dating Tucker this last month is that absolutely nothing fazes this guy. He takes everything in stride, adjusting and adapting as needed. I don't even know what he looks like when he's annoyed.

"I should warn you—Nana's a bit...outspoken." That's my tactful way of saying *rude bitch*. As we head for the kitchen, I pray that my grandmother won't be a jerk to Tucker.

She's at the table when we walk in, flipping through an issue of *US Weekly*. "Did Ray forget his key again?" Nana asks without looking up.

"Um. No." I shift awkwardly. "Nana, this is Tucker."

Her head flies up. Immediately, interest fills her gaze. She studies Tucker from head to toe, so blatant in her ogling that I feel my cheeks heat up.

"Nana," I chide.

She snaps out of it. "It's very nice to meet you, Tucker." She emphasizes the word *very*.

Great. My grandmother is hitting on my...well, I'm not sure what he is. But Nana's seductive tone still isn't cool.

"I'm Joy, Sabrina's grandma."

"It's nice to meet you, ma'am." He extends his hand for a shake, and she holds it a little too long. Long enough that he looks uncomfortable when he steps back.

"Sabrina didn't mention she had a boyfriend."

"We're just friends," I answer.

Tucker's shoulders tense.

Aw fuck. I wasn't trying to hurt his feelings. I simply don't want Nana getting all nosy and asking us when the wedding is or some shit.

"I thought you were too busy for friends." She lifts a mocking brow.

I grit my teeth. "I'm not too busy for friends. I hang out with Hope and Carin, don't I?"

Rather than answer, she turns back to Tucker. "So, what are you two *friends* up to tonight?"

I speak before he can. "We're going to hang out in my room for a while. Maybe watch a movie or something."

A knowing smirk curves her lips. "All right then. Try to keep the volume down, hmmm?"

And we all know she's not talking about the television volume.

Cheeks scorching, I drag Tucker out of the kitchen. "I'm sorry," I say when we're in the hall. "She can be inappropriate."

His steady gaze finds mine. "Why would it be inappropriate for her to ask what we are to each other?"

I avert my eyes. He's got me there.

Truth is, the reason I don't want Nana asking questions is because I don't have any answers. I don't know what Tucker and I are to each other. All I know is that I miss him when he's not around. That every time a text from him pops up on my phone, my heart soars like a cluster of helium balloons. That when he looks at me with those heavy-lidded brown eyes, I forget my own name.

We go to my bedroom, where he sits on the edge of the bed while I close and lock the door. A couple seconds tick by. Then he pats his lap and says, "C'mere, darlin'."

I'm on him in a heartbeat, my legs wrapped around his waist and my fingers in his hair. "I really did miss you," I whisper, pressing my lips to his.

Kissing Tucker is like sinking into a hot bath. It makes my skin tingle and turns my limbs to jelly, surrounding me in a cocoon of heat that I never want to emerge from. His tongue drags over my lower lip before easing into my mouth. His hands are warm and solid as they slide underneath my tank top and stroke my bare hips.

Before I know it, we're tangled together on the bed, clawing at each other's clothes even while our mouths stay locked. Once we're naked, my body strains against him, aching for release. Tucker is just as frantic. There's no foreplay, no words exchanged. I grab a condom from my nightstand, toss it to him, and he puts it on without delay.

It's the quietest sex we've ever had. It has to be, because Nana is right down the hall. And there's something so hot and dirty about the silent way we fuck. He fills me completely, sliding in and out of my pulsing core in a slow, sweet pace that drives me wild.

"Gonna come soon," he whispers in my ear.

I open my eyes to find his handsome features stretched taut, his teeth digging into his bottom lip as he struggles to keep quiet.

The gorgeous sight succeeds in splintering the tension building inside me. As the orgasm crashes to the surface, I gasp and cling to his broad shoulders and hold him tight as he shudders on top of me.

Afterward, he rolls over and pulls me against him. His fingers thread through my hair as I curl one leg over his lower body. We snuggle wordlessly for a while, until Tuck finally breaks the silence by telling me what he's been up to lately. We text regularly, so I know most of the stories already, but this guy's voice is so sexy that I would listen to him recite a restaurant menu if it meant hearing that southern drawl purring in my ear.

I smother giggles behind my hand when he tells me how Dean's girlfriend—figure that one out—knocked Dean unconscious with a paperweight last night. I kiss his shoulder when he confesses how much he's looking forward to seeing his mom for the upcoming holidays. And when I admit how stressed I am over finals, he strokes my back and assures me that I'm going to kick ass.

Eventually we throw our clothes on and do put on a movie, but he's the only one watching it. I crack open a textbook and start highlighting passages that I want to source in my paper. Tuck chuckles softly at the raunchy comedy on the small TV mounted to my wall.

Every so often he leans over and kisses my temple, rubs my cheek, tweaks my nipple.

Every so often I lean over and suck on his neck, stroke his beard, pinch his ass.

It's the most perfect night I could've ever imagined. And in the back of my mind, a little voice keeps whispering, *I could get used to this...*

16

TUCKER

After I get off the plane in Dallas, Mom is waiting at the bottom of the escalator with three balloons. You'd think I was coming home from the battlefield instead of a posh Eastern college.

"Look at you!" she cries.

I pick her up and swing her around before setting her back on her feet. She leans in, the familiar smell of hairspray and ammonia wafting up.

"What should I be looking at?" I tease.

She gives me a sappy mom smile before wrapping one thin arm around my waist and squeezing. "How handsome you are. You look wonderful."

I shrug as we begin to make our way to the exit. "I feel pretty good."

"Thank goodness. I thought you'd be depressed over how your season is going." Our games aren't televised often, but she follows the results online.

"Is that what the balloons are for?"

"Did you think the balloons are for you? Because they're not."

"Is that why the silver one says 'Welcome Home, Son'?"

"It was discounted. I would've bought the 'I'm the Greatest Mom in the World,' but it cost five dollars more."

"Man, the patriarchy is even ruining balloon sales?"

Thrusting the attached streamers toward me, she laughs. "It's a terrible world, which is why we need balloons."

"This feels suspiciously like the pink apron incident," I say in mock protest, but I take the balloons anyway and bend down to press a kiss on the top of her head. Like the pink apron my roommates gave me, carrying a few balloons through the airport isn't going to dent my ego.

"If I were you, I'd give them all something pink in return."

I contemplate the pink dildo that Dean likes to take baths with. "That's not a bad idea. I've got to pick up a few gifts before I head back. I'll make sure everything I buy is either pink or full of glitter. Both, if possible." Garret and Logan would die laughing at the thought of giving Dean a pink, glittering dildo. I make a mental note to text the guys later.

"You didn't check a bag?" she asks as we bypass the baggage carousels.

"No, ma'am." I don't need to look at her face to know she's disappointed. "You know I've got to get back for practice. Even if the season is sucking wind, I'm still required to lace 'em up. That's the price of my scholarship."

My busy schedule during the holidays has always been a source of dismay for my mother, who goes all out celebrating stuff. She lives for Christmas, which is why I made the trek home even though a lot of the guys stayed back at Briar.

"I thought maybe because this is your last year and you guys weren't doing well, that you'd be allowed to spend the entire break with me."

"Doesn't work that way. Besides, soon I'll be underfoot all the time and you'll be begging me to leave," I warn her.

But even as I say it, my mind zips back to Sabrina. She's going to be in Boston for the next three years. I wonder how we're going to make that work.

I wonder if she even wants to make it work.

It'd be a lot easier if we'd met last year. Or hell, even last semester, but we've only got a few more months where we'll be in the same zip code, and for reasons I'm not fully prepared to examine, especially with Mom at my side, the coming distance between us bothers the shit out of me.

I fight the urge to climb back on the plane and return to Boston. But I'll have to settle for texting, phone calls, and maybe if I'm lucky, a little video chatting. I'd like to see how she uses her toy when I'm not around.

I nearly run into Mom's SUV, lost in my thoughts about Sabrina and her vibrator. I clear my throat. "Mind if I drive?"

She tosses me the keys. "I'd never complain about you being around too much. You know I'd love it if you came back and lived with me."

"Yeah, that's not happening. No woman alive wants to go out with a guy who lives with his mom," I say, holding the door open for her.

She climbs in with a frown. "What's wrong with living with your mother?"

"Everything, and you know it." Then I lean forward and press another kiss on her forehead to take away the sting.

During the four-hour ride home from Dallas, she catches me up on the local gossip of Patterson. "Maria Solis's daughter is home from UT. She gets her hair cut in Austin now, but she still has the nicest manners. She stopped in the other day just to say hi."

I nod absently, wondering if I had invited Sabrina to come home with me for the holidays if she would have said yes. I figured the invitation would be unwelcome, not just because she'd view it as a sign we were moving too fast, but because she needs the money from work. Before I left, she was nearly beside herself with happiness about the time and a half she was going to be making.

"You should ask her out." Mom's voice penetrates my daydreams again.

"Who?" I ask.

"Maria Solis's daughter," she replies impatiently.

I glance away from the road to give her an incredulous stare. "You want me to date Daniela Solis?"

"Why not? She's gorgeous and smart." Mom sits back in her seat and crosses her arms.

"She's also gay."

Her mouth falls open. "Dani Solis is gay?"

"I guess the appropriate term is *lesbian*," I say, remembering my gender studies course.

"No," my mother protests. "She's far too beautiful."

"Mom, beautiful girls can be lesbians."

"Are you sure? Maybe she's bi. I know they say kids experiment in college."

"She took Cassie Carter to prom! You did both their hair."

"I thought they were friends."

"They had to go as friends because the prom folks wouldn't let them attend as a couple."

The small West Texas town I grew up in is a tad on the conservative side. Dani and Cassie *were* friends, only ones that kissed and felt each other up in the hallway. And drove every teenage boy in eyeballing distance right out of their ever loving minds. I'd spent many a teenage night fantasizing about the things those two girls did in private. It was probably inappropriate, but the majority of my thoughts from about age ten to seventeen fell into the inappropriate category.

Mom slumps in her seat. She'd obviously worked out an elaborate plan in her mind about Dani and me getting together.

"Remember when I told you that I met a girl?" I say slowly,

deciding that I better get this out there now before she starts trying to pair me off with every single girl in Patterson.

"Oh?" Her voice is guarded. "I thought it wasn't a thing?"

"It is now. Look, you'd like her. She's got perfect grades, works two jobs, and just got accepted into Harvard Law."

"Harvard? Isn't that in Boston?"

The worry is heavy in her voice. I get it. She's concerned that if I fall for a girl in Boston, I won't move back home, which is why she sprang the Dani Solis thing on me before we even finished the drive home.

"Yeah. Cambridge." I can't even give her assurances, because at this point, I don't know what I'm doing about Boston, Patterson, or any of it. The only thing I'm sure of is that I want to be with Sabrina.

"How long is law school?"

"Three years." AKA too long to be separated.

"Your plan is still to come home and buy a business, right? I was talking with Stewart Randolph the other day. You remember him? He owns the real estate business over on Pleasant. He's thinking of retiring, and that kid of his doesn't want to move from Austin. It sounds like Randy would be interested in entertaining offers."

I grip the steering wheel a little tighter. Sabrina asked if anything got to me. Well, making my mom unhappy is on the top of that list. But the idea of buying Stewart Randolph's real estate business might be a close second. In fact, the actual idea of sitting in Randolph's office, wearing a tie every day, makes my skin itch. I've got some ideas about what I'm going to do when I graduate and being a realtor isn't one of them, particularly in Patterson, population 10,000.

"I'll talk to him," I hear myself saying.

"Good." At least someone's satisfied. "Oh, by the way, the Solises are coming to dinner tonight."

"Jesus Christ, Mom."

"Don't curse, John."

I drag in a deep breath and pray for patience, wondering when I'll be able to text Sabrina.

"MY MOM HAS OFFICIALLY DUBBED you a 'good catch.'" Dani takes a seat next to me on the back steps of the small two-story house where I've lived all my life.

I tap my glass of sangria against hers. "That's solid. I'm going to put that on my Tinder profile."

"She also says that you have a secret cache of money that you'll shower on me when I provide you the requisite firstborn." Dani's grin stretches from ear to ear. She's clearly loving this.

"My mother told me you were gorgeous and smart." I stifle a sigh, thinking of the other gorgeous and smart girl who I haven't gotten to text since I sent her the *I landed* hours ago.

Her response of *Yay! Glad to hear it* isn't providing me with my necessary Sabrina daily intake. I guess absence does make the heart grow fonder, because I miss the shit out of her.

"And you said?"

I jerk my attention back to my friend. "That I thought you were a lesbian and Mom replied that maybe you were bi."

This sets Dani off. She folds in half, laughing so hard that the sangria spills all over the rim.

I lift the glass out of her hand so I don't get showered with the drink, and set it on my other side. It takes a while for Dani to get her shit together, so I finish my drink and then down the rest of hers.

"Tuck, I'm sorry," she gasps, wiping a wine-drenched hand across her face. "The idea of Mama Tucker hoping that I'm bisexual so we can pair up is just too funny."

"Good thing I'm confident about my appeal," I say dryly. "Or all this cackling might've made my balls shrivel."

Dani sobers up immediately. "Oh hell, did I offend you? Do you...have feelings for me?"

"Nope, and I'm not saying you aren't a babe, because you are, but I've known you swing a certain way since we were in junior high."

"Yeah, I've always known." She bites her lip. "Was your mom upset?"

"She didn't think less of you, if that's what you're asking. She's just disappointed."

Dani gives me a pensive nod. "Patterson is so small-minded, you know? I'm okay for a visit, but I could never live here." She punctuates her declaration with a shiver of distaste. "I'm surprised you're coming back."

"Why's that?"

"Tuck, you play hockey." She says the last word like it has extra meaning, but I'm dumb, so I have to ask for an explanation.

"There's a hockey team in Dallas," I remind her. "It's not that unusual."

"It is too. This is a football state, but no, you, a Texas boy, love the ice and cold. I'm surprised you aren't staying up in Boston."

I kick out my legs and peer up at the darkening sky. Patterson's one of those relic towns—once it was self-sustaining, but nearly all of the small businesses were squeezed out by regional stores that offered cheaper prices and more choices. Most folks who live here either farm or work at the tractor plant two towns over. Living in Boston is something I've thought about, but every time I've brought it up to my mother in the last four years, she's rejected the idea.

"Mom loves it here. This is my daddy's house that he bought when they were married." I pat the steps. "She doesn't want to leave it."

"So there's no one you met at Briar? You spent four years there and are just coming home to settle in and be Patterson's number-one realtor?" She holds up her index finger and deepens her voice.

Gotta admit, that doesn't sound good. "You know about those plans too?"

"Yeah, that was part of the sales pitch. Along with your huge bank account, you'd be able to keep me in luxury for the rest of our lives by selling houses in this place. The good news for your mom is that every single girl in Patterson would give their left tit to be John Tucker's woman."

There's only one girl I want to slap that label on, and I'm not entirely certain she wants it.

"I've got a girl back in Briar," I confess. Talking about Sabrina makes her feel a little closer. Man, I've gotten sappy. I guess I don't care that I am, because I pull out my phone. "Wanna see?"

Dani nods eagerly.

I thumb to a picture I took of Sabrina at a pub where we grabbed dinner the last time I drove up to see her. Her dark hair is loose and cascading down her shoulders, and her eyes are gleaming impishly because she'd just smacked my ass as we were leaving.

"Jesus, she's hot!" Dani grabs my phone to pinch and zoom, first on Sabrina's face and then the rest of her body. "Are you sure she's not bi? Because it's a crime that she has to suffer through life with a man."

"Hey, I'm good with my tongue."

Dani gives me a somewhat contemptuous look. "No man is ever as good at oral as a lesbian. It's a scientific truth."

"Yeah? Then spill your secrets, Solis. If not for me, then for poor Sabrina."

Dani's lips curve into a sexy smile. "You know what? I will."

And then she proceeds to give me a very graphic lesson in what makes good oral.

17

SABRINA

Ran into old HS friend. She's an L. Told me no man can ever deliver what a woman can. Got her drunk on sangria and forced her 2 reveal her secrets. Prepare urself. I'm going to wreck u.

Tucker's text pops up during my break at the club. As I slip off my six-inch heels, I type in a reply:

Promises. Promises.

When there's no immediate response, I put my phone away and try not to be disappointed. I guess he's busy with his mom and his old friends.

The rock that settled into my stomach when he left today grows a little larger. I miss him. And if I'm honest with myself, I think I'm falling for him. John Tucker has slid deftly into my life, filling spaces that I didn't realize existed.

And he's not the distraction I thought he would be. When I need quiet, he gives it to me. When I need fun, he's there with a ready smile. And when my whole body aches, he has no problem fucking me until I'm a boneless mess. He likes being with me. And I like being with him.

I squeeze the back of my neck. Am I in too deep already? Should I get out now? Can I continue this without one of us getting hurt?

Tucker had guessed that I had my whole life planned out—and I did. The vision I had of four years of college followed by law school followed by a well-paying summer internship which precedes the perfect job at a Big Six law firm ending with retirement in some sunny place on the beach...it's a plan that didn't ever include a man. I don't know why. It just didn't.

Men are for...sex. And it's easy to get and easy to let go. Or at least, it *was* easy to let go. Now, not so much, because the idea of not having Tucker makes that rock in my stomach feel like a boulder. Actually, the rock is making me feel queasy. I take a few deep breaths and try to remember the last time I ate something.

"You okay, honey?" Kitty Thompson asks in concern. Kitty is one of the owners of Boots & Chutes. She and three other former strippers run the club, and it's one of the best places I've ever worked.

I rub my temple before answering. "Just worn out."

"Only a couple more hours." She clucks sympathetically. "And it's slow tonight. I'll probably let you go early."

We both take in the handful of occupied tables.

With a decisive nod, she says, "Yes, you might as well take off. You wouldn't earn much more than twenty dollars. Go home and get some rest."

I don't need her to tell me twice. Having a couple more hours of sleep before I need to be at the post office to sort mail sounds like a dream. So I hurry home and then fall into bed without checking my phone again. It'll still be there in the morning.

At three-forty my alarm goes off. When I push up into a sitting position, I nearly pass out from dizziness. The contents of last night's hastily gulped supper at the club threaten to make a reappearance.

I close my eyes and take several deep breaths. Once I feel like I can stand without throwing up all over my feet, I bend over to grab my phone.

Which is a huge mistake.

My stomach revolts. Vomit is in my mouth before I can make it to the bathroom, and I'm already throwing up before I can snap the toilet lid up. I drop to my knees as everything I'd eaten for what seems like the last week comes out and dumps into the porcelain bowl.

Oh God. I feel awful.

I heave until there's nothing but pale watery bile. Still on my knees, I reach for a towel and wipe my face off. I'm sweating, I realize. Shaking, sweating, and sick as a dog. Weakly, I flush the toilet twice before dragging myself upright.

At the sink, I swish my mouth out with water and then stare at my pale reflection. I have to go to work. During every holiday season, there's a shortage of workers and the full-time employees receive time and a half. I can't afford to stay home.

I totter back to my bedroom only to stop at my door. Uh-oh. The water I swallowed isn't sitting well. Sweat breaks out across my forehead, forcing me back to the toilet.

As I flush the mess away, I come to the realization.

I'm going to have to call in sick. There's no way I can go in.

The clock beside my bed says it's five past four. I'm already late. I pick up the phone and dial. My supervisor, Kam, answers right away.

"Kam, it's Sabrina. I've been throwing up—"

"Do you have a doctor's note?" he demands.

"No, but—"

"Sorry, Sabrina, you need to come in. It's all hands on deck. You asked for these shifts."

"I know, but—"

"No buts. Sorry."

"I've been puking all—"

"Look, I have to go, but as a favor I'll go punch your time card so you aren't docked or written up for being late. But you need to get in here. We've got so many frickin' boxes to sort, I can't even see the other side of the room. Doesn't anyone shop at the mall anymore?"

It's a rhetorical question, apparently, because he hangs up immediately after.

I stare at my phone and then push to my feet. I'm going to work, I guess.

"You look terrible," one of the temporary workers comments when I stumble in twenty minutes later. "Don't stand by me. I don't want to get sick."

I squint at her through narrowed eyes and am tempted to barf all over her starchy uniform. "Me neither," I say shortly.

Kam arrives with a frown and his iPad. "Get over into bay four and start sorting. We're so freaking behind it's not even funny."

I resist the urge to salute. I agree with him, though—there's nothing funny about this situation. I feel terrible.

The whole morning drags on. I feel like I'm covered in tar, each movement of my body requiring so much effort. I must've gotten a flu bug. I'm worn down, just like Hope had warned, due to the two jobs, the full load, the worry about Harvard. I pushed myself too much this semester and now I'm paying for it.

When the shift is over, I barely have the energy to pour myself into the car and drive out of the parking lot. I make it home, but the minute I hit the kitchen, another wave of nausea strikes. I slap a hand over my mouth and rush to the bathroom.

"What's wrong with the two of you?" grumbles Ray, who's standing at the open door. He's wearing one of his stained white tank tops untucked over a pair of gray sweatpants. In one hand is a beer.

You. You're what's wrong with us.

Then the meaning of his words sinks in. "What do you mean the two of us? Is Nana sick?"

"So she says. She didn't finish making my breakfast. She got sick and had to go pass out in the bedroom." He jerks his head toward Nana's room.

I drag myself to my feet and stumble into her room. "Nana, you sick?" I ask.

The room's dark and she's lying on the bed with an eye mask on her face. "Yeah. I think I came down with the flu."

"Shit. I've got it too."

"I heard you puking this morning."

"Sorry."

She pats the bed. "Come over here and lay next to me, baby. You done with work?"

I nod, even though she can't see me. "Yeah, I'm off until tomorrow morning. No club tonight."

"That's good. You work too hard."

I crawl onto the space that she's made for me. Back when I was little, I used to sleep with Nana. I'd get scared and she'd find me huddled under my blankets, crying into my pillow. Mom was off with Ray or one of the many men she had before Ray. Nana would carry me into her room and tell me that the monsters weren't going to get me as long as we held on to each other.

I find my grandmother's hand and twine my fingers through hers. "It's only for a few more months."

"Don't kill yourself before then."

"I won't."

She squeezes my fingers. "I'm sorry about what I said."

"What's that?"

"That you're uppity. That your momma thought about getting rid of you. I'm glad she didn't. I love you, baby girl."

Tears prick my eyes. "I love you too."

"I'm sorry I'm not a better parent to you."

"You've done a good job," I protest. "I'm going to Harvard, remember?"

"Yeah. Harvard." The word is filled with disbelief and wonder.

"What about me?" Ray whines from the doorway. "You never finished cooking breakfast and it's now fucking lunch time."

Next to me, I can feel Nana's slight body shake and I don't know whether it's from anger or sickness. I force myself to sit up. "You stay here, Nana. I'll get it."

She turns her head away from the door, away from Ray, but also away from me. I guess, secretly, I wanted her to tell Ray to go fuck himself.

He grunts as I pass him on my way to the kitchen.

"What do you want?" I open the fridge and find it surprisingly empty. I wonder if Nana's been feeling sick for a while and I haven't noticed.

"Grilled cheese and tomato soup," he says. He drags a chair away from the kitchen table and drops his skinny ass into it.

"Go watch TV," I tell him as I pull out a block of cheddar cheese, butter and milk.

"Nah, I like seeing your ass in the kitchen. It's just as good as any show." He folds his arms behind his head and leans back. I can feel his beady eyes following my every sluggish move.

The bread looks surprisingly inviting and I tear off a small piece, chewing it slowly to see if I can keep it down. When my stomach doesn't send it straight back in revolt, I eat another small piece. After a few moments, the dizziness and queasiness subside.

The cast-iron pan is already on the stove, and I have the sandwich ready to brown in no time.

"Don't forget the soup, missy."

I rub the side of my neck with my middle finger before crossing the room to grab a can of soup out of the cupboard.

"Why are you such an asshole?" I ask conversationally as I root around in the drawer for the can opener. "Is it because you're a worthless sack of shit and can't bear to look at yourself in the mirror? Or is it because the only woman you can con into your bed these days is a member of the AARP?"

"I've got plenty of pussy, don't you worry about me. Someday you're going to fall off your high horse and come crawling to me." He makes a gross smacking sound with his mouth. "And maybe I'll agree to fuck you, or maybe I'll just let you suck me off when I feel like it."

I'd rather kill myself.

No, I correct, I'd kill him first.

As I operate the can opener, I fantasize about the sharp lid coming off and winging across the room and slicing Ray's dick off. Then the acid of the tomato hits my nose, and an overwhelming urge to vomit washes over me.

I drop everything and race to the bathroom, where I throw up for the third time today.

18

TUCKER

New Year's Eve

At quarter past two, Sabrina appears at the entrance of the club. Her brown hair is pulled up in a high ponytail and she's thrown a long coat over her skimpy waitressing uniform. An older lady exits behind her. The two exchange words, pausing under the dimly lit entrance.

My heart starts thumping erratically. I didn't get to kiss her tonight at midnight to ring in the New Year, but I plan on kissing her all night long to make up for that. I missed her like crazy down in Texas, and even though my mom worked me like a dog, Sabrina wasn't far from my mind.

I fixed the railing on the porch, helped Mom repot some of the perennials she was keeping in the garage, changed five light bulbs, the batteries on all the smoke detectors, cleaned out her furnace, and ran errands from the moment I got up until the moment I lay down. I'd also met with Mr. #1 Realtor and made all the right noises, but as hard as I tried to envision Sabrina in Patterson, the image never came into focus.

"Hey, handsome," she greets me. "I didn't know you were coming here. I thought I was meeting up with you tomorrow."

"Couldn't wait," I say truthfully. "Happy New Year, darlin'."

"Happy New Year, Tuck."

I gather her up against me and bury my face in her exposed neck. She quivers in response to the light caress, and the half-hard cock in my pants rises to full mast.

Reluctantly, I set her aside and pull open the car door. "We better get going or all my good intentions are going into the shitter."

"I thought your good intentions were to fuck me into tomorrow," she teases, referencing one of the texts I managed to shoot off to her in between the chores my mom thought up.

I nearly tackle Sabrina to the ground, but despite her light words, I can see exhaustion in every line of her gorgeous face.

Instead, I nod toward the others trudging toward their cars. "Why give these folks a free show?"

"Good point." She twirls the key ring around her finger. "Slight problem. My stepfather is home and I don't know if we want a repeat of that last scene."

I can't imagine why. The fucking perverted bastard needs a fist in his face and a boot up his ass, but I don't want to bring him into the equation. I've got a whole series of events planned out and they don't include spending a second on that dickhole.

"I don't give a rat's ass about your stepdad," I admit, "but I figured since it's the holidays and I didn't get you a present, that we'd do something different. Why don't you get in?"

She swings her keys around again and then tosses them over to me. "You drive. I'm tired."

I catch them easily and unlock the doors. Reaching in, I push the seat back so I'm not driving with my knees around my neck.

Sabrina climbs into the passenger seat. "Where are we going?"

"Downtown."

"Oooh, sounds like a mystery. I like mysteries."

And I'd like to eat you up. I stare at her mouth for way too long before giving myself a mental head slap and putting the car in drive.

"How was everything? You feeling better?"

"I'm okay. It comes and goes. Nana is better, though, so I figure I just need to sweat it out a few more days and I'll have worked the bug out of my system."

I stretch my arm across the car and slip my hand behind her head. It's been a long time since I've touched her, and I need this small connection.

"You want me to take you to a doctor?" I offer.

"Do I look that terrible?"

"No, you're gorgeous, but you said you've been sick," *and you feel fragile—like brittle glass—under my hand,* "And I want to take care of you."

"No, I don't want to go to a doctor."

"Is it the cash? Because if you don't want me to cover it, we could go to Hastings to the campus clinic."

She shakes her head, a slow roll back and forth on my palm. I slide my grip lower to massage her neck, and she moans. The sound goes straight to my neglected cock.

"I've got insurance. I just need to rest," she insists. "And it's Sunday tomorrow, which means I get to spend the whole day bumming around and doing nothing."

I decide not to push the issue. "What a coincidence. That's my plan."

This time when our eyes meet, her gaze is as hot as mine. I punch the gas a little harder than I intend to.

"A hotel?" she squawks when I pull up in front of the Fairmont ten minutes later.

I grin. "Merry belated Christmas."

The valet reaches her side and opens the door. I hop out and round the front bumper, thanking him as I throw him the keys. This is all costing me a pretty penny, but I don't care. Nor do I care that the doorman is smirking at Sabrina's outfit and our car. He probably thinks I'm going to get ripped off by bringing a hooker back to my room.

"Your present is at my house," she says mournfully as I join her on the sidewalk.

Draping an arm around her back, I gently push her forward. "You can give it to me tomorrow during our bumming-around time."

"Deal."

I lead her directly to the elevators and then stare at the digital display so I don't attack her in the lobby of this swanky hotel.

"I'm pretty sure everyone here thinks I'm a prostitute," she says dryly.

"If they do, it's because that's the only way someone as hot as you is allowing me to put my grubby mitts all over your body."

"Bullshit, but that's a nice compliment."

"I'd kiss you right now, but since I haven't seen you in ten days, I'd probably lose control and try to hump you in the lobby."

"I can wait." She stares pointedly at the bulge in my jeans. "Although, from the outline of your monster, my guess is that no one would be surprised."

The dinging of the elevator doors covers my growl, but judging by the smirk that spreads across Sabrina's face, I can tell she hears it.

We get off on the fourth floor. I barely make it inside the room before I have her pressed up against the door, my tongue inside her mouth, my hands pushing open her coat to grope her tits.

She moans, but it's not a cry of passion.

Instantly, I drop my hands. "Did I hurt you?"

"No." She quickly draws me back against her. "My boobs are extra sensitive for some reason."

I run my hands down her sides. "Then I'll be extra tender tonight." I allow her to tug me in for another kiss before backing off. Reaching down, I adjust myself. "Give me a minute, darlin'. I didn't plan to attack you the minute I saw you, but, hell, you know you drive me crazy."

"Same." She swipes a palm across her forehead, and her hand looks mighty shaky to me.

I wonder if part of it's from hunger. "Why don't you sit down?" I gesture toward the little couch against the wall.

Sabrina nods and walks farther into the room. Meanwhile, I press the heel of my hand against my cock and order myself to act like I've had sex before.

"How much did this cost?" She collapses on the loveseat and looks around in dismay.

"It's nothing," I assure her. "The guy who owns this joint is a Briar alum. He gives us a special rate. Don't tell the NCAA."

"Is that even a violation?"

"Don't know. I'm operating under the don't ask, don't tell policy."

"Gotcha." She slips off her shoes and folds her coat over the arm of the couch, leaving her wearing only her tiny shorts and the bra.

God, she's the hottest thing on the planet.

"What's that?" she asks, her gaze landing on the gift-wrapped box sitting on the center of the bed.

"Your present." I had checked in earlier and left her gift in the room. Reaching out, I swipe the package off the bedspread and join her on the sofa. "Happy holidays."

Her face lights up as she takes the box from me. I lean back and watch. I can't wait to see her face when she opens it.

"What is this?" she asks warily. "It feels expensive."

I snicker. "You can tell whether it's expensive or not based on how much it weighs?"

"Of course. The heavier it is, the more it costs." She bites her lip. "I hope you didn't spend a fortune on me."

"I promise you I didn't." I'm lying. It's definitely more money than I've ever spent on a girl before, but I couldn't resist.

One of Mom's clients makes custom leather goods and sells them online, and she let me buy Sabrina's gift at cost because there was a flaw in the leather. The defect is on the inside, but apparently for the prices she charges, even that requires a discount. I was thrilled to buy it. My mom? Not so much. She felt it was too expensive to buy for a girl I barely know, but this had Sabrina stamped all over it.

Beside me, she rips open the paper and then lifts off the lid. When the rich smell of leather wafts up, her mouth forms a perfect circle of surprise.

"What did you get?" she asks, but it's not a question I'm required to answer. Her hands rip away the tissue paper to reveal the burnished leather and brass buckles of a briefcase.

"Oh my God, this is so gorgeous!"

I don't have to ask if she loves it. It's in every gasp and loving caress of the leather. Oh yeah, nailed it.

"Did I do okay?" I smile as I watch her lift every flap and unzip every zipper. She examines it, flipping it over and over. She even stands up to pose with it.

"You did *amazing*." She finally sets the bag to the side and launches herself at me. "Amazing," she repeats, punctuating that word with a kiss. "Now it's my turn to give you a present."

Licking her lips, she proceeds to move down my body and unzip my jeans.

My dick jumps out like it's on a spring. She circles me with her hand and then gives me the dirtiest, most devilish grin before swallowing me to the back of her throat.

Holy shit, that's good. I cup her head as she blows me, admiring the way her ass juts in the air as she bends forward to take more of me in her mouth. I reach over and slide my hand underneath the satin of her shorts until my fingers meet her soaked pussy.

And suddenly her mouth on my cock isn't enough. I've got to be inside her.

I lift her up and in three strides have her down on the bed. She claws at my clothes. I tear at hers. We're hasty, somewhat uncoordinated, and full of need.

I grab the condom from my jeans and am inside her in the next breath. She's coming three strokes later.

"It's been a while," she gasps.

Sweat beads on my forehead as I slow down, trying to prolong the pleasure for as long as humanly possible.

But as usual, Sabrina has other ideas.

"Come on, Tuck. Fuck me hard."

She digs her nails into my ass and I'm gone.

I hammer into her hard enough to drive her from one side of the bed to the other. She comes again and I finally let go.

I love this girl. Love her to death. The words are on the tip of my tongue and I barely manage to swallow them back. She's not certain of me yet. I need to bide my time, but as long as I'm in the game, I'm not worried about the outcome.

"Gonna take care of the condom," I murmur, and she nods sleepily.

When I get out of the bathroom, she's tucked under the covers, fast asleep.

Smiling, I crawl in next to her, propping myself up on an elbow to stare at her beautiful face. Her thick lashes lay on her cheeks, and there's a satisfied smile on her lips. To the outside world, Sabrina James puts on a good show of being tough and impervious to it all, but in reality, she's vulnerable and sweet and precious.

I slide an arm under her neck, and even in slumber she turns into me, her legs twining with mine. We sleep wrapped up in each other. Two halves of a bigger, better whole.

THE SOUND of retching wakes me up. Someone is puking her guts out in the bathroom. I glance at the clock—it's not even six.

I stumble out of the bed, naked and not quite fully awake yet.

In the bathroom, I find Sabrina on her knees, bent over and heaving into the toilet.

I'm instantly alert. I grab a towel off the rack and wrap it around her shoulders. "What do you need?" I ask in a gentle voice.

She shakes her head wordlessly and then slumps against my legs.

I reach down to smooth her hair away from her head, worry spiking in my blood. What the fuck should I do?

Without moving her, I reach behind me and fill a glass with water, then drop down on my haunches and offer her the glass.

"Thanks." She accepts the glass with a trembling hand.

I stroke her back as she takes a timid sip. "Take your time."

In my head, I'm already dialing up doctors and wheeling her into the emergency room, but I've got to frame it right or I know she'll object. Before I can even broach the subject with her, she lurches forward and throws up the water she just drank.

I wait until she settles down again before lifting her into my arms and carrying her back to bed. "I'm taking you to a doctor," I announce.

"No." She grabs my wrist, but her grip is limp. "I'll be fine in a few hours. I just overdid it this week." Tears stain her face. "God, that was gross. I'm sorry."

"Fuck, baby, who cares?" I hold her against my chest as I clear the sheets away for her.

Once I have her tucked in, I leave to get a washcloth and another glass of water. On my way back to the bed, I snag the trashcan and place it on the floor next to her.

I hate how miserable she looks, and my nurturing side kicks in as I lay the washcloth across her forehead. "You've been throwing up like this every day for how long?"

"I don't know. A while. I caught a bug. Nana had it first and she's finally gotten over it. I just need to wait it out. I'll feel better in a few hours."

"You got a fever? Should I get you some aspirin?" I press the back of my hand against her face. It doesn't feel flushed.

"No fever," she mumbles. "Just queasy and tired."

An alarm bell rings in my head.

Biting the inside of my cheek, I run through her symptoms. The sickness in the morning, tapering off in the afternoons, the really tender breasts, her feelings of fatigue. No signs of fever. The fact that she's never once had her period, or at least mentioned it, in the two-odd months we've been screwing.

"Are you pregnant?" I blurt out.

Her eyelids snap open. "What?"

"Pregnant." I tick off her symptoms on each of my fingers, ending with the lack of period.

"No. I'm not. I just had my period..." She pauses and thinks. Her face goes white. "Close to three months ago," she whispers. "But...I've always had light periods, even on the pill. And I've been spotting the last couple of months. I thought..."

I get to my feet and hunt down my clothes.

"Where are you going?" she whimpers.

"To buy a pregnancy test." Or five. I swipe a package of crackers from the minibar and toss them toward her. "Try to eat, okay? I'll be right back."

She's still protesting as I leave the room.

There's a twenty-four-hour pharmacy eight blocks away. I sprint toward it like I'm trying to qualify for the Olympics, unconcerned that I totally forgot my coat at the hotel.

Inside the pharmacy, I find three different tests. I buy them all.

The clerk gives me a sympathetic look and opens his mouth to say something stupid. The death glare on my face has him clamping his lips together.

When I get back, Sabrina is sitting on the edge of the bed eating the crackers. I feel like the tests are superfluous at this point. She could be a commercial for pregnant chicks.

I'm surprisingly calm as I open each box. "Here you go. Three different ones."

"We've been safe," she says, her tone faraway as if she's talking to herself rather than me. "I'm on the pill."

"Except that first time."

She grimaces. "It was just the tip."

An involuntary laugh comes out. "Then peeing on the sticks only gives us peace of mind, right?"

She finishes her cracker in silence. I don't know whether to sit beside her or on the loveseat. I opt for the couch to give her space. Sometimes Sabrina can be hard to read. Right now, I have zero idea what's going through her head.

Slowly, she gets up and approaches the small cardboard boxes stacked on the desk as if they contain venomous snakes. But eventually she gets there, gathers the boxes in her arms, and disappears into the bathroom.

I don't stand at the door with a cup against the wall, even though I'm tempted as fuck to do it. Instead, I turn on the television and watch a couple ladies try to sell me a velour tracksuit in various types of animal print—only $69.99.

I watch this mind-numbing display for ten eternal minutes before the bathroom door opens. Sabrina's face is about the same shade of white as the hotel robe she's wearing.

"Positive?" I ask unnecessarily.

She holds up an empty box. "You need to go buy ten more of these."

I pat the sofa cushion next to me. "I'm not buying any more. Come and sit down."

Like a belligerent child, she stomps over. Then she drops down next to me and covers her face with her hands. "I can't have a baby, Tucker. I can't."

A sick feeling curdles in my stomach. It's a weird mix of relief and disappointment. The words *I love you*—the ones I wanted to say earlier when I was buried inside her—are stuck in my throat. I can't say them now.

"You do whatever you need to," I whisper into her hair. "I've got you."

It's all I feel like I can say at this point, and I know it's not enough.

19

TUCKER

I always thought that if I knocked someone up, I'd be able to talk to my friends about it. But I've known for nearly a week that my girlfriend is pregnant, and I haven't said a single word to anyone.

Actually, no one even knows I *have* a girlfriend.

For that matter, neither do I.

Ever since Sabrina peed on three sticks and got three positive results, she's been avoiding seeing me in person. We've texted every day, but she insists she's too busy to meet up because she wants to get a leg up on the new semester. I've been trying to give her the space she clearly needs, but my patience is running thin.

We need to sit down and discuss this. I mean, we're talking about a possible baby. A *baby*. Jesus. I'm freaking out here. I'm the guy who's unshakable, the guy who can take any lickin' and kick on tickin', but the only thing ticking right now is my heart—at double time.

I don't know how the hell to handle this. Sabrina said she

couldn't have a kid, and I plan to support whatever she decides, but I want her to include me, damn it. It rips me apart to think of her going through this alone.

She *needs* me.

"You making something to eat or just staring at the stove for funsies?"

Garrett's voice draws me out of my misery. My roommate strolls into the kitchen with Logan on his tail. Both guys make a beeline for the fridge.

"Seriously," Logan gripes as he peers into the refrigerator. "Feed us, Tuck. There's nothing edible here."

Yeah, I haven't shopped for groceries all week. And when you live in a house full of hockey players, skipping out on the shopping is bad news.

I stare at the empty pot I'd placed on the burner. I didn't have a menu in mind when I wandered into the kitchen, and with the sad assortment of ingredients we have on hand, there's not much I can work with.

"I guess I'll make some pasta," I say glumly. Carbs at this hour isn't the smartest idea, but beggars can't be choosers.

"Thanks, Mom."

I cringe at that word. *Mom.* He might as well have said *Dad.* As in, I might be a fucking dad.

I draw a calming breath and fill the pot with water.

Logan beams at me. "Don't forget to put on your apron."

I give him the finger on my way to the pantry. "One of you lazy asses make yourself useful and chop some onions," I mutter.

"On it," Garrett says.

Logan flops down at the kitchen table and watches us like a jerk as we prepare a late dinner. "Make enough for five," he tells us. "Dean's working one-on-one with Hunter tonight. The kid might come back here with him."

Garrett glances at me in amusement. "Naah, I think we'll only make enough for four—right, Tuck? If Hunter's here, he can take Logan's spot."

"Awesome idea."

Our roommate rolls his eyes. "I'll tell Coach you're trying to starve me."

"You do that," Garrett says graciously.

I set the pot on the burner. While I wait for the water to boil, I scrounge around in the crisper for anything green. I find one pepper and two carrots. Whatever. Might as well chop 'em and throw 'em in the sauce.

We chat about nothing in particular as we prepare dinner. Or rather, they chat. I'm too busy internally freaking out about Sabrina. I guess that's a testament to my acting skills, because my roommates don't seem to notice that anything is out of the ordinary.

I'm about to dump two packages of penne in the boiling water when Garrett's phone rings.

"It's Coach," he says, sounding slightly confused.

I set the pasta on the counter instead of in the pot and watch as Garrett takes the call. I don't know why, but there's a nervous feeling crawling up my spine. Coach Jensen doesn't usually phone us off-hours for no reason. Garrett's team captain, but it's not like he's getting nightly calls from the man.

"Hey, Coach. What's up?" Garrett listens for a moment. His dark eyebrows knit, and then he speaks again. Warily. "I don't understand. Why did Pat ask you to call me?"

He listens again. For much longer, this time.

Whatever Coach Jensen is telling him, it's turning Garrett's complexion to paste. By the time he hangs up, he's as white as the walls.

"What's wrong?" Logan demands. He doesn't miss Garrett's change in demeanor either.

Garrett shakes his head, looking stunned. "Beau Maxwell died."

What?

Logan freezes.

I drop the spatula I'm holding. It clatters to the floor, and in the silence of the kitchen, it sounds like an explosion from a war film. We all flinch at the noise.

I don't pick up the spatula. I just stare at Garrett, stupidly asking, "What?"

"Beau Maxwell died." He continues to shake his head, over and over again, as if he can't make sense of the words coming out of his own mouth.

"What do you mean, *he died?*" Logan growls in outrage. "Is this some kind of sick joke?"

Our team captain braces both hands on the counter. He's actually shaking. I don't think I've ever seen Garrett lose his cool like this.

"Coach just got off the phone with Pat Deluca. Beau's coach. Pat said Beau died."

Without a word, I turn off the stove and stumble over to the kitchen table. I sink into the first chair I collide into and rub my fists over my forehead. This isn't happening.

"How?" Logan snaps. "When?"

He sounds angry, but I can tell it's all shock. Logan and Beau are close. Not as close as Dean and Beau, but—oh Jesus. Dean. Someone needs to tell Dean.

"Last night." Garrett's voice is barely above a whisper. "Car accident. He was in Wisconsin for his grandmother's birthday. Coach said the roads were icy. Beau's dad was driving the car and he swerved to avoid hitting a deer. The car flipped over and flew off the road and..." His words are choked now. "Beau broke his neck and died."

Oh sweet Jesus.

Horror swirls in my gut like poison. Across from me, Logan is blinking back tears. We're all just sitting there. Silent. Shocked. I've never...had a friend who died before. No relatives, either. My dad passed away when I was too young to really grieve for him. That was a car accident too. God. Why the fuck do we drive cars?

In the back of my mind, there's a nagging thought that I should be doing something. I swipe a hand over my stinging eyes and force myself to focus.

Sabrina.

Fuck, that's what I need to do. I need to call Sabrina and tell her the news. She used to date Beau. She cares about him.

Before I can move from my chair, the front door creaks open. The three of us tense up.

Dean's home.

"Fuck," Logan whispers.

"I'll tell him," Garrett says hoarsely.

Dean's blond head is lowered as he wanders into the kitchen. He's engrossed with his phone, his fingers tapping out a text message, probably to Allie. He doesn't notice us at first, but even when he does, I don't think he's registering our expressions.

"What's up?" he asks in an absentminded tone.

When none of us say a word, Dean frowns and puts the phone away. His gaze lands on Logan, and he stiffens when he sees our friend's tears.

"What's going on?" he demands.

Logan wipes his eyes.

I press my lips together.

"Seriously, if someone doesn't tell me what's going on right this fucking second—"

"Coach called," Garrett interrupts in a low voice. "He just got off the phone with Patrick Deluca, and, uh..."

Dean looks confused.

Garrett keeps talking, though I wish he wouldn't. I wish we didn't have to tell Dean about Beau. I wish we didn't even know about Beau.

I wish...lots of things. But right now, wishes mean shit.

"I guess Deluca called him because he knows we're friends with Beau—"

"This is about Maxwell? What about him?"

Logan and I both stare at our hands.

Garrett has more courage than us, because he doesn't shy away from Dean's anxious gaze. "He...ah...died."

Just like that, Dean falls into a trance. It's painful to watch, and I have no idea how to draw him out of it. Garrett repeats what he told Logan and me, but it's obvious our teammate isn't listening. Dean's green eyes are glazed, his mouth parted slightly as he sucks in uneven breaths.

It's only when Garrett says that Beau died on impact that Dean blinks himself back to reality. "Can you tell it to me again?" he croaks. "What happened, I mean."

"Goddamn it, why?"

"Because I need to hear it again." Dean is adamant.

We watch as he marches to the cupboards and grabs a bottle of whiskey from the top one. He takes a deep swig right out of the bottle before staggering over to sit beside me.

Garrett starts talking again. Christ. I don't know if I can hear this awful story again. Dean passes me the whiskey and I take a small sip before passing it to Logan. I can't get wasted right now. I plan on driving tonight.

Once Garrett is finished, Dean pushes his chair back and stands up. He clutches the Jack Daniel's bottle in both hands like it's a security blanket. "Going upstairs," he mumbles.

"Dean—" I start, but our teammate is already gone.

We hear footsteps climbing the stairs. A thump. A door clicking shut.

Silence falls over the kitchen.

"I have to leave," I mutter to Garrett and Logan, unsteadily rising to my feet.

Neither of them ask me where I'm going.

SABRINA

I STARE AT TUCKER, unable to comprehend what he's saying. When he texted to say he was coming to Boston to see me tonight, I expected a serious discussion about our unplanned pregnancy. I panicked, told him I was studying, and he all but said *tough shit*. I think his exact message was: *I'm coming. We're talking.*

The entire hour I was waiting for him, I gave myself pep talk after pep talk. I ordered myself to put on my big-girl pants and deal with this pregnancy the way I deal with everything else in my life— head on. I reminded myself that Tuck had said *I've got you*, that he'd support whatever I chose to do.

But none of that had succeeded in ridding me of the fear clinging to my throat.

Now the fear is even worse, for a whole other reason.

"Beau is dead?" My heart pounds dangerously fast. I'm scared it's going to give out on me.

I'm scared of the grief I see in Tucker's eyes.

"Yes. He's gone, darlin'."

I can't understand it. I *can't*. Beau is Briar's starting quarterback. Beau is my friend. Beau's dimples always pop out when he's flashing you a particularly naughty grin. Beau is...

Dead.

A car accident, apparently. His father survived but Beau died.

The tears I've been fighting spill over and stream down my cheeks in salty rivulets. I try to breathe between sobs, but it's hard, and eventually I'm hyperventilating. That's when Tucker wraps me up in a warm, tight embrace.

"Breathe," he whispers into my hair.

I try, I really do, but the oxygen isn't getting in.

"Breathe." Firmer this time, and his hands are moving up and down my back in comforting sweeps.

I manage to take a breath, and then another, and another, until I'm not feeling quite so dizzy. The tears are still falling, though. And my chest feels like someone sliced it open and is poking it with a hot blade.

"He's..." I gulp. "...*was*. He was such a good guy, Tuck."

"I know."

"He was good and *young* and he shouldn't be dead," I say fiercely.

"I know."

"It's not fair."

"I know."

Tucker holds me tighter. I burrow against him until there's nowhere left to go. His strong, solid body is the anchor I need right now. It allows me to cry and curse and rail at the world, because I know Tuck is here, listening to me and steadying me and reminding me to breathe.

A loud knock causes both of us to jump.

"Keep it down in there," comes Ray's horrible voice. "'The hell am I s'posed to watch the game if I can hear you bawling all the way from the living room? You on the rag or somethin'?"

A strangled sob flies out of my mouth. Oh God. Nothing like an interruption from Ray to highlight what an emotional mess I am—an emotional mess who *isn't* having her period. Because she's goddamn pregnant.

My breathing grows shallow again.

Tucker keeps stroking my back as he answers my stepfather. "If you can't hear the TV, turn up the volume," he calls tightly.

There's a beat, then, "Is that you, jock boy? Didn't realize Rina had company."

"We walked right past him when you let me in," Tucker mutters to me.

Yeah, we had. But Ray's drunker than usual tonight. He spent the whole day at a sports bar with his buddies, getting loaded while they watched the afternoon football games.

"He could barely walk in a straight line when he got home this evening," I mutter back.

Ray pipes up again, slurring like crazy. "Mus' not be too good in the sack if you're making the bitch cry!"

I grab Tucker's arm before he can stand up. "Ignore him," I whisper. Then I raise my voice and address Ray. "Go watch your game. We'll keep it down."

After another beat, his footsteps thump away.

Tears stain my face as I nestle against Tucker again. "W-will you..." I clear my aching throat. "Will you stay with me tonight?"

"Not even a question," he murmurs before dropping a soft kiss on my forehead. "I'm here for as long as you need me, baby."

20

TUCKER

The stadium is a sea of black and silver. Thousands of people are in attendance, and a good number of them wear Briar football jerseys beneath their unzipped coats. Those who aren't wear the school colors.

On the field, a large stage has been raised, where Beau's teammates and family sit. Alumni flew in from all over the country to honor our fallen quarterback. Kids who didn't even know Beau are here. Faces are somber and the mood is subdued.

It's fucking awful.

I'm sitting in the bleachers behind the home bench, with Garrett on my left. Hannah's beside him, then Logan and Grace, then Allie—who's alone.

Dean has been a total mess this week. He's in a destructive spiral, skipping practices and locking himself in his room, drunk out of his mind most of the time. The other night he got so high that he passed out on the living room couch, half his body on the cushions, the other sprawled on the floor. Logan carried him upstairs while Allie trailed after them, near tears.

I keep wanting to reassure Allie that Dean will get through this, but honestly, my mind has been all over the place this week.

The reason for my anguish is sitting on my other side. I don't think Garrett and the others even realize Sabrina's here—their gazes are fixed on the field, where a huge projection screen is showing highlights from Beau's four years at Briar University. Actually, make that five years. Beau redshirted his freshman year, so this is technically his fifth year. *Was* his fifth year. Lord, it's hard to remember that he's actually gone.

It's cold out, so the sleeve of my bulky coat kind of disguises that I'm clutching Sabrina's hand. I want to put my arm around her, kiss her cheek, hold her close, but I don't think Beau's memorial is the time to be announcing our relationship to the world. It's surreal to me, though, that the girl next to me is pregnant with my child and nobody has a clue.

We haven't spoken about the baby at all. I don't know if Sabrina is planning on scheduling a procedure. Hell, for all I know she's already gone through with it. I'd like to think that she'd include me if and when the time comes, but she's been so distant this week. Beau's death hit her hard. And witnessing what it's done to Dean makes me even more hesitant to push Sabrina to talk, not when she's dealing with the loss of a friend.

A quiet sob sounds from a few seats over. It's Hannah. The choked noise alerts me to the fact that the slideshow of Beau's life has ended. His older sister Joanna is rising from her seat.

I tense up, because I know things are about to get even more heartbreaking.

Joanna's a beautiful woman, with a chin-length dark bob and blue eyes like Beau's. Those eyes are so lifeless right now. Her face is haunted. So are the faces of her parents.

In her simple black dress, she sinks onto the bench of a black grand piano on the other side of the stage. I was wondering about the piano, and now I have my answer. Joanna Maxwell was a music major when she went to Briar, landing a job on Broadway right after graduation. Hannah says she's an incredible singer.

I wince as microphone feedback screeches through the stadium.

"Sorry," Joanna murmurs, then adjusts the mic and leans closer. "I don't think many of you know this, but my brother was actually a pretty good singer. He wouldn't dare to sing in public, though. He had his bad boy reputation to maintain, after all."

Laughter ripples through the bleachers. It's eerie combined with the wave of grief hanging over us.

"Anyway, Beau was a big music buff. When we were little, we would sneak into our dad's den and mess around with his record player." She sheepishly glances at her father. "Sorry you're just finding that out now, Daddy. But I swear we didn't break into the liquor cabinet." She pauses. "At least not until we were older."

Mr. Maxwell shakes his head ruefully. Another wave of laughter washes through the stands.

"We loved listening to the Beatles." She adjusts the mic again and poises her fingers over the ivory keys. "This was Beau's favorite song, so—" Her voice cracks. "—I thought I would sing it for him today."

My heart aches as the first strains of "Let It Be" fill the stadium. Sabrina clutches my hand tighter. Her fingers are like ice. I squeeze them, hoping to warm her up, but I know mine are equally cold.

By the time Joanna finishes singing, there isn't a dry eye in the bleachers. I'm rapidly blinking back tears, but eventually I give up and let them stream down my cheeks without wiping them away.

Afterward, Joanna gracefully rises from the piano bench and rejoins her parents. Then come the speeches, and the tears only fall harder. Coach Deluca gets behind the podium and talks about what a talented player Beau was, his dedication, his strength of character. A few of his teammates speak, making us laugh again with stories about Beau's shenanigans in the locker room. Beau's mom thanks everybody for coming, for supporting her son, for loving him.

I feel ravaged when the memorial finally reaches its conclusion.

Sorrow thickens the air as people shuffle out of their seats and make their way down the aisles. Sabrina releases my hand and walks ahead of me. Hope and Carin sandwich her between them like two mother hens, each one wrapping an arm around her shoulders as the trio descends the steps.

On the landing, I come up behind her and lean in to murmur in her ear. "Want me to come to Boston tonight?"

She gives a slight shake of her head, and disappointment and frustration flood my stomach. She must see it in my eyes, because she bites her lip and whispers, "We'll talk soon, okay?"

"Okay," I whisper back.

With my heart in my throat, I watch her walk away.

"What was that about?" Garrett appears beside me, focusing on Sabrina's retreating back.

"Just offering my condolences," I lie. "That's Sabrina James—she used to date Beau."

"Oh." He frowns. "Dean's Sabrina?"

My Sabrina.

I choke down another rush of frustration and offer a careless shrug. "I guess."

I'm sick of this. So fucking sick of it. I want to tell my friends about Sabrina. I want to tell them about the baby and get their advice, but she made me promise not to say a word until we'd made a decision. Then again, if that decision results in no baby, there'd be no point in telling them anyway. What would I even say? *I knocked someone up, but she had an abortion, so there's nothing to talk about?*

I swallow through my suddenly dry mouth. I have no idea how I got to this place. My friends tease me about being a Boy Scout, and truthfully I thought I had the "be prepared" thing down pat. But one careless mistake and now I might be a father. I'm twenty-two, for fuck's sake.

I don't know if I can do this.

Panic bubbles in my throat. I'm a patient guy. Rock solid. Good head on my shoulders. I want to have a family someday. I want kids and a wife and a dog and a goddamn picket fence. I want all that —*someday*.

Not today. Not nine months from now. Not—

You might not have a choice.

Christ.

"C'mon," Garrett says, gently nudging me forward. "We're all going back to the house."

Swallowing my panic, I let my friends herd me out of the stadium and into the parking lot. I rode to campus with Garrett and Hannah, so I climb into the backseat of Garrett's Jeep. Allie slides in beside me. The four of us don't say a single word during the drive home.

The moment we walk through the front door, Allie hurries upstairs to Dean's room. I still can't believe he skipped out on Beau's memorial, but I get the feeling Dean hasn't experienced much loss in his life. I don't think he knows how to handle it, and I find myself praying that Allie can get through to him.

The rest of us ditch our coats and boots and traipse into the living room. Hannah and Grace make some coffee, and we sit in silence for a while. It's like we all have PTSD or something. We've lost a friend and can't make sense of it.

Eventually, Garrett loosens his tie and then tugs it off, dropping it on the arm of the couch. With a weary sigh, he says, "Graduation is in a few months."

Everyone nods, though I'm not sure if it's in agreement or just a form of acknowledgment.

He glances around the living room, his expression going sad. "I'm going to miss this house."

Yeah, me too. And I still have no idea where I'll be in May. The plan was to move back to Texas, but there's no way I can do that when there's so much uncertainty between me and Sabrina. Granted, by May I'll already have an answer about the baby. I looked it up online, so I know that if Sabrina chooses to have an abortion, her window will end in early March.

I swallow a strangled groan. God. I hate not knowing where I stand. Where *we* stand.

"I'm excited to go apartment hunting," Hannah says, but despite her words, there isn't a trace of excitement in her voice.

"We'll find something great," Garrett assures her.

She glances at Grace. "You guys are still looking for something halfway between Hastings and Providence?"

Grace nods and snuggles closer to Logan, who's tenderly running his fingers through her long hair.

Envy ripples through me. They have no idea how lucky they are that they can actually make plans for their futures. Garrett's agent is in negotiations with the Bruins, which means Garrett and Wellsy will be living in Boston once he signs with the team. Grace still has two more years at Briar, but Logan's already signed with the Bruins' farm team, so he'll be playing in Providence until he's hopefully called up to the pros.

And me? Who the fuck knows.

"Are you heading back to Texas right after graduation or sticking around for the summer?"

Logan's question brings a knot of discomfort to my chest. "I'm not sure yet. It all depends on what kind of business opportunities there are."

No, it all depends on whether my girlfriend is going to have my baby.

But the other thing is true too, I guess.

"I still think you should open a restaurant," Hannah teases. "You could come up with fun Tucker-related names for all your dishes."

I shrug. "Naah. I don't want to be a chef. And I don't want the stress of owning such a high-pressure business. Restaurants are constantly closing down—it's too big of a risk."

I plan on being careful with my dad's insurance money. I've been saving it for years and I'm not sure I want to gamble it all on a restaurant. But it's not like I have any other ideas, either.

I'd better come up with something, though—and fast. Graduation is looming. Real life is beckoning. My girl is pregnant. A million decisions need to be made, but at the moment, I'm in limbo.

I can't make a single decision. Not until Sabrina makes the most important one of all.

21

SABRINA

February

There's a bitter chill in the air as I walk down the snow-lined path in Boston Common. My gloved hands are buried in the pockets of my coat, and my red knit hat is pulled so low on my forehead it nearly covers my eyes.

It's so cold out today. I suddenly regret suggesting that Tucker and I meet in the park. He wanted to meet at my house, but both Nana and Ray are home, and I couldn't risk them eavesdropping on us and finding out about the pregnancy. I haven't told them yet. I haven't told anyone.

I assume Tucker is going to bring up the baby from the word *go*, but when I reach Brewer Fountain five minutes later, the first thing he says to me is, "I hate fountains."

"Um. All right. Any particular reason why?"

"They don't have much of a purpose." Then he tugs me into his arms for a long hug, and I find myself sagging against him, clinging to his warm, solid body.

I haven't seen him since Beau's memorial. That was two weeks ago. *Two weeks.* I swear, John Tucker has the kind of patience I can only dream of having. He hasn't bugged me to meet up. Hasn't pushed me to talk about our situation. Hasn't done anything but stand by and follow my lead.

"But they're pretty," I murmur in response to his remark.

His lips brush mine in a brief kiss. "Not as pretty as you." And then he hugs me tighter and I try hard not to burst into tears.

I'm a hormonal mess lately. Constantly on the verge of sobbing, and I don't know if it's the pregnancy or because I miss Tuck.

I miss him so fucking much it breaks my heart, but I don't know what to say when I'm with him.

I don't fucking know what to do.

The hug finally breaks up, and we both step back awkwardly. A dozen questions flicker in his expression, but he doesn't voice a single one. Instead, he says, "Let's walk. If we stay on the move, maybe we won't freeze to death."

Laughing again, I allow him to sling his arm around me, and we take off down the path, our boots crunching over the thin layer of snow beneath them.

"How are classes going?" he asks gruffly.

"Okay, I guess." I'm lying. It's not okay at all. I'm finding it impossible to concentrate on anything other than the subtle changes in my body. "You?"

He shrugs. "Not great. It's been tough to focus ever since..." He trails off.

"Ever since this?" I gesture to my stomach.

"Yeah. And Beau too. Dean's not doing too great, and there's lots of tension in the house."

"I'm sorry."

"It'll get better," is all he says.

God, I wish I had his faith. And his resilience. And his courage.

I'm lacking all those things right now. Just the thought of opening my mouth and bringing up the pink or blue baby elephant in our vicinity makes me want to throw up. Or maybe that's the morning sickness.

But as usual, Tucker doesn't push the subject. He simply changes it. "Did you come here a lot when you were growing up?" He gestures at the beautiful display of nature all around us.

"When I was little," I admit. "Back when it was just me and my mom and Nana, we'd come here every weekend. I learned how to skate on Frog Pond."

He gives me a sidelong look. "You don't talk about your mom much."

"There's nothing to talk about." Resentment crawls up my throat. "She wasn't around much. I mean, she used to make an effort when I was really young, up until I was six, maybe. But then the men in her life became more important than me."

Tucker's gloved hand squeezes my shoulder. "I'm sorry, darlin'."

"It is what it is." I glance over at him. "You're close with your mother, right?"

He nods. "She's the best woman I know."

Emotion clogs my throat. Tucker might've lost his dad at a young age, but obviously his mother did everything she could to make up for that. From what he's told me, she worked her butt off so her son could have a good life. My own mother could take a few lessons from Mrs. Tucker. So could Nana.

"Our childhoods were so different," I find myself saying.

"And yet we both grew up to be awesome people."

Him, maybe. Me, I don't feel so awesome right now. But I keep the thought to myself. "Does your mom want you to move back to Texas after college?"

"Yeah." He stops in the middle of the path, releasing a tired-sounding breath.

"Do you want to move back?" I ask, then hold my breath as I wait for his reply.

"I don't know."

He rakes a hand through his auburn hair, and I track the motion of his hand. His hair looks so soft to the touch. It *is* soft to the touch—I know this because I've run my fingers through it on many occasions. I want to do it again now, but I'm scared that if I touch him, I won't be able to stop.

"My plan was always to go back after graduation. I want to be close to my mom, take care of her, you know? But when I was there for the holidays..." He groans softly. "There are no opportunities in Patterson. None. It's a tiny town that hasn't grown at all in a hundred years. And I wouldn't even be able to commute to Dallas because it's a four-hour drive. I originally thought I'd live in Dallas during the week and stay in Patterson on the weekends, but that sounds exhausting the more I think about it."

"So what are you going to do?"

"I have no clue."

I wait for him to turn it around on me, ask *me* what *I'm* going to do about this baby, but he doesn't.

"You want to go watch the skaters for a bit?" he suggests.

"Sure."

We start walking again. His arm is still around me. His familiar scent wafts into my nostrils and makes me ache. I want to kiss him. No, I want to drag him back to wherever he parked his truck and *maul* him. I want to feel his lips on mine and his hands on my breasts and his cock moving inside me.

The happy squeals of children greet us before we even reach the pond. A bittersweet feeling washes over me as we approach the railing. Dozens of people whiz past us on the shiny surface of the rink. Kids bundled up in colorful coats and scarves and mittens. Families skating together. Couples gliding hand-in-hand.

Tucker reaches for my hand and laces our gloved fingers together, and we stand there watching the rink for a while. My heart skips, because it feels like we're a real couple. Just two happy people spending the afternoon in the park, enjoying each other's company.

"Oh shit, see that man over there?" Tucker suddenly says.

I follow his gaze toward a tall, gray-haired man in a blue parka and black skates. "Yeah... Do you know him?"

He squints. "No. For a second I thought I did, but he's just a lookalike."

"For who?" I ask curiously.

"Coach Death."

I almost choke on my tongue. "Okay. Let's back this up. Did you just say *Coach Death?*"

His boom of laughter tickles the side of my face. "Yep. Not even joking, darlin'. My very first hockey coach was named Paul Death. Apparently it's an old British name. Or maybe Welsh? I can't remember now."

I shift around so my back is to the railing. "Was he as evil as his name suggests?"

"Nicest dude you'll ever meet," Tucker declares.

"Seriously?"

"Oh yeah. He's the first person who told me I had potential. I was five at the time. Begged my mom for hockey lessons, so she drove me to this arena an hour away because Patterson doesn't have a rink. Coach Death popped a squat, shook my hand, and said, 'Yup-yup, I see it, kid. You've got potential.'" Tucker chuckles. "That was his catchphrase—*yup-yup.* I started saying it around the house and it drove Mom crazy."

I laugh. "So Coach Death was your idol growing up?"

"Pretty much." He slants his head. "What about you? Who was your idol?"

"I had five." I grin at him. "They were called NSYNC."

His jaw drops. "Oh no, darlin', say it ain't so. You were into boy bands?"

"So into them it's not even funny. Nana took me to an NSYNC concert when I was twelve. I swear I had my first orgasm that night."

He throws his head back and hoots.

"I told you, it's not funny," I grumble. "I was obsessed. I used to doodle *Sabrina Timberlake* in all my school notebooks."

"I honestly can't picture that."

"Why not?"

"Because you're so serious all the time. When I picture you as a kid, I see you reading textbooks for fun and studying for the SATs four years in advance."

A wry smile tugs on my mouth. "Yeah, I did all that too. But I always made time for Justin. I'd take study breaks and kiss his picture. With tongue."

Tucker hoots. "Jesus, Sabrina. I don't know if I can be with you anymore."

Just like that, my good humor fades. Not because of what he said —I know he's joking—but because... Because of the pink or blue elephant, damn it.

Tucker and I had only been dating for a few months before this baby bomb. Would we have even had a future? I love being with him. It's *easy* being with him, easier than it's ever been with anyone. I was *starting* to see a future for us, but what about him? What if he'd gotten sick of me and wanted to dump me?

If we keep this baby, then the future is set. We'll be a part of each other's lives, whether we want to or not. Whether he wants it or not.

"What's wrong?" he asks in concern.

I gulp through the lump in my throat. "I..." My face crumples. "I haven't made a decision yet."

His voice turns hoarse. "I know."

"I'm...scared." I stare down at my boots. "I'm really scared, Tuck."

"I know," he says again. Then he rubs his face. "So am I."

My gaze flies to his. "You are?"

"Are you kidding me? I'm goddamn terrified." A groan slips out. "I'm trying to be strong for you here, Sabrina. I'm really fucking trying."

I blink back tears. "I'm usually the strong one. But right now I don't feel strong at all."

He draws me into his arms and suddenly we're clinging to each other again. I'm pretty sure everyone on the ice is staring at us, wondering why we're power-hugging like a couple of maniacs, but I don't care. I'm on emotional overload, and maybe that's what drives me to say, "I don't think I want to keep it."

Tucker eases back slightly. His expression is somber. "Are you sure?"

"No."

"Then you need to take some more time to think about it," he says softly. "Okay?"

"Okay," I mumble.

After a long beat, he reaches for my hand again. "Come on, let's keep walking. I'll tell you more about Coach Death and you can tell me all about how you French-kissed your Timberlake posters."

I croak out a laugh. God. This guy... just... this guy. I want to thank him. Kiss him. Tell him how amazing he is.

But all I do is twine my fingers through his and let him guide me back to the path.

22

SABRINA

The phone feels like a brick in my hands. I have to schedule the D&C soon or I'll be outside my window. I should've done it a month ago, damn it. It's nearly the end of February and I'm fifteen weeks along. I don't know why I've let it go so long.

Well, I do know why. Because I can't make up my mind. Half the time, I think I'll be better off without a child. The rest of the time, I can't get the image of Beau's casket out of my head.

Wetness dribbles down my cheeks and I swipe the tears away with an angry hand. Great. I'm crying in public. You would've thought I cried all my tears at Beau's memorial. That was hideously brutal.

I knew it was a bad idea to study at Starbucks today, considering how hormonal I've been lately, but I didn't want to be at home in case I finally worked up the nerve to call the clinic. I still haven't told Nana about the pregnancy and I didn't want her accidentally on purpose finding out.

For the first time in my life, I feel like I'm completely without direction. I haven't seen Tucker since our day in the park, and I stopped answering his texts about a week ago. These days, I can't focus on anything other than the impending decision that's hanging over my head.

And it's not just Tucker I've been ducking. I've only been to one weekly lunch with Hope and Carin since Beau's death. I've blamed it on increased work hours, but I don't think they're buying it.

"Sabrina?"

My head jerks up. Joanna Maxwell is standing in front of my table. She's got a cup of coffee in one hand and a stylish white clutch in the other. Draped in a royal-blue wool coat, she looks every inch the Broadway star that she's going to be.

"Joanna." I leap to my feet and give her a hug. "How are you?" Her bones feel about as sturdy as twigs in my embrace. I give her another squeeze before letting her go.

She smiles wanly. "Okay."

"What are you doing in Boston? Is your show traveling?"

"No, it's still playing in Manhattan." A slow flush creeps up her neck. "I...ah...quit."

Shock silences me for a second. "You quit?"

"Yes. I had an opportunity to do something else and I took it." Her words are a mixture of defiance and embarrassment, as if she's tired of having to justify her choices, which she certainly doesn't have to do with me.

"Well, good for you." But I'm confused, because when I hung out with Beau, he said that Broadway was Joanna's dream.

"Right? I'm young, so if there's ever a time for me to try new things, it's right now."

Trying new things terrifies me, but I nod anyway because I'm not the girl who lost her beloved brother.

I'm just the girl who's knocked up.

"Absolutely. What are you doing?"

"I'm cutting a demo," she admits.

I'm not part of the Briar arts crowd, so I have no idea what she's talking about. "Oh. Cool."

The bewilderment must show on my face, because Joanna adds, "It's pretty much a sample that I can send to various A&R people in the industry. They listen to it, and, hopefully, someone signs me and I get a record deal. If that doesn't work, I'll sing covers and post them on YouTube, maybe try to gain visibility that way. It's all kind of up in the air."

"That's great," I tell her, but in my head, I don't understand.

Why in the world would anyone leave a paying singing gig for something that seems risky as hell? If I had a good job right now, maybe I'd keep this baby. I think that if I'd gotten pregnant at the end of law school instead of the beginning, I'd view things differently.

"It's terrifying, actually. I had to get a job waiting tables, which I've never done before. But there's no other way to pay my bills. And by leaving Broadway now, I might never be able to go back."

"I, ah, I—" I stutter. The potential of losing everything I planned for all my life because of this pregnancy has paralyzed me. Joanna sounds like she purposely jumped off a cliff with no safety net. "I hope you follow your dream," I finish lamely.

"That's exactly what I'm doing." She sighs. "And despite what my parents believe, I'm not having an existential crisis because Beau died. In fact, he'd totally be on board with this, don't you think?"

Beau loved his sister, so yeah, if this made her happy, then he would have supported her. "He'd want you to be happy," I agree.

Joanna bites her lower lip. "Did you know that Beau didn't really want to go pro? I mean, the team sucked last year and he had offers to go to other schools, maybe win another championship. That would've put him in a better position to be drafted, but he loved his team and he wasn't interested in playing at the next level. Beau was all about being happy." She starts to choke up, and I pray to God those tears don't spill over, because if she cries, I'm going to start sobbing too.

Pregnancy has turned me into a weepy, emo bitch.

"Then you should do this," I say firmly.

"I know."

She wipes her face with her sleeve while I dig into my purse to see if I can find a tissue. There's a crumpled one in the corner, but it's clean, and Joanna gratefully takes it.

"He really liked you," she says in a soft voice. "You guys could've made a great couple, but maybe it's better that you didn't fall in love with him." Her face collapses as the grief she's been holding at bay swamps her. "Then you wouldn't be a mess like I am."

Without a word, I guide her to the table, drag an empty chair next to mine, and then sit beside her while she cries. A few of the other patrons give us weird looks. I return their nosiness with a death glare.

Fortunately, Joanna composes herself in no time. Soon she's blowing her nose and casting me a chagrined look out from under the veil of her hair. "Fuck. I hadn't cried all day," she mumbles. "It was a new record."

"If I were you, I wouldn't even get out of bed."

"I did that for the first couple of weeks, and then I woke up and thought, Beau would kick my ass if he saw me shitting my life away. So here I am, trying something stupid and new."

"Doesn't sound so stupid to me." And it doesn't anymore. Joanna *is* young. If pursuing a different career in music is her dream, better to chase it now than later.

"You really believe that?"

"Of course I do."

She stuffs the tissue in her coat pocket. "Beau always said you were so driven. I figured this was the sort of thing you'd look down on."

I frown. "You make me sound like a callous asshole."

"No. I didn't mean it that way. It was a compliment." She pauses. "I was the same way. I had everything planned out—I'd get a degree in performing arts, get a fantastic role in a Broadway play, and ride my star to the top of the marquee. Then Beau died and all of it just seems unimportant now, you know what I mean?"

I think I might.

"Anyway, I better get going." She leans forward and hugs me again. This time her grip is surprisingly fierce. "Take care of yourself, Sabrina. I hope you live your life making yourself happy."

Yeah. If only I knew what path that required.

THE NEXT DAY, I find myself in front of my advisor's office. Professor Gibson has her head bent over her desk, grading papers. I knock softly so I don't startle her.

"Sabrina, come in." She waves me forward with a welcoming smile. "How's your last semester going?"

"Easy. I know how to take a test now."

"Or you've trained yourself to think more critically and be able to parse through scads of information to find the simple tenets that underpin all theories?"

"Or that." I laugh as I take a seat.

"Are you excited about Harvard this fall or looking forward to summer break?"

"Harvard, definitely. I'm going to miss this place." I take in Professor Gibson's cozy office with its oversized stuffed chair that she gets recovered every four years, and the towering stack of books that threaten to tumble over at any second but never do. She has pictures everywhere—with her students, with her husband.

And it hits me. The reason I've never thought about having kids is because from the minute I met Professor Gibson, I wanted to be her. She's smart, successful, kind-hearted, and so well respected. Everywhere she goes, people look up to her. And for a kid like me, from the South Boston slums, that sort of admiration was a dream—one that I've pursued relentlessly here at Briar.

I don't know any female with a child who's as successful as Professor Gibson. Which I know, intellectually, is wrong, because there are thousands of mothers who are doctors, lawyers, bankers, and scientists. Even Hope and Carin talk about motherhood, someday. But that someday is in the nebulous future for them, whereas it's right fucking now in my belly.

"Do you wish you had kids?" I blurt out as I stare at the picture of her and her husband standing in front of some ancient castle.

Professor Gibson narrows her eyes, and somehow, she knows. I can see it in her face.

"Oh, Sabrina." There's a question implicit in her sigh.

I nod.

She closes her eyes, and when she opens them, all traces of judgment are gone. But I saw that initial flicker of disappointment, and it stings.

"Sometimes," she says in response to my question. "Sometimes I do, and sometimes I'm glad that I don't. I've been the special auntie to my brother's three kids, and that's filled most of my mothering instincts. I have my students, and that's tremendously fulfilling, but I won't lie and say I haven't wondered what it would be like to have a child of my own."

"Do you think I can do it? Have a kid and make it through Harvard?"

She makes a small, sad sound at the back of her throat. "I don't know. Your first year is time-consuming and overwhelming, but you're very smart, Sabrina. If there was anyone who could do this, it would be you. But it may mean sacrifices. Maybe you don't graduate *summa cum laude*—"

I wince, because being at the top of my law school class is definitely one of my goals.

"Or Law Review—"

I swallow a moan of dismay.

"—But you'll still be a Harvard grad. I have no doubt about that." She pauses. "What does the father say?"

"It's up to me. He supports me either way."

The smile that spreads is genuine. "Ah, you've got a good one then."

I do. Tucker has been very good to me, and that's part of the problem. If I keep this baby, I'm impacting his life in a thousand different ways—and not all of them are good.

"I'm sure you'll make the right decision, whatever it is."

"Thanks." I push to my feet. "I know that this is weird, me coming to you, but my mom..." I trail off.

"I'm glad you came to me," Professor Gibson says firmly.

I thank her again and leave the office. I know I should talk to my girls, but they'll say the same things as Professor Gibson. In fact, the reason I went to her was because I thought for sure she'd tell me to get the abortion.

Five minutes later, I sit in my car, staring unseeingly at the dashboard. I miss my mom right now. She was hardly ever around and we weren't close, but she's still my mother and I wish she were here. I want to know why she kept me when she clearly didn't want me in her life.

When I get home, I pull out a sheet of paper and start listing the pros and cons. Halfway through the cons, I tear the sheet in half and throw it away.

My answer has been there all along. I didn't need to see Joanna, or Professor Gibson, or commune with my absentee mother. The fact is, I haven't scheduled the abortion because I don't want to get one. It might be the best option, but I've spent my whole life feeling unwanted.

I tuck a protective hand over my still-flat stomach. A smarter girl would get the procedure done, but I'm not that smart girl. Not today.

Today, I'm keeping it.

23

SABRINA

I lie in wait outside Tucker's eleven o'clock class. Rather than ask him when we could meet up, I stalked him online and found a post on the Briar YikYak that had all of the players' schedules. That's not creepy.

As students stream out of the ivy-covered building, I recognize maybe one in thirty, if that. My time at Briar is coming to the end, and I don't have much to show for it. Some kids graduate with a raft of friends that they carry into their postgraduate life. Me? I've got my degree, Carin, and Hope. And now a baby. I guess the baby outweighs the entire sisterhood of a sorority.

Tucker strolls out with Garrett Graham. They're both gorgeous, but Tucker is the one who commands my attention. Not that Graham isn't good-looking, but Tucker's all I see. He shaved his beard. I don't know how I feel about that—I liked the beard—but I can't deny that his clean-shaven face is equally appealing. He's got a dimple in his chin that was hidden by all the scruff. God, I want to explore that dimple with my tongue.

The rest of him is equally tempting. He's wearing a tight, long-sleeve knit shirt with one corner tucked into the side of his jeans. A pair of sunglasses is perched on the top of his auburn head, which is thrown back as he laughs at something Graham is murmuring out of the corner of his mouth. Behind them trails a line of hungry girls who desperately want the attention of these guys. But they're both more interested in exchanging quips than scoping out the women.

A flutter of relief washes over me. Since the night at the hotel, we haven't slept together. There was the pregnancy discovery and then Beau's death and then Beau's memorial and then...nothing really. My head hasn't been in a good place since New Year's.

I bite my lip. I didn't want to drag him down with me, but that's exactly what I'm doing.

He cuts off mid-chuckle when his eyes land on me. His lips move, saying something like, "I'll see you later, man. I've got something to take care of."

Garrett's gaze swings toward me, and he probably says, "She's going to suck your soul out. Stay away from her."

Tucker's lips curve up. He's either replying that he can handle me or likes the way I suck or maybe even, "Too late." As he saunters toward me, Garrett's glare moves from Tucker's back to my face.

I smile wide, showing a little teeth.

"You're avoiding me," Tucker murmurs when he reaches me.

I switch my attention to him, tuning out Garrett, the adoring girls, and the rest of our classmates. They're a distraction and I owe it to Tucker to be focused.

"I've had a lot on my mind," I admit.

"Yeah. Me too."

When he quirks up an eyebrow, I tilt my head toward the crowd. "Got a moment?"

"For you, always."

My heart squeezes. I've been AWOL for weeks and he still finds a way to look at me like I'm the only girl in his orbit. I don't fucking deserve him.

He takes my elbow and I follow him toward a row of benches along the quad. "You seeing anyone?" I ask in the most casual voice I can muster.

He stops so abruptly that I nearly take a header on the cobblestones. He hauls me upright, planting both hands on my shoulders to orient me so I'm facing him.

"Are you kidding me with that?"

"You stopped texting me." I hate the uncertainty in my voice.

His expression softens. "I've been giving you space."

I force a shrug. "It'd be okay if you were."

A muscle in his jaw jumps, and the grip around my shoulders grows uncomfortably tight. Okay. I pegged that one wrong.

Finally, he sighs and pulls his sunglasses on. "No, I'm not seeing anyone." Under his breath, I hear him mutter, "Apparently not even you."

"I'm sorry," I blurt out. "It wasn't meant to be an insult. I just wanted you to know that this—" I wave my fingers in a circle around my belly "—shouldn't be holding you back."

His features tense again. "I need some food before we continue this conversation. Come on."

"Where are we going?"

"Somewhere private." He doesn't break stride even as he redirects us from the lecture hall toward the parking lot behind the building.

A number of people wave to him as we pass, but he doesn't stop for any of them, nor does he talk to me. When we reach his pickup, he nudges me into the passenger side and then stares expectantly at me.

"What?" I mutter.

"Seatbelt."

"I'll do it when you get in the truck."

"Now."

"Is this because I asked if you were seeing anyone?"

The jaw muscle moves again. "No. It's because you're pregnant."

An eyebrow creeps above the rim of his sunglasses. "You still are, right?"

I flush. But I guess I deserved that. "Yes. I wouldn't do anything without telling you first."

"Good. Buckle your seatbelt."

I do as he orders because it's obvious we're not moving an inch until he hears the click. Then I hold my hands out and say, "Okay?"

He nods and shuts the door.

We don't say a word as he starts the truck and leaves the lot. He drives us about three miles away, where we pull to a stop in front of a small outdoor rink. The ice is melted, and instead of skaters, the rink is filled with picnic tables. Only a few people, none of them students, occupy the tables.

"Why don't you grab a seat?" Tucker says as he helps me get out of the car. "Want anything to eat? Drink?"

"I'll take a water."

He heads off to the concession stand while I claim a table in the far corner, situating myself so I can watch Tucker stride across the pavement.

If I had to choose the father of my child, I couldn't have done better than John Tucker. He's gorgeous, tall, athletically gifted and smart. But most of all, he's decent. No matter what happens in the future, he'll never turn away from his kid. He'll never make him or her feel unwanted. He'll never threaten his or her life in any way. No matter what happens—even if I screw up, and I know I will—Tucker will be there to clean up my mess.

It's because he's so good and decent that this decision to keep the baby was so fucking difficult. If I'd gotten the abortion, I think he would have grieved, but now that I'm keeping it, his life will be forever changed. And it'll be because of me.

I keep having to remind myself of that. I can't rely on him too heavily or ask too much from him, because he'd give me everything without complaint. But I'm not a taker and I'm not a user. It would be so easy to fall in love with Tucker and allow him to take care of everything.

It would be easy. But not fair.

A minute later, he settles into his seat and pushes a water bottle across the table. He bought himself a hot dog and a coffee, and neither of us speak as he quickly inhales his food. Once he's done, he balls up his napkin and shoves it in the empty hot dog container. He tucks his sunglasses into his neckline, curves his large, capable hands around his coffee cup, and then waits. It's my show.

I lick my lips once, twice, and then just go for it. "I'm keeping the baby."

His eyes flutter shut, hiding whatever emotion that washes over him. Relief? Fear? Unhappiness? When he flicks his lids up, his gaze is clear and expressionless. "How can I help?"

A reluctant smile surfaces. Such a Tucker thing to say. Which reinforces my resolve to make sure that he suffers almost no burden and that he's free to find whomever or whatever he wants in the future. The minute that he wants out, I won't fight it.

"I'm good for now. I actually have insurance through my postal job. I've been working there since I graduated from high school. I used to grumble about my health premium since I never used it, but now it's coming in handy."

"All right. So healthcare is taken care of. What about after you have the baby? You still going to law school?"

"Yes, absolutely." The thought of quitting hadn't even occurred to me. "It's like college. You have three or four hours of classes a day. The rest of the time, I'll be home studying."

His mouth thins out in the first sign of any kind of emotion. "With your stepfather?"

It's hard not to flush with shame. "He's an asshole, but he's never touched me."

"That's not much of an endorsement."

I roll the water bottle between my hands a few times. Tucker waits me out. He's got more patience than a saint.

"I had to quit my job at the club," I say quietly. "I was banking on that money to help with my law school tuition. I can't afford to live anywhere else than where I am now. Plus, I'm hoping that Nana will watch the baby when I'm at school."

"What about me? Do you trust me?"

My head jerks up to meet his slightly frustrated expression. "Of course."

"Then why don't I take care of the baby while you're in class?"

"Because you've got to get a job, right? Nana doesn't work. She lives off her social security money."

Tucker rubs a hand across his forehead, as if the enormity of the task we're about to undertake is finally settling in. "You're right. I need to find a job."

"You haven't found a business yet?"

"There are dozens of them, but if there's anything I learned about business management, it's that if you don't love what you're doing it's bound to be a failure." He takes a sip of his coffee. "I'll sign on to a construction crew for the summer. I've done that in the past and it's good money. During my time off, I'll keep looking at different opportunities until I find the right one."

"So until that time, it makes sense for Nana to help."

He thinks it over, but he can't come up with a better solution. "For now. Until we can find something better." He pauses. "I need to tell my mom. And my teammates."

The churning that starts in my belly has nothing to do with the pregnancy and everything to do with embarrassment. Which triggers a jolt of self-directed annoyance, because getting pregnant isn't some horrible, shameful occurrence. I'm an adult. I'm having a baby. That's not a big deal.

"Will you wait a bit longer? I mean, I'm okay with you telling your mom, but can you keep it quiet with your friends for now?" I hesitate, then confess, "I haven't told anyone."

"No one?" he says, incredulous.

I nod miserably. "You're not the only person I've been avoiding. I've barely seen Carin or Hope."

"So you admit you're avoiding me."

I can't look him in the eye. Instead, I pretend to be fixated with the wood grain of the picnic tables. I want so badly to tell him how much I've missed him. Because I have. I've missed kissing him and joking around with him and hearing him call me "darlin'" in his southern drawl.

I've been a largely solitary person my whole life, avoiding Nana and Ray when I could. At Briar, I made friends with Carin and Hope but didn't feel the need for a bigger, more extensive circle. So the acute loneliness brought on by not seeing Tucker took me by surprise.

But how can I be with him knowing that I'm the one who turned his whole world upside down? The weight of guilt would crush me more than the weight of loneliness.

I take a deep breath, pushing out the words that I don't want to say. "If you want to see other people...you can. I'm not going to. I don't have time for that, but if you want to, I don't mind."

Silence falls between us.

A long finger finds its way under my chin and lifts it up until I either have to shut my eyes or stare into Tucker's. I choose the latter, but it's impossible to read his expression.

He gives me a long, contemplative look before saying, "How about this? I'll tell you if I've found anyone new. And you and I, we can just be friends." He gentles his tone. "If you decide you want more, we can talk about it then."

"Friends?" I echo faintly. "I'll take friends." And then, because he's so decent, I blurt out, "I've never had a boyfriend. I only know how to hook up and how to screw up."

"Darlin'—"

Hearing those two soft syllables only heightens my panic. "I can't believe I'm going to be a parent. God, Tuck, I've only thought about one thing my entire life—crawling out of my hellhole. And now I have to drag someone down with me and I don't know if I can do it."

Tears that I've been holding at bay for weeks spill over. Tucker cups my cheek with one warm hand and stares firmly into my eyes.

"You're not alone," he says, fierce and low. "And you're not dragging anyone down. I'm here with you, Sabrina. Every step of the way."

That's what I'm afraid of.

TUCKER

IN HOCKEY, nearly everyone plays with a partner. The offense forward line is made up of a left wing, a center, and a right wing. The defense skates in pairs. Only the goalie is alone and he's always weird. Always.

Kenny Simms, who graduated last year, was one of the greatest goalies at Briar and probably the reason we won three Frozen Fours in a row, but that guy had the strangest fucking habits. He talked to himself more than he talked to anyone else, sat in the back of the bus, preferred to eat alone. On the rare occasion that he came out with us, he'd argue the entire time. I once got into it with him over whether there was too much technology available to children. We argued about that topic for the entire three hours we were knocking back beers at the bar.

Sabrina reminds me of Simms. She's not weird, but she's closed off like he is. She thinks she's alone. Basically, she's never had anyone skate with her—not even her friends, Carin and Hope. I kind of understand it. The guys outside of my hockey team that I've been friendly with are decent, but I haven't bled with them, cried with them, won with them. I don't know if they'll have my back, because we've never been in a position where that loyalty has been tested.

Sabrina doesn't know what it's like to have someone stand beside her, let alone behind her. And it's for that reason that I don't give in to the urge to shake her like a piñata for saying shit like I'm free to see other women. The fear in her eyes is palpable, and I remind myself that patience is the key here.

"Want me to follow you home?" I offer as I pull into the campus lot where she left her car. "We can hang out a bit, make some plans?"

She shakes her head. Of course not. The girl hasn't been able to look at me since she broke down in tears. She hates crying in front of me. Hell, she probably hates crying in general. To Sabrina, tears are a sign of weakness, and she can't stand being viewed as anything less than Amazonian.

I stifle a sigh and climb out of the truck. I walk her to her car and then drag her stiff body against mine. It's like hugging a frozen log.

"I want to go to the next doctor's visit with you," I tell her.

"Okay."

"Don't get too excited about all of this. You'll wake up the baby," I say dryly.

She flashes a pained smile. "That's weird, right? Saying that we're having a baby?"

"There are weirder things. Simmsy, our old goalie, used to eat circus peanuts before each game. That's pretty strange. A woman having a baby seems to fall into the fairly ordinary category."

Her ears pinken. "I mean, *us*." She wiggles her index finger between us. "Us having a baby is weird."

"Nope. Don't think that's weird either. You're young—and super fertile, apparently—and I can't keep my hands off of you." I lean down and plant a hard kiss on her surprised mouth. "Go home and take a nap or something. Text me when you know when the next appointment is. I'll see you later."

And then I take off before she has the opportunity to argue with me. Weird? It's not weird. It's terrifying and awesome at the same time, but it's not weird.

When I get home, the house is empty, which is a good thing. If my roommates were around, I might end up spilling the beans, and I've got to respect Sabrina's wishes. We're a team now, whether she likes it or not. She's scared out of her mind, filled with guilt, and overwhelmed with what's going to happen next. I figure at this point all I can do is be there for her.

When you have a new teammate, they don't always trust you right away. They'll play puck hog because that's the way they're used to scoring, to achieving success. Raising a kid is a team sport. Sabrina needs to learn to trust me.

But while I won't tell my roommates until she's ready, there is someone who needs to know.

So I head upstairs, sit on the edge of my bed, and text my mom.

Me: *Got a minute?*

Her: *In 20, baby! Finishing a color for Mrs. Nelson.*

I spend the next twenty minutes googling shit about babies. I hadn't allowed myself to do that before. I didn't know if Sabrina was going to keep the baby, and if she'd decided to go through with the abortion, I didn't want to become attached and then be heartbroken.

Now, I'm free to throw myself into fatherhood. Unlike Sabrina, I'm not feeling as terrified about it anymore. I've always envisioned myself having a family. Granted, I didn't think it was going to happen for a while, at least not until I was done with college, had a good business, and was making decent coin. But life is always changing and you just have to adapt.

I do some sloppy math in the margin of my business property notes about whether I can buy a home in Boston and quickly realize that I can't afford to buy a business and a house on the funds my dad left me. Housing is ridiculously expensive in Boston. I guess I'll have to rent for a while.

Okay. So. I'm going to need a place to live, a job, and I need to figure out what I'm going to do with my fucking life beyond college. I've been half-assing the business search because there wasn't any urgency, but with a kid on the way and Sabrina living in the shithole she's currently in, I need to get all my ducks in order.

I'm ordering a couple of books on Amazon about pregnancy and parenting when my mother calls.

"Sweetheart! How is everything going? Only a couple more months and you'll be back home!" she sings into my ear.

My stomach plummets. If there's one person I hate disappointing, it's my mom, and me not coming back to Texas is going to crush her. But if I'm honest, I've been on the fence about Texas for a while now. In some ways, the baby is saving me from that.

I make a mental note to tell Sabrina this, because I know, in her head, she's thinking she's ruined my life.

"Actually, about that. My..." I hesitate, because I don't know what we are after our little talk this morning. "Girlfriend," I finish, for lack of a better term. Our relationship is too complicated to go into depth with Mom right now. Besides, I can't poison that particular well, because Mom's already going to be upset. "Remember I told you at Christmas I met a girl?"

"Yes..." She sounds cautious.

I rip the bandage off. "She's pregnant."

"Is the baby yours?" Mom asks immediately. There's a note of hope in her voice, which I quickly squash.

"Yeah, Mom, that's why I'm calling you."

There's a long, long moment of silence. So long that I almost wonder if she's hung up on me.

Finally, she says, "Is she keeping it?"

"Yes. She's like sixteen weeks along." I've already done the math. The date of conception is probably the first time we had sex, when I was in such a hurry to be inside her tight pussy that I forgot about the condom.

Sabrina James makes me lose my mind, in more ways than one.

"Sixteen weeks!" Mom yelps. "Did you know at Christmas and didn't say anything?"

"No, of course not. I didn't find out until later."

"Oh, John. What are you going to do?"

I let out a slow, steady breath. "Whatever it takes."

24

SABRINA

Three Weeks Later

W hen I arrive at Della's, the booth in the corner is empty. That's a good sign. I tug the side of my coat over my belly. It's getting too warm for my long jacket, but I'm starting to show. Thank goodness for yoga pants. I don't know how much longer I'll get away with wearing regular clothes.

I've been researching everything I can about pregnancy, and one sad fact I found is that no one's experience is the same. For every woman who's gained only the exact baby weight plus a few extra pounds, there are five who swear they swallowed an entire field of watermelons. A lot of them admitted that at some point they had to give up driving because the steering wheel pushed into their stomach, not to mention that seatbelts aren't made for pregnant ladies. I can already testify to that.

Everything is changing for me and I'm scared shitless. I still haven't told Nana or my friends. Tucker still hasn't told *his* friends, because I've ordered him not to. I know it's irrational, but it's like a part of me believes that if we don't say anything, then life doesn't have to change. When I told Tucker that over the phone last night, he responded with a gentle laugh and said, "It's already changed, darlin'."

And then I woke up this morning and couldn't do up my jeans, and reality came crashing down on me like the hammer of Thor. I can't hide this pregnancy anymore. This shit is real.

So today is let's-drop-a-baby-bomb day. I'm hoping that once I stop hiding, I can reclaim control of my life and start steering my ship again. Maybe then I'll be able to sleep an entire night without waking up in a cold sweat.

"Want to wait for your friends, or should I bring you something?" Hannah asks as I slide into the booth.

My gaze involuntarily falls to her slender waist, and a twinge of envy hits me. I wonder if mine will ever be the same. My body is starting to feel alien. The hard bump in my stomach isn't something I can diet away. There's a *human being* in there. And that mound is only going to grow.

"Milk," I say, albeit reluctantly. Soda is on the list of things that are bad for my system, along with everything else that is good and wonderful in this world.

As Hannah trots off, Hope appears. "What's up? Your text sounded so ominous." She shrugs out of her trench and flops down across from me. "Everything is still a go with Harvard, right?"

"Let's wait 'til Carin comes."

She frowns deeply. "You okay? Nana isn't sick, is she?"

"No, she's fine. And Harvard's still a go." I peer at the door, willing Carin to arrive.

Hope continues to grill me. "Did Ray fall off a cliff? No, that would be good news. Oh God, he broke his leg and you have to literally wait on him hand and foot."

"Shut your mouth. We don't even want to tempt fate with suggestions like that."

"Ah, she can still joke. The world isn't coming to an end." Hope signals for Hannah before fixing her gaze on me. "Okay, so if it's not your grandma and Harvard is on track and Ray's still the same asshole as always, what is it? We haven't seen you in weeks."

"I'll tell you when Carin gets here."

She throws up her hands in frustration. "Carin's always late!"

"And you're always impatient." I wonder what my kid will be? Late, impatient, driven, laidback? I hope laidback. I'm always so fucking anxious. I wish Tucker had shot me up with some of his patience rather than his sperm. Sadly, it doesn't work that way.

"True." She shifts in her seat. "How's Tucker? You guys an actual thing?"

"We're something," I mutter.

"What's that supposed to mean? You've been seeing him since the end of October. That's more than four months. In Sabrina Land, you might as well be engaged."

Actually, eighteen weeks and three days, but who's counting besides me and my OB?

Before Hope can push me some more, Carin breezes in with a, "Sorry, I'm late," and one-armed side hugs for each of us.

Hannah pops over, delivering my milk and two more menus before disappearing to tend to the next table.

Hope grabs Carin by the wrist and drags her into the booth. "We forgive you," she tells her. Then she turns to me with a stern look. "Spill."

"Carin doesn't even have her coat off," I protest, although I don't know why I'm delaying the inevitable. It's embarrassing that I don't know how to use contraceptives correctly, but having a baby is normal. At least, that's my current mantra.

"Fuck Carin and her coat. She's here. Start talking."

I take a deep breath, and because there's no easy way to say it, I just spit it out. "I'm pregnant."

Carin freezes with her coat halfway down her arms.

Hope's mouth falls open.

With one of her trapped arms, Carin nudges Hope. "Is it April Fool's Day?" she asks, not taking her eyes off me.

Even as she answers Carin, Hope also keeps her gaze pinned on my face. "I don't think so, but I'm having my doubts."

"It's no joke." I sip my milk. "I'm almost five months along."

"*Five months?*" Hope screams so loud that every head in the diner swivels toward us. Leaning across the table, she repeats the words, this time at a whisper. "Five months?"

I nod, but before I can add anything else, Hannah arrives to take our orders. Hope and Carin's appetites are apparently ruined by my news, but I'm hungry, so I order a turkey sandwich.

"Are you showing at all?" Hope still looks a tad dazed.

"A little bit. I can still wear stretchy pants. No skinny jeans, though."

"Have you been to the doctor?" she asks. Beside her, Carin remains silent.

"Yes. I have insurance through work. Everything looks good."

"Were you planning to tell us after you had the baby?" Carin blurts out, hurt coloring her words.

"I wasn't even sure I was going to keep it," I admit. "And once I decided, I was...embarrassed. I didn't know how to tell you guys."

"You know, it's not too late," Hope says with an encouraging smile.

Carin brightens at the thought. "Right. Like, you can still get the A any time up until the third trimester."

Their lack of support stings, but somehow it makes me all the more resolute. My whole life has been about showing doubters I can succeed.

"No," I say firmly. "This is what I want."

"What about Harvard?" Hope demands.

"I'm still going. Nothing's changed."

My friends exchange a look that says I'm hopeless and which one of them is going to break the news to me. I guess Hope wins, because she says, "You really think nothing is going to change? You're having a *baby*."

"I know. But there are millions of women who have babies every day and still manage to be functioning adults."

"It's going to be so hard for you. Who's going to take care of the baby while you're in class? How are you going to study?" She reaches across the table to squeeze my limp hand. "I just don't want you to feel like you're making a mistake."

My face grows hard. "I'm still going to Harvard. "

I don't know if it's my tone or my expression that convinces them that my mind is made up, but either way they get the message. Despite the lingering skepticism on their faces, they move on.

"Is it a boy or girl?" Carin asks. "Wait—Tucker's the dad, right?"

"Of course Tucker is the dad, and I don't know. We haven't had the ultrasound yet."

"What did he say when you told him?" Hope butts in.

That I'm not alone. "He's okay with it. He didn't burst into tears or shout in anger. He didn't flip over a table or rage about the unfairness of it. He just held me and told me I wasn't alone. I think he's a bit scared, but he's going to be with me every step of the way." I swallow the lump in my throat. "And as much as I want to protect him, I'm going to hold on to his hand for as long as possible. It's so damn selfish of me, but right now the idea of facing the future alone keeps me up at night."

"That's good, at least," Carin says gently.

"He's amazing. I don't deserve him." God, if my best friends are struggling with this, I can't even imagine what's going on in Tucker's head.

Hope frowns. "What makes you say that? It's not like you got pregnant alone."

"He didn't have a choice."

"Bullshit. Every time you have sex, there's a risk. No form of contraception is a hundred percent effective, not even a vasectomy. You want to go for the ride, you have to pay the price."

"That's a steep price."

She waves her hand. "Which you're paying too."

"Can we stop being so depressing?" Carin pipes up. "Let's talk about the important stuff. When are you getting the ultrasound? I want to start buying baby things."

I open my mouth to say I don't know when we're interrupted by Carin's phone. "Shit." She digs it out and slides out of the seat. "It's my advisor. I've got to take this."

As she disappears toward the bathroom, Hope turns her worried gaze toward me. "Damn, B. I really hope you know what you're doing."

"So do I." I know she loves me and that's why she's so concerned, but like Carin, I don't want to dwell on the negatives. My mind is made up and all this second-guessing is only going to make me feel bad.

"I only want you to be happy," she says softly.

"I know." This time it's my turn to reach across the table. "I'm scared, but this is what I want. I promise."

She grips my hand hard. "Okay. I'm here for you then. Whatever you need."

Carin comes back and pushes Hope over. "I'm going to learn how to knit," she announces.

"Knit?" I echo wryly.

"Yeah, baby booties. You're five months along? That gives me about four months to learn how to knit, so be prepared to be amazed and awed by my new skill."

I finally crack a smile. "Consider me prepared."

In more ways than one, but hey, I've got my friends and I've got Tucker, which is more than I thought I'd ever have and more than I probably deserve.

But I'll take it.

25

TUCKER

The kitchen is so silent, I feel like I'm in church. Not that I've been to church often. Mom dragged me to a few Sunday sermons when I was a kid, until finally admitting that she'd way rather sleep in on the weekends. I was totally on board with that plan.

But right now, it's not God and Pastor Dave passing judgment on me—it's my closest friends.

"Why the hell didn't you tell us sooner?" Garrett.

"You're seriously keeping this kid?" Logan.

"Sabrina fucking James?" Dean.

I tighten my grip around my beer bottle and scowl at Dean. I blame *him* for this little powwow. Two seconds after I told him and Allie the news, he'd sent an SOS to Garrett and Logan ordering them to get their asses home. They'd been at the dorms with their girl-friends, and now I feel like a jerk for spoiling their nights.

"Guys, why don't you let him talk instead of shouting questions at him?" Allie speaks up in a cautious tone.

I can tell she doesn't want to be here for this, but Dean dragged her into the kitchen with us, latched his hand onto hers, and hasn't let go since. I don't get why he's so pissed about this. It's not like *he's* the one about to become a father. And I know for a fact he's not still into Sabrina, because he looks at Allie like she hung the damn moon. The two of them hit a rocky patch after Beau's death, but the last couple of months they've been disgustingly in love.

"Tuck?" Allie prompts, tucking her blonde hair behind her ear.

I take a terse swig of my beer. "I don't have much else to say. Sabrina and I are having a kid. End of story."

"How long have you been seeing her?" Logan demands.

"A while." Their frowns tell me they don't like my response, so I add, "Early November."

Logan looks startled. Garrett doesn't, which makes me narrow my eyes at him in question.

"I suspected," he admits.

The other guys swivel their heads toward him in accusation. "What do you mean, you suspected?" Logan echoes.

"It means I suspected." Garrett glances across the table at me. "Saw you holding her hand at Beau's memorial."

When a flash of guilt passes through Dean's eyes, I know he's thinking about how he got piss-drunk in his room instead of attending the memorial service for one of his best friends.

Logan turns back to me. "So it's serious with you two?"

Laughter sputters out. "We're having a baby. Of course it's serious."

Or at least I'm planning for it to be. Sabrina still needs time, though. Time to fully get a handle on this pregnancy stuff. Time to lower her guard and realize she can trust me. Time to lower that guard even more and realize that she loves me. Because I know she does. She's just too scared to admit or acknowledge it, to me and to herself.

"Why didn't she get an abortion?"

Dean's question elicits a gasp from Allie, frowns from the guys, and an angry scowl from me.

"Because we decided to keep it," I say harshly.

Everyone flinches. I'm pretty sure they've never heard me snap at anyone before. Usually I don't, but Dean is treading dangerously close to I'm-going-to-beat-him-senseless territory. I get that he doesn't like Sabrina, but he will damn well show her respect, even when she's not in the room.

"Hey. Let's relax, okay?" Garrett proves why he's our team captain by speaking in a calm, pacifying voice.

Though, I realize, he's not Dean's captain anymore, because Dean got kicked off the team back in January. I think failing that drug test was one of the catalysts for his dragging himself back to the land of the sober. That, and Allie.

"This is Tuck's life," Garrett goes on. "We have no right to judge his decisions. If this is what he wants, then we're going to support him. Right?"

After a beat, Logan nods. "Right."

Dean's jaw tightens. "This is going to ruin your life, man."

It's getting harder and harder to control the anger simmering in my gut. "Well, it's my life to ruin," I say coldly. "You don't get a say in it."

"What about Harvard?" he pushes. "Is she still gonna go?"

"Yes."

He shakes his head. "Does she get how time-consuming law school is?"

"Of course."

Another shake of his head. "So she's dumping all the responsibilities on you?"

I instantly come to Sabrina's defense. "No, we're sharing the responsibilities."

More head-shaking.

Swear to God, if he doesn't stop doing that, I'm going to rip his blond head right off his neck.

"Dean," Allie warns.

"I'm sorry, but I think this is crazy," he announces. "That girl is colder than ice. She's judgmental. She's—"

"The mother of my child," I growl.

Dean growls back. "Fine, whatever. Go ahead and destroy your life. What do I care?"

My mouth falls open as he marches out of the kitchen. Seriously?

There's a long silence, and then Allie gets up too. "I'll go talk to him," she says with a sigh. "Ignore him, Tuck. He's just being a dickhead."

I don't answer. I'm too pissed to talk.

"For what it's worth, you have my support. I think you're going to make a great dad." Her hand rests lightly on my shoulder before she heads to the door.

Once she's gone, I stare at my remaining friends. "You meant what you said? I have your support on this?"

They both nod. Logan's lips are twitching, though, as if he's trying not to laugh.

"What's so funny?" I ask warily.

"Dude. Do you even realize all the gross things coming your way?"

I blink in confusion.

"Go look up childbirth videos on YouTube," he advises. "We had to watch some for the women's studies class I took freshman year. They're goddamn horrifying." Logan shudders. "Did you know that eighty percent of chicks shit on the table?"

Garrett snorts. "You're totally making up that stat."

"Okay, maybe not eighty percent. But it fucking happens, and it's *gross*. Oh, and the placenta? A huge bloody sac that just drops on the floor after the kid pops out? After you see that, I guarantee you'll never want to stick your dick in there again."

"I suddenly feel really sorry for Grace," Garrett remarks.

"I'm going to push for a scheduled C-section," Logan says haughtily, but the twinkle in his eye tells me he's only kidding. You can always count on Logan to lighten the mood.

"Look," I say, "I know this is a huge shock. And trust me, I still haven't wrapped my head around it either. But I lo—care about Sabrina." I correct myself before the L-word leaves my mouth. No way am I saying it to my friends before I say it to her. "Dean is all wrong about her. She's driven, yeah, but she's not cold or judgmental. She's got the biggest heart of anyone I've ever met. She's...pretty fucking amazing."

A lump obstructs my throat. Damn it. I wish Sabrina could see herself through my eyes. She thinks she's dragging me down into the gutter with her, but she's wrong. She's giving me the one thing I've always wanted—a family. Sure, it's happening earlier than I planned, but life doesn't always follow a schedule.

"So you're really doing this, huh?" Garrett sounds a bit awed.

"Yup."

"Do I get to be the godfather?"

"Fuck that!" Logan objects. "He's picking me. Obvs."

"Bullshit. I'm clearly the better choice."

"You're clearly the bigger egomaniac, that's what you are."

I snicker. "Keep this up and I'm picking neither of you. But it's good to know you're both eager for the job. I think I'll come up with some kind of competition, make you two battle it out."

"I'll win," Garrett says immediately.

"Fuck that!"

They're still arguing about it as I duck out of the kitchen. Dean might've been a jackass about my big news, but it's a relief to know that at least I have G and Logan's support.

I'm sure as hell going to need it.

I'M HERE. Where u at?

Fitzy's text pops up as I park in the lot in front of Malone's. I drove here straight from the house, because telling my roommates about the baby isn't the only item on tonight's agenda. I still need to find a place to live, and I'm really hoping Fitz can help me with that.

I quickly type a response.

Me: *Just got here. Walking in now.*

Him: *Corner booth in the back.*

Putting away my phone, I lock the truck and head into the bar. Fitzy is sipping a beer when I slide onto the booth seat across from him. He's ordered one for me too, which I gratefully accept.

"Hey. Thanks for meeting up."

He shrugs. "No prob. I was getting stir crazy anyway. My apartment is too fucking small."

Huh. I didn't expect an opening this early in the conversation, but damned if I'm going to pass it up. "That's actually what I wanted to talk to you about."

Fitzy arches a brow. "My small apartment?"

"Sort of." I trace my finger over the label of my beer. "You said your lease is ending in May, right?"

"Yeah. Why?"

"You given any thought to what you're doing about that? Are you signing another lease? Moving somewhere else?"

A grin tugs on the corners of his mouth. "What's with the Twenty Questions?"

"Just trying to figure out where your head is at." I take another sip. "I'm not going back to Texas after graduation."

He peers at me over the neck of his bottle. "Since when?"

"Since I'm having a kid in August."

Loud choking noises break out from his side of the booth. I probably shouldn't have sprung that on him while he was mid-sip. I feel bad as I watch him cough wildly.

"Y-you—" He coughs again. Clears his throat. "You're having a kid?"

"Yeah. Sabrina's pregnant."

"Oh." One tattooed arm lifts so he can rub his temple. "Shit. Well. Congrats, I guess?"

An unwitting smile touches my lips. "Thanks."

He studies me carefully. "You seem cool about this."

"That's because I am," I say simply. "But yeah, I definitely need to find a place in Boston. And I remember you mentioned you wouldn't be against living in the city, so..." I shrug. "Figured it wouldn't hurt to ask if you're in the market for a roommate."

"Ah." Regret flickers in his expression. "I decided not to do that. I thought I'd be cool with the commute, but I talked it through with Hollis and he reminded me what a bitch it is to drive from Boston to Hastings in the winter, so I'm going to stick around here for my senior year."

I swallow my disappointment. "Oh, okay. That makes sense."

"Stupid question, but...why aren't you moving in with Sabrina?"

Stupid question, no. Good question? Hell yes.

"We're not there yet," I reply, because the alternative is fucking embarrassing. *Because she doesn't want to be with me.*

"Okay. Well. If you're serious about living in Boston, I actually do know someone who needs a roommate."

I brighten up. "Who?"

"You're not going to like it," he warns.

"Who?" I press.

"Hollis' brother. His landlord hiked up his rent and he's not sure he can keep the place on his own."

Aw fuck. Brody Hollis, king of the douches? The man who puts the *bro* in *Brody*? I'd rather—no. There's no *I'd rather*. I'm not exactly swimming in options at the moment. Brody might be...fratty, but his apartment was big and clean and had two bedrooms.

And it's only a five-minute drive from Sabrina's house.

As much as I hate the idea, I can't deny that it's a good, convenient option.

I take another long sip of my beer. Then I say, "Can I have his number?"

26

SABRINA

"I'm nervous." I whisper the words in Tucker's ear so that the other expectant moms in the waiting room won't hear me. They all have this happy excited glow to their faces, and I don't want to ruin it for them. Just because I'm a basket case doesn't mean I should freak anyone else out.

But I'm freaked. This is the first appointment that Tuck has come along for, and it's the one that will reveal the sex of the baby—if we can reach an agreement about it. I want to know. He wants to be surprised. And this is the perfect illustration of the kind of people we are.

I'm the one who likes to be in control. If I know the sex of the baby, I can plan for it. Buy cute little girlie stuff or cute little boy stuff. Come up with names.

Tucker is a go-with-the-flow guy. He thinks we should just buy yellow clothes and be done with it.

"There's nothing to be nervous about." He squeezes my hand and leans in to kiss my cheek.

I give an involuntary shiver. His lips are soft and warm and I want to feel them against my mouth, not my cheek. I want to kiss his neck and suck on it until he moans. I want to slide my hand inside his pants, grip his cock, and stroke him off until he comes all over my hand.

Did I mention I'm horny as fuck?

I don't know if it's all the increased sensitivity or the three or so months of sexual dormancy, but holy hell do I need to get laid. Even the accidental brush of my own hand against my boobs gets me hot and bothered. I read that women are usually super aroused during the first trimester, but my sex drive didn't kick into overdrive until the second one. Every time I see Tucker, I want to rip his clothes off.

And he knows it.

"You ready to be more than friends yet?" he murmurs.

I glare at him. "I'm telling you I'm nervous and you're thinking about sex?"

"No, *you're* thinking about sex." He grins. "Your eyes are begging me to fuck you."

I hastily glance around to make sure nobody heard that, but the other pregnant women are either talking to their partners or have their heads buried in baby magazines.

"Nope," I lie. "My eyes are too busy worrying about what they're going to see on the ultrasound. I read that we might be able to see the baby's face, and the fingers and toes." Panic flutters in my belly again. "What if it only has three fingers, Tuck? What if it doesn't have a nose?" My breathing grows labored. "Oh my God, what if we have a mutant baby?"

Tucker hunches over and starts to shake. It takes me a second to realize he's shuddering with silent, hysterical laughter. Wonderful. The father of my child is laughing at me.

"Oh hell. Goddamn, darlin'." He's wheezing as he lifts his head. "I knew I shouldn't have let you watch *The Hills Have Eyes* last night."

"There was nothing else on," I protest. *And I didn't want you to leave.*

I'm so pathetic. This past week, I've been finding reasons to have Tucker over. Like, "we need to research breathing classes," and, "my back is killing me—do you feel like coming by to rub it?" and, "maybe I should have a water birth." He urged me to reconsider that last one, but I wasn't serious about it to begin with. The idea of my pregnant ass submerged in a tub full of water and childbirth fluids makes me want to throw up.

But because he's Tucker, he's driven to Boston every time I've called. In the back of my mind, I'm scared I'm taking advantage of him, but he keeps assuring me that this is what he signed up for.

"We're not going to have a mutant baby." His chuckles have subsided, and he's holding my hand again. "He or she is going to be perfect. I promise."

I nod weakly.

"Sabrina James?" a voice calls from the doorway.

"That's me." I shoot to my feet so fast that I wobble for a moment. Tucker steadies me by placing one muscular arm around my shoulders.

"That's us," he corrects.

We follow the pink-scrubs-wearing nurse down a wide, well-lit hallway. She guides us into an exam room and instructs me to sit up on the table. The ultrasound machine is already set up beside it, and my heart does an excited little flip.

"I really want to know," I blurt out once the nurse leaves the room.

Tucker pouts. "But think about how exciting it will be when the doctor shouts out 'It's a boy!' or 'It's a girl!'"

This is his go-to argument. But frankly, I don't need any more excitement in my life right now. My home situation is already way too charged, what with Nana lecturing me daily about getting knocked up, chastising me for keeping the baby, and constantly reminding me that she's not dishing out free childcare just because

I'm her granddaughter. And of course, then there's Ray, with his snide comments about my promiscuity, my fat stomach, and my stupidity for not knowing how to use a condom.

Ray, I don't give a shit about. Nana...well, I'm sure she'll come around once she holds her great-granddaughter or grandson in her arms. She's always been a sucker for babies.

"I want to know *now*," I whine, not caring that I sound like a five-year-old throwing a tantrum.

"How about this? We'll Rock, Paper, Scissors for it."

Yeah, we're going to make great parents, all right.

"Fine." I crack my knuckles, which makes him snicker. "Ready?"

"Ready."

We count in unison. On three, we reveal our hands. He did paper. I did rock.

"I win," he says smugly.

"Sorry, baby, but you lose."

"Paper covers rock!"

I smirk. "Rock weighs down the paper so it can't fly away. It traps it."

A loud sigh fills the room. "I'm not going to win on this, am I?"

"Nope." But he looks so cute right now that I offer a compromise. "How about this? You can leave the room while the doctor tells me, and I swear I won't give it away. I'll hide all my baby purchases in my closet so you can't see what I'm buying."

"Deal."

We're interrupted by the arrival of the technician, who greets me warmly and then orders me to pull up my loose-fitting shirt so she can slather cold goo all over my belly.

"Is your bladder full?" she asks.

"My bladder is always full," I answer dryly.

That gets me a laugh. "Don't worry. This won't take long. Soon you'll be able to pee to your heart's content."

"Awesome. Living the dream."

I've already had an ultrasound, so I'm not concerned when the tech shuts up once we get going. Every now and then she points something out, like how the baby's spine resembles a teeny string of pearls, or how—thank the Lord—we've got ten fingers and ten toes.

Tucker stands there in silent wonder, watching the grainy images on the screen. At one point he bends down and kisses my forehead, and ribbons of warmth unfurl inside my body. I'm glad he's here. I really am.

"Okay. All done." After wiping the goo off my belly, the tech presses a button and the machine makes a whirring sound as it spits out a picture of the ultrasound. She doesn't hand it over yet, instead saying, "The doctor will be in shortly to talk to you. If you need to empty your bladder, the bathroom is two doors down, on your left."

Tucker chuckles as I instantly shoot off the table. "I'll be right back," I tell him, ducking out of the room.

I do my business, wash my hands, and when I step back into the exam room, Doctor Laura is already there, chatting with Tuck. When I first met her, I wasn't sure what to think. Calling a doctor by their first name is weird to me. I guess maybe I thought it was a sign of unprofessionalism or something, but the woman seems to know her stuff. She's in her mid-thirties and talks in a no-nonsense way that I appreciate.

"So Daddy here says you've been arguing about whether to find out the sex of the baby," she teases when I walk in.

"Daddy here is being stubborn," I grumble.

Tucker's jaw drops. "Nuh-uh. Mommy is the stubborn one who doesn't like surprises."

I sweep a hand over the protruding belly that has popped out in a big way in the last month. "This wasn't surprise enough for you?" I ask primly.

Doctor Laura snorts before glancing down at the file folder in her hand. "Well, we got a very clear image from the ultrasound. Since Sabrina is my patient and you're not, John, I'm going to tell her the sex if that's what she wants."

"Traitor," he says with a mock glare.

"I want to know," I tell the doctor before cocking my head at Tucker. "You may leave the room now, Daddy."

"Naah. I've changed my mind. I want to know."

I eye him anxiously. "Are you sure?"

He responds with an earnest nod.

"All right, then. Hit us," I tell the doc.

Her eyes twinkle. "Congratulations. You're having a baby girl."

I gasp, all the oxygen sucking into my lungs and then getting trapped there. My pulse speeds up, and it's like my surroundings, my entire world, come into sharper focus. Colors seem brighter and the air feels lighter and this whole experience—this life growing inside of me—suddenly feels *real*.

"We're having a girl," I breathe, turning to Tucker.

His gaze is almost reverent. "We're having a girl," he whispers.

Doctor Laura lets us marvel in silence for a few seconds before clearing her throat. "Anyway, everything looks great. The baby is healthy, the heartbeat is strong and steady. Keep taking your prenatal vitamins, try not to push yourself too hard, and I'll see you again in four weeks."

At the door, she pauses and winks at Tucker over her shoulder. "As for the other matter you were asking about, all systems are a go."

After she's gone, I frown at him. "What other matter?"

He shrugs, the epitome of mystery. "Just a dad question." He reaches for my hand. "Come on, let's get going. I want to show you something before I drop you off at home."

My forehead creases. "Show me what?"

"It's a surprise."

"Didn't we just establish I don't like surprises?"

He chuckles. "Trust me, you'll like this one."

27

SABRINA

"What are we doing here?" I ask fifteen minutes later, examining the street Tucker had just turned onto. This neighborhood is sketchy. I mean, it's only a five-minute drive from my place, so of course it's sketchy.

"Patience," he chides, parking at the curb in front of a ten-story brick building.

I will up some of that patience and wait for him to open my door. This guy refuses to let me open doors. It's like he doesn't understand that I have hands.

When my flats land on the pavement, Tucker takes my hand and leads me to the entrance of the building. I fight back a million questions, because I know he won't answer them, and obediently follow him into a small lobby with an even smaller elevator. We take it all the way to the tenth floor, walk down a short hall, and stop in front of apartment 10C.

Tucker pulls a key ring out of his pocket and unlocks the door.

"Who lives here?" I demand.

"I do."

"What? Since when?"

"Since three days ago," he admits. "Well, technically I don't move in until the end of the week, but three days ago was when we reached an agreement."

"We?"

"Me and Brody Hollis, a teammate's brother."

"Oh." I'm so confused, because this entire week he didn't once mention moving to Boston. "What about your house in Hastings?"

"The lease is up in June. I would've had to move out anyway." He shrugs. "It made more sense to find a place here in Boston. That way I can be close to you and the baby." He holds out a hand. "Do you want the grand tour?"

"Um. Sure." I'm still a bit stunned.

Tucker laces his fingers through mine and leads me through the apartment. While the exterior of the building is kind of crappy, the interior is surprisingly nice. The apartment has great outdoor light, pine floors, and an open layout. Down the hall are three doors that lead to the bathroom and two bedrooms.

"I haven't brought any of my shit over yet," he says.

We walk into a large, empty bedroom with a huge window that lets in so much sunlight I wish I had my sunglasses with me.

"No, really?" I tease, wandering around the bare room. I approach the window and peer out. "Oh nice. Your room's got the fire escape."

"And even nicer—it leads right up to a roof patio. Only the tenth floor apartments have access to it. There's a barbecue up there, and lots of patio furniture."

"Oooh, that's awesome."

We head back to the kitchen, where Tucker opens the fridge to survey the contents. "You want something to drink? There's OJ, milk, and water. And a shit ton of beer, but you don't get to drink that."

"I'll take a water." As he pulls a pitcher out and pours me a glass, I run a hand over the spotless countertops. "It's super clean in here."

"Yup. One of Brody's redeeming qualities is that he likes things clean. You know, because chicks are turned off by clothes on the floor."

"He's not wrong."

"That dude's entire decision tree consists of 'will this get me laid?'"

I grin. "Predictability can be nice."

"Mind if I have a beer?"

"Knock yourself out. Where is he, anyway? At work?"

"Yup. He works nine-to-five at Morgan Stanley. He's in financial planning, which, from all I can figure out, is basically selling annuities to old people."

I sip on my water while Tucker cracks open a beer for himself. On the counter near the microwave are a bunch of colorful brochures stacked on top of inch-thick binders.

"What are these?" I trace my fingers over the top one that says 'Fitness. Your Time. Her Time. Any Time.'

"More prospectuses. Or is it prospectii? I picked this stuff up the other day during a business research expedition." He paws through the stack, flicking one toward me. "This is for a women's waxing and laser treatment business. Hollis said that it's like being a gyno without having to go through med school. Pussy for days."

My lips twitch. "He knows that just because he's waxing a girl's private parts doesn't mean he gets to touch them again, right?"

"No, I'm pretty sure he thinks it gives him a free pass to fuck them."

"Lovely."

I leaf through a couple of glossy pictures of long hairless legs set next to bold type that declares this particular laser is the next best thing. Hmmm. If Tucker buys a laser hair-removal salon, maybe he'd offer me the services for free. Already, my growing belly is starting to make simple tasks difficult. I have to sit down to shave because I'm afraid of tipping over doing my one-legged, flamingo grooming dance in the shower.

Tucker flips over another brochure. "This one is to sell shovels. Door to door."

I grimace. "That sounds terrible. There's money in that?"

"According to the franchise documents, yep, but I have my doubts."

"What else do you have?"

"Sex toys, laundromat, fitness clubs, a bazillion food options. Fast casual is all the rage."

"You sound enthused by a whole big zero of them."

"I know." He scoops the pamphlets into a pile and tosses them into a recycling bin. "Maybe a franchise isn't for me."

I nibble on my bottom lip, hesitating for a moment. "What would you be doing if it weren't for this?" I circle my hand around my belly.

"Stringing myself up by my tie," he says. "Mom wanted me to buy the local realtor's business—"

I bite my lip even harder.

"—but I'd rather be waxing some guy's ass crack than selling houses in Patterson, so you can get that anxious look off your face."

His gaze strays to my belly again. Since the ultrasound, he can't stop staring at it. I'm not much better. I always have my hand over the curve or under it, and now it feels even more special because I know my baby girl is right beneath my palm.

I climb onto the counter stool and gesture for him to come closer. "Wanna touch?"

"Always." He swings around the counter to squat down in front of me, his hands framing the bump on either side. "Hey gorgeous. Daddy's here." He peers up at me, auburn hair tousled, light-brown eyes full of affection. "Has she been kicking at all?"

"Some." I pull his hand to the side where the baby often tries to kick her way out of my uterus. "Try here."

We wait, holding our breath. Tuck's hand presses firmly against me, and the warmth of his palm sinks into my skin, spreading until all my nerve endings begin to tingle.

Inappropriate! He's communing with his child, not trying to fondle you.

Except...it feels so good. Tucker and I haven't slept together in months. And lately, fucking him is about all I can think about.

Sure, it's what got me into this condition in the first place, but at night, when the baby is keeping me awake, I remember how he felt between my legs. His hair-roughened thighs scratching against my skin as he plunged inside. I remember the thickness of his cock and the delicious way he'd stretch me when he entered. I remember his teeth on my breast, scraping downward until he caught a nipple in his mouth. I remember it all and it makes my breath short and my skin so sensitive.

The fingers on my stomach tighten. "Sabrina," he says gruffly. "What're you thinking about, darlin'?"

My unfocused gaze zeros in on his face. As I lick my lips, I remember the heavy weight of his shaft on my tongue. "You."

His breath hitches. "Me as your friend or me as something else?"

"Something else," I whisper.

He slowly drags his hands down my stomach to the tops of my thighs. My legs part involuntarily, and his thumbs graze the waistband of my yoga pants.

"Be specific," he whispers back.

I'm suddenly transported to the first night we spent together, when he lounged like a sultan in his truck telling me—no, ordering me—to come take what I want.

"I'm thinking about your cock in my mouth."

His fingers dig into my thighs. "Really? Because I'm thinking how much I want to shove your pants down and lick your pussy until all that worry is driven out of your head."

Said pussy clenches at his words. "I'm...damn it, I'm fat now."

"No. You're perfect." Then he surges to his feet, lifting me up against him.

"Wait." I squirm in his grasp. "I'm too heavy."

"You're full of bullshit," he retorts and strides to the living room. Without releasing me, he lays me down on the black leather sofa.

I squeak in protest. "This is your new roommate's couch!"

"What my new roommate doesn't know won't hurt him. Now strip. I'm hungry, woman."

All the blood in my body pulses under his heated gaze. We stare at each other for a moment, and then we're both hurrying out of our clothes. His shirt comes off and is tossed across the room. My shirt and pants follow. His jeans and boxer briefs are next. When I remove my bra, he curses.

"Holy *fuck*." There's a note of awe in his voice as he stalks forward to join me on the couch. His hard cock bobs with each step he takes.

"I know. They've grown."

He kneels between my legs, reaching up to cup my heavy boobs. "They're fucking amazing."

I shiver when his thumbs rub across my erect nipples. "And very sensitive," I pant out.

An evil glint lights his eyes. "Think you can come if I suck on them?"

"Don't know." I drag a hand through his hair. "Let's find out."

Without delay, his mouth latches on to one breast while his hand squeezes the other. The hard pull of his mouth makes me arch off the cushions. Oh God. It's like there's a direct line between his tongue and my pussy. When he groans, I feel it everywhere. My hips come off the couch, seeking pressure to alleviate the ache but finding nothing.

"Fuck me," I plead.

He falls backward on his ass and pulls me down on top of him, somehow never once losing contact with my breasts. I straddle him and try to rub my wet core against his cock, but my stupid belly gets in the way and a moan of frustration escapes.

His response is to slip a hand between us. Shoving my panties aside, his fingers find my slick skin and begin to rub. Two fingers glide along my pussy while his thumb strums my clit like a guitar string. And suddenly it's almost too much. I come in a mindless rush of pleasure, moaning his name, and even when I float down from the blissful high, it's still not enough. I reach down and give his cock a desperate stroke.

"This," I gasp. "I want this."

"Yes, ma'am."

With a glittery, hungry gaze, he tears my panties off and nudges me onto my back. Then he grips his shaft and guides it to my entrance. I suck in a breath at the first push of his broad head spreading me.

He stops abruptly in mid-glide. "You okay?"

I can see his arms straining as his lust pushes hard against his self-control. I want to be taken hard, though. I want him to remind me that I'm beautiful, that I'm lust-worthy, that I'm still rocking his world.

I curve my legs around his hips and try to pull him in deeper. "I'm more than okay. I need you to fuck me. Please."

The fierce look that passes over his face is breathtaking. He jacks in deep, hard and hot, filling me up with his cock until that's all I know. I haven't felt him close to me like this in so long. It feels like...a homecoming.

His mouth finds my neck, the tender skin behind my ear. He trails wet kisses along my shoulder and collarbone. He sucks on my nipple again, and stars flash in front of my closed eyelids. One hand slips beneath my ass, holding me slightly off the couch, and his hips move, stroking, stroking, stroking until he hits that one spot that has me crying out again.

He's relentless, plunging inside me again and again. The head of his shaft rubs against that soft bundle of nerves inside me until I'm a gasping, writhing mess.

"I missed you," he chokes out. "So fucking much."

I don't say it back because I've forgotten how to talk. The pleasure is too intense, fogging up my brain. He continues to ravage my breasts, one and then the other. And then he sits up, takes hold of my hips, and thrusts into me harder and faster than before.

The leather beneath my shoulders chafes my skin. My hair is plastered across my face and I'm having a hard time drawing each breath, but none of that matters as I'm lost in the maelstrom of sensation. All I register, all I know, is *him*. How good he feels, how much my body craves him, how hard my heart beats for him.

How I'm deeply in love with him.

"Come for me," he rasps. "Come all over my dick, Sabrina."

The pleasure builds inside of me until finally it detonates, shattering my composure, melting my body. Tucker whips his head back and groans out his own release, while I lay a wrecked mess beneath him.

How he finds the strength to get up and walk to the kitchen, I don't know. I'm too out of it to do anything but murmur a thank you when he comes back with some wet paper towels and gently cleans up the moisture trickling down my thigh.

Before I can protest, he rejoins me on the couch and throws a blanket over our naked bodies. He pushes an arm under my head and cocoons me in his heat, while I pray that this isn't the day Brody Hollis decides to come home early from work.

As Tucker strokes my hair, the words of love that sit like lead in my throat fight to get out, but I swallow them back. It was just sex. We both needed the release, that's all. I can't read anything more into it, and I can't even trust my own feelings these days, not with all the pregnancy hormones running rampant in my blood.

I snuggle into his sweat-dampened body. This is enough for me. Whatever he can give me is enough. I won't ask for more.

"What were you and the doctor whispering about before?" I ask eventually.

He chuckles. "This."

"This?"

"Yeah, *this*." He reaches under the blanket and tweaks one of my nipples. "I asked her if we were allowed to have sex."

My jaw drops. "You asked our OB for permission to fuck me?"

"I wanted to make sure it wouldn't hurt the baby," he protests. "Jeez. Sorry for being a concerned dad."

I can't help but smile.

We both grumble in displeasure when a phone chimes. It's his, and he reluctantly leans over the side of the couch in search of his pants. He fishes out the phone and then he's nestled beside me again, swiping a finger over the screen.

Feeling curious—fine, nosy—I peek at the display.

And release a horrified scream.

Shooting up into a sitting position, I snatch the phone out of Tucker's hand. "Oh my God!" I shriek. "What *is* that?"

28

TUCKER

I know I shouldn't laugh. The mother of my child is upset. The last thing I should do is laugh at her, but the horrified expression on her face is priceless.

"Tucker!" She punches my shoulder. "Stop laughing and tell me what the hell that is."

I glance at the picture and lose it again. "It's comforting," I croak.

Sabrina punches me again.

"Logan," I choke out. "He made this for the baby. It's the comforting test."

"I swear to God, Tuck, if you don't start making sense, I'm going to send this picture to the police and tell them I'm the victim of a hate crime."

I hiccup uncontrollably.

"Tucker!"

Wheezing, I manage to sit up. I cough for a full minute to get the humor out of my system. Then I stare at the stuffed thing on the screen.

I think it's supposed to be a teddy bear, but somewhere during the process, shit went horribly wrong. The stitching is something out of a Tim Burton movie. One eye is a button while the other is a serial-killer style X sewn with black thread. There's a patch of fur missing on the side of its head, and the arms and legs are all different sizes.

Underneath the pic, Logan wrote:

Grace thinks this'll scare the BB. She's wrong, right?

She's not wrong.

"Why did Logan do this to us?" Sabrina demands.

I snort. "He's vying for godfather."

"Start making sense!"

Swallowing another roar of laughter, I hastily clarify. "He and Garrett both want to be our baby's godfather. I made this stupid offhand joke about how I'm gonna make them compete for the title, and they decided that was a great idea. So now they're competing."

Sabrina arches a brow. "And did you ever think that maybe I don't want either of them to be the baby's godfather?"

"Of course. I figured we'd talk about it at some point, but honestly, I think Garrett and Hannah would be awesome godparents."

"They're going to have to fight it out with Hope and Carin. But you're already cutting Logan out?"

My gaze strays back to the phone. "Um. Yes."

She finally cracks a smile. "Okay. So how does this competition of theirs work?"

I sigh. "It's complicated. Stupidly complicated."

"That doesn't surprise me in the slightest," she says cheerfully.

"There are five, I dunno, categories, I guess. Each one is designed to showcase a necessary parenting skill." Jesus. I can't believe I'm even saying this right now. I already had to sit through Logan's ridiculous explanation. I feel like I'm endorsing the crazy by repeating it.

Sabrina, however, looks fascinated. "What are the categories?"

I scan my brain. "Comforting. Grace under pressure. Solid

support system. Um...finances. And...shit, I can't remember the last one."

"How is buying a stuffed animal a sign of comfort?"

"Buying? Darlin', that creature is homemade. They got these sew-your-own-stuffed-animal kits."

Her jaw drops. "Oh my gosh. That's...dedication."

"They're hockey players. Dedication is in our DNA."

"How do they know who wins? Do they get awarded points?"

"I'm supposed to pick a winner in each category." Because my friends hate me, apparently.

"Did they show you copies of their tax returns to determine who wins in the finances department?" she asks dryly.

"Naah. But that one's a draw because they'll both be playing for the pros. Same with support system—no way was I going to choose between Hannah and Grace. I like my balls where they are."

She snickers. "So who wins comforting?"

"Unless Garrett sews something even more nightmare-inducing than that—" I jerk a thumb at my phone, "—I'm pretty sure he'll win this round."

"Your friends are fucking weird, Tucker. You know that, right?"

"Well aware of it." I hesitate for a beat. "Hey, are you working at the post office tomorrow afternoon?"

"No. Why?"

"I was hoping maybe you'd come by the house and help me pack up some stuff. The guys will be there. And Hannah, Grace, maybe Allie. I rented a U-Haul, so everyone's helping me load the furniture I'm taking with me." I hurry to add, "Obviously I won't let you lift anything heavy, but I figure you could help with the light stuff, like clothes. We're ordering some pizzas, so there'll be food..." I let the word *food* hang enticingly, because I know how voracious her appetite has been lately.

But Sabrina's forehead is creased with reluctance. "Are you sure they won't mind that I'm there?"

"Of course not. They really want to get to know you. Wellsy was saying the other day how she's bummed that you never come around."

"Wellsy?" she says blankly.

"Hannah. Her last name is Wells, so Garrett dubbed her Wellsy." And all of a sudden I'm troubled that I've been with Sabrina since the winter and she hardly knows anything about my closest friends.

"I don't know, Tuck..."

"Please?" I flash her my best aw-shucks smile. "It'd mean a lot to me."

"Oh." Her expression melts like butter in the sun. "Okay. I'll come."

———

SABRINA STAYS true to her word and shows up at my house around two o'clock the following day. When she arrives, she nearly gets sideswiped by the mattress that Logan and Fitzy are hauling out to the moving truck. It's chaos in here.

I whisk her out of harm's way and plant a kiss right on her lips. "Hey darlin'. Thanks for coming."

A blush rises in her cheeks when she realizes that Hannah and Grace are standing directly behind me and had witnessed the kiss. I, on the other hand, don't care if they witness us banging against the damn wall. Sabrina looks so fucking beautiful in her flower-print blue sundress, with her dark hair pulled back in a low ponytail. These last couple of months her cheeks have been perpetually rosy, giving credence to that whole pregnancy glow thing.

"Hey," she says, her tone oddly shy.

I introduce her to the girls. They greet her warmly, and Sabrina quickly warms up to them too. Apparently she already knows Hannah from the diner, and Grace has a cute habit of babbling when she's nervous, so she's talking Sabrina's ear off before the introductions are even over.

"You want something to drink?" I offer, guiding her into the kitchen while Hannah and Grace trail after us.

"No, it's fine. Just put me to work."

"We were going to take a break now anyway. Fitzy showed up earlier than planned and he has to leave in an hour, so we've already moved all the furniture out of my room. All that's left is emptying out my closet and drawers." I nudge her toward a chair. "Sit down. Water okay?"

"Sure."

As Hannah and Grace join her at the table, I don't miss the way both their gazes keep darting toward Sabrina's stomach. She's clearly pregnant, but not quite watermelon-big yet. Maybe a soccer ball?

Either way, that's my daughter in there, and every time I think that, pride fills my chest. My daughter. Christ. Life is strange and unpredictable and so freaking awesome.

"How are you feeling?" Hannah is asking Sabrina. "Are you still getting morning sickness?"

"No, that stopped a couple months ago. These days I'm just tired and hungry and need to go to the bathroom every other minute. Oh, and it's getting harder and harder to see my feet. Which is probably a good thing because I think they're swollen to twice their size."

"Aw, that sucks," Grace says sympathetically. "But at least you get an adorable, chubby-cheeked miracle for all your pain and suffering. That's a decent tradeoff, right?"

"Ha!" Sabrina grins. "How about I call you at three in the morning when my chubby-cheeked miracle is screaming her lungs out and *then* you can tell me if it's a decent tradeoff."

Hannah snickers. "She's got you there, Gracie."

I hand Sabrina a glass of water and then lean against the counter, smiling as the girls continue to joke about all the "wonderful" things Sabrina and I can look forward to—no sleep, diaper changes, colic, teething.

Truthfully, none of that scares me. If you don't have to work hard for something, then how can it ever truly be rewarding?

Footsteps approach the kitchen. Garrett wanders in, wiping sweat off his brow. When he notices Sabrina, he brightens. "Oh good. You're here. Hold on—gotta grab something."

She turns to me as if to say, *Is he talking to me?*

He's already gone, though, his footsteps thumping up the stairs.

At the table, Hannah runs a hand through her hair and gives me a pleading look. "Just remember he's your best friend, okay?"

That doesn't sound ominous.

When Garrett returns, he's holding a notepad and a ballpoint pen, which he sets on the table as he sits across from Sabrina. "Tuck," he says. "Sit. This is important."

I'm so baffled right now. Hannah's resigned expression doesn't help in lessening the confusion.

Once I'm seated next to Sabrina, Garrett flips open the notepad, all business. "Okay. So let's go over the names."

Sabrina raises an eyebrow at me.

I shrug, because I legitimately don't know what the fuck he's talking about.

"I've put together a solid list. I really think you're going to like these." But when he glances down at the page, his face falls. "Ah crap. We can't use any of the boy names."

"Wait." Sabrina holds up a hand, her brow furrowed. "You're picking names for our baby?"

He nods, busy flipping the page.

My baby mama gapes at me.

I shrug again.

"Just out of curiosity, what were the boy names?" Grace hedges, clearly fighting a smile.

He cheers up again. "Well, the top contender was Garrett."

I snicker loud enough to rattle Sabrina's water glass. "Uh-huh," I say, playing along. "And what was the runner-up?"

"Graham."

Hannah sighs.

"But it's okay. I have some kickass girl names too." He taps his pen on the pad, meets our eyes, and utters two syllables. "Gigi."

My jaw drops. "Are you kidding me? I'm not naming my daughter *Gigi*."

Sabrina is mystified. "Why Gigi?" she asks slowly.

Hannah sighs again.

The name suddenly clicks in my head. Oh for fuck's sake.

"G.G.," I mutter to Sabrina. "As in Garrett Graham."

She's silent for a beat. Then she bursts out laughing, triggering giggles from Grace and eventually Hannah, who keeps shaking her head at her boyfriend.

"What?" Garrett says defensively. "The godfather should have a say in the name. It's in the rule book."

"What rule book?" Hannah bursts out. "You make up the rules as you go along!"

"So?"

"Besides, you haven't been crowned godfather yet," I point out with a smirk, just as Fitzy and Logan drift into the kitchen. I jerk a thumb toward Logan. "This dumbass is still in the running."

"Actually..." Garrett beams at us. "Logan's out of the race."

I twist in my chair to look at our teammate. "Since when?"

Logan's expression instantly goes shuttered. "I decided to bow out," he mutters. "It's a big responsibility."

A loud snort sounds from Garrett's vicinity. "You decided to bow out? Is that what we're calling it?"

Logan glowers at him. "It's what we're calling it because it's true."

"Yeah?" Garrett hops to his feet. "Be right back."

Sabrina and I exchange puzzled glances as he steps out of the kitchen. I hear him moving around in the living room. A moment later he pops back into sight and whips up his hands in front of Logan's face.

"Then how do you explain *this*?"

Sabrina yelps in horror.

Me, I'm just really curious to hear why Garrett is holding a tiny newborn doll.

Which is missing its head, by the way.

"You fucking took it home?" Logan sounds outraged.

"Hell yeah I did. What use were they going to have for it there? It doesn't have a head, bro."

"Where's 'there'?" I ask carefully, though I'm not sure I want to know the answer.

"Newborn CPR," Garrett explains. "We took a course at the campus health center this morning."

"Newborn CPR?" Sabrina shakes her head, dazed.

"It was the grace under pressure test." Garrett smiles smugly. "Which he failed. I, of course, passed with flying colors."

"Is it my fault I don't know my own strength?" Logan protests.

"Yes!" Garrett says in a spurt of laughter. "That is *totally* your fault." He holds up the doll and waves it around tauntingly. "Show me on the doll where your brain is. Oh right, you can't. Because you fucking decapitated it."

Sabrina turns to me. "Can we go upstairs and pack now?"

"You guys are scaring Sabrina," Hannah grumbles at the bickering idiots. "Babe, put that doll away. And Logan, remind me to never let you babysit my future children." With that, she refocuses her attention on Sabrina. "Okay, assuming we're putting a pin in Gigi, what other names are you thinking about?"

Sabrina and I exchange another look. "We haven't even discussed it," she admits.

"Are there any names you like in general?"

Sabrina ponders it. "I like the name Charlotte."

"Oh, I love that!" Grace exclaims. "Charlotte Tucker. It has a nice ring to it."

"Charlotte James," Sabrina corrects.

I glare at her. "Her last name is going to be Tucker."

"No it's not. It's going to be James."

"What about Tucker-James?" Fitzy calls out as he grabs a beer from the fridge.

"No," we say in unison. Not because we're against hyphens, but because we're both stubborn jerks.

I didn't realize I felt so strongly about my daughter having my last name, but I do. Hell, if it was up to me, Sabrina would have my last name too. But that would require us getting married, which would require me to propose, and I'm pretty sure she'd flee to another continent if I did that. We might be sleeping together again, but I can tell she's still fighting the idea that we're in an actual relationship.

For some reason, the silly girl thinks she has to do everything alone.

"Okay." Hannah grins. "How about we table the first name discussion until you've solved the surname quandary?"

That sounds like a good idea. The last thing I want to do is argue with Sabrina in front of all my friends. "Let's go upstairs and do some packing," I tell Sabrina.

Nodding, she allows me to help her out of her chair.

From his perch at the counter, Garrett's expression turns glum. "I can't believe you're moving out."

I roll my eyes. "You guys are moving out too."

"Yeah, but not for two more weeks."

I notice that Logan looks equally bummed at the prospect of my leaving today. They wanted to throw me a goodbye party, but I said no, because technically this isn't goodbye. I'm just moving to Boston, which is where they'll both be in a few months anyway.

Dean's heading to New York, though. He's bailing on law school and got a job teaching at a prep school. Allie landed a role on a TV show that's filming in Manhattan, so I guess they'll be moving in together.

Truthfully, I'm equal parts sad and relieved that Dean will be living in another state. He hasn't exactly been supportive about my impending fatherhood, but he's still one of my best friends, damn it.

"You guys decide yet who gets the master bedroom?"

Garrett is speaking to Fitzy now, who shrugs his tattooed shoulders. "Me. Obviously."

"I don't know," Logan warns. "Hollis and the freshman are gonna try to fight you for it."

Fitzy raises an eyebrow and then flexes his big biceps. "Let 'em."

I stifle a laugh. Yeah, Hollis and Hunter don't stand a chance against Colin Fitzgerald. Though, considering what a private person he is, I'm still surprised that he agreed to take over our lease with them. I figured he'd look for another place on his own, but I guess Hollis twisted his arm into it.

Sabrina and I head upstairs, where I sweep my gaze over my empty room. The bed's gone and there's nowhere to sit. I notice Sabrina rubbing her lower back, so I make a mental note not to let her stay on her feet for too long.

"Okay," she says in a decisive voice as she opens the closet door. "Should we fold everything up nicely? Or just toss it in the boxes willy-nilly?"

"What boxes?" I swipe a cardboard container of garbage bags off the hardwood. "The clothes go in here."

"Oh my God. You are *such* a guy."

"Am I?" Smirking, I drift my hand down my abs and then cup my junk over my jeans. "Do you want to inspect the goods to make sure?"

"Did you ask me here to pack or to fuck?"

"Both?"

She waves a hand around the room. "There's no bed."

"Who needs a bed?"

"My poor fat pregnant body does," Sabrina answers with a self-deprecating smile.

"How about this?" I counter. "Let's pack as fast as we can, and then I'll follow you back to Boston and we can fuck up a storm on your big comfy bed."

She stands up on her tiptoes and plants a kiss on my lips. "Deal."

SABRINA

I WAS nervous about spending time with Tucker's friends, but really I had nothing to worry about, because they're pretty awesome. Hannah and Grace are so easy to talk to. Garrett and Logan are hysterical, and a lot more laidback than I expected. I mean, they're drop-dead gorgeous hockey players. Shouldn't they all be super conceited like—

"We need to talk."

Like *this* guy.

I stiffen when Dean Di Laurentis appears in the doorway. Tucker just went outside to say goodbye to Fitzy, leaving me to empty out the last dresser drawer on my own, but I stop what I'm doing when Dean enters and closes the door behind him.

The mere sight of him irritates me. It's not fair that someone so jerky is so ridiculously attractive. Objectively, Dean is probably the best-looking guy I've ever seen outside of a movie screen. He's got blond hair, chiseled male-model features, a spectacular body. And he's charming as hell—that's how he got me into bed in the first place. Well, that and the three daiquiris I drank. I might have even seen him again, if I hadn't learned that he was sleeping with our TA in exchange for good grades.

"We do, huh?" I drawl. "And what do we need to talk about, Richie?"

He flinches, as he always does when I use the mocking nickname. I dubbed him Richie Rich after I discovered that he uses his money and looks to get ahead.

"You know exactly what we need to talk about."

I frown. "If you mean *this*—" I gesture to my stomach, "—then there's nothing to discuss. My baby and I are none of your business."

"Tucker's my business," he says coolly, crossing his arms over his muscular chest. "I mean, damn, Sabrina, I always knew you were an ambitious bitch, but I didn't think you were a selfish one."

Anger climbs up my throat. "Wow. Beau always tried to convince me that you were a decent guy, but he was so clearly wrong."

Dean hisses out a breath. "Leave Beau out of this. We're talking about you and Tuck."

"Do you really want to pick a fight with a pregnant chick right now? Because I'm warning you—my hormones are all over the place. I might claw your eyes out."

He looks unfazed. "You're fucking up my boy's life. You really think I'm just going to stand by and let you do that?"

Gritting my teeth, I slam the dresser drawer shut and mimic his pose, positioning my arms tight across my swollen breasts. "Tucker is a grown-up. He also happens to be the father of this baby. If he wants to have a hand in raising her, I can't exactly stop him."

Frustration clouds his expression. "This will ruin his whole life. Don't you get that? He's giving up everything he's worked toward for a chick who doesn't even love him."

My jaw almost hits the floor. Where the fuck does he get off saying this shit to me?

"What makes you think I don't love him?" I shoot back defiantly.

"Because if you did, then you'd already have a ring on your finger. Tuck doesn't do things half-assed. He loves you, you're having his kid —if he thought for a moment that you loved him back, you'd be getting married in City Hall before this kid pops out. Instead, he's staying in Boston when all he's talked about since freshman year is going back to Texas—"

Guilt pricks my throat. Hard.

"And now he's going to take the first job he finds, instead of opening a business that he's actually taken the time to research and think about." Dean shakes his head. "Don't you see that?"

I falter. He's right. Tucker *doesn't* half-ass it. And yet here he is, moving in with a guy he barely likes, considering buying shitty franchises he's not passionate about, and all because I was so overcome with lust one night that I forgot that "just the tip" is as effective in knocking you up as having a guy ejaculate in you.

He's changing his entire life for me. He's changing his goals and his plans and his lifestyle to accommodate this baby. And *I'm* the one who caused him to do that.

Despite my threat about clawing Dean's eyes out, I don't feel at all feral anymore. I feel...wrecked.

So wrecked that I'm helpless to stop the sob that flies out. So wrecked that I fall apart right in front of Dean fucking Di Laurentis.

I sink to the floor and bury my face in my hands, crying so hard that I can't even draw a breath. I gasp for air while hot tears slide down my cheeks and soak my palms. I'm a shuddering, pathetic, pregnant mess, and it's not until a firm hand clasps my shoulder that I realize Dean is sitting on the floor beside me.

"Fuck," he mumbles, sounding as helpless as I feel. "I didn't mean to make you cry."

"I deserve to cry," I choke out between sobs.

"Sabrina—" He touches my shoulder again.

"No!" I wrench away from his grip and stare at him with tear-filled eyes. "You're right, okay? I'm ruining his life! Do you think I'm fucking happy about that? Because I'm not!" I gulp rapidly, trying to remember how to breathe. "He's kind and sweet and so goddamn incredible and he doesn't deserve to have his world turned upside down like this! He should be making all these plans right now and being excited about graduating college and starting a new chapter in his life, and instead it's *end of fucking story*. The best guy on this whole planet is stuck with me—*forever*—all because of what was supposed to be a one-time hookup!"

I finish in a panting rush, viciously swiping at my tears. Beside me, Dean looks totally and utterly stunned.

"Aw hell," he finally says. "You do love him."

I hang my head. "Yes."

"But you haven't told him."

"No."

"Why the hell not?"

"Because..." My face collapses again. "Because I'm trying to make this as easy as I can for him. Love complicates things, and shit is complicated enough right now. And..."

"And what?" Dean asks.

And I don't know if he loves me back.

Sometimes I think he does, but in the back of my mind there's always a little nugget of doubt. I'm honestly not certain if Tucker wants to be with me because he loves me, or because he thinks we should be together for the sake of our baby.

"It doesn't matter," I say hoarsely. "You're right. This baby is screwing up his plans." I wipe my face again. "The least I can do is make sure it doesn't ruin more than it has to. I'll take on the bulk of the responsibility. That'll free up a lot of his time so that he can open a business he loves."

Dean hesitates. "What about Harvard?"

"I'm still going." Bitterness joins the sorrow clinging to my throat. "Don't worry, you'll have three more years to hate me and call me a bitch."

"Actually, I won't be there," he confesses.

I frown. "Since when?"

"I accepted a teaching job at a private school in Manhattan." He shrugs. "I realized law school isn't where I want to be."

"Oh." I wonder why Tucker didn't mention that, but I guess it doesn't surprise me. He's already admitted that Dean hasn't exactly been Mr. Supportive about the baby.

"After Beau died," Dean starts, but his voice cracks and he stops to clear his throat. "After he died, I kind of went batshit crazy for a while. But then I crawled out of the hole I dug for myself and really took stock of my life, you know?"

I nod slowly. Joanna Maxwell had done the same thing. So had I. Beau's death made me realize how important life is, how short it can be. I wonder if losing Beau was a game-changer for everyone who knew and cared about him.

"It changed stuff for me too," I confess.

It's Dean's turn to nod. "I can tell." He pauses ruefully. "Sometimes I can't believe you and I ever hooked up. It seems like a million years ago."

I manage a laugh. "Yup."

"You really love Tuck, huh?"

"I do."

He lets out a heavy breath. "You should tell him."

"No." I swallow. "And you're not going to tell him either."

"He needs to know—"

"No," I repeat, firmer this time. "I mean it, Dean. Don't say anything to him. You owe me."

Humor flickers in his eyes. "How do you figure?"

I jut out my chin. "You didn't deserve that A in Statistics sophomore year."

"Ah. So keeping my mouth shut is my punishment for the undeserved grade?"

"So you admit it was undeserved!"

"Of course it was." His tone becomes pained. "Trust me, I did everything I could to try to get the professor to fail me."

"Bullshit."

"It's true. After I aced that project we teamed up on and you only got a B, I realized the TA was fucking around with my grades. I asked the prof to go over all my tests and papers, and turns out I was supposed to be failing."

"Oh my God. I *knew* it." Though I don't feel as smug about it as I thought I would. My beef with Dean suddenly feels incredibly unimportant. And, like he said, as if it happened a million years ago.

"Well, I didn't," he says frankly. "I know you think I was boning the TA for the grades—" He flashes a grin, "—but I was boning her because she had a great rack and the sweetest ass."

I pretend to gag before going serious. "Why didn't you ever tell me any of this?"

He snickers. "Because we're not friends."

I snicker back. "True." I mull something over. "But maybe we should call a ceasefire."

"Jesus. Has hell frozen over?"

Embarrassment tickles my belly. "You're one of Tucker's best friends. I'm about to have his kid. It makes sense for us to try to co-exist."

"Makes sense," he agrees.

Dean hops off the floor and holds out a hand.

I hesitate for only a second before allowing him to help me to my feet. "Thanks."

An awkward silence stretches between us, which I don't try to fill by talking. I'm still not convinced that Dean isn't a superficial play-boy, and I'm sure a part of him still thinks I'm a bitch. But the hostility is gone, and even though we're never going to be best buds, I know Tucker will appreciate it if I make an effort to get along with Dean.

It's the least I can do, considering how much Tucker has already sacrificed for *me*.

29

SABRINA

June

"Holy crap, babies need a lot of shit." Carin staggers into my bedroom loaded with three bags. "I think your incoming babelette has more gear than Hope."

"Not possible," says Hope's boyfriend, who we corralled into picking up a crib I found at a garage sale over in Dunham.

He and Tucker muscle the pieces inside and look around at the small space.

"You going to fit everything in here?" D'Andre asks dubiously.

I rub a hand over my belly. Nothing seems to fit anymore. Not my clothes. Not my shoes. And now, not the crib. My bedroom is big enough for a desk and a bed but not a desk and a bed and a crib.

I sigh. "I guess the desk is going to have to go."

Tucker keeps his mouth shut, but I see frustration flare briefly in his eyes. We've been over this before. He wants me to move out, but I refuse to.

We've settled into a nice routine this past month, in which I've been doing exactly what I told Dean I would do—trying to make life as easy as possible for Tuck.

I don't ask him for anything. I won't let him pay for or even split the cost of all the baby stuff I'm buying. I don't call him in the middle of the night when the baby kicks me awake and my back is throbbing. And I'm definitely not going to commit to an apartment with him. I'd never be able to afford anything decent and I need to pay my way or this is never going to work.

Still, asking John Tucker not to help out is like asking the sun not to rise. He comes to my doctor's appointments, rubs my back and feet every time we're on the couch together, has read as many baby books as we can get our hands on, and is always picking me up little snacks —a pint of cookie dough ice cream, a bag of double-stuff Oreos, a jar of olives. I've started to keep my random cravings to myself, because if I even hint that something sounds enticing, Tucker's in his truck on his way to the grocery store.

"Where are you going to study?" Carin asks in alarm.

D'Andre grunts and tries to re-adjust his grip on the crib.

"Out in the kitchen," I answer. Pointing to the closet door, I ask the guys to set the pieces down. "Over there, and then I guess we'll put this desk out on the curb and hope someone picks it up."

As the two men maneuver the crib parts into the room, I start cleaning out the desk drawers, dumping papers on the bed. Carin hops over to help.

"Good call on Dunham," I tell Tucker. It was his idea to head over to that posh town twenty minutes outside of Boston.

He shrugs as if it was no big deal. "I looked at property over there and the cheapest place was six figures. Figured it would have some good stuff for us."

"What you doing over in Dunham?" D'Andre asks.

"Looking around at some businesses for sale. I'm buying one with my dad's insurance money." Tucker crouches beside me and starts to paw through the pieces of the crib.

"Find anything interesting?"

"Lots of franchises, but nothing feels right. I can't see myself making sub sandwiches for the rest of my life, even if the P&L statements are good. I could buy a couple of small rentals. Good cash flow with that."

D'Andre nods. "Yeah. You'd be able to do most of the maintenance too. What else is out there?"

"In my price range? Mostly small businesses. There are a couple gyms, lots of foodie places, and a few other things which I think are a big money drain."

"Gotta find something you like."

"You know it." Tucker hops to his feet. "I'm going to get the rest of the shit from the truck."

I give him an absent nod as he leaves. In no time, we have the desk cleared out. Hope and I start to move it, but D'Andre stomps over and pushes me away.

"Are you fucking kidding me? Get over there and sit down." He shakes his head. "Fool girl. The size of a house and she's still trying to pretend she's not pregnant," he mutters, but it's loud enough for everyone in the room to hear him.

Chastised, I make my way over to the bed to start sorting things. I'm going to have to clean out my closet and dresser drawers because, as Carin said, babies require a lot of shit. Diapers are already stacked in the corner of the closet—they were a gift from Hope. I can't imagine going through all of them, even if the books say that you change a diaper six to ten times a day.

The books I picked up at the used bookstore were old, so I'm guessing some of the information is outdated. Because six to ten times a day? Who's got time for that? Tucker has some newer books, so I can compare notes with him later.

Hope joins me on the bed. "'Most Likely to be a Lawyer, 8th Grade.'" She makes a face. "You were a barrel of laughs as a kid, weren't you?"

I snatch the stupid certificate out of her hand. "I suck at science but didn't mind telling people exactly what I thought of them, so doctor was out and lawyer was in."

"I think that's talk show host, not lawyer." She reaches out to glide her hand across my stomach. "How's our baby today?"

"Sleeping."

"I want to feel her kick. Wake her up."

Hope has baby fever. Every time I see her, she wants to rub my belly like I'm the lucky Buddha statue at a Chinese restaurant. Unfortunately for Hope, the baby and I are not on the same schedule. When I'm moving around, she's sleeping. The moment I get into bed, she decides to wake up. Doctor Laura told me it was because my movement lulls the baby to sleep. That's all well and good, but it doesn't help me get a good night's sleep, does it?

"How am I supposed to do that? Jumping jacks?"

"Would that make the baby fall out? Like if you were near your due date, could you shake shake shake it out?" Carin wriggles her arms like she's a member of Taylor Swift's dance squad.

I stare at her. "Please tell me that whatever science field you end up studying in grad school, it won't be important."

Carin flips me off and shimmies her way across the room before bending down to pick up one of the bags we filled at Goodwill. She dumps them on the floor and starts sorting the whites from the colors. We agreed at the store that everything had to be washed in the hottest water possible given the smell of some of the items.

"Did you know that when the baby starts moving that it's called the quickening?" Hope says.

I snicker. "So she's going to burst out of my stomach with a sword declaring there can be only one?"

"Possibly. Women have died in childbirth, right? The baby is essentially a parasite. It lives off your nutrients, saps your energy." She taps the bottom of a hanger against her lip. "So yeah, I think the Highlander motto could fit."

Carin and I look at her in horror. "Hopeless, you can shut up any time now," Carin orders.

"I was just saying, from a medical standpoint, it's a possible theory. Not here, but maybe in other less developed nations." She reaches over and pats my belly. "Don't worry. You're safe. You should've gotten more maternity clothes," she says, moving on to another topic while I'm still digesting that my baby is a parasite.

I shake my head. "No. That stuff was hideous. I already look like a boat. I didn't need to look like an ugly one."

"I think if I were pregnant, I'd wear muumuus or housecoats like Lucille Ball," Carin muses.

"Are those even a thing?" Hope asks.

"They should be."

I nod in agreement because hell yeah, I'd wear something like that over the awful jeans and polyester gear and their white expandable waist pouches. I know I'm going to appreciate those in a few weeks, but right now I'm not looking forward to getting bigger.

"I tried to bend over and touch my toes this morning," I tell the girls. "I tipped over, hit my head on the desk, and then had to call for Nana to get up. I'm literally the size of an Oompa Loompa."

"You're the most beautiful Oompa Loompa in the world," Hope declares.

"Because she's not orange."

"Oompa Loompas were orange?" I try to conjure up a mental picture of them but can only recall their white overalls.

Carin purses her lips. "Were they supposed to be candies? Like orange slices? Or maybe candy corn?"

"They were squirrels," Hope informs us.

"No way," we both say at once.

"Yes way. I read it on the back of a Laffy Taffy when I was like ten. It was a trivia question and I'd just seen the movie. I was terrified of squirrels for years afterwards."

"Shit. Learn something new every day." I push my body upright, a task that takes a certain amount of upper body strength these days, and toddle over to inspect the crib.

"I don't believe you," Carin tells Hope. "The movie is about candy. It's called *Willy Wonka and the Chocolate Factory*. Since when are squirrels candies? I can buy into a bunny because, you know, the chocolate Easter bunnies, but not a squirrel."

"Look it up, Careful. I'm right."

"You're ruining my childhood." Carin turns to me. "Don't do this to your daughter."

"Raise her to believe Oompa Loompas are squirrels?"

"Yes."

Hope laughs. "Here's my theory on parenthood. We're going to screw up. Badly. Many, many times. And our kids are going to need therapy. The goal is to reduce the amount of therapy they'll need."

"That's a dark parenting outlook," I remark. "How do these things go together? Are we missing something?" There are two matching end pieces, but the rest of the boards on the floor are like a Lego set with no instructions.

Carin shrugs. "I'm a scientist. I can estimate the volume and mass of the pieces, but I'm not going to hurt myself trying to assemble it."

D'Andre appears in the doorway, sweat glistening on his dark skin. All three of us turn toward him with pleading eyes.

"Why you all looking at me like that?" he asks suspiciously.

"Can you put this crib back together?" I ask hopefully.

"And if you do, will you please take off your shirt?" Carin begs.

D'Andre scowls. "You gotta stop treating me like a piece of meat. I have feelings."

But he whips off his shirt anyway and we all take a moment to praise God for creating a specimen like D'Andre, whose chest looks like it was sculpted out of marble.

He smirks. "Had enough?"

"No, not really." Carin props her chin on a hand. "Why don't you take off those shorts too?"

I admit I'm curious. D'Andre's a big man. I'm not opposed to seeing his equipment.

Hope throws a palm up in the air. "No, no stripping. We're here to help put the crib together. Baby, what can you do?"

"I'm an accounting major," he reminds her. "Remember? I'm good with numbers and lifting. Tucker'll put it together. He's out there talking some stranger into hauling away the desk." He directs a pointed glance to my belly. "So we wait for your man."

"She doesn't need a man," Hope says. "She has us."

"Then why am I here?"

"Because you love me and don't want to sleep on the sofa," Hope says sweetly.

"That's not a sofa, Hope. That's a piece of wood with some foam on it."

I giggle. Hope's new place in Boston is full of items from her grandma's attic, which contains enough furniture to fill about three houses.

"That's an original Saarinen."

"Still don't make it a sofa," he insists.

"You sit on it. It has three cushions. Hence, it's a sofa." She sniffs. Conversation over. "We need an engineering friend." She points a finger at Carin. "Go back to Briar and hook up with an engineering student."

"Okay, but I'll need to actually have sex with him beforehand, so I won't be back until," she pretends to check the time, "ten or so."

"We're all college graduates," I proclaim. "We can put this together ourselves."

Clapping my hands, I motion for everyone to get on the floor with me. After three tries of trying to lower myself to the ground and making Hope and Carin nearly pee their pants laughing in the process, D'Andre takes pity on all of us and helps me onto my knees. Which is where Tucker finds us.

"Is this some new fertility ritual?" he drawls from the doorway, one shoulder propped against the frame. "Because she's already pregnant, you know."

"Get yo ass in here, white boy, and put this thing together," D'Andre snaps. "This is ridiculous."

"What's ridiculous?" Tucker stops next to me, and I take the opportunity to lean against his legs. Even kneeling is hard when you're toting around an extra thirty pounds. "We took it apart. How can you not know how to put it back together?"

D'Andre repeats his earlier excuse. "I'm an accounting major."

Tucker rolls his eyes. "You got an Allen wrench?"

"Are you mocking us right now?" I grumble. "I don't have any wrenches, let alone ones with names."

He grins. "Leave this to me, darlin'. I'll get it fixed up."

"I want to help," Hope volunteers. "This is like surgery, except with wood and not people."

"Lord help us," D'Andre mutters.

"Come on." Carin tugs on my arm. "Let's start washing some of this stuff we bought."

With a boost on my ass from Tucker, I get to my feet and waddle after Carin.

"How does it feel to not be waiting tables?" she asks as we make our way into the laundry room.

"Weird. It's hard finding a job for three months that doesn't require some heavy manual labor. I went to a temp agency to see if they had anything for me, but they weren't hopeful. Apparently pregnant women aren't on the top of the candidate list."

"So Tucker's really not going back to Texas?"

"Nope. He wants to stay close to the baby." I grimace. "But his mom...he's so close with her. I think there are problems there."

"Oh Lord. You don't want to mess with a southern boy's mama," Carin warns. "I've heard endless complaints about grits from Hope."

I have too. Still, what are my options? "So I should leave Harvard and move to Texas?"

"No. Just eat your grits. Whenever she offers them to you. No matter how sick they make you."

"That's morbid."

"Have you thought about what you're going to do about the baby when you're in class?" she asks as we load the washing machine.

"I don't know yet. Harvard doesn't offer day care. I'll try to find an in-home care provider, I guess."

Thinking about all these issues is stressing me out, but I don't want to complain about it too much. Carin and Hope are already feeling guilty about not being able to help out more, but fuck, they have their own lives to worry about.

"What about your grandmother?"

"God. You should've seen her face when I asked. She told me she'd already raised one kid—" I point a thumb at my chest, "—that didn't belong to her, and she wasn't raising another one."

"Harsh."

We move into the kitchen and start in on the baby bottles. "Harsh but true. I can't dump this load on her."

"What about Tucker?" Carin shakes out a clean bottle and sets it in the dish rack.

"What about him?"

"He's the dad. He has to help. You can take him to court and force him to pay you child support."

My jaw drops. "I'm not going to do that. And he *is* going to help." I pause. "As much as I'll let him."

Carin makes a disgusted noise. "You're so stubborn. You don't have to do this all on your own, B. You make it sound like he's just along for the ride. What's going on with the two of you?"

I pick up one of the clean bottles and twist a nipple, trying to imagine myself holding the baby and feeding it with one of these. "He never intended on staying here. He's just here because of me and the baby, and I feel like I'm ruining his life."

She scoffs. "He was part of this too. You're not the Virgin Mary. There was no immaculate conception."

"I know. But I still could have gotten an abortion." Honestly, that's a thought that weighs on me every minute I spend trying to figure out how I'm going to make this all work.

"But you didn't, so stop looking backward."

"I know," I say again.

"You have feelings for him."

I busy myself with finding a place for the clean bottles and other baby gear. "I like him."

"You can say the other L word. It won't kill you."

Annoyed, I glare at Carin. "Like you're any better, Miss Commitmentphobe. Since when have you run around telling guys you've hooked up with that you love them?"

"Never, but I'm not afraid of it like you are."

"I'm not afraid of it." Am I?

She rolls her eyes.

"Whatever. It's irrelevant, anyway. Tucker's in this because he's in love with the baby and that's good enough for me."

Carin opens her mouth to rebuke me, but Tucker strolls into the kitchen before she can get a word out. "Ready?" he asks me.

I flick a gaze toward the microwave clock. Crap. It says we have about twenty minutes before class starts.

"Yup. You guys are going to have to leave," I tell Carin. "Tuck and I are going to a breathing class."

She raises a brow. "For what?"

"To help her when she's in labor," Hope explains as she enters the kitchen with D'Andre on her heels. She comes over and gives me a kiss on the cheek. "Call us later, okay?"

"I will. And thanks for helping out today. All of you."

"No thanks necessary," Hope says, and Carin and D'Andre nod in agreement. "We're here for you, B. Now and always."

Emotion wells up in my throat. I have no idea how I wound up with such amazing friends, but I'm sure as heck not complaining.

"YOU DON'T SOUND TOO excited about this," Tucker comments twenty minutes later. He holds the door to the community center open for me.

"And you are?" A yellow sign decorated with balloons greets us.

"This process is so hard that I have to learn how to breathe? That's not normal."

"You watch any of those YouTube videos?"

"God no. I didn't want to psych myself out. Did you?"

"A few."

"And?"

He gives me a thumbs-down. "I don't recommend them. I'm wondering why we use *brass balls* to describe someone who's really strong, because after the second video, my balls tried to climb inside my body. Plus, my YouTube history is officially fucked."

"Ha. Exactly why I didn't watch any." I wag a warning finger at him. "Stay by my head during the birth or you'll never want to have sex with me again."

"Naah, I can separate the two." He drags his hand down my spine to rest it on top of my butt, which, like my boobs, is growing in size. "This ass is made for tapping."

"So anal is all I'm going to get after childbirth?"

He grins broadly. "Why not both?"

Before I can respond, a curly-haired older lady wearing a rainbow-colored peasant skirt sweeps forward to greet us. "Welcome to Labor of Love workshop! I'm Stacy!"

"John Tucker and Sabrina James." Tuck introduces us both.

Stacy doesn't shake his hand. Instead, she makes a prayer gesture. "Please find a mat on the floor."

"This is going to be too hippy dippy for me," I murmur as we make our way to the three rows of yoga mats spaced out on the floor. The room is mostly full, but we find an empty mat in the back.

"It's a lesson on breathing. I think that's the definition of hippy dippy." Tucker helps me into a seated position. "Want me to practice giving you injections instead?"

"Maybe?" I'm only half joking. I read that there are complications with medications, and I haven't decided if I'm going to opt for the epidural.

The lights dim and Stacy moves deeper into the room, hands still folded in prayer.

"I think she knows something we don't," Tucker murmurs in my ear. "That's why she's praying all the time."

"She knows that no amount of meditation is ever going to make childbirth pain free."

The man next to us clears his throat. Tucker chuckles softly, but we both shut up.

In the front of the room, Stacy turns on a projector. The words "Welcome to Labor of Love" appear. And then she proceeds to read off the slide.

"We're here to help ease you through the labor process. The mainstream media and health organizations feed you an endless supply of fear and paranoia, but the truth is that childbirth does not have to be a painful experience. Today we will start our journey to a joyful and pleasurable labor. These three classes will help you refocus your negative feelings, drawing in serenity and pushing out fear."

"Are we in a breathing class or signing up for a cult?" Tucker whispers.

Cult. Definitely cult.

"Partners, helpers, move into position behind the mama."

"I already hate this woman," I hiss as he crouches behind me.

"Because she called you *mama* or because she says it's not a painful experience?"

A man a few mats down raises his hand. "Where should we put our hands?"

"Great question, Mark."

Oh God, she remembers all our names.

"During labor, the appropriate position will be the lower back, but for today, we're concentrating on relaxation, so please place your hands on your partner's shoulders."

Next to me, one expectant mother is taking copious notes, as if

Stacy in the peasant skirt is the oracle of laborhood, speaking the ten commandments of birthing.

"If she says, 'There's nothing to fear but fear itself,' we're out of here," I say a little too loudly.

The gunner and her equally serious partner turn around to glare at me. A burble of laughter threatens to escape. Can we get arrested for disturbing the peace in a breathing class?

Stacy waves her hand toward the projection screen. "First we'll watch a short video of the appropriate breathing pattern, and then we'll practice."

The video consists of five minutes of a woman panting, her lips forming different shapes while her partner counts off.

"You think she's really got a baby in there or is it one of those foam things?" Tucker asks, his hands lightly squeezing my shoulders.

"Foam," I say instantly. "She's not even sweating. I sweat just trying to get my shoes on."

After the video ends, Stacy goes around the room to check on all our breathing positions. "Deeper breaths, Sabrina. John, please rub a little harder. Place your fingers closer to her neck. Her neck needs more attention."

His fingers start rubbing a long path along the side of my neck, drawing out a low moan. Shit, that does feel good. I guess Stacy's right. I did need more attention on my neck.

"Good job, John," Stacy coos. She straightens and addresses the class. "Now, I'd like you all to imagine a favorite memory. Something very good in your life. Close your eyes and bring that recollection to the forefront. Pin it to the wall of your mind's eye."

"I'm envisioning one of us is a Cyclops." Tucker's breath tickles my ear, and I start to feel something completely inappropriate downstairs.

"Maybe the one eye is your dick," I counter.

The couple next to us huffs loudly. We both ignore them this time.

"All this shushing reminds me of the library." His lips brush my earlobe. "Actually, it's worse than the library because there's no tables to hide my hand creeping inside your skirt."

I squirm. "Shut up."

"She told me to go to a favorite memory. Most of those involve either my big head or little head between your legs."

"The important thing," Stacy says with a raised voice and a pointed glare in our direction, "is to find peace. Now close your eyes and picture your happy place."

Tucker hums.

Gotta admit, my recent good times all involve Tucker too, but this is definitely not the time or place to get horny. So I pull up the crimson shield and try to channel the euphoria of the news of my law school admission. That was a good memory too.

"Partners, as your mama is breathing, please give her a good massage around the neck and shoulders. Many mamas hold their tension there. Don't be too gentle. Your mamas are pillars of strength. The next video we will watch is of the birth itself."

Stacy taps something on the laptop attached to the projector. An image of a pair of giant cooking tongs appears on the screen. Okay, maybe they aren't *cooking* tongs, but they look a hell of a lot like them. The camera pans out and we see the tongs being held by a masked surgeon. As the scene unfurls, a gasp fills the room.

A woman's spread legs appear and it's not pretty. I cover my eyes. Tucker's hands tighten around my neck.

Stacy's cheery voice narrates the scene. "Remember your happy place as we watch these next few videos. The implement being used is not a torture device but rather a forceps. If you're not able to push with sufficient strength, your doctor will be forced to use these to pull the infant from your uterus, which can affect the shape of your child's head and possibly lead to brain damage. Keep breathing, mamas. Partners, keep massaging. This is what will happen if you can't conquer your pain. Remember that your mind controls the outcome."

There's another collective intake of breath as the screen shows a scalpel cutting into the flesh of a woman.

Tucker's grip grows tighter.

"You're choking me," I mutter.

He doesn't release me. If anything, the constriction gets tighter.

"And here we have the C-section. The infant will shy away from the light when the stomach cavity is cut open. The doctor has to reach in and drag the baby out of your stomach. Again, if you are unable to do your duty as a mother and push your baby down the vaginal canal, your doctor will be forced to cut the baby out."

I tug on Tucker's fingers. "You're choking me," I repeat.

Stacy taps to another scene. A gush of fluid and blood and, *is that shit?* pours out of the woman on the table.

"This is the most natural thing in the universe as evidenced by births in nature," she says in a dreamy voice.

A montage of the bloody birthing scenes of different mammals follows.

I grab Tucker's middle finger and wrench as hard as I can.

"What's wrong?" he asks, falling away immediately.

"You were choking me!" I snap.

"I thought you said I was joking you!"

We stare at each other, filled with equal parts horror and hilarity.

"Communication is always the key," Stacy sings from the front.

Laughter wins out. Tucker and I collapse against each other. We can't stop laughing, and after a few seconds of calling our names and clapping for attention, Stacy finally asks us to leave.

30

TUCKER

Fourth of July

"On a scale of one to I'm-ready-to-jump-out-of-this-speeding-truck, where are you on the freak-out scale?"

Sabrina jerks her head away from the car window. She's been staring at the Boston scenery as if she's never seen it before, never mind that she's lived here her whole life.

"You can tell I'm anxious?" She grimaces, her pouty lips flattening out.

"Your fingers are white, so either you're suffering from a serious condition that needs immediate medical attention or you're squeezing the blood out of them intentionally."

Out of the corner of my eye, I see her slowly uncurl her fingers until they're straight and pink again.

"I've never met a guy's parents before," she admits, fiddling with the radio station.

"Good thing there's only one," I joke. Then her words sink in. "Wait—never?"

I remember her telling me she's never had a boyfriend before, but I took that to mean college. Sabrina is gorgeous. If I saw her in high school, I would've laid in front of her locker every day until she agreed to go out with me.

It all makes sense now, why she's been so on edge ever since I told her that my mom was coming up to meet her. At first, we tried to make a plan for Sabrina and me to fly to Texas, but the cost of two plane tickets and a rental car didn't make sense, even though it meant Mom rescheduling a few appointments. Besides, turns out a lot of airlines balk at pregnant women flying. I guess they aren't really keen on deliveries happening on board.

The bonus about staying in town is that I'm able to work this holiday weekend and get some of that extra time and a half that Sabrina's always bragging about. I've been working part-time on a construction crew in the city and making decent money, which is awesome because I'm trying not to dip into my savings unless I absolutely have to.

"I already told you," Sabrina mumbles from the passenger side. "No boyfriends."

Abandoning the radio, she sits back with a sigh. Her stomach is big enough that she can't even cross her arms unless she rests them on top of the bump. Which is not a shelf, she's reminded me more than once.

"Thought you meant college. Were the boys in your high school deaf, dumb and blind?"

"No. They chased after me, but I didn't have time for them." She absently reaches down and rubs the curve of her stomach.

Every time I look at her, I'm struck anew with awe at the fact that my little girl is inside of her body. It also makes me fucking horny as hell. Thank Christ we're having regular sex again.

"I was constantly hustling for scholarship money," she goes on. "Working almost full-time at the post office since I was sixteen. In the summers I waited tables at night and worked at the post office during the day. Guys were...unnecessary. Other than, you know," she waves vaguely toward her crotch. "Plus they didn't know what to do with their equipment in high school. I was better off taking care of myself at home."

My dick twitches against my zipper. The idea of her playing with herself makes me light-headed, and I have to wait a moment until some of the blood migrates back up to my brain.

"What about you? Did you date a lot in high school? Were you homecoming king?" she teases.

"Nope. I dated three girls. And homecoming kings in Texas are always football players."

"You didn't play football?"

"Not after ninth grade. I played hockey year round. Coach Death's rink was an hour north and I'd drive there pretty much every day."

"So tell me about these three girls."

"You're that desperate for a distraction?"

"Yes," she says eagerly.

I tap my fingers against the wheel, pulling up my dusty memories. "I dated Emma Hopkins in seventh grade until she got asked to the homecoming dance by a ninth grader. After that, she was only interested in older men."

"This is fascinating. Tell me more."

I grin. I can suffer a little personal embarrassment if it keeps her from worrying about meeting Mom.

"June Anderson was my ninth grade crush. We had nearly all of our classes together, but the clincher was that she could tie a cherry stem into a knot with her tongue. At ninth grade, that was up there with a tightrope walk across the Grand Canyon."

Sabrina laughs. "I think for some guys it still ranks as one of humanity's greatest achievements. I bet Brody lists it as a requirement for hooking up with him."

Her scornful tone doesn't go unnoticed. The first time that

Sabrina and Brody had met didn't go well. It started with him suggesting that her pussy would be destroyed by childbirth and ended with her telling him that regardless of the state of her lady garden, he'd still never be invited to see it.

"That guy is such a douche," she grumbles. "Is it terrible living with him?"

Yep.

"I've had better roommates." Glumly, I think about the awesome time I had in college with Dean, Logan, and Garrett.

My problem with Brody isn't that he's a horndog who chases skirts from the moment he gets up until he passes out at night. I mean, my old roommates slept around regularly. Hell, even I had my share of shenanigans, including a booze-soaked foursome one crazy New Year's Eve. It's hard not to go a little nuts when you're playing hockey at the level we were playing. There was a non-stop stream of girls in the house.

And yet even having experienced three sets of tits rubbing up against me and three tongues on my dick, I'd still pick Sabrina over a drunken orgy any day. That's not really a thing I can tell a girl, though. Not even Hallmark can make a greeting card that conveys the message that you once banged three chicks at the same time, but none of them are as good as her.

Brody's problem is that he has zero respect for the opposite sex.

"Does he really refuse to take selfies with a girl, or was he making that up to toy with me?" Sabrina asks.

"No, that's a real thing for him. He thinks that any pictures of him with a girl pressed up to his side would drive other potential hookups away. Selfies are a sign of commitment." He'd expounded on this topic at some length after instructing me to keep my Tinder account active and to not tell anyone I was having a kid.

"Ugh. He's so gross."

"I signed up for a fake Instagram account so I can troll him. When he posts something, I'll wait a day or so and then pop on to comment about how cool it is that he and my grandpa are rocking the same shirt. I've done that twice now and each time, I've seen him shoving the shirt down the apartment's trash compactor."

Sabrina throws back her head and cackles. "You do not."

"Hey, we all have to get our jollies somewhere, right? For me, it's negging Brody on Instagram and choking my baby mama in breathing classes."

She laughs even harder, her belly bouncing up and down. I reach over and stroke the curve myself. It feels good to see her laughing again.

"Mom's going to love you," I assure her. "You'll see."

MOM HATES HER.

Or at least, she's doing a good job of hiding her love. The initial meeting wasn't so bad. We picked Mom up at the Holiday Inn and drove her back to my apartment, which is thankfully free of Brody at the moment. He and Hollis are celebrating the Fourth in New Hampshire with their family.

On the ride over, Mom and Sabrina had chatted awkwardly, but the tension had been manageable.

Now, that tension is damn near suffocating me.

"Where do you live, Sabrina?" Mom asks as she surveys my two-bedroom apartment.

"With my nana and stepfather."

"Hmmm."

Sabrina winces at this obvious lack of approval.

I shoot Mom an irritated glance. "Sabrina's saving money so her debt won't be too big when she gets out of law school."

Mom raises a brow. "And how much debt will that be?"

"Too much," Sabrina jokes.

"I hope you don't expect John to pay it off for you."

"Of course not," Sabrina exclaims.

"Mom!" I say at the same time.

"What? I'm looking out for you, baby. Just as you'll be tasked with looking out for your daughter." She tips her head toward Sabrina's belly.

Sabrina smiles tightly and decides to change the subject. "I wish we'd been able to come to Patterson. I bet it's a great place to raise children. You certainly did an amazing job with Tucker."

Sincerity bleeds out of every word, and even my mother can hear it. Thankfully, she softens slightly. "Yes, it's a wonderful place. And they have a delightful Fourth of July picnic. This year, Emma Hopkins was the organizer."

"Your old girlfriend, Tuck," Sabrina teases on her way to the refrigerator. "We should've tried harder to fly down."

"The airline wouldn't let us. Besides, we can get drunk and shoot off bottle rockets here, and it'll be just like we were there," I say dryly. "Speaking of drinking—Mom, you want a glass of wine?"

"Red, please," she says, settling into a stool at the counter.

Sabrina pulls out the beef patties she'd carefully constructed earlier today. I'm more than capable of cooking, but she wouldn't allow me to lift a finger. Everything from the potato salad to the baked beans had been prepared by her.

We manage to make it halfway through dinner without any hostility, as Sabrina asks Mom a ton of questions about Patterson, Mom's salon business, and even Dad. It's the stuff about my father that really gets my mother talking.

"He said his car broke down, but I don't believe him," she declares between bites of her burger.

Sabrina's eyes widen. "You think he faked it so he could stay there and get to know you?"

My mother smirks. "I don't think so. I know so."

I've heard the story a thousand times, but it's as entertaining this time as it ever was. More so, actually, because this time Sabrina's the audience and she doesn't believe in love. But Mom's devotion to my father is unmistakable.

"John Senior, Tucker's dad, admitted to it when I got pregnant with Tucker. He said he pulled the spark plug out of the car and that he got the idea from watching *The Sound of Music* with his mama. I even asked Bill—he's the local mechanic—who confirmed that the only thing wrong with John's car was a missing plug."

"That's the most romantic story I've ever heard."

I don't miss the way Sabrina is pushing the salad around on her plate. For the most part, she's done a good job of hiding her ongoing nervousness, but her lack of appetite is a dead giveaway. I make a mental note to fix up a plate for her after I take care of the dishes.

"I'm sorry for your loss," Sabrina adds, her tone soft with sympathy.

"Thank you, sweetie."

I smile to myself. Mom's definitely thawed.

Sabrina turns to me. "How old were you when your father passed? Was it three or four?"

"Three," I confirm, popping a potato chunk in my mouth.

"That's so young." She makes an absent pass of her hand along her stomach.

"You didn't know?" Mom interjects, the chill back in her voice.

"No, I knew," Sabrina fumbles. "I just forgot the exact age."

"Have the two of you talked about anything important, or is it simply a physical thing? Because you certainly can't raise a child on lust alone."

"Mom," I say sharply. "We've talked about important things."

"Will you be living together? How will you share finances? Who will take care of your child when you're in class?"

Sabrina gets a hunted look in her eyes. "I—I... My nana is helping out."

"John says she's reluctant. I'm not sure a reluctant caregiver is a good one."

Sabrina aims a glare of betrayal in my direction.

"I said we didn't know what kind of help she'd offer." I lay down my fork. "It'll all work out." This is directed to both of them, but neither take it well.

"You can't raise a child flying by the seat of your pants, John. I know you want to do the right thing. You always do, but in this case, if the two of you can't take care of it, you should think about other options. Have you considered adoption?"

Sabrina's face goes ashen at the implied insult that she's not up to being a mother.

I reach for her. "Sabrina, it's going to work out—"

But she's already darting out of the kitchen, a sob catching in her throat as she mutters something that sounds like *bathroom* and *sorry*. Her feet slap against the wood floors as she moves faster than an eight-month pregnant woman should.

I jump out of my chair. "Sabrina—"

"Give her some time," Mom says behind me.

A door slams, and I flinch at the sharp sound. I start for the doorway and then stop in the middle of the kitchen and spin around.

"Sabrina's a good person," I say gruffly. "And she's going to make a good mother. And even if she was the worst, you'd still have to accept her because that kid in her stomach is half of me."

This time it's my mother's face that blanches. "Is that a threat?" Her voice quivers.

I drag an agitated hand through my hair. "No. But there's no need for us to be on opposite sides of the ice here. We're all on the same team."

Mom tilts her chin up defiantly. "That remains to be seen."

I shake my head in disappointment before heading down the hallway to see if Sabrina is still talking to me.

Her eyes are red when she opens the bathroom door. "I'm sorry about running out like that."

"It's fine, darlin'." I push her inside and shut the door behind me. She lets me gather her close—or as close as we can get with a bowling ball between us. "You're going to be a great mom. I believe in you."

Her body feels slight despite the weight she's gained. "Don't be mad at your mother," she whispers against my chest. "She's looking out for you. She wants what's best for you. I know that."

"She'll come around." But I sound a hell of a lot more confident than I feel.

31

TUCKER

August

"Oh my God! Oh my *God*! Brody! Yes! Yes, yes, *yes*! Right there, baby! *Oh my Godddddddddd!*"

Not even the full-blast TV volume can drown out the sex noises wafting out of Brody's bedroom. If I had a pair of pliers on me, I'd rip my ears off so I wouldn't have to listen to this anymore. Unfortunately, Brody doesn't even own a toolbox—I found that out when I first moved in and looked around for tools to fix the leaky kitchen faucet with. Brody had shrugged and said, "Shit leaks, man. Life doesn't always give you tools."

I'd wanted to point out that yes, life *does* give you tools—that's why we have fucking Home Depot. But arguing with Brody's logic is an exercise in futility.

I don't know how much longer I can take this. Hollis' brother is impossible to live with. He has a different chick over every night, and they're either porn stars or just very good at articulating what they like, love, and *really* love in bed. He leaves wet towels on the bathroom floor. His idea of cooking is throwing a frozen pizza in the oven, announcing it didn't fill him up, and then ordering an actual pizza.

"Oh gosh, yes! Harder, baby!"

"This hard?"

"Harder!"

"Oh yeah, you dirty girl!"

Jesus H. Christ. I hate this apartment with the fire of a thousand suns.

I heave myself off the couch and head for the door, texting Sabrina as I slip into a pair of flip-flops.

Me: *Hey bb, want me to come over and rub ur back?*

She must have her phone handy, because she texts back right away.

Her: *Not 2nite. Ray has his poker buds over and they're all kinda drunk.*

I frown at the screen. Damn it, I can't stand that she's still living in that house with that creep. But every time I bring up the idea of finding a place together, Sabrina brushes it aside. And she's been kind of distant ever since Mom flew back to Texas.

I love my mother to death, but I'm pissed at her, if I'm being honest. I get that she's worried about me and thinks that having a baby at my age is a terrible idea, but I didn't like the way she interrogated Sabrina. Not just on that first day, either. The whole visit was riddled with passive aggressive remarks and veiled criticism. I think Sabrina felt defeated by the time Mom left, and I'm not sure I blame her.

I send another text.

Me: *Honestly? Don't like the idea of u being around drunk dudes. Ur due date is in 4 days. U need 2 B around responsible adults.*

Her: *Don't worry. Nana's sober as a judge. She doesn't drink, remember?*

At least that's something. Still, I hate not being there with her.

"Oooooooh! I'm coooommming!"

Okay. Enough. I can't stay here for one more second listening to Brody Hollis get his nut off.

Shoving my phone and wallet in my pocket, I stomp out of the apartment and take the elevator down to the lobby. It's past nine, so the August sun has already set and a nice breeze tickles my face when I step outside.

I walk down the sidewalk with no destination in mind, other than *not my apartment*. With the part-time construction jobs, the visit from Mom, and driving back and forth from Sabrina's, I haven't had a chance to fully explore my new neighborhood yet. Now I take the time to do it, and discover that it's not as sketchy as I originally thought.

I pass several cafes with quaint outdoor patios, some nice low-rise office buildings, a handful of nail salons, and a barbershop that I make a mental note to visit one of these days. Eventually I find myself in front of a corner bar, admiring the redbrick facade, the small patio sectioned off by a wrought-iron railing, and the green awning over the door.

The sign is old and dated and slightly crooked. It reads "Paddy's Dive", and when I step past the creaky wooden door, I find a dive, all right. The bar is bigger than it appears from outside, but everything in here looks like it was built, bought, and operated in the seventies.

Aside from one barfly at the end of the long counter, the place is empty. On a Friday night. In Boston. I've never been to a bar, anywhere, that hasn't been jam-packed on a Friday night.

"What can I getcha?" the man behind the counter asks. He's in his early to late sixties, with a shock of white hair, tanned wrinkled skin, and exhaustion lining his eyes.

"I'll have a..." I pause, realizing I'm not in the mood for alcohol. "Coffee," I finish.

He winks. "Living on the edge, are ya, son?"

Chuckling, I sit on one of the tall, vinyl stools and fold my hands on the counter. Okay, wait, bad idea touching this counter. The wood is so weathered that I'm pretty sure I just got a splinter.

I absently pick the sliver of wood out of my thumb as I wait for the bartender to make my drink. When he places a cup of coffee in front of me, I accept it gratefully and glance around the room.

"Slow night?" I ask.

He smiles wryly. "Slow decade."

"Oh. Sorry to hear that."

I can see why that is, though. Everything in this bar is outdated. The jukebox is the kind that still requires quarters—who even uses coins anymore? The dartboards are all punctured with holes so big that I don't think a dart could ever embed into the board. The booths are tattered. The tables are crooked. The floor looks like it could cave in at any second.

And there aren't any TVs. What kind of bar doesn't have a TV?

Yet, despite all its obvious flaws and drawbacks, I see potential in the place. The location is amazing, and inside are high ceilings with exposed beams and gorgeous wood paneling on the walls. A few renos and some modernizing, and the owner could totally turn this place around.

I take a sip of coffee, studying the bartender over the rim of my cup. "Are you the owner?"

"Sure am."

Hesitation has me going silent for a second. Then I set down my cup and ask, "Ever thought about selling?"

"Actually, I'm—"

My phone rings before he can finish. "Sorry," I say hastily, reaching into my pocket. When I see Sabrina's name, I'm instantly on alert. "I need to take this. It's my girl."

The older man smiles knowingly and backs away. "Gotcha."

I press *TALK* and shove the phone to my ear. "Hey, darlin'. Everything okay?"

"No! It's not okay!"

Her shriek nearly shatters my eardrums. The anguish there makes my pulse kick up a panicky notch.

"What's wrong? Are you all right?" Did that son of a bitch Ray touch her?

"No," she moans, and then there's a gasp of pain. "I'm not all right. My water just broke!"

32

TUCKER

There is no worse feeling in this world than seeing the woman you love in pain and being unable to do a damn thing about it.

For the past eight hours, I've been about as helpful as a fish out of water. Or a fish *in* water, because what the fuck do fish really offer to society?

Every time I try to encourage Sabrina to do her breathing, she glares at me like I slaughtered her treasured family pet. When I offer her some ice chips to chew on, she tells me to shove them up my ass. The one time I peeked over Doctor Laura's shoulder at Sabrina's lady parts, she told me that if I did that one more time, she'd break my hockey stick and stab me with it.

The mother of my child, folks.

"Four centimeters dilated," Doctor Laura reports during her latest check-in. "We still have a ways to go, but things are progressing nicely."

"Why is it taking so long?" I ask in concern. "Her water broke hours ago." Eight hours and six minutes, to be exact.

"Some women deliver their babies within hours of the water breaking. Some don't start having contractions as late as forty-eight hours after it. Every labor is different." She pats my shoulder. "Don't worry. We'll get there. Sabrina, let the nurse know if the pain becomes too much for you, and we'll administer that epidural. But don't wait too long. If the baby is too far down the birth canal, it won't do any good. I'll be back in a bit to check on you."

"Thank you, Doc." Sabrina's tone is as sweet as sugar, probably because Doctor Laura is the one who controls the drugs.

And yep, the second the doctor is gone, my woman's smile fades and she fixes me with a scowl. "*You* did this to me," she growls. "*You!*"

I fight a laugh. "Takes two to conceive, darlin'. At least according to science."

"Don't you dare bring science into this! Do you even care what's happening to my body right now? I—" A groan rips out of her throat. "Noooooo! Oh, Tuck, another contraction."

I snap to action, rubbing her lower back just like Hippie Stacy instructed me to. I order her to breathe and count out each breath, while diligently checking the monitor she's hooked up to, which is measuring and timing her contractions.

It passes quickly, and the next one doesn't come for a while, which disheartens me. I read up on the labor process, and it seems like Sabrina is still in the early stages of it. She hasn't even hit active labor yet, and I pray to God that this baby doesn't take days to pop out.

"It hurts," she moans after another contraction ends. There's a sheen of sweat on her face and her lips are so dry they're turning white.

I rub an ice chip over her mouth and lean down to kiss her temple. "I know, darlin'. But it'll all be over soon."

I'm lying. Four more hours pass before she dilates to five centimeters, and then another three before she's at six. That brings the tally to fifteen hours, and I can see Sabrina's energy beginning to drain. Plus, the pain is getting worse. Her latest contraction has her gripping my hand so tight I feel the bones shift.

When it ends, she collapses against the bed in a sweaty mess and announces, "I want the epidural. Fuck, I'll even take the forceps of doom. Just get this baby out of my body!"

"Okay." I smooth her damp hair away from her forehead. "We'll tell Doctor Laura when she comes back to—"

"Now!" Sabrina yells. "Go tell her *now*."

"She'll be here any minute, baby. And the contractions are three minutes apart. We still have time before the next—"

Before I can finish, there's a lethal little hand bunching up my shirt. Sabrina hisses like a cornered jungle cat and murders me with her eyes.

"I swear to God, Tucker, if you don't go find her *right now*, I will rip your stupid head off your stupid neck and FEED IT TO THE BABY!"

Nodding calmly, I pry her fingers off my collar and drop a kiss on her forehead. Then I get the fuck out of there and look for the doctor.

***

THE TALLIES KEEP RACKING UP.

Time in labor: 19 hours.

Time between contractions: 60 seconds.

Number of times Sabrina has threatened to kill me: 38.

Number of broken bones in my hand: who knows.

The good thing is, we're finally at the finish line. Despite getting the epidural, Sabrina is still suffering. Her face is flushed a deep crimson and she's been in tears ever since Doctor Laura instructed her to start pushing. She's not a screamer, though. In bed? Yes. In childbirth, nope. The only sounds she makes are anguished moans and low grunts.

My woman's a trooper.

A few hours ago I was able to duck out of the room to take a leak and text my mother and my friends, but since the hard part began, Sabrina hasn't let me leave her side. That's fine, because I'm not going anywhere until our baby girl is safe and sound in our arms.

"All right, Sabrina, one more push," Doctor Laura orders from between Sabrina's legs. "I can see the head. One more push and you'll get to meet your daughter."

"I can't," Sabrina moans.

"Yes, you can," I say gently, tucking her hair behind her ears. "You've got this. One more push, that's all. You can do it."

When she starts crying again, I cup her chin and meet her hazy eyes. "You've got this," I repeat. "You're the strongest person I've ever met. You worked your way through college, worked your butt off to get to law school, and now you're going to work a teeny bit harder and deliver this baby. Right?"

She takes a breath, fortitude hardening her features. "Right."

And then, after nearly twenty hours of huffing and puffing and blowing the house down, Sabrina delivers a healthy baby girl.

After the tiny, slimy infant drops into Doctor Laura's hands, there's one split second of silence, and then a high-pitched wail fills the delivery room.

"Well, lungs seem healthy," the doctor remarks with a smile. She turns to me. "You want to cut the cord, Daddy?"

"Fuck. Yes."

"Don't swear," Sabrina chides, while Doctor Laura chuckles.

My heart is in my throat as I cut the cord that's tethering my daughter to her mother. I catch a fleeting glimpse of a red gooey thing, but a nurse sweeps her out of sight so fast that I croak out a protest. But they're just weighing her, and while they do, the doc does some discreet stitching between Sabrina's legs.

I ache for everything she's gone through, but Sabrina looks more serene than I've ever seen her.

"Seven pounds, three ounces," the nurse announces as she gently places the baby in Sabrina's arms.

My heart expands to triple its size.

"Oh my gosh," Sabrina whispers, staring down at our daughter. "She's perfect."

She is. She's so frickin' perfect that I'm near tears. I can't take my eyes off her tiny face and the tuft of auburn hair on her tiny head. She's no longer crying, and she's got big blue eyes that stare up at us, curious and unblinking. Her lips are red and her cheeks are rosy. And her fingers are so damn small.

"You did good, darlin'." My voice is hoarse as I reach down to stroke Sabrina's hair.

She peers up at me with a wondrous smile. "*We* did good."

HOURS LATER, we're both lying in Sabrina's hospital bed, marveling over the little creature we brought into the world. It's been about twenty-four hours since Sabrina called to tell me she was in labor. She's supposed to stay here for two nights so the doctors can monitor her and the baby, but both of them seem to be healthy.

A lactation expert stopped by an hour ago to teach Sabrina the proper techniques for breastfeeding, and our daughter has already proven how she's better than every other baby alive, because she latched on right away and suckled happily at her mom's breast while we both watched in pure wonder.

Now she's full and sleepy and lying half in Sabrina's arms, half in mine. Never in my life have I felt more at peace than in this very moment.

"I love you," I whisper.

Sabrina stiffens slightly. She doesn't respond.

I suddenly realize that she probably thinks I'm talking to the baby. So I add, "Both of you."

"Tucker..." There's a note of warning in her voice.

I instantly regret opening my mouth. And since I don't particularly want to hear her say she doesn't love me back or make excuses about why she can't say it, I paste on a cheerful smile and change the subject.

"We really need to pick a name."

Sabrina bites her lip. "I know."

I tenderly run my thumb over our daughter's perfect little mouth. She makes a sniffling noise and stirs in our arms. "Should we tackle the first name or the last name?"

I'm hoping she picks the former. We haven't even discussed first names because we've been too busy arguing about the James-Tucker dilemma.

Sabrina surprises me by saying, "You know...I guess James-Tucker isn't a terrible idea."

My breath hitches. "James Tucker."

"That's what I said."

"No, I mean, that should be her name—James Tucker."

"Are you nuts? You want to name her James?"

"Yeah," I say slowly. "Why not? We can call her Jamie. But the birth certificate will say James Tucker. That way she's equal parts both of us, without the hyphen we both seem to hate."

She laughs and leans in to kiss our baby's perfect cheek. "Jamie... I like it."

And that's that.

33

SABRINA

Little James is in the back of the truck. The nurse waves to us from inside the foyer. I have a bag full of free shit sitting at my feet. Tucker's hands are on the steering wheel. But we're not moving.

"Why aren't we moving?"

Tucker swings his bloodshot eyes toward the backseat. "We have a baby in this truck, Sabrina."

"I know."

He swallows hard. "This is fucked up. We shouldn't be allowed to leave the hospital with a kid. I've never even had a pet before."

I shouldn't laugh at Tucker's misery. In fact, it sort of hurts to do anything but sit in a still, slightly reclined position. But his frustrated, somewhat terrorized expression is so unlike him that I can't stop a giggle from escaping. I cover my mouth to muffle the sound, having learned quickly in the forty-eight hours since the delivery that sleep is a precious and all-too-scarce commodity for new parents.

"I love that you're the one freaking out. Start the car, Tuck. The family behind us wants to leave."

He twists to peer through the back windshield. "They already have two kids. Let's follow them home."

"Let's not."

Gingerly, I reach over to Jamie's car seat and tug the blanket down, because even though baby Jamie is sleeping and I should definitely not disturb her, I can't help but want to stare into her beautiful, wrinkly face again. Her tiny baby mouth is slightly parted and her little baby fists are clenched tight by her side.

"Let's go home," I say firmly. "I want to hold her."

My arms feel empty. Yes, Tuck and I are only twenty-two years old. Neither of us have steady jobs. I'm living at home with my angry nana and my asshole stepfather. Tucker's living with a guy whose dream is to be an extra on the set of *Entourage*. And now we have a child together.

But looking at Jamie's sweet face, all I can think of is how much I love her—and Tucker.

I ease back into my seat and watch as Tucker gets the truck into gear and pulls out slowly. I could walk faster than he's moving the pickup along, but at least we're leaving. Still, it takes us nearly forty-five minutes to make the drive home because Tucker maintains a steady speed of five miles under the speed limit.

"I'm surprised that even the Boston cop flipping you off and honking didn't make you drive faster."

"That asshole should be written up," he retorts. "Stay there and I'll come and help you out."

I've learned in these last ten months that Tucker really gets off on helping me out of the truck, and I'm not gonna lie, I'm getting used to it.

He's got these old-school courtly manners. Like, doors are always held open. I have to walk on the inside of the sidewalk in case there's a drive-by shooting. He even holds my coat.

Mama Tucker raised him right. I could learn a lot from her. And since we're bound together by this child, by her son, I've decided that we're going to get along. No matter how many arrows she slings my way, I'm going to take them and prove to her that I'm good enough to be the mother of her grandchild.

"I wonder if I should get one of those baby-on-board signs. That way the assholes behind me can learn a little patience instead of laying on the horn like we're all in some motherfucking emergency," Tucker grumbles as he helps me out.

"What's going to happen when one of those fuckers comes to your door wanting to take Jamie out on a date?"

Tucker stops abruptly, causing me to collide with his stiff back. "She's going to an all-girls school."

"Okay, so what happens if one of those fuckers is a female wanting to take Jamie out on a date?"

"None of this would be a problem," he accuses, "if we stayed in the hospital like I suggested."

I giggle and brush him aside so I can get to my girl. "She's still sleeping."

His solid frame presses into my back as he leans over to peek inside. "She's so gorgeous. I can't believe we made her," he says quietly against my ear. "I'm buying a chastity belt."

"I don't think she needs one yet."

"I'm thinking ahead." He gently moves me aside to pluck the carrier out of the base.

I arch a brow. "I heard you once had a threesome."

He nearly trips on a non-existent crack in the sidewalk. A light cough precedes his query, "A threesome? Who'd you hear that from?"

Ha! He doesn't deny it. Amused, I brush by him to get the front door. "Carin heard it. Said it was always the quiet ones."

"No threesomes for Jamie," he declares. "Maybe we should homeschool her until she's thirty."

"We're turning into hypocrites."

Tucker nods enthusiastically. "Yup, and no guilt here." Right before he ducks into the house, he murmurs, "By the way, it was a foursome."

I gasp. "Two guys and two girls?"

He smirks. "Three girls and me."

"Wow." I'm more impressed than angry. "Good for you, stud."

Snickering, he pushes into the front hall and kicks off his flip-flops.

Inside, the house is surprisingly quiet. Ray must still be in bed, because the television is on but the volume is low, and instead of ESPN, a game show is playing.

"That you, Sabrina?" Nana calls from the kitchen.

"I'll take the baby to the bedroom," Tucker says, trying to keep as quiet as possible.

I head to the kitchen. "Hey, Nana. I, ah, survived." I raise my hands in a lame victory pose.

She wipes her hands on a towel. Behind her, bacon is sizzling in a pan and the smell of eggs and vanilla fill the air. My stomach rumbles in appreciation. Hospital food is terrible.

"The baby sleeping?"

"Yup." I open the oven door. Thick slices of golden French toast rest in a syrup of peach juice. My mouth waters. "This looks so good."

"You should eat and then go lie down. These first few weeks aren't easy." She nudges me toward the table, her tone and her touch surprisingly loving.

"Do you want to see Jamie?" I ask, trying not to sound too hopeful. Carin and Hope had visited yesterday, whereas Nana had stayed away. It definitely hurt my feelings, but since Nana is my go-to caregiver, I don't want to be a jerk about this.

"She's sleeping," Nana says dismissively. "There'll be time enough for holding when the little thing wakes up. Babies never sleep for long—you have to take advantage of it while you can. Your man here?"

"Right here, Ms. James. What can I help with?" Tucker strides in with purpose, filling up the small room with his tall frame and broad shoulders. Whatever trepidation he had upon leaving the hospital seems to have worn off.

"You sit down too. We're having breakfast. French toast and bacon."

"I wish I could stay, but I have to go. My boss called and one of the crew members fell off a ladder on a job. He said he'd pay me extra if I came on short notice."

"Extra money's good," Nana says with a nod.

Tucker leans down to kiss my cheek. "Walk me out?"

I get up without question and follow him outside to the truck. Now that I don't have a baby bump between us, things feel awkward. He's seen me at my worst, though, and is still sticking around. "Thanks for everything."

"I haven't done much."

"You were there with me. That's a lot."

He runs his thumb along my jawbone. "You were out of it in the hospital. Do you remember much of it?"

Like how you told me you love me?

"I don't remember much," I lie. "I was operating on pure exhaustion."

His face tightens with disappointment. "All right. If you want to play it that way, I'll let it go for now." He opens the driver's door. "I'll see you after work. Call me if you need anything."

I want to tell him I need him to say he loves me when I'm not screaming my head off in pain or when I'm not weeping about how scared I am of motherhood.

A dozen emotions slide and pulse beneath the thin membrane of my self-control. Feeling vulnerable, I step back. "We'll be fine. Come when you can."

From the way his jaw hardens into granite, I know it's not the answer he wants.

With a small wave, I hurry inside, not waiting to see him roar away. In the living room, I find Nana holding Jamie.

"She was crying," Nana says defensively.

"It's fine," I tell her, fighting a smile. "Mind if I hop in the shower? I feel gross."

"You go on ahead." Her gaze is glued to Jamie's face. "This little one loves her grandma, don't you? Don't you?"

With a lightened heart, I hit the shower. Nana's clearly halfway in love with Jamie already. Who wouldn't be, though? She's the most amazing thing in the world.

I take a good, long, hot shower, which they didn't allow in the hospital due to the epidural. Despite the pain, it feels good to be out of that hospital bed. After drying off, I throw on a pair of old sweats and a T-shirt and then examine my reflection in the mirror.

My body still feels weird and not my own. The capillaries in my eyes burst during labor, so I look demonic, all red-eyed and wild hair. I could give Helena Bonham Carter a run for her weird, crazy money. My tummy is still large and round—only now it's squishy and soft. My breasts have grown to enormous, comical sizes.

It's a good thing I can't have sex for six weeks. I can't even look at my post-partum shape without flinching, let alone want *Tucker* to look at it.

"You still doing the breastfeeding thing? I always used formula, and both you and your momma turned out fine." Nana eyes me expectantly as I join her in the living room.

"They've said it's the best."

"Hmmmph. I may've read something like that in *People*. Well, you should probably feed the poor tyke then."

She hands the baby over, and I carefully tuck Jamie against my chest and carry her to my bedroom. Sitting on the edge of the bed, I lift up one side of my shirt, holding it against my chest with my chin, and then lift Jamie up to my boob. She roots around like a little animal until she finds the nipple. Thankfully, she latches on.

I sigh with relief and scoot backward on the mattress until my shoulders hit the wall. The lactation consultant warned me that breastfeeding is hard as fuck—well, she didn't use those words exactly, but that was the gist—so I'm grateful that this is going okay for now.

Picking up my phone, I one-hand type a couple of texts.

Me: *I'm home.*

Hope: *When can I come over?*

Carin: *NO!!!!!!! I haven't finished the booties. Go back to the hospital!*

Me: *U sound like Tucker. He didn't want to leave either.*

Carin: *Listen to ur BB daddy.*

Hope: *She's not going back to the hospital bc UR not done knitting. Hospitals only keep you 2 days for a V birth. How RU feeling?*

Me: *Tired. Scared. Tucker told me he loved me at the hospital.*

Hope: *OMG.*

Carin: *OMG.*

Hope: *What'd u say?*

Carin: *She said she doesn't believe in love, right?*

I stick out my tongue at the phone.

Me: *I pretended I didn't hear him.*

Hope: *OMG.*

Carin: *See!*

Hope: *That's the worst.*

Is it, though? Is it really?

Me: *It was an emotional time. Not holding him to it.*

Hope: *UR dumb. I'm ending my friendship with u.*

Carin: *She's being unselfish.*

Me: *Thank u, C.*

Hope: *UR still dumb.*

Me: *Not dumb. Mom hates me. T's forced to live in Bos. Don't want him tied down. T shld b out there, hitting bars, tapping asses.*

Carin: *I take that back. UR dumb.*

Hope: *See!*

Carin: *You'd kill any chick who looked twice at him.*

An image of Tucker with another woman, holding another baby besides Jamie, forms in my head, and a dull ache springs up in my chest. Carin's not wrong at all. I'm not prepared for Tucker to move on, no matter how nonchalant and uncaring I try to be.

Jamie releases a sharp cry and I peer down to see her precious baby mouth rooting around for the nipple again.

Me: *Gotta go. Baby crying.*

Hope: *Good luck.*

Carin: *Don't wish her good luck. It's not a sporting event.*

Hope: *:P What's the worst response to I <3 you?*

Carin: *Silence and then, "I wish I felt the same."*

Hope: *I'm thinking "Why?"*

Carin: *How about "That's nice."*

Hope: *Brutal.*

Me: *I'm done here.*

Jamie opens her mouth, and the volume that comes out of her lungs surprises even me. It's like there's an amplifier in her throat.

"Shhhh. Shhhh." I whirl around and pluck the blanket out of her car seat. It takes a few tries before I have her bundled up like a burrito. All the while, I'm shushing her. A ton of people online swear by a system called the Five S's where you shush, swaddle, swing, side or stomach position, and...dammit, I can't remember the other one.

Jamie doesn't like that I've forgotten. Her face contorts into a puckered, unhappy mess as she belts out her opinion of my mothering skills.

"Shush, swaddle, swing, side or stomach, sing?" I hum a few bars. Jamie wails on.

"Jesus Christ, what the hell is going on in there?" Ray's up and pounding on my door.

"Come on, Little Jamie. Stop crying. Mommy's here."

Little Jamie doesn't give a fuck. She screams even louder.

"Suck!" I shout in triumph. "Suck is the other one!"

I lunge for the dresser in the corner, where all of Jamie's paraphernalia is stored. The door bursts open and Nana comes bustling in.

"What are you doing to that child?" she yells over the baby.

"Told you she was going to fuck up." Ray's right behind her and can't wait to offer his unwanted two cents.

"Ray, that's enough. You go eat your French toast." Nana pushes me aside. "What're you looking for?"

"Pacifier." I fumble through tiny onesies, blankets, and burping cloths until I find a paci.

"Thought you were breastfeeding," Nana comments as I try to shove the pacifier into Jamie's mouth. Her tongue is stronger than Tucker's ninth grade girlfriend's. I give up after she spits it out for the fifth time.

"What do I do?" I ask Nana in desperation.

"She wants the nip," Ray says from the door.

Is he right? Panicked, I flip up my shirt, not even caring that Ray can see my bare breast. Jamie latches on almost immediately, her whole body shaking from the crying. Small hiccups interrupt her sucks, but at least the crying has stopped. I sag onto the bed in relief.

In the middle of the room, Nana shakes her head. "You shouldn't have ever got her hooked on the boob. Now that's all she's ever gonna want."

"I like it." Ray gives me a smarmy thumbs-up. "Nice tits, Rina."

"Get out," I snap, letting go of my top. Jamie gives a little cry as the fabric falls over her face. "Seriously, just get out. Nana, please."

"You should've used a bottle," Nana chides.

"You should take your shirt off," is Ray's helpful suggestion.

I clench my teeth. "I need some privacy. Please."

"How you going to feed her while you're at class?" Nana asks.

Jamie starts crying again. I pull up the shirt despite the fact that Ray is leering at me. I send another pleading glance to Nana, who finally moves toward the door.

"You go on now, Ray. Your breakfast is going to get cold."

"This isn't going to work, Joy," he mutters. "That kid can't be attached to Rina's tit all day."

"Leave them alone." Nana shoots him a dirty look before addressing me. "Babies cry."

Even before the door shuts, I whip off my shirt. Jamie quiets as I direct my nipple into her mouth. When she latches again, the tension starts to leech out of me.

Holy shit.

I don't know if I can survive this. Her little head is dwarfed by my giant boob, but when her eyes open and her hand starts kneading me, so much love floods through my system that I grow weak.

The whole feeding process takes less than fifteen minutes. It's the only fifteen minutes of peace I have for the next two hours. I can't put her down. Every time I try, she starts to cry, which sets off a bout of screaming between Ray, Nana, and me. So I end up carrying her around, learning to eat with one hand, changing her diaper using three diapers because I tear off the tapes of the first two.

By the time Tucker checks in at noon, I'm an exhausted mess.

"Your daddy's calling," I tell Jamie as she stares at me out of slitted eyes. I've collapsed onto the floor, holding her bundled frame in my arms.

"How's it going?" he asks when I answer the phone.

"I've had better days." I hitch Jamie a tad higher on my shoulder. Her face burrows into my neck. "But I think you're right. We shouldn't have left the hospital."

"There's no going back now."

"You have no idea."

"Tell me about your morning."

And I'm so grateful to hear his calm voice, I nearly burst out in tears. Somehow I manage to hold it together, telling him about how Jamie's going to win Olympic medals in weightlifting because she's already strong as fuck or that she could be a magician because she's able to wiggle out of every blanket I've tried to wrap her in.

Tucker laughs and encourages me, and by the time I get off the phone, I'm convinced I can do this.

34

SABRINA

September

Motherhood is hard. Harder than I ever imagined anything could be. It's harder than studying for my SATs. My LSAT. More challenging than that paper I had to write for the Women's Studies course in my freshman year that came back to me looking like two red pens had engaged in a murder/suicide all over my typewritten words. More tiring than working two jobs and taking a full load of classes for four years.

My respect for Nana is through the roof. If I had to raise one kid after the other, I'd be a little cranky too. But with her help and Tucker's, I've fallen into a routine that seems to work, and by the time the second week of classes launches, I'm convinced I've got this. After all, I'm only in class three hours—at the most—a day. And I'm not working two jobs.

This is easy.

Easy.

Until I stumble out of my last class Friday of that second week, laden with my bottles, tubes, five pounds of books, and my computer with a class assignment of more than a thousand pages of reading for the weekend. They keep piling up. When Professor Malcolm announced we'd need to read the entire chapter on culpability and intent, I waited for someone—anyone—to object. But no one did.

After class, none of my peers appear to be affected by the fact that we're pretty much required to read what seems like an entire semester's worth of coursework in two days. Instead, three kids in my row decide to conduct an intense discussion about Harvard's grading system, which they already should've known about before they even enrolled.

I wait impatiently for them to wrap up the conversation so we can all get the hell out of the classroom. I need to start reading, but more importantly, my breasts feel like they're about to burst. I haven't fed Jamie for nearly three hours and if I don't get to the library's lactation room, I'm going to end up leaking all over my damn shirt.

"I don't like this no letter grades thing. Honors, Pass, Low Pass, and Fail?" grouses the sharp-nosed blond boy next to me.

"I heard that LPs are really discouraged. It's either Honors or Pass. You really have to fuck up to get a Fail," says the girl beside him. Her cheekbones are so fierce they could cut through my entire textbook.

I make a big show of gathering up all my shit and stuffing it into my messenger bag, but no one's moving. Instead, another girl, wearing a peasant skirt that triggers bad memories of Hippie Stacy, chimes in.

"My cousin graduated from here a year ago and said that BigLaw calculates their own grades based on your H, Ps, and LPs, so it works all the same. H is an A, and so forth."

"My big complaint is that only one person gets to be summa cum laude. At any other law school, if you get the grades, you get the designation. Having only one is shitty," Cheekbones declares.

Peasant Skirt reassures her. "You can get the DS, though."

"Still, only a couple people get the Dean's Scholar too."

"They're so stingy with their honors," the guy adds.

I clear my throat. They continue to ignore me.

"But it's Harvard, so the bigs are going to look at you anyway," Cheekbones says with the nonchalance of someone who's secure in her postgraduate prospects. "How soon can you start bidding in EIP?"

"Early interview program?" Peasant Girl smirks. "Settle down, gunner. Second year only. Learn how to write a memo first."

She shares a look of derision with the boy as Cheekbones flushes slightly. It's no fun to be the butt of jokes, which spurs me to unwisely jump in.

"I'm not so worried about the grades as I am the amount of reading we're going to have to do. I'd like to get a head start on it this afternoon." Hint. Hint. Move the hell along, people.

Cheekbones lifts her chin, happy to be the insulter instead of the insulted. "That isn't hard. Hard is picking the right Law Review article topic. Reading and digesting a few cases is a cakewalk."

She turns with a contemptuous swish of hair, gathers her books and leaves me open-mouthed behind her. The two other students follow. The guy whispers to Peasant Skirt, "Hey, I heard there's an application-only study group. I'm interested. How do I get in?"

She sniffs. "If you have to ask, you don't belong."

Lovely. At least we're moving.

My boobs ache as if my body is getting ready to let all the milk out. Hurrying, I move toward the door, brushing by two classmates who have stopped to chat with another student. Don't these kids have anything better to do than stand around and shoot the shit?

Outside, a student is handing out brochures. I grab one and stop in my tracks. It's an invitation to attend an informational course on how to get on Law Review. The meeting is in fifteen minutes. My chest throbs.

"Your shirt's sprung a leak," an amused male voice says.

I drop my chin to see what he's talking about and blanch at the sight of two damp spots right around my nipple areas.

"I don't know what's going on, but maybe you should see a doctor for that infection. That's nasty."

I recognize him instantly. Kale something or other, the asshole from the legal clinic. His hair is Ken-doll neat, plastered to the side of his face. Everything about him screams expensive and privileged. He nudges the guy next to him, who looks utterly grossed out.

I slap the brochure against his chest. "I'm breastfeeding, you douche."

I swear I hear a mooing sound behind me, but when I turn around, both guys are walking away.

It takes me fifteen minutes to walk across campus. With each step, I drip more. My emotions are a cross between embarrassment, anger and frustration. Embarrassment that I'm leaking all over. Anger that I even care what that fuckface thinks. And frustration that all my precious breast milk is filling my bra cups and staining my shirt. Crossing my arms over my chest doesn't do any good. The pressure makes the milk come out faster.

By the time I get to the library, I'm a fucking mess. The reference clerk who holds the keys to the lactation room gingerly hands it over, careful not to make any contact with my flesh.

A woman is just leaving as I arrive. "All yours," she says cheerfully.

"Thanks," is my dour response.

She catches the door as I start inside. "Bad day, huh?"

Her voice is so kind and understanding, I nearly break down. "You have no idea," I answer, but then realize she, of all people, probably does have an idea. "Or maybe you do. But yeah, it's been a shit day."

"Hold on a sec." She digs around in her bag. "Here." She hands me a small plastic package. "I actually have a second set and I've never used them."

"What's this?" I turn the package over, examining the petal-shaped silicon pads.

"You stick them on your nipples and they stop the leaking."

"Seriously?" I gape at her.

"Yep. They're not perfect, and if you wait too long, the milk will eventually wear the adhesion off, but they do work."

I clench the package tight in my fist, filled with overwhelming relief. I have to fight off the tears again. "I would hug you right now if I wasn't all gross. But thank you so much." I spot a distinctive red textbook with black and gold lettering on the spine sticking out of her bag. "1 L?" I ask.

"Third year, actually. I was hoping to wait until I was done with school before this all happened." She waves her hand at the insulated lunch bag she's carrying. Her milk must be in there. "How about you?"

"1 L."

She grimaces. "Good luck, honey. Just remember, every year gets easier after the first one. And the first one is really just a war of attrition." She pats me on the back. "You'll be fine."

I slip inside and attach myself to the medical grade pump. It's a trek to get to Widener Library from the law school, but the pump engine is here, which means I only need to carry my bottles, horns and tubes, and I didn't have to spring for the cost of an expensive portable pumping machine. My checking account is already weeping from the ravaging that my textbooks did to it.

I undo my silk button-down and pull off my bra. I should be grossed out, but I'm too damn tired. I'm mostly vaguely irritated given that it takes twenty minutes for the stupid machine to pull out two ounces of food from my boobs that Jamie doesn't even want to eat.

Rocking in the chair, I pull out my phone to read my texts. Hope and Carin messaged me, but I skip those and tap on Tucker's name.

Tucker: *Went over to see J over lunch.*

Underneath the message is a picture of Jamie sleeping in the crook of his arm. My heart squeezes, and the place between my legs—which I figured was dead from labor—pulses wildly. There's nothing sexier than a loving dad.

Tucker makes all my hormones do a giddy dance.

Me: *She's such an angel.*

Tucker: *I hate leaving her.*

Me: *I leaked breast milk all over my shirt. It was horribly embarrassing.*

Tucker: *Awww. Poor baby. I'll come over later and rub ur back.*

Me: *I have 1000 pages to read and that's not even an exaggeration.*

Tucker: *I'll take care of J. U study.*

Me: *I'll take u up on that.*

Tucker: *Good. U never let me do enough.*

Because I don't want to drive you away.

Of course, I don't type that.

Me: *You're the best dad J could ever ask for.*

Tucker: *U have low standards, babe, but I like it.*

Me: *:)*

Me: *I'm going to take a nap now while all my life blood is sucked out of me. I look like I'm part of the Matrix, plugged into a machine.*

Tucker: *Did u take the red pill or the blue one?*

Me: *Which one makes Jamie go to sleep? That's the one I'll take.*

Tucker: *I'll go buy an rx of Ambien.*

Me: *Too bad I'm not allowed to take that.*

Tucker: *My mom said her mom used to rub brandy on her gums to get her to go to sleep.*

Me: *Hopefully DHS isn't spying on these messages. Did it work?*

Tucker: *I dunno. I'll leave a bottle of brandy next to the Ambien.*

Me: *See. Best dad ever.*

Tucker: *LOL. Go to sleep, darlin.*

HOPE AND CARIN bought me a book called "Go the Fuck to Sleep." I've read it to Jamie a hundred times. It doesn't work. That thing is trash. Over the weekend Jamie decides she's allergic to sleep. The only time she even closes her eyes is when I'm moving.

While I can read and walk at the same time, simultaneous sleeping and walking is beyond my abilities, which is why I start my third week of law school eight hundred pages behind. I drag myself into class, having not read even one word for my contracts class. I made it through criminal law, but that was it.

Hopefully Professor Clive will call on anyone but me today.

"Last week, we went over the first two elements forming a contract. Mr. Bagliano, please share with the class those two elements and the holding of the 1898 *Carlill* case."

Mr. Bagliano, who looks as Italian as his last name sounds, obediently recites the two principles we learned earlier. "Offer and acceptance. The 1898 *Carlill* case discussed whether an advertisement could be construed as an offer. The case was decided by the English Court of Appeals, who held that yes, it was a binding unilateral offer that could be accepted by anyone responding to the advert."

"Excellent, Mr. Bagliano." Professor Clive consults his sheet of paper that I presume has all of our names.

I close my eyes and pray that my name magically disappears.

"Ms. James, tell us the third element of a contract and the holding of the *Borden* case."

As my heart plummets to my stomach, I desperately scan the room as if somehow I can read the answer in the eyes of one of my classmates. No light bulb appears over anyone's head, least of all mine.

Beside me, a guy whose name I haven't made the effort to learn mutters something out of the side of his mouth. It sounds like *confederation*. That doesn't seem right. He coughs "confederation" again into his hand. Nervous laughter spreads across the room while my cheeks light up like twin flames.

Down in the front of the lecture bowl, Professor Clive's lips thin.

"Mr. Gavriel is saying *consideration*, Ms. James." He shifts his gaze to the poor guy next to me. "Mr. Gavriel, since you know the answer, perhaps you can share the holding of the case?"

Mr. Gavriel shoots me a sympathetic look before whipping out his perfectly constructed notes and proceeding to discuss mutuality and illusory promises and other shit that I don't have the first clue about.

I casually draw a notebook over my own chicken scratching where the ink is smeared and bleeding through the page from where I drooled on it when I fell asleep, along with a healthy dose of breast milk and baby spit.

It's hard to hear the last of the lecture with embarrassment roaring in my eardrums, but I take copious notes in the hopes that when I review this crap later, it will all make sense.

After class is over, Professor Clive gestures for me to join him in the front of the room.

He steeples his fingers below his chin. "Ms. James, Professor Fromm shared with me your home circumstance, and while I can appreciate how difficult that must be, the standards in class are not modified due to motherhood."

Stiffly, I reply, "I didn't think that they would be. I apologize about today and promise that there won't be any lapses in the future."

"I certainly hope not, but then again, we grade on a curve and someone has to be on the bottom."

I raise my hand to scratch my neck, not because I itch, but because of the overwhelming urge to flick him off.

"It won't be me," I assure him.

He peers at me for a long, uncomfortable moment before dismissing me with a slight nod. "We'll see."

35

TUCKER

Sabrina shows up at my apartment on Friday afternoon carting enough stuff to fill an entire baby store. Ever since Jamie was born, I've learned I can no longer leave the house with only my wallet, phone and keys.

Nope. Just taking Jamie for a short walk requires a diaper bag overflowing with everything from baby wipes to pacifiers to the tiny stuffed duck that she screams bloody murder if you try to take away from her. Plus the stroller, her hat, extra clothes in case she spits up on herself.

And with all that gear on hand, half the time I don't end up using more than a diaper and bottle, rendering the rest of the stuff useless.

I don't mind, though. I love being a dad. I wish I got to see Sabrina and the baby every day, all day, but right now I only get a few full days a week and my nightly visits to Sabrina's house. Each time I'm there, I offer to spend the night and she gently shakes her head. I think she feels uncomfortable having me around her shady stepfather, and the more I get to know Ray, the more I hate him. The bastard is rude, crude and lewd. He's not a good dude. Yep, Dr. Seuss could write a series of adult rhyming books about that creep.

"Hey." Sabrina pushes the stroller through the narrow front door, and I don't miss the dark circles under her eyes.

When we spoke earlier this morning, she said she hadn't caught a wink of sleep because Jamie woke her up every other hour. Our daughter has a voracious appetite, and I know for a fact that she loves Sabrina's tits as much as I do, because whenever you try to bottle feed her with breast milk, it takes twice as long as when she's on the breast.

"Hey. How's my girl today?" I ask with a smile.

"Surprisingly chipper considering she kept me up all night."

"I meant you, darlin'." Rolling my eyes, I lean in to kiss her.

She's wearing some fruity-tasting lip-gloss—strawberry, I think. And it's so delicious that I dip my mouth for another taste. I swipe my tongue over her bottom lip and groan softly.

Fuck, I want to stand here and kiss her forever. Or even better—rip her clothes off and lose myself in her body for a week straight. But our six weeks aren't up, and even if they were, I'm not sure Sabrina even wants sex. She's so tired all the time, well on her way to becoming a zombie.

I don't know how she's managing to attend classes, get her reading done, write papers, and still be there for our daughter. It's a testament to her strength and determination, I guess, though I wish she'd let me do more to ease her stress. Hell, even asking her to come over today, where she can study in silence while I take care of the baby, required a thirty-minute debate before she eventually caved. She's having a tough time studying at home, with her grandmother constantly chatting her ear off about what the Kardashians are up to while Ray stumbles in and out of the kitchen to get a fresh beer.

Here, I have a roommate who works during the day, so it's nice and quiet. Plus, I haven't been getting much construction work lately due to a recent spate of non-stop rain, so this last week I've been at home, bumming around and researching various business ventures.

When a disgruntled squawk comes from the stroller, I chuckle softly.

"The little princess doesn't like being ignored, huh?" I squat in front of the stroller and carefully undo the various snaps and buckles that are keeping Jamie secure. Then I lift her into my arms, one hand cupping her tiny butt, the other supporting her neck as I hold her up in front of me.

As always, the sight of her takes my breath away. She's the most beautiful baby in the world. Even my mom says so. I send her pics every day and she's constantly marveling about the perfection that is James Tucker. Mom is dying to meet Jamie in person, but she can't get away until the holidays, which are still a couple of months out. For now, the daily pictures seem to be pacifying her.

"How's Daddy's little angel this morning?"

Jamie gurgles and flashes me a toothless smile. And yes, it's *totally* a smile. Sabrina keeps insisting it's gas, but I think I know when my own daughter is grinning at me, thank you very much.

I kiss her impossibly soft cheek and she nuzzles her sweet face against my pec. A sharp sting immediately jolts through my nipple. I yelp as her eager mouth tries to latch on.

Shit, I forgot I wasn't wearing a shirt. Brody doesn't like to turn on the air conditioning if we don't have to, so most of the time we leave the windows open. I've taken to walking around in basketball shorts and nothing else.

"Easy, darlin'," I chide, easing her face away.

Her mouth opens and closes rapidly as she tries to suck on air, which melts my heart.

I look up to share a smile with Sabrina, only to find that her dark eyes are glazed and her mouth is hanging open.

I wrinkle my forehead. "What?"

It takes her a second to answer. When she does, her voice is a tad husky. "You've just provided me with about hundreds of hours' worth of spank bank material."

I choke out a laugh. "Jesus, Sabrina. You're getting off on our daughter trying to nurse on me?"

"No, I get off on *that*." She gestures to us.

I still don't get it.

"A gorgeous, bare-chested man holding a tiny infant?" she prompts. "It's the hottest thing I've ever seen in my life."

Damned if my dick doesn't stiffen beneath my shorts. "Yeah?" I say slowly.

"Oh yeah." She sighs. "Damn you, Tuck. Now I'll never be able to concentrate on Contracts today."

"I'll put on a shirt," I offer graciously.

"You do that." Sabrina sets down the diaper bag, but holds on to the messenger bag hanging off her other shoulder. She stalks toward the living room table, drops the bag, and starts taking out her books.

I whistle under my breath. Man, she's been lugging around that heavy diaper bag in one hand and all those textbooks in the other? She's the freaking Hulk.

"How was class this morning?"

"Long-winded." She glances over her shoulder. "Should I study out here or in your room?"

"You might as well stay out here." I shift Jamie to my other arm, loving the small weight of her and the little cheek pressed against my bare shoulder. "I was thinking of taking the princess for a walk around the block."

Sabrina nods. "Okay, but make sure you keep her out of the sun."

I nod back. We've both read the same books, so I know direct sunlight is harmful for babies. Whenever I take Jamie out, I make sure she's wearing her hat and is hidden safely beneath the stroller's shade screen. I pretty much treat her like she's a vampire.

"Mind holding on to this precious cargo while I throw on a shirt?"

Sabrina opens her arms, and I deposit Jamie into them. My chest turns to hot goo as I watch Sabrina bend down to smack tiny kisses on Jamie's cheeks and forehead. In response, Jamie wiggles around like a worm and pumps her fists in the air. She hasn't learned to laugh yet, at least not with her vocal cords, but I've discovered that her squirming body is a sign that she's having fun.

I duck into my room and throw on a wife beater, then roll on a pair of athletic socks and shove my wallet and phone in my back pocket. In the front hall, I lace up my sneakers before collecting Jamie and her mountain of stuff. Once she's buckled up in the stroller, I wheel it toward the door, while Sabrina gives us a little wave.

"Study hard, Mommy," I tease.

"Have fun," she answers absently. She's already scribbling something on a yellow legal pad, her gaze focused on one of her law books.

It takes a bit of strategic maneuvering to push the stroller into the cramped elevator. A few minutes later, Jamie and I stroll along the sidewalk. The sun has decided to duck behind a thick gray cloud, leaving the sky overcast, so I raise Jamie's shade screen a couple inches so she can enjoy the scenery.

And she's not the only one enjoying it. Another thing I've learned since I had a kid? Women go nuts when they see me with the baby.

Every time I'm pushing the stroller down the street, I find myself with dozens of groupies. Chicks will stop me out of nowhere to gush and coo over Jamie. They almost always scope out my hand to check for a wedding ring and then nod in satisfaction when they don't see one. The bolder ones have zero problems flat-out asking if the little angel's mom is still in the picture.

They're always thoroughly disappointed when I inform them that the mother is very much in the picture. Then I'll flash a polite smile, bid them good day, and keep on walking. The one time Logan joined me for one of these strolls, he'd shaken his head in amazement, remarking that it was a shame none of us were single, because Jamie's a chick magnet.

My friends adore her. I know they wish they got to see her more often, but we've all got our own busy lives to lead. Since the hockey season started, Garrett's been practicing hard and is constantly on the road for away games. Logan's training equally hard with the development team, and he and Grace are still settling in to their new apartment. Despite that, they all drive out to see Jamie any time they have a free moment. Hannah, especially, who's only working part-time at the moment and writing songs on the side.

"Hey, look at that, little darlin'," I tell my daughter as we stop at the crosswalk. "It's a doggie."

Said doggie tries to sniff the stroller as he and his owner sidle up to us. And damn, I should've kept my mouth shut, because now I've attracted the owner's attention.

"Oh my! Look at this precious little angel!"

She crouches down and starts pawing at Jamie, which makes me bristle. Is this normal? Strangers constantly trying to touch your baby? Because it happens way too often for my liking.

The woman presses a kiss to Jamie's tiny fingers, and I make a mental note to wipe them down the second we're out of sight. Hell, I'd hose her down if I didn't think it'd hurt her. I don't want all these germs all over my kid.

"What's her name?" the woman asks.

"Jamie." I stare steadily at the crosswalk signal, willing the little green man to pop up before the chick starts flirting.

"And what's her daddy's name?"

Too late. "Tucker, but my wife calls me Tuck."

That shuts her up fast. Normally I'm not this rude during these random street pick-ups, but I really don't like the way she touched my child without permission. Fuck that.

Once the light turns green, I swiftly push the stroller forward, murmuring goodbye at the woman and her dog.

"Well, at least the doggie was cute, right, darlin'?"

She doesn't answer, but it doesn't matter. I've taken to carrying on entire conversations with this kid. I find it kind of soothing.

"See that over there? That's a swing set," I inform her as we walk by a small park. "When you're a bit older, Daddy's gonna take you there and push you on the swing."

I walk two more blocks, speeding up when we near an adult toy store. "And *that's* a place you'll never go into," I say cheerfully. "Because you're never, ever going to have sex, right, princess?"

There's a loud snort.

I glance over my shoulder to see an elderly couple walking behind me. They remind me a bit of Hiram and Doris. Man, I wonder what those two are up to. I kind of wish we'd gotten their contact info after that kickass naked painting date.

"Good luck with that," the man calls to me with a crooked grin.

"Four daughters," the woman confirms. "Poor Freddie over here couldn't convince a single one of 'em to stay virgins."

I grin back. "Obviously he didn't try hard enough. Did you consider purchasing a shotgun?"

The couple roars with laughter.

Jamie and I keep strolling for a few more minutes, until I suddenly come to a dead stop at a familiar corner. I haven't been to Paddy's Dive since the night Sabrina went into labor, but somehow I've found my way back to it now.

And there's a FOR SALE sign in the window.

36

SABRINA

"I'm sorry I'm late," I apologize as I slide into a chair at Della's. Carin and Hope already have their drinks, and by the pool of condensation on the table, I'm later than I realized. Or they were early. Ever since Jamie was born, I have a hard time getting anywhere on time.

"Where's the baby?" Carin asks, dismissing my tardiness with an airy wave of her hand.

"She's with Nana." I grab the menu, quickly searching it for the juiciest, meatiest thing I can find.

Both girls pout. "We wanted to see the baby!" Hope cries.

"Yeah. The whole point is for you to bring Jamie so we can coo over her. I'm almost done with the booties." Carin pulls out a mess of yarn that looks nothing like a shoe or even a sock.

"What is that thing?" I lay down the menu to get a better view of the object she's holding up. It's kind of like the wool equivalent of Logan's horrifying teddy bear.

"It's a sock. Is it too big or too small?" She stretches it out and I vaguely see something shiplike in the mess.

"It's...are you sure that's a sock?"

Hope giggles behind her menu.

Carin scowls at me. "Have you ever tried knitting? It's hard as fuck, thank you very much." With a sniff, she stuffs the mottled mess in her bag.

"Besides knitting, which I do appreciate, how's MIT?"

Hope lights up. "Carin knocked *beard* off her bucket list."

"Nice." I give her a thumbs-up. "Tell me about it."

"Nah, it's nothing." Carin lifts the menu up to hide her face.

"Mr. Beard is Carin's TA," Hope explains. "She thinks you'll be pissed."

"He's not my TA," Carin objects.

"Okay, fine," Hope relents. "He's the TA in another class, which Carin will likely take next year."

"Eh. I'm fine with it." I pick up my menu again and study my choices.

I'm torn between the burger with blue cheese and the Philly steak sandwich. Can I even eat blue cheese? I lower the menu to ask Hope, only to find my friends staring at me.

"What?" My eyes drop to my chest in a panic. "Am I leaking?" No, my shirt is dry, thank God. Those little silicon nip pads are working great.

"We thought for sure you'd be upset over this because of the Dean thing," Carin explains.

"Dean and I kind of made up." If me breaking down and Dean giving me awkward pats on the back counts as making up. Which, in my book, does. Plus, as far as I know, he hasn't said a word to Tucker about the fact that I'm madly in love with the guy.

"Well, that's good."

The waitress shows up and we all order. Hope gets a salad, Carin orders soup and salad, and I order the Philly cheesesteak with a side of fries because I'm so hungry.

"How's med school?" I ask Hope.

"It's going okay. The course load is crushing."

"I hear you."

"Med school is sapping all my energy to the point that I don't have time for D'Andre. He keeps talking about skiing from sunup to sundown over Christmas break, and all I want to do is lie in front of the lodge fireplace and sleep. I don't know how you're doing it."

"I wouldn't be able to do it without Tucker. He's always there. Well, most of the time," I correct. Because lately, he's been really busy and I've been quietly panicking.

Hope frowns. "Oh no. Is there trouble in paradise?"

"No, not really. He's doing more than I ever dreamed of, actually. It makes me feel guilty."

"Oh fuck that," Carin says. "This is his kid too. Is he slacking off? Because I will kick his ass from here to the harbor for you."

"No, not at all. It's..." I pause, hesitant to give my fear a voice, as if saying the words will make them true. But these two are my closest friends, so I give in to the urge. "I think he's found someone else."

"No." Hope denies it immediately. "When would he have the time? You said he comes over almost every night and you see him on the weekends too."

"That's just it. Before, he was around all the time, but in the past couple weeks, he's been really busy."

"Maybe there's a bunch of builders trying to get projects done before the snow comes," Carin suggests. "And so everyone's working double shifts or something."

"Maybe." I heave a sigh. "It's not just that he's not around as much. He's distracted and quiet, more so than usual. I feel like he wants to tell me something but is afraid of how I'll take it."

"Just come out and tell him you love him," Hope orders, shaking her fork at me. "Actually, I'm shocked you haven't slipped up and done it already. Even in texts and stuff."

"It's beyond hard," I admit. "The other day he was reaching for a glass of water and his shirt slipped up and I almost dropped to my knees with lust. And when he's with Jamie? It becomes nearly impossible. He was sitting on the couch the other night, feeding her. And I started to say *I love you* and caught myself, but not before I had the first two words out. I ended up saying *I love your socks*."

"I love your socks?" Carin exclaims.

"It's beyond ridiculous. I know."

"Why don't you just tell him?"

"Because if I tell him, then he'll feel bound to me. He's so honorable and so decent, he won't even look at another woman."

"Just come out and ask him if he's seeing anyone. If he says no, then tell him you want him all to yourself," Carin advises. "If he says yes, at least you know. It's better to know than to drive yourself nuts wondering."

"Certainty is best," Hope agrees.

I give them a tight smile and change the subject by asking Carin more about the hot, bearded TA she's currently banging. She happily obliges, although all the sex talk reminds me of how little of it I've had lately. It was hard to find a position that was comfortable before I had the baby, and now that the six-week ban has been lifted, I'm not sure I want Tucker seeing my body. He's used to hot, college girls with zero body fat and abs of steel. I'm more like abs of Jell-O at this point.

Our food finally arrives. I dig in, under the pretense that I'm starving, but mostly I'm hiding from my friends because I don't agree with their advice. Knowing Tucker loves someone else will break me.

I'd rather go my whole life in limbo than have him tell me that he's fallen in love with a woman who isn't me.

WHEN I GET HOME, Nana is napping with Jamie, allowing me to get a few hours of studying in before dinner. Ray's on the sofa, blaring the television, which means I can't read in the kitchen. I'm getting tired of being shut in my cramped bedroom with the crib, my twin bed, and a thousand and five baby items, but I don't have much of a choice. Sticking a pair of earplugs in, I manage to read through all of my crim law and torts before I hear the thin wail of my hungry child.

"You home, Sabrina?" Nana calls through the door.

I hop up and greet her. "Yup. Got home a couple hours ago. You two were sleeping." I reach out and pluck Jamie from her arms. My baby doll whimpers and roots around, mouthing me over my shirt. "I better feed her."

"You do that. I'm going to run to the store for a few things. We're almost out of milk and cheese."

"'Kay." I start to close the door, but Nana stops me.

"You should get out of there," she says, peering over my shoulder into the confined space. "You'll go nuts."

"It's fine," I reply, even though she's right. The room is feeling smaller every day.

She shrugs, her body language telling me that it's my funeral.

Before I get the door closed, I hear her yell at Ray. "That TV is too loud, Ray. It'll hurt the baby's ears."

He mumbles something indistinguishable. I'm sure it's some variation of "fuck the baby."

Three more years. Three more years and then I'll land that BigLaw job and get the hell out of this place.

Nana and Ray exchange a few more terse words—her voice is sharp and his is angry. The energy in this house is so damn negative.

I cuddle Jamie closer to me. "We're going to get out of this place soon."

She cries, a plaintive, hungry sound. I unbutton my shirt and pull it to the side, bouncing her in my arms as I do. She keeps crying, though.

A moment later, Ray pounds on my door. "Shut that fucking baby up. My game is on."

I close my eyes and pray for patience. Jamie shouts her annoyance and I look down to discover that the silicon nipple pad is hindering her efforts to feed. I rip it off and throw it on the dresser.

Ray knocks again. "I'm talking to you, Rina!"

I wrench open the door, Jamie latched on to my boob, and confront the asshole. "She's a baby, not a machine. I don't turn her on and off at will, okay? And it's not like I enjoy hearing her cry, you asshole. I'm doing everything I can to make her happy."

"Doesn't look like you're good at anything but being a suck toy," he grunts. His hot beer breath washes over me.

Anger burns in my gut. I swing the door closed, but it bounces back toward me as he slams his hand against it.

"Get out," I order. I don't want this man anywhere near my daughter, and I don't care if I have to kick him in the balls to make that clear.

Ray's not much taller than me and is skinny as a rail, but he manages to kick the door out of my hand and stalk forward.

I back up, my legs hitting the mattress. "Get out," I repeat.

My heart starts beating rapidly. Ray has never been violent, never raised a hand to me, but in this moment, the look in his eyes makes every hair on my body stand on end. I clutch Jamie closer to me. She whimpers and I force myself to loosen the hold.

"Your tits are huge." His tongue peeks out from between his lips.

I draw one side of my shirt closed. But the other one still has Jamie latched to it.

"What's that milk taste like?"

A chill races down my spine. My milk is sweet, but the fear tastes like copper against my tongue. "You need to leave right now," I growl.

"You've got two tits and only one mouth on 'em." He reaches toward me, slowly and creepily.

I scramble backward, keeping a protective hold on my daughter. "Stay away from us, Ray. I mean it. Come any closer and I swear I'll rip your eyes out."

"Why don't you give me a taste? I've been thinking about what a juicy piece you must be. And I've had your mama and your grandma. Why not the youngest? It'll be my Ray Donaghy hat trick."

I reach behind me in search of a weapon, but the need never

materializes. Instead, there's a roar at the door, and then a six-foot, three-inch torpedo launches itself at Ray and spins him around.

Tucker drives a fist into Ray's face before the bastard even realizes there's another person in the room with us.

I huddle in the corner, drawing a blanket up over my chest as if to cover Jamie's eyes from the scene in front of her. Tucker throws Ray against the wall, lifting my stepfather's skinny ass up with one strong hand against his throat.

"You sick fuck. You're lucky my kid and woman are in this room right now or I would fucking *end* you."

His grip tightens, and as much as I think Ray deserves to have the snot choked out of him, I don't want Jamie visiting her daddy in a Massachusetts state prison for the next twenty years.

"You should really wait until after I'm done with law school to kill Ray," I tell Tucker, weak with relief.

He squeezes Ray's throat once more before letting the creep drop to the floor.

"Come on," Tucker barks, turning to me. His pupils are dilated and his nostrils flare as he struggles to gather his composure. "We're out of here."

I don't argue.

"HOW LONG HAS that been going on?" Tucker demands as he pulls out of the driveway. I turn away from Jamie's gurgling, happy face and meet his grim expression.

"Ray being an asshole? Since the beginning of time. Him trying to feel me up while I was feeding Jamie? That's the first."

Although his creepiness must have always been in the back of my mind or else I wouldn't have felt compelled to hide in my bedroom all the time.

"You can't stay there," Tucker says flatly.

I drag a shaky hand over my face. "I don't have another option at this point. Babies are expensive and my bank account is bleeding out. Hope gave me this diaper cake and it had like two hundred and fifty diapers—I laughed when I counted them. Well, I used that up in the first three weeks. And you're living with Brody, who pretends his bedroom is a Cirque de Soleil tryout, complete with the accompanying soundtrack."

"I know." Tucker bites his lip. "I wasn't ready to do this because I wanted to wait for the right time, but I'm going to have to."

I gnaw nervously on the inside of my cheek. "The right time for what?"

Is he breaking up with me?

Oh God.

I fight the urge to vomit all over the inside of Tucker's clean truck.

"For this." He stops the pickup in front of a corner bar. It's classic Boston with its redbrick exterior, green awning and a postage-stamp sized patio toward the rear.

"I can't drink while I'm breastfeeding," I remind him.

"Yeah, hold that thought," he says, and then slides out of the truck.

As he's pulling Jamie out of her carrier, I climb down and meet him on the sidewalk. "We can't bring a baby into the bar."

"We're not." He places his hand on my lower back and steers me toward the side of the small building. There's a set of stairs leading up to the second floor. "Go on," he says when I hesitate.

"Did you rent an apartment?" I try to keep the worry out of my voice. It's his money and he should do what he wants with it, but renting a place by himself because I'm having problems at home seems like a waste of his money. "Because Ray's all talk and no action."

"Right. Like him attacking you in your bedroom was all a bunch of words."

"He was drunk." Jeez. Why am I even making excuses for that psycho?

Tucker gives me another shove. "Are you going to drag your ass upstairs or do I have to carry the both of you?"

"I'm going." I cave. The doorknob turns under my hand and I notice a freshly installed electronic keypad.

"It works via near-field communications," Tucker informs me.

"English, please."

"It unlocks when a paired device is close to it. That way if you have your hands full, you can still get in."

"Cool," I say faintly. And that's only the first of many surprises.

Upstairs, I find a huge two-bedroom apartment. The kitchen is small and the appliances are old, but there are windows everywhere. The living room is filled with dust and exposed brick.

"I've been tearing down the drywall." Tucker gestures at the walls. "I haven't touched the bedroom because I figured you'd want a say, but the stuff in here was rotting. Come on."

This time he takes the lead. Down the hall are two bedrooms. He pushes open the first one, drops the carrier inside the door, and then kneels down to pull sleepy Jamie out. The little pill always falls asleep in the car.

I creep toward the door as if there's a serial killer behind it. But the only thing I find is a beautifully decorated nursery.

"Oh my gosh," I breathe.

It's painted a pale pink. White curtains hang over the big windows. An off-white crib sits against one wall, and a dresser with a changing table is pushed up against another. Between them is an upholstered glider, one that I'd sighed over and posted on my Instagram account.

I shoot an astonished look at Tucker, but he's too busy loving up Jamie. God, he's too gorgeous for words. His biceps is bigger than her head, but he's as gentle as a lamb with her.

That whole picture is Tucker, though. Strong, steady, with exactly the right touch to make his ladies melt. I know I do.

I wrench my gaze away from his bent head so I don't launch myself at his poor unsuspecting frame. To my right, at the end of the room, a door sits slightly ajar. I head over to investigate and find an en suite bathroom. It's too much.

"What's going on? Did you win the lottery?"

He gives me a crooked smile. "Nope. I bought a bar. This came with it."

"This?" I wave my hand around the room. "The pink room, the crib, the electronic keypad entry!"

"Okay, the building came with an apartment. I'm not done with the renos up here. That's going to take a while. I was hoping to surprise you around November when the bar opened."

Feeling weak, I lean against the wall. "I don't know what to say."

He strides across the room and tucks a hand under my chin. "Say that this is home. For you, Jamie, and me."

I close my eyes so he can't see the emotion in them—the relief, the gratitude, the overwhelming love I have for him. I don't deserve him. Not one bit, but for some reason he wants me in his life.

I turn my face into his palm and press my lips against the warm skin. "I love this place. It's amazing. You're amazing." And because I can't help myself, I rise up on my tiptoes and throw my arms around his neck. "Thank you."

One muscular arm clutches me close while the other holds our baby close. "This is going to work," he murmurs. "You'll see."

I hope so. God, I hope so.

37

TUCKER

November

"Holy shit! This place is *sick*."

I flush with pride at Logan's exclamation. Weeks of hard work have led to this moment, but my backbreaking efforts are made all the more worthwhile as I witness my friends' reactions.

And I'm so fucking touched that everyone showed up to be here for me tonight. Dean and Allie rode in on the train from New York, and Coach Jensen actually canceled an evening practice so that all my former Briar teammates could attend my big opening.

But the most important guests are my two girls. Jamie's strapped to my chest in a BabyBjorn, wearing a custom-made pink onesie that reads "Tucker's Bar" in gold glitter.

Sabrina is beside me, dressed a little less fancy in faded jeans and a tight green sweater. Her full tits are nearly pouring out of the deep V-neckline, and every time I glance her way my dick turns to granite.

I almost wish she was still moaning about the baby weight she's carrying and refusing to let me touch her, because even though she doesn't have her pre-baby body back, I'm horny twenty-four/seven.

"Hitting the head," Logan says. "BRB."

As he disappears into the crowd, Garrett sweeps his gaze over the packed bar. "I can't believe how well the renovations turned out," he marvels.

I look around, trying to see the room through his eyes. After I'd completely restored the wood paneling and exposed beams, I went on a hunt for sports memorabilia to hang on the gleaming walls. This isn't technically a sports bar, but hey, I'm a hockey player. I can't *not* have framed photos of athletes in my bar.

And it helps to have friends in high places. Garrett got me signed jerseys from several of his new teammates—many of whom are here tonight. One of the chicks by the pool table wasted no time blasting it on social media, and within an hour of opening my doors, I had people lining up to get in, hoping to land an autograph or chat up the professional hockey players.

The groupies, however, have been surprisingly unobtrusive, letting Garrett's teammates drink in peace without harassing them too much. I appreciate that, because the vibe I'm going for is "neighborhood bar." A place where people can come after work (or hockey practice) and just relax. Somewhere that's not too loud and not too rowdy.

So far, it's exactly what I wanted it to be.

"Thanks for all your help," I tell Garrett, who shrugs off my gratitude. He deserves it, though. He gave up way too many days off to come here and help me rip up flooring and gut the bathrooms.

"You too," I say to Fitzy, who drove to Boston every weekend after I bought the bar, crashing on the floor of Jamie's nursery and waking up at ungodly hours to help me out.

I hired people to do the jobs that my friends and I couldn't do ourselves. Staffed the place too, since I have no interest in tending bar unless I have to; management is more my thing. Samira and Zeke, the two bartenders working tonight, are awesome. They already bicker like an old married couple and this is only their first night working here.

"It was fun," Fitzy grunts before taking a sip of his Coors.

"Dude," Dean says, coming up to slap Fitz on the shoulder. "That was a hell of a game last weekend. You guys crushed Yale."

Fitzy frowns. "You saw it in New York? I didn't realize it was televised."

"Naah, someone was live-tweeting it. I was tracking his posts."

So was I, actually. I'd wanted to drive out to Briar to watch it live, but Jamie had been fussy the night before, and Sabrina and I were wiped. The team's kicking ass this season, though. Last year's shitty record is all but forgotten now that Briar is on a five-game winning streak.

"Hunter scored a total beauty in the third," Hollis says from his stool. "I almost came in my pants."

"Don't be crude in front of the baby," I say immediately.

"Bro, you brought a baby to a *bar*. Go throw glass stones in your own house." When everyone snickers, Hollis is visibly confused. "What?"

"That's not the phrase," Hannah says helpfully.

"Sure it is."

"It's really not."

Hollis waves a hand. "You know nothing, Jon Snow."

She sighs and wanders off to the booth where Allie, Hope, Carin and Grace are sitting. "You coming?" she asks Sabrina over her shoulder.

"Yup." My woman glances at me. "Want me to take her?"

"No way," Dean says instantly. "You can't take her away from us! She's barely spent any time with her uncles!" He plucks Jamie out of the BabyBjorn and snuggles her up against his chest. "Give your Uncle Dean a kiss, princess."

Sabrina rolls her eyes as Dean presses our daughter's mouth to his cheek and proceeds to make kissing noises as if she's actually smacking him a good one.

"I'll be over there with the normal people," Sabrina says dryly, then heads for the girls' booth.

My friends pass Jamie around amongst themselves until eventually she ends up in Fitzy's arms. Since he's wearing a T-shirt, his tattoos are fully visible, and for some reason they fascinate the baby. Every time he holds her, she stares wide-eyed at the tats and forms an O with her red rosebud mouth.

"Jesus, that's one cute kid," Garrett says, shaking his head.

Logan returns from the bathroom to hear Garrett's remark. "Right? I swear, I was so fucking worried he'd end up with an ugly baby and then I'd have to fake it. Day before I met her, I was practicing '*Awwwwww! She's so cute!*' for an hour in the mirror."

I flip him off.

"It's true—ask Gracie. And relax, man. I didn't have to lie, did I? She's fucking precious."

"Tuck's got magic sperm," Dean agrees.

Hollis snorts. "No, Tuck's got a smokin' hot baby mama. Genes, bro."

"Speaking of the baby mama..." Dean cocks a brow at me.

I frown. "What about her?"

"You two officially together or what?"

"We live together," is all I can think to say.

"Okay. But that doesn't answer my question."

My gaze strays across the room. Sabrina is laughing hysterically at something Hope just said. With her bottomless dark eyes and flawless face, she's hands-down the hottest woman in this bar. I fucking *ache* for her. And yeah, I love her. So much it hurts.

But damned if I'm going to say it again after she totally brushed it off the night she delivered Jamie.

"We're together," I finally say. "Is it serious?" I shrug. "I want it to be. But I'm following her lead."

Dean wears a troubled expression, but he doesn't say anything more on the subject. Instead, he changes it completely, turning to grin at Fitzy. "Hey, I keep forgetting to text you, but I should probably give you a heads up about something."

"A heads up about what?"

"Remember Summer?"

"What about it?"

Dean laughs. "Not it. *Her.* My sister Summer."

I hide a grin when I see Fitzy narrow his eyes. It's no secret that Summer Di Laurentis's visit last winter had freaked him out. I wasn't there to witness it, but apparently Dean's incredibly forward sister had all but thrown herself at the big guy.

"What about her?"

"She's transferring to Briar next semester."

Fitzy's face turns as white as Jamie's spit-up. Which is pooling on the sleeve of his T-shirt. He hasn't noticed it yet, and I'm hoping someone else points it out so I don't have to.

"Why?" Fitzy is clearly speaking through clenched teeth.

Dean sighs. "She officially got kicked out of Brown. Or rather, politely asked to leave, as she likes to phrase it. But yeah, my dad is friends with the head of admissions at Briar, so he called in a favor. Summer will be there starting January."

"Does she still want to see Fitzy's dick?" Hollis pipes up.

The owner of said dick passes my baby back to me, then picks up his beer bottle and chugs the entire thing.

My grin surfaces. Poor guy. The ladies go wild for Colin Fitzgerald, but in all the years I've known him, he's been incredibly selective about who he goes out with. I think deep down he's as old-fashioned as I am.

"Tuck!" Zeke calls from behind the counter. "Got a quick question for you about this drink menu!"

I slide Jamie back into the Bjorn and gesture to my friends that I'll be a minute. Then I dart off to take care of business. *My* business.

"HEY," Sabrina says hours later, smiling at me as I stagger into our bedroom.

She's lying in the middle of the bed with a textbook in her lap, a sight that doesn't surprise me. Sabrina takes her studying any way she can get it, and the best times for her to do it are when Jamie's asleep. Most nights, she'll have her nose buried in a book long after I've fallen asleep.

The good thing is, now that the bar renovations are done and I'm officially open for business, I'll be able to take care of Jamie during the day while Sabrina is in class, and then we'll switch off—she'll be on baby duty while I go downstairs to work. We don't have the easiest schedules, but we're doing our best. And shit's been a lot easier since she moved in with me.

Well, easier *and* harder. I'm still not sure where we stand. We haven't had sex in three months despite sleeping in the same bed. One of us is usually pacing the nursery with Jamie while the other catches up on much-needed sleep. She hasn't told me she likes me, let alone loves me. Sometimes I think she does, but other times it feels like we're just two people who happen to be raising a child together.

But the one thing I know about Sabrina—pushing her gets you the opposite result of what you're hoping for. I get it, though. She's been on her own all her life. Her dad bailed before she was even born. Her mom abandoned her. Her grandmother, as much as she claims to love her, always acts like she did Sabrina some huge favor by raising her.

Sabrina James isn't used to people loving her. Sometimes I wonder if she even knows how to love someone back, but then I see her with our daughter, the way her face softens with love and adoration every time she looks at Jamie, and I know she's capable of feeling deeply.

I just wish she'd feel deeply about *me*.

"Why do you look so serious?" she teases, setting aside her textbook. "You killed it tonight. You should be grinning from ear to ear."

I undo my jeans and let them drop to the floor. "I'm grinning on the inside." I tackle my plaid button-down next. "I'm too exhausted to move my facial muscles."

"Really? That's a damn shame, because I'm not tired at all."

The mischievous note in her voice makes my body roar to life. Oh fuck. Please please *please* tell me she's saying what I think she is.

"Jamie's fast asleep in the other room," she adds, waving the baby monitor around enticingly. "Lately she can go for a whole two hours before she starts screaming her lungs out..."

Two hours.

My dick springs up and tries to tunnel its way out of my boxer briefs.

Sabrina doesn't miss my body's response. Licking her lips, she reaches for the hem of her sweater and tugs it up and over her head.

"Darlin'," I start hoarsely.

"Hmmm?"

"If this is some sick joke and you're *not* planning on fucking me right now, I need you to tell me. My cock won't be able to handle the disappointment."

She bursts out laughing, then claps a hand over her mouth to stifle the sound. Fortunately, the baby monitor stays quiet.

"Not a joke," she assures me. Then she unclasps her bra, and holy hell, her tits are glorious. "I've wanted to jump you all night."

I stalk toward her like a predator. "Yeah?"

"Mmm-hmmm. I've been thinking about this all day. And tonight, the thinking turned into obsessing. You have *no* idea how hot you are when you order your staff around." She's already wiggling out of her yoga pants and bikini underwear.

My breath stalls when I lay eyes on her pussy. It's completely bare. Oh yeah, this isn't a spur of the moment thing. She totally prepared for this.

I'm on top of her before she can blink, my mouth crushing down on hers in a kiss that leaves us both breathless. But as much as I love her mouth, that's not what I want to be kissing right now.

Three months. It's been three goddamn *torturous* months since

I've had my tongue in paradise. I tear my mouth away and slide down the bed until my face is level with her pussy. Her very wet, very gorgeous pussy.

"Hold yourself open, babe. I haven't eaten in a very long time and I'm hungry as fuck."

Sabrina's hands come down and spread her lips apart. I dive in and drag my tongue once from front to back, coating my taste buds with her. My already aching dick throbs with need. God, I've missed this. I've missed her.

"Tucker, please," she begs.

My cock is so hard it might break in half, but I don't care because my face is buried between my woman's legs. Her heels dig into my shoulders, urging me on. Above me, she thrashes, making the sexiest noises ever.

Come on, baby. Come for me.

"Yes, ah, yes. Right there." She cries out and then claps a hand over her mouth again.

We both freeze, waiting for a peep from next door. When nothing happens, I breathe a sigh of relief, reach for a pillow and throw it to her.

I grin devilishly. "As much as your sexy sounds drive me nuts, it's probably best you scream into the pillow."

She drops her head back, throws the pillow over her face and gives me the thumbs-up. Laughing, I reapply myself to the awesome task at hand, but as soon as my mouth is back on, my chuckles quickly die out.

Each taste of her makes me more ravenous. Her thighs tighten under my palms and her pussy vibrates against my tongue, signaling that she's close. I suck harder. I lick faster. I bite and kiss and tongue her until she screams into her pillow and comes all over my face.

It's fucking glorious.

Sitting up, I swipe a hand over my mouth. "Condom?" I ask.

She shoves the pillow aside. "I'm on the pill. Got the prescription at the last checkup."

I grip my cock and run the tip along her wet core. Her breath hisses when the broad head breaches her entrance. It's been a long time since I've been inside her, and despite the fact that she pushed a bowling ball out of her vagina, she's still tight as fuck. The female body is a thing of magic.

As I slide inside, I can't stop my own groan from escaping. It feels so damn good. When I'm fully seated, I stop. Her inner muscles pulse around me.

"Fuck, I wish I rubbed one out before the bar opened," I grind out. "I'm going to shoot my wad in under ten seconds."

"Please don't. This feels so good." Her tone is slightly surprised.

"You thought it would suck?" I pull her legs up around my shoulders so I can drill in deeper.

"I had a baby."

"Your body is perfect." I kiss a pretty ankle. "Any more perfect and I'd be dead. You're still tight as hell, wet as heaven."

She giggles. "Heaven is wet?"

I rotate my hips and we both moan. "My heaven is wet and hot and belongs to this babe called Sabrina."

Smiling, she clenches around my dick.

"Stop it." I gasp. "You want to come again, or do you want me to embarrass myself?"

She responds by squeezing me even tighter. I clamp my eyes shut and search for an ounce of control. Once the urge to come inside of her passes, I start moving at a slow and steady pace.

Her gaze clings to mine and I telegraph everything I feel, everything I can't say, everything that's in my heart for her.

You're the only one for me.

My sun rises and sets on your smile.

My heart beats because yours does.

Her hips cant upward, welcoming every thrust.

"Hold on to me, babe." Sweat beads on my forehead as I dig a knee into the mattress to drive into her harder, deeper.

She pulls me down until her tits rub against my chest with every plunge forward. "I'm close," she whispers. "Kiss me. I want your tongue in my mouth when I come."

Fucking hell.

My mouth crashes onto hers. Our tongues greedily tangle together. This is all I'm ever going to want. Her body beneath mine. Her taste on my lips. Her scent in my lungs.

She cries against my mouth as she comes. I swallow her cry of ecstasy and then allow my own orgasm to rip through me, slamming into her so hard that I'm probably going to leave bruises. After the pleasure finally subsides, I collapse next to her, barely managing to throw my body to the side so I don't crush her.

"Give me about ten minutes and I'll be good to go again," I mumble into the mattress.

A soft hand strokes its way down my spine and cups my ass, sending shivers throughout my frame. My dick twitches with interest.

"Make that five."

She laughs.

I flop onto my back and tuck an arm under her shoulders to pull her against me. "You've killed me, Sabrina. I'm dead."

She runs a finger along my inner thigh. Predictably, my dick hardens. "If this is you dead, I'm a little afraid of how long our next round is going to last."

"You might want to get a sandwich. I'm gonna keep you in bed for a long time."

Her legs twine through mine as if she can't handle even an inch of her being separated. Which is totally fine with me.

"Everything seems to be working," she murmurs, her lips moving against the side of my chest. She sounds surprised again.

"Why wouldn't it? We both want this to work, don't we?"

I hold my breath as I wait for her answer. It's as hard as I've pushed her lately and I half expect her to leap up and run for the door.

Instead, she inhales deeply. "Yeah, we do."

"Does that mean I can stop looking for a different woman?"

"It means you *have* to stop," she declares. Her delicate fingers dig possessively into my skin, and I grunt with pleasure.

"Good. I've already told a few women around here that I'm married."

"Why?"

"Jamie's a chick magnet. I've never had so many women hit on me."

And then, as if I'd summoned her, my phone chirps to announce that Jamie's crying in the other room.

"What's that?" Sabrina sits up, wiping the hair out of her face.

"Fitzy set it up. There are monitors in the crib that send an alert to my phone to let us know if she stops moving or if she's crying. I'll install the app on your phone later." I swing out of bed. "Stay here," I tell her as she scrambles to her knees. "I'll bring Jamie in."

When I reach the door, I look back. Sabrina has positioned herself against the padded headboard, arranging the pillows around her sides as she gets ready to feed our baby. She lifts her head and smiles, looking like a fucking angel.

This isn't how I planned my life to be, at least not this soon, but I wouldn't give it up for all the gold in the world.

Heart in my throat, and feeling happier than any man has the right to feel, I go get our little girl.

38

SABRINA

December

I limp into the apartment after my study group, an hour late and feeling guilty about it. I call out an apology to Tucker as I swing inside, my arms full of books and a small bag of groceries, which contains only half the items I was supposed to bring home an hour ago. "I'm so *so* sorry. I had my phone turned off and—"

The rest of my excuse dies in my throat when I find Tucker's mother in my kitchen.

She turns a death glare in my direction and speaks up from her spot behind the counter. "John went to pick up some things from the store. He tried to text you to see if you'd pick up the items on your way home, but you never answered."

Her words are colder than the winter winds off the bay. I shiver under my down coat.

"I thought you weren't getting in until Friday," I stammer.

"The wedding I was supposed to style was postponed, so I

decided to take advantage and come early. That way I get to spend extra time with my granddaughter."

"Oh. Cool. That's...cool."

I've turned into an idiot. I can't help it, though. Tucker's mother is so damn intimidating. I haven't seen her since that disastrous visit over the summer, and even though Tucker texts her daily and arranges for video chats between her and Jamie, she hasn't once asked to speak to me.

"Why were you late?" It's an accusation and we both know it.

I gulp. "I was in a study group. Finals are coming up."

She nods toward the living room. "I suppose that's why the place isn't as clean as you'd like."

I follow her gaze with deepening dismay. This week had gotten away from me, and the apartment shows every bit of my distraction. The kitchen cupboards are embarrassingly bare. Dishes—clean at least—are stacked on the counter. I was going to put them away tonight after Jamie was fed. In the living room, textbooks and outlines and supplemental study guides take up every available surface. Jamie's bathroom—the one Mrs. Tucker will be using—looks like a hurricane. Everything is terrible because I thought I had two more days to fix it.

Which is what I say to her. "I planned on tidying up before you arrived."

Her arched eyebrow conveys that my excuse is embarrassing. "You're trying your hardest, aren't you?"

The dagger strikes deep. My hardest isn't good enough in Mrs. Tucker's eyes.

Breath tight in my chest, I slowly toe off my boots and make the short trek across the open-concept room toward the kitchen, dragging my stocking-covered feet with each step. The apartment is bigger than my childhood home, and on most days I'm giddy over the space, but Mrs. Tucker has a way of vacuuming up all the air in the room.

Silently, I put away the milk, eggs, and butter. The convenience store was over-priced, but it was close by and I was feeling a little desperate. Now? I'm feeling small and incompetent.

"Is Jamie with Tucker?" I ask. The apartment's as quiet as a study carrel at Harvard.

"She's in her crib sleeping," Mrs. Tucker says tersely, not glancing up from the onions she's chopping.

I make an attempt to smile. "Did you enjoy seeing her in person for the first time?"

"What kind of question is that? Of course I did. She's my only grandchild."

My half-hearted smile fades. I gulp again. Oh God, this visit is going to be brutal.

"I'm going to run in and check on her." I shove a carton of juice in the fridge before fleeing the kitchen.

In the nursery, the unmade bed Tucker and Fitzy had hauled up here last weekend taunts me. The sheets stacked on one end only serve to highlight my ineptness as a mother and a housekeeper. If those are traits that Mrs. Tucker values in a daughter-in-law, then I'm failing miserably.

Jamie's sleeping blissfully in her crib, wrapped up tight in her blanket. I resist the urge to pick her up, despite knowing that holding her sweet, nonjudgmental body will make me feel so much better. But she needs to sleep and I have shit to get done.

As quietly as possible, I make the bed and then creep out to join Mrs. Tucker in the kitchen.

"Can I get you something to drink?" I offer. She has the onions in a pan, and the apartment is filling with the fragrant smell of sweet herbs and tangy garlic.

"No. I'm fine."

"Can I help you make your..." I wave my hand toward the stove.

"Chili?" she fills in. "No."

Okay then. I lick my lips and consider my options. My first preference is to hide in the bedroom until Tucker comes home, but as my gaze falls on the mound of dishes, I decide that tidying up should come first. Even if I have to make conversation with someone who clearly thinks I'm about as low as a slug.

"Has Tucker shown you the bar yet?" I ask, stacking the bowls first. "He's done a great job and it's already making decent money." Tucker's Bar has been full since it opened its doors.

"It's early yet. Most bars fail after a couple of years. It's not what I would've wanted for him to spend his father's insurance money on." Her lips pinch. "I would've told him that if he'd asked me."

Good thing he hadn't. Tucker is clearly in love with his bar. He's already talking about buying another one since his estimated cash flow from year one would allow him enough profit to invest in another business. He's a businessman, not a bartender, as anyone who listens to him for five minutes can attest to. He talks about leveraging risk, returns on investments, profit margins, and hidden opportunities.

"I think it's going to be a big success," I declare confidently.

"You would think that." She huffs. "Tucker could've bought the realty business back home. He should be in an office, not working in a bar."

She says *bar* like someone else might say *whorehouse*.

"And now he's living over it." She heaves another huge, disappointed sigh. "This isn't what his daddy would've wanted."

I don't know how to respond, so I turn the conversation to Jamie because surely she couldn't be critical of Jamie.

"Was Jamie awake when you got home? She's so smart. We've been reading to her every day. I found an article that says if you read to your infant at least two hours a day, she'll be an advanced reader."

Jeez. I'm beginning to sound like Nana, spouting off pseudo-facts that are presented in click bait articles as if they're gospel.

Tucker's mother ignores my remarks. "Tuck says you're breast-feeding and that she's only in the fifth percentile for weight. That sounds dangerously underweight. In my day, we all used formula. It filled those tummies up and helped them grow."

I resign myself to the fact that there's not a thing associated with me that Mrs. Tucker won't find fault with.

Grabbing for the threads of my fraying patience, I say, "Most doctors really push for breastfeeding these days. The mother's milk is calibrated to match the infant's needs, and there are studies—"

"There are studies that prove anything," she says disdainfully. She flicks the burner to low and moves toward the sink, where she begins to wash her hands vigorously. "I heard there was a study that said kids who are around alcohol tend to grow up to have a lot of problems. I hope that isn't the case with Jamie."

I place one foot over the other and stomp down, hoping the pain will serve as a distraction since grinding my molars isn't doing the trick. I remind myself that Mrs. Tucker loves her son and that all her criticism, some of it founded, comes from a place of love. Not for me, but for her son. I should respect that.

"We aren't going to live here forever," I say with false cheerfulness.

I finish up with the dishes and then swing into the living room. Maybe the distance will keep me from saying something stupid out of anger. That would only cause more damage to the already difficult relationship I have with Tucker's mom.

If I'm going to stay with Tucker, I need to make this thing with her work.

"Law school is going well. I got in with a great study group. They're super important because we all help each other see the bigger picture. When I first started, I thought I wasn't going to make any friends, but it was early day jitters for all of us." I'm rambling as I tidy up my coursework. "There's this one guy in my group—Simon— who's a genius. He has a photographic memory plus this keen ability to really narrow in on the important issues. I get bogged down in the details too much."

"Simon? You study with other men?"

I jerk upright at her suspicious tone.

"Yes, there are men in my class," I answer carefully.

"Does John know about this?" She crosses her arms over her chest, looking at me as if I'd just confessed to boning another student in front of her son.

"Yes. He's met Simon. We've studied here." Well, actually at the bar. My study group loves to come here.

She shakes her head, the red-gold strands highlighted by the kitchen light behind her. "This is..." Another head shake. "Exactly what I expected," she finishes.

A frown puckers my mouth. "What do you mean?"

"I mean that you take advantage of my son and have been doing it since the day you two met."

I suck in a breath. "W-what?"

"How soon after you learned about his inheritance did you decide to trap him, Sabrina?" Her expression is colder than ice. "It's pretty convenient how he pays for everything while you go off *studying* with another man."

Are. You. Fucking. Kidding. Me.

I straighten fully, indignation injecting into my bloodstream.

It's one thing for her to criticize my housekeeping. I suck at it.

I can handle her objection to the breastfeeding. I'm concerned about Jamie's weight too, even though the doctor assures me it's perfectly normal for breastfed babies to be underweight.

I don't care if she derides my parenting, housekeeping or mothering skills from one side of Boston to the other.

But I won't—I fucking *won't*—stand for her whispering awful and unfounded suspicions in Tucker's ear.

I can survive on my own. I don't need Tucker—I *want* him. I want him so much that I'd give everything up to have him and Jamie.

With as much dignity as I have, I face Mrs. Tucker.

"I have so much respect for you. I've only been doing this mothering sh—stuff for four months and I've screwed up probably a thousand times. It's hard, and I have Tucker, your amazing son, helping me every inch of the way. I can't imagine how you did it on your own. But I'm not going to let you insult everything I do in this place. This is my home. Yes, I'm not perfect, but I'm trying. I love Jamie and I love Tucker and if, at any time, Harvard or work or anything threatens their happiness in any way, I would give it all up in a minute."

Her brown eyes widen.

But I'm not done. "He and Jamie are the most important things in my life," I say fiercely. "And everything I'm doing right now is to make sure that I keep them in my life, to make sure I can contribute to our family and give Jamie a better childhood than the one I had to deal with, even if it means studying with a *man*. Who, by the way, is happily married and has two kids of his own."

There's a rustling noise behind Mrs. Tucker, and the blot behind her head slowly comes into focus. It takes a second for me to realize it's Tucker. He's standing at the front door.

He leans an arm on the doorframe, a smile slanting across his face.

"You love me, huh?"

39

TUCKER

S abrina looks like she wants to crawl under a rock. Or maybe jump out one of the many windows in our apartment. I know she doesn't like being put on the spot, and I probably wouldn't even blame her if she decided to flee.

But whatever my mother said to her before I came home—and I intend on finding out every last word that was spoken—has clearly given Sabrina a dose of courage. She frowns briefly at my mom, then turns to me and meets my gaze straight on.

"I love you," she confirms.

I take a step closer. "Since when?"

"Since fucking always." When my mom winces, Sabrina gives her a sheepish look. "Sorry. Tuck and I are still going through a language transition. We don't always remember to say 'fudge' and 'sugar,' okay?" She lifts an eyebrow. "Are you going to lecture me about that too?"

Mom's lips twitch as if she's trying not to laugh. "No," she says faintly. "I'm not. In fact..." She makes a big show of slipping into her winter boots and coat. "I think I'll take a walk around the block. I love looking at all the snow."

"Bullshit," I cough into my hands. My mom despises winter and we both know it.

She glares at me on her way to the door. "Please speed up this language transition, John." And then she's gone, and Sabrina and I exchange grins.

The humor doesn't last long, though.

"I'm sorry," Sabrina tells me.

"For what?" I bridge the distance between us and plant both hands on her slender hips.

"I didn't mean to be rude to your mother. It's just...she said some...hurtful things." She holds up her hand when she sees my dark expression. "They're not worth repeating, and I have a feeling she won't say that kind of stuff anymore."

I nod slowly. "You mean now that she knows you love me?"

"Yeah."

I search her beautiful face for a moment before smiling again. "Since fucking always, huh?"

"Well, maybe not always," she concedes. "I won't lie, Tuck. That connection you talked about when we first met? About our eyes meeting across the room and how you felt something in that moment?" Sabrina sighs. "All I felt was lust that night."

"I know."

"But it's not just lust anymore. It hasn't been about that for a long time."

"When?" I can't help but tease. "When did you figure out you're madly in love with me?"

"I don't know. Maybe on that ridiculous double date? Maybe when you took care of me when I thought I was sick? When you got me the briefcase? When you punched out Ray in my honor?" Each word is lined with wonder. "I don't know exactly when, Tuck, but I know I love you."

A lump rises in my throat. "Why didn't you say anything

sooner?"

"Because I was scared. And because I wasn't sure if you actually loved me back—"

"Are you kidding me? I lost my head for you the second we met. You know that."

She stubbornly sticks out her chin. "I figured you were thinking with your dick. Guys do that."

I'll give her that. But I've never been one of those guys.

"And then I got pregnant, and I was worried you were confusing your feelings for the baby with your feelings for me." She rakes a hand through her silky dark hair. "But the biggest thing is...was...that I...I..."

I stroke her hips. "You what?"

Tears cling to her long eyelashes. "I can't be the person who ruins your life. I already turned you into a father earlier than you wanted to be one. I didn't want love to complicate everything. I didn't want..." She blinks rapidly. "I didn't want you to wake up one day and hate me."

I growl. "Hate you? Jesus, woman." Hauling her tight against me, I bury my face in her neck. "You still don't get it, do you?"

"Get what?" she asks in a small voice.

"You. Me. Us. This." I spit out words as they pop into my head. "You're the one, Sabrina. There's no one else for me in this world, nobody but you. If I was driving and saw you on the side of the road? You better believe I'd rip out a spark plug or two if it meant getting to spend even five seconds in your presence. You're the fucking one."

Her breath hitches.

"Even if you didn't give me Jamie—which is the greatest goddamn gift in the world, by the way—I'd still want to be with you. Even if you hadn't said you loved me back, I'd take whatever scraps you were willing to give me as long as I could be with you. I don't give a shit if that makes me pathetic—"

"You're not pathetic." Her expression is fierce now. "You could never be pathetic."

"I wouldn't care if you thought I was." I cup her face in my hands and wipe away her tears with my thumbs. "You're the best thing that's ever happened to me, Sabrina James."

"No." She smiles. "You're the best thing that's ever happened to *me*."

Before I can lean down to kiss her, a hearty cry wails through the apartment.

"And *that*," I murmur, "is the best thing that's ever happened to either one of us."

A tear breaks free from her lashes and slides down her cheek. "Yes. It is."

Jamie lets out another bloodcurdling shriek, and we both hurry toward the corridor that leads to the bedrooms. Right outside the nursery door, though, I stop Sabrina by taking her hand.

"She can cry for five more seconds," I decide. "We're trying out that self-soothing thing anyway, remember?"

Her lips quiver with humor. "I thought you were against it." She deepens her voice and gives it a drawl to mimic me. "'I ain't gonna let my princess suffer, darlin'. What kind of father does that?'"

My jaw drops in outrage. "I did not say *ain't*."

"You may as well have."

Rolling my eyes, I tug her toward me and capture her bottom lip between my teeth. Sabrina moans in response, which wakes up my cock.

"I wanted a kiss," I grumble against her mouth. "Not sex noises."

"Too bad. You're getting both." She proceeds to stick her tongue in my mouth and kiss the shit out of me until we're both making sex noises.

When we break apart, we're both laughing and breathing hard, and Jamie is still screaming her displeasure to anyone who'll listen.

"C'mon, let's go wait on the princess," Sabrina says with a smile.

She gives my ass a playful smack, and then we walk into the nursery, hand-in-hand, to see our daughter.

EPILOGUE

SABRINA

One Year Later

Tucker walks ahead of me into the private box at TD Garden. He's holding a squirming Jamie in his arms, but her efforts to wiggle out of his grip are futile, because her daddy's strong as fuck. Ever since she started walking, she's demanding to go everywhere on her own two little feet. And she's frickin' fast. I swear, I turn my head and the kid is *gone*. Lately I've been rethinking my opinion on parents who leash their children.

"Sorry we're late," Tucker tells the room.

Several heads turn in our direction. I don't recognize half the people in this executive suite, but the ones I do recognize bring a happy smile to my lips.

"You're here!" Grace jumps up from her seat and races over to us. "Logan is going to be so psyched that you made it."

"We almost didn't," Tucker says ruefully. He ruffles our daughter's reddish-brown hair. "The little princess couldn't decide which uncle's jersey she wanted to wear."

"Ha," I say with a snort. "*She* couldn't decide?" I give Grace a warm hug and then turn to do the same to Hannah, who's wandered over to say hi. "Tuck is the one who was moaning and griping about it."

"And yet you chose neither," Hannah points out, grinning at Jamie's pink hockey jersey, which has the words "Daddy's Girl" stitched onto the back.

Custom-made, of course. Tucker likes to get things custom-made. Probably because the ridiculous shit he comes up with in his head isn't available to normal consumers.

"She'll start alternating," Tucker promises. "One game she'll wear G's jersey, the next she'll wear Logan's. Hey, Jean. Good to see you." He steps forward to hug Logan's mother, who is beaming with pride.

I don't blame her. Her son is about to make his debut in the pros, after spending a year playing for something Tuck calls the 'farm team.' I still haven't bothered to study up on hockey. I'm too busy working my butt off in my second year at Harvard. Somehow, I managed to make it through my first year without having a nervous breakdown. I even made Law Review, much to Lettuce Head's—aka Kale's—dismay.

Tucker's doing well too. The bar turned a bigger profit in its first year than either of us had expected. Some of the money was set aside for a college fund for Jamie, but he's planning on investing the rest in a second location. Downtown, this time, which will either be a huge bust or a smashing success. I have faith in my man, so I'm going with the second one.

"Sugar," Tucker curses, his gaze shifting to the huge window that overlooks the arena. "The game's already started?"

"Only two minutes into the first period," Hannah assures him. "Logan hasn't even played a shift yet."

"He might not play at all," Grace says glumly. "He warned me they might not give him any ice time."

"Of course they will," Jean declares. "He's a superstar."

I hide a smile behind my hand. Yeah. I know what it's like to be a proud mother. Jamie said her first word last week—"Boo," and yes, it fucking counts as a word—and I damn near shouted it from the rooftops. I recorded her saying it three times and then sent the video off to Tucker's mom, who immediately called me up and we spent thirty minutes raving about how smart she is.

Mama Tucker and I have gotten along splendidly ever since she accepted that I love her son and that I'm not going anywhere. I'm not sure if it'll still be the case when she moves to Boston next spring. I'm a bit nervous about having her close by, but after Jamie's first birthday, which Mrs. Tucker wasn't there for, Tuck's mom decided that she simply *cannot* stand to be so far away from her precious granddaughter. She's saving up some more money first, and then she's moving east to open her own hair salon. Tucker, of course, is insisting on providing the capital for it.

My soon-to-be husband is a saint. When he proposed after the small birthday party we threw for Jamie, I almost said no. Sometimes it scares me how incredible this man is. I'm terrified that I'm somehow going to screw this up, but Tucker constantly reminds me that this is *it*. He and I are it. Forever.

"Where's Dean?" I ask, searching the room for his blond head.

"He couldn't have made it in time," Hannah explains. "He coaches the girls' hockey team at his school and they practice Tuesday and Thursday evenings."

I nod. I had to bail on a study session to be able to attend this Tuesday night game. But it's harder for Dean and Allie to drop everything when they're living in Manhattan. They made it to Jamie's party, though. Dean bought her a stuffed unicorn that she carts around everywhere.

Hannah, Carin, Hope, Grace and I get together once a month, no matter what, to commiserate over school, life, and love. Carin's moved on from her TA and is madly in love with a guest lecturer from London. She says that everything's sexier with a British accent.

I can't disagree. I love Tucker's southern drawl and hope he never loses it.

Hope told me she and D'Andre are talking about marriage and a family. They're jealous over Jamie and talk about how they want to be young parents.

All in all, we're a happy group.

Sometimes I worry that we're *too* happy, but then a visit to Nana's house brings things into focus. We're happy because we want to be, because we're pouring our energy and emotion into each other in the best possible way.

My goal, once upon a time, was to succeed. I didn't realize that success wasn't grades or scholarships or achievements, but the people I was lucky enough to have in my life.

As I look around the room, I want to give everyone a hug and a thank-you. A hug to express how much I love them and a thank-you for loving me back.

Because love is the ultimate goal. It's not the one I had strived for, but I was lucky enough, so damn lucky, to achieve it.

AUTHOR'S NOTE

I can't believe this is the fourth (and final) book in the Off-Campus series! It's always so sad for me to say goodbye to characters I adore, but don't you worry, dear reader...there is a spinoff in the works!

As always, I couldn't have survived this project without the help of some very awesome people.

Early readers Viv, Jen, Sarina and Vi for the invaluable feedback and general best-friendship.

My editor Gwen, who is the second biggest dog-lover (after myself, of course) on the planet and therefore the best person ever.

My publicist/cheerleader/soul mate Nina Bocci for loving this series as much as I do.

Sarah Hansen (Okay Creations) for the abs-licious cover!

Nicole and Natasha—my angels sent from heaven.

Kristy, for all the work you do in the FB group!

Sharon Muha, just because.

And finally, YOU! The bloggers and reviewers who continue to rave about the series and spread the word. The readers who send me the sweetest, most enthusiastic messages about these books. The members of my Facebook group (Everything Elle Kennedy) who make me laugh on a daily basis.

So, yes—*you*. Thank you for taking the time to read my books!

ABOUT THE AUTHOR

A *New York Times*, *USA Today* and *Wall Street Journal* bestselling author, Elle Kennedy grew up in the suburbs of Toronto, Ontario, and holds a BA in English from York University. From an early age, she knew she wanted to be a writer and actively began pursuing that dream when she was a teenager. She loves strong heroines and sexy alpha heroes, and just enough heat and danger to keep things interesting!

Elle loves to hear from her readers. Visit her website www. ellekennedy.com or sign up for her newsletter to receive updates about upcoming books and exclusive excerpts. You can also find her on Facebook (ElleKennedyAuthor), Twitter (@ElleKennedy), or Instagram (@ElleKennedy33).

CPSIA information can be obtained
at www.ICGtesting.com
Printed in the USA
BVHW060729260321
603431BV00006B/389